Siren's Song

Trish Albright

LEISURE BOOKS NEW YORK CITY

To Mom and Dad.

A LEISURE BOOK®

July 2008

Published by

Dorchester Publishing Co., Inc.
200 Madison Avenue
New York, NY 10016

ISBN 10: 0-8439-6086-8
ISBN 13: 978-0-8439-6086-0

Printed in the United States of America.

10 9 8 7 6 5 4 3 2 1

Visit us on the web at www.dorchesterpub.com.

ACKNOWLEDGMENTS

There are many people who help a book reach the reader. First, I must thank my amazing editor, Leah Hultenschmidt, for her brilliance in plucking me out of the contest circuit followed by her patience, trust, and excellent editing while ushering this first book through the publishing process. Next my agent, Meredith Bernstein, for her guidance and support. My two bosses, Kevin Rice and Joe Garlington, who keep giving me great assignments around the world, but would be just as happy (for me) if I wrote full-time. My family is the best in the world and I thank them for putting up with me during the editing and revision process, and to my parents for passing on the tenacious gene. Aunt Ann and Uncle Richard, for their love and also for giving me a beautiful place where I can escape and write. Thanks to Jim Cerrone, my first fan, critic and supporter. Theresa and Keith Austin, for notes on maritime history—all mistakes are my own. Tom Cerrone, for supporting me no matter what I do. All my friends at the office, especially Mark Mine, who cheered me every step of the way these last two years leading to publication. My friends who fed me, especially Lori, Steve, and Julie. All the book-club "Lit Chicks." The amazing and unconditional support of Los Angeles Romance Authors. My sisters in writing, and the ones I could not survive without—Gina Bono, Robena Grant, TJ Bennett, D'Anne Avner, and the fabulous Lynne Marshall.

Last, my readers, thank you so much for buying this book and sharing it with your friends. Visit me on the Web where you can read more about sirens, fin whales, ancient treasure, and the new exploits of the Stafford family.

Enjoy the adventure,

Trish Albright

www.TrishAlbright.com

Siren's Song

Chapter One

1787, Morocco

Moments like this made her life legendary.

Being a practical sort, she preferred being a living legend.

An Arabian guard yanked her thick, long braid, demanding attention she refused to give. Undeterred, he hooked her bound arms, currently tied from behind, and dragged her sideways toward the auction block. It was uncomfortable, not to mention the height of rudeness.

Stumbling, but stubborn to the end, Alexandra Stafford levered bare feet against the hardwood steps and pressed backward against the guard with all her strength, her body nearly horizontal, stretched open to the crowd of attentive buyers.

Another figure sauntered into her peripheral vision and the face of her kidnapper appeared as he bent down nonchalantly to observe her distress. His hand lifted to halt the guard. Tilting his sun-darkened face parallel to hers, he frowned with a disingenuous expression of worry, shaking his head over her situation. The sour smell of tobacco emanated from his breath and skin, and Alex grimaced in disgust, before unleashing her fury.

"I swear if you do this, my family will hunt you down, cut you limb from limb, gut you like a pig, and feed you to the sharks, you miserable, son of a—"

She cut off, choking, as Reginald Paxton blew smoke in her face. Her body convulsed with hacking coughs, and the guard took advantage to yank her back into standing position. Alex kicked out at Paxton with rage, her bare feet doing little damage to the parts she could reach. He laughed. It infuriated her further to think he was laughing at her puny efforts. Once freed, she would kill him. With any luck, a few different ways.

"Tell me where the map is, and I can make this all go away, Miss Stafford."

"I told you." The guard painfully tightened his grip on her. "I don't know anything"—she slammed her heel down on the guard's foot—"about some stupid map."

The guard whacked her in the side of the head, causing her brain to rattle.

Alex faked a recovery she didn't feel, raised her head and smiled.

Incensed, Paxton waved for the man to proceed.

"No! You bastard! I'm an American. I'm a free woman," Alex screamed, fighting violently as she was forced toward the platform. Her efforts were so fierce another guard came to assist.

"Someone help me!" she begged, searching desperately for a sympathetic face or word from the crowd. There were none. Only the foreign sounds of Arabic. She understood enough to heighten her fear, as she was dragged onto the small stage and held in place.

In her short life she'd had many roles—daughter, heiress, sea captain, and now she thought bleakly, slave. Boston was a lifetime away and she was at the wrong end of a sale gone bad. Very bad. Fear no longer prickled the hairs at the back of her neck, but suffocated the life from her with dizzying force. She swore to kill Paxton for this—if her father didn't get to him first.

Forcing self-pity aside, she took stock of escape options.

They appeared dismal at best.

To her left, the door she entered was protected by a long hallway of armed guards. Paxton stood aside waiting to collect his earnings for the night. She had not been his only sale, but the other woman had appeared blessedly incoherent. Forward, she faced the eyes of a hundred dark predators, staring, eager for conquest. She couldn't breathe without tasting their steamy, musky sweat. Finally, to her right, stairs to a place she didn't want to know about. The place they took the slaves. Her stomach wrenched with dread.

Panic hit hard and fast.

She woke up from her temporary daze and leapt. Unfortunately, the arm encircling her neck caught and tightened. Turning her head sideways inside his grip, Alex bit hard into the salty, hairy flesh. Disgusting, but effective.

A remarkably high-pitched yelp rewarded her efforts before the air at her throat was cut off. Her vision blurred, and her body trembled. The guard gave an inch. She hissed in a sharp breath. The second she regained her focus and footing she spat, "Obviously, your mother didn't teach you any manners, you stinking, filthy, brainless bastard."

She croaked more than cursed, but the slurs felt good nonetheless.

Alex regretted the outburst immediately when a murmur of curiosity, expectation, then appreciation, spread across the room. As if her struggle excited them. Her eyes burned with terror. God help her. They were all animals.

Joshua Leigh looked up at the commotion. He'd been having an exceptional night out with his friends—until now. Right now, he felt sick. His cohorts thought to impress him with admittance to one of the special markets—a Moroccan slave auction. To the buyers, a very civil affair. To the slaves, the beginning of a nightmare.

Joshua raked a hand through his hair, yearning for escape. They had missed most of "the evening's highlights," and thankfully the experience was nearly over.

He surveyed the small square room, crammed with lustful buyers, and suffused in cigar smoke. Although he was in the back, his height gave him a clear view of the makeshift auction block and the buyers eager to make a purchase. They no doubt had experienced every known pleasure and out of boredom sought more. There was no thought of moral consequences. When you were this rich you could control the consequences.

A howl from the barrel-chested guard escorting the current captive caught his attention. The girl choked on a scream, her long braid coming undone, and spilling rich, auburn tresses over her shoulders. A buzz began in the room. Joshua tensed, watching the girl struggle in vain against the enormous creature twice her size.

Witnessing her vulnerability, he was forced to think of his own. Of everything he had worked and sweat for in the last four years. He was making a life for himself. An honest one. One that had nothing to do with his bastard father, and nothing to do with this. His current shipment would put him in the black. If he delivered it on time.

Why then, would the thought of losing it all even come into consideration?

He quickly assessed the possible exits, as was his habit in a tricky negotiation. The trading business was oftentimes dangerous and he knew from experience when to walk away before it got messy.

Every rational thought told him to walk away now.

He looked at the girl again and sighed regretfully, stepping backward to blend more into his surroundings.

Alex continued to look out, not sparing anyone her disdain. If she could remember their faces it would give her focus in the days to come. She fully intended to kill every one of them. In this lifetime. For now, she must face reality and find a way to survive. She was a Stafford after all. She would survive. Somehow, she prayed, she would survive.

Alex cursed every man in Morocco, and then herself for wanting to come here. This trip had been a chance to prove herself. Her first voyage as the youngest captain for Stafford Shipping. True, she had been accompanied by her father's and brothers' ships, but at sea she'd been in charge.

This last month had been all she ever imagined. Of course, many parts of Morocco were crowded, dirty, and dangerous. Her father didn't trust her to go anywhere alone. After the humiliation of being kidnapped, she grudgingly admitted he might be right. If she survived, this current setback could last years. That thought alone was abysmally depressing. She would be forever proving herself.

She licked her lips, parched and desperate for one drop of

water. Deep weariness made every limb seem twice its weight. Even her hands ached from the guard's tight hold. Undoubtedly, he had ceased the blood flow to her fingers. Hopelessness caused a burning sensation in her eyes, and her head wilted, causing wild strands of hair to stick to her cheeks. She wanted to give up.

A man came up to her, his personal odor preceding him. She saw only feet and some flowing robes. He was a potential customer, and Alex understood clearly his command that she look up. She also considered it fair enough that she was not in the mood to cooperate.

The buyer was smug and undeterred. He grasped her chin in demand. To be relieved of his touch, she gave in and forced herself to gaze past his stout body. She recognized the words of appreciation as well as the scrutiny up and down meant to denigrate.

Defiance disappeared as she smiled tentatively, forcing herself to look him in the eyes. He froze, surprised, then grinned oafishly. Alex felt not an ounce of remorse at his disconcerted look. If he was that stupid, he deserved what he got.

He was still smiling dimwittedly when the shin of Alex's leg connected with his groin. The guard immediately pulled her back. Using the hold from behind as leverage, Alex jumped up, lifting both her legs, and pushed the man off the stage. There was a gratifying thump. A rush of satisfaction gave her new strength.

The fallen man got up with a murderous look. Joshua started instinctively, then stopped. He needn't have worried. The "goods" were well protected, and the humiliated buyer was escorted aside amid laughter and lusty admiration.

His stomach twisted again as the girl straightened her back and lifted her head. Her eyes sparkled clear and pure, and her hair was the color of rich cherrywood with a warmth and texture that lured him, even through the dirty haze of smoke. She was young, which might account for her somewhat strange clothing—a tailored shirt, that could have been designed for a man, was torn at the throat, revealing more than it was meant to. Her skirt was not a skirt, but loose gentleman's pants that must have been made to order. A large belt cinched them at her waist with a decorative buckle. They were some kind of work clothes, but for what profession he knew not. From the surprisingly strong voice that spit out at the room in Arabic, he'd mark her as a survivor. That, at least, was a good sign.

"You will all rot in bloody hell, and I promise to send each one of you foul, pathetic, immoral scum there myself."

Joshua winced. There were a few guffaws from the locals. Educated, but obviously not the daughter of a diplomat. The girl then added what curses and slurs she seemed able to summon in Spanish, French, Italian, the local dialect, and what he thought might be Chinese. No, he decided recognizing some of the words, definitely no diplomats in the family. A resounding slap echoed in his ears as she was struck across the face, her head snapping, stunning her into temporary silence.

A ferocious rage struck him just as quickly, and his friend grabbed his arm in warning. He swallowed impatience, fighting for control, and found himself urging her on. Praying she could magically absorb a little of his strength to survive her torment.

The next seconds seemed like hours as he waited to see if she would recover from the blow, uncertain she was not already unconscious. Then, very slowly, with painstaking control, she lifted her chin. A clenched jaw made the angles of her face even sharper, and he sensed her strength to move came only from blood-sizzling fury and sheer determination. He stepped back unconsciously at the fire in her eyes and watched with admiration as she returned the strike with one of her own.

She spat.

The Moroccan slowly wiped a hand across his chin and mouth. He raised his arm again threateningly, but she refused to cower. She did make the concession of keeping her mouth shut. For that, Joshua was relieved. Most of the men likely didn't understand her threats and slurs against their manhood, but the way her lips curled with disgust conveyed the meaning just as well. She was haughty as a queen, yet he knew she was frightened. Hell, if she wasn't, then she was downright stupid.

The guard wrenched her arms from behind and earned a sharp flinch from his captive. It was an act of brutality merely for the pleasure of it. Joshua had experienced it often as a boy, and empathy twisted his guts at the memory. He acknowledged then what he had known the instant he'd seen her—she was doomed, and somehow, God help him, he had to save her.

What a damned mess.

There was an intimate description of the goods before the bidding took off feverishly. It stopped when a bid from the side won silence. Joshua recognized the round, middle-aged sultan who had just doubled the last offer. The man was richer than any king in Europe and known to keep harems in each of his many palaces. He was also known for a cruel streak in ruling his people. He would no doubt take great pleasure in breaking this girl of her spirit.

Throwing caution to the wind, Joshua stepped forward and raised the bid. He had no idea how he would get his hands on that kind of money, but he didn't care.

There was a collective murmur of shock in the room. Not because of the costly price he realized, but because he dared to bid against the sultan.

The sultan bid again, but Joshua voiced a higher price, heedless of his own increasing peril. The sultan then offered a small fortune, and the bidding ended.

Joshua watched the girl curse and fight as they dragged her off the stage to the other side of the platform. His blood burned. All the injustices he had ever experienced came to a head. He couldn't bear to see another innocent creature ruined by the egos and will of greedy men.

"It is over, my friend. Let's go." His companion, the sultan's nephew, pulled his arm urgently.

"Where are they taking her?"

"There are quarters upstairs," Prince Raja explained. "Al-Aziz gets her only for tonight. She is not allowed to leave the rooms here. He paid well to be the first. Soon there will be another auction. A rare piece like that will bring them much money." The prince read his friend's expression. "Please, my friend, do not do anything foolish."

Joshua's lips curved slightly. "Me?"

Raja sighed. "I cannot be involved. I am easily recognized, and my cousin is my responsibility."

Joshua recalled his cousin was currently laid out drunk in Raja's carriage.

"But . . . if you live long enough . . ." Raja hesitated, then whispered some directions indicating a meeting place on the edge of the city. "They will expect you to go where it is busy. Do not. I will find you." He paused with warning. "If that is still an option."

Joshua gripped Raja's hand gratefully.

The prince rebuked, "Do not thank me. I should have never brought you here."

Joshua watched as the auctioneer paid the slave trader, then turned back to Raja, grinning. "It was fate, my friend. Fear not."

Alex cursed as Paxton collected an obscene amount of gold. It was entirely unjust. He lifted it toward her in a salute, then handed it to a companion while a new guard undid her bonds. Paxton wasn't more than fourteen feet away. She could kill him. With a knife. Perhaps the one being used to free her. It had cut through the ropes efficiently enough. But then she had to reach him. Too many people moving about. Not a direct throw.

Not to worry.

Saying words of thanks in Arabic to the guard who freed her, she turned around and added a respectful nod. The guard looked into her eyes. She smiled for good measure, distracting him. Two seconds later she had the knife. Four seconds later she was in striking distance of Paxton.

Paxton didn't anticipate trouble coming his way. He turned at the sudden noise. Not expecting her. Not expecting the shadow of a knife to flash before him.

Alex leapt, triumph in her last breath.

Someone caught her ankle.

She stretched, determined, victory near. Her target clear.

Paxton's eyes met hers. She reached for his throat.

And missed.

Paxton turned his head away defensively as she struck. Blood spurted free as the knife opened skin down the side of his left cheek. He cried in rage as Alex fell forward to the ground, several guards instantly on her, a foot crushing her knife-wielding hand. Paxton tried to get at her in the fray, seeking revenge, but was held back.

Someone gave him a rag. Held apart, he faced her as she was lifted to her feet, a look of pure evil burning in his eyes. "You will live to regret this, Stafford."

"Not," she gasped, being pulled away, "while there is a breath left in my body!"

Paxton's face contorted into something monstrous. "Then start counting your days."

Chapter Two

She couldn't find anything to use as a weapon.

Her best chance was suffocation with the ridiculous number of pillows scattered throughout the room. Somehow Alex thought that possibility was unlikely. She rubbed her sore wrists and tried to strategize. There was one window, but it was too small and too high to reach. Panicked, she circled the room and debated throwing a pillow up at a candle in the hopes of starting a fire. Footsteps beyond the entrance stopped her in her tracks. There was an abrupt discussion outside. She waited behind the door in a vain attempt to hide and run for it. There was a grunt from a guard, and then, with remarkable stealth, a man entered.

Alex gasped in dismay. He was a giant. Much taller than she'd first gathered. She darted for the opening but was quickly grabbed by the arms, picked up, and put aside. She ran to the other side of the room, realizing her time was up. There was no such thing as knights in shining armor, or chivalry, or even gentlemen—at least not in this savage country. Not even her family could get her out of here with all the guards. But of course, no one knew where she was.

Alex choked back tears as the sultan pulled off his long *jellaba*. He wore European clothes underneath, and even with her blurred vision she could see thick golden streaks of hair. She tried to refocus, thinking her eyes tricked her.

As if sensing her fear, he spoke quickly. "Don't be afraid. I've come to rescue you."

He was young. From what she could see in the candlelight, somewhat handsome. And by the sound of his accent . . . English! Alex blinked in disbelief, but nodded. Every awful thing she was ever brought up to believe about the English she forgave. However, one critical word slipped out. "How?"

"How?" he repeated. "Good question."

He grabbed the hooded robe from the floor and stood by the door. "Stand in the center and let him see you. As soon as the door is closed, start screaming."

She nodded that she understood.

The round sultan entered. He didn't seem to expect her to be waiting, docile.

As the door closed, Alex saw her rescuer cover the sultan's head. Immediately, she started screaming—it helped to cover the sound of the loud punches being administered to the surprised Moroccan. She ran to lock the door.

Then all hell broke loose.

Two guards, sensing something amiss, pushed at the door, sending Alex to the floor. A knife glittered briefly in the candlelight. Her guardian turned in time to stab one man and charged the second before a sword could come down. Alex gasped as he grabbed the guard's throat with one hand and the sword with his other. With great force the Englishman slammed the guard against the wall. The entire room shook, and Alex swore if the city hadn't been alerted already, they were now. She swallowed her shock as the Englishman dispatched the nearly unconscious man with his own weapon.

Alex had seen death before, but never this close, nor on her behalf. She wondered if she really would have been able to kill Paxton. Gathering her wits, she decided this was no time to question herself. She ran to the door and slammed it shut—on more guards.

The Englishman looked at her, sword in hand. "How many?"

"Three."

"And more on the way, no doubt."

Alex decided he was either truly courageous or truly insane. Still, she felt anything was possible. "You can take 'em. They're small."

"Your confidence inspires me."

"But they are armed."

"Of course."

Alex plucked the dagger fiercely from the first guard's back. "I'm ready."

He nodded, she thought in admiration, then pulled a burning candle from high off the wall, reaching it with ease.

"Stay behind me."

Alex thought that would be the safest place as well. She sensed rather than saw his smile in the dim room. It gave her courage, and she took a deep, steadying breath.

Patiently they tracked the sound of guards to the top of the stairs. Using the element of surprise, the Englishman burst out the door with great enthusiasm and dashed hot wax in the face of the first guard. He then kicked the blinded man with enough force to send him toppling into two guards behind him. All three tumbled down the narrow steps in a spectacle of arms and legs.

"And let that be a lesson to you," Alex said, before the Englishman grabbed her hand and pulled her through the corridors toward a large window. He kicked the panels open and looked around. She nudged him aside to judge the situation herself. They were on the top floor, and it was a long way down.

He looked up. "Hope you're not afraid of heights."

Before Alex could enjoy a much-needed breath of fresh air, the Englishman lifted her onto his shoulders. Balanced against the wall, she could just reach the rooftop. He lifted higher, her feet in his palms, then with no time to waste, launched her over the side of the roof, where she landed safely in a stunned heap.

Recovering, Alex ran back to the edge, grabbed the sword from her rescuer, and watched as he climbed the small balcony wall and pulled himself onto the roof with surprising agility. She returned the long saber to him, and was just starting to think they would make it when a guard appeared on the roof, gun in hand, and aimed at her heart.

The Englishman gallantly pulled her behind him, pressing

her hand into his back so tightly it hurt. She thought he was being protective until she felt something hard against her hand. A small flintlock. They were good at close range, but only gave you a single shot.

The guard motioned for her protector to put down his sword. He did so—very, very slowly, giving her time to pull out the gun.

Dear God, Alex prayed, don't let me miss.

She stepped to the left, underneath the Englishman's raised arm, and aimed with precision. The explosion vibrated up her arm and the gun's heat burned into her palm, but she remained steady.

She breathed again, satisfied. She'd hit the man's hand, knocking his gun away. Her protector looked at her in surprise, then at the guard who pulled out a long dagger and gave a murderous cry before charging. "You should have killed him."

"Sorry."

He pushed her out of the way and stood fiercely before the savage-looking man now running toward him.

Alex didn't breathe as she watched her intrepid Englishman stand frozen against the advancing assault. The guard roared, appearing all the more dangerous, and she feared she'd made a terrible mistake in not killing the man herself.

In the very last second the Englishman bent to the ground, as if in prayer, and tripped the attacker at his knees. Giving an animal-like cry, he stood back up, and with a great heave, rolled the guard off his back and sent him flying off the side of the roof. Just as she heard a satisfying thump, another hand reached over the side of the roof. Alex ran for the former guard's gun, turned, cocked the pistol, and shot at the head coming up from the balcony. The head disappeared.

"Thanks," the Englishman acknowledged. There was a loud commotion below. He pulled out a leather bag and grabbed the pistol on the ground. "Can you load?"

Alex nodded, abandoned the Arab's gun, and took the ammunition along with the smaller weapon. He pulled a larger pistol out from his long coat and picked up the sword he had surrendered earlier.

"What happened to your shoes?" he asked.

"They took them so I couldn't run away."

He smiled, understanding. "Guess it didn't work."

"No." She grinned, encouraged.

"You can make it?"

Alex didn't think there was a choice. "I can make it."

Armed, they ran across the roof preparing for the worst. Her companion laid a wood plank across to the next roof. The sound of guards climbing to the roof was all the urging she needed.

He looked dubiously at the makeshift bridge and Alex thought he was going to be gallant and lead the way. She tugged at him quickly. "Let me go first. The wood may crack under your weight."

"Thanks," he said, wryly.

Alex looked down, took a deep breath, and carefully stepped across the shaky bridge with as much false confidence as she could muster, gun in one hand, ammunition and dagger in the other. With one final leap, she landed on the other side and exhaled with relief.

When Alex turned around, a trio of men were charging her brave rescuer on the opposite rooftop. He yelled for her to run, but she mutely shook her head, urging him to follow.

"Go!"

"No!" She wouldn't let him die after he risked all to save her. What kind of woman did he think she was? Loading the gun quickly, Alex knelt at the small rooftop wall for protection and took aim. At this range she thought the spray would be only a minor irritation. Still, it worked. The sound of gunfire was threatening even if the end result was meager. The guards took cover. Alex reloaded. When she glanced up again, the Englishman was halfway across the board and leaping through the air.

Guns fired everywhere.

Alex ducked but knew she would never forget the image caught in the moonlight of this bold, fierce, blond avenger flying through the air, sword in hand, as if he were one of God's own angels. Then again, maybe he was. She blessed herself quickly and took another shot.

The Englishman rolled near her, then jumped up and pushed the wood plank to the ground. She was about to shoot again when he suddenly knocked her flat on her back, covering her completely with his huge frame. A shot took off a piece of wall where her head had been. Alex gulped as debris shattered against her face.

"Sorry, my lady. It'd be a damned shame to lose you after all that."

Alex merely nodded. She saw his smile up close this time. It was a dashing, boyish smile, and she realized he was younger than she first thought. Perhaps early twenties. He was also as tall and broad as any of her brothers.

"How did you get into this mess?" His intent gaze demanded the truth.

"Just shopping."

"Well." His smile widened. "That explains it."

Their brief interlude ended with an explosion of bullets nearby. He hunched over her, and his large hand tucked her face to his throat, forcing her lips to his skin. Alex fought the sudden sensation to taste him, her lips burning from his body heat. She swallowed hard. Entirely bad timing all around.

When it was safe, he lifted his head again, giving her much needed air.

It was too dark to tell the color of his eyes, but Alex was certain they were blue. In the moonlight she thought he was the most handsome man she had ever seen. He was certainly the most courageous. She knew at least for the moment, she felt safer than she had ever felt in her life. Her heart opened to him, and her eyes locked on his as if to hold him to her forever. Unconsciously, her free hand traced his square jaw.

He didn't move.

His smile vanished and his lips moved perceptibly closer. Alex inhaled as his exhale of breath caressed her mouth, awakening a shocking desire in her to lean upward and . . .

He stopped her with a whisper. "I find I must take something from you."

Alex shivered with anticipation. "Yes."

His eyes never left hers as calloused fingers slid down her arm, leaving goose bumps in their wake. Reaching their mark, a large hand gently covered her own—before taking hold of the gun she clutched.

"I think there's one more," he informed. "Get ready to run."

Lightning fast, Joshua sprang to his knees and shot both the guns at his disposal. He couldn't believe his luck when the man went down. He couldn't believe his luck again when he heard shouts below. A crowd of soldiers were approaching, led by the sultan, his face swollen and disfigured. For the second time that night, Joshua did what any self-respecting hero would do: He grabbed the girl and ran.

The next twenty minutes left them both breathless as they ran furtively rooftop to rooftop across a maze of square buildings, moving in a direction certain to confuse the best tracker.

Finally, they stopped, both panting for breath. Joshua caught the girl as she reached out to steady herself. They had lost their pursuers for the moment but that didn't mean they weren't near. He tried to make out any movement in the dark night, listening intently for a sound that did not belong. It was silent. Eerily so.

They weren't far from where Raja said to meet. He was certain his friend would be there. Unless Raja had been detained by the sultan's troops. If so, he needed to find a hiding place where the girl could rest for a few hours.

Joshua looked down at her thoughtfully. Her cheek rested against his chest. Long, tangled hair streamed around her shoulders and over his arm in thick waves. He lifted her face gently and his breath caught. She was so lovely. Whether it was the dangerous escape or the worshipping expression on her face, Joshua couldn't say, but he felt rather cocky and dashing at that moment. Damned if it wasn't a miracle they were both alive. Still, if he listened carefully, he could hear the sound of soldiers searching, perhaps closing in. He took hold of the blade she clutched defensively and tucked it safely in his belt.

"Do you trust me?"

Alex's eyes widened at the question. The man had just taken on one of the most powerful men in the country and half his army, saved her from a fate worse than death, protected her from getting her head shot off, and all for someone he didn't even know. She could only guess this was an example of that English sense of honor and chivalry of which she had heard, but never seen until now. Damn, those Brits were strange.

She stared straight into his eyes. "Yes. I trust you with my life."

"Good," he stated, but with a tone that said he didn't think her trust would last long. Hastily, he lifted her into the cradle of his arms. "Please don't scream."

He squeezed her to him briefly, and before she had a chance to enjoy the moment or wonder at his words, Alex was lifted over the side of the building. Her eyes met his in complete panic. Followed by shock.

He let go.

Her last thought as she flailed for purchase was that her hero was a damned, bloody Brit after all.

Chapter Three

Alex immediately forgot his warning. A choked howl escaped her throat involuntarily as she sailed through the air. Before she had a chance to think she would die, Alex landed on her bottom, atop a heap of very hard hay. She was still stunned when the blond brute landed next to her with a pained curse.

"Next time, kindly warn me when you plan on tossing me like a sack of potatoes," she flashed indignantly. Alex continued to glare at the man, but he just sat there, grinning helplessly, straw poking out of his head. "Well? Have you lost your mind?"

"I surely have. And I do believe I may have injured my delicate backside as well."

Alex quickly smothered a burst of laughter, remembering they were not yet safe. She gingerly moved to the edge of the cart.

"You're American," he said.

"Yes." Alex reached out to him and he grasped her waist, easily lifting and sliding her to the ground. She shivered at the contact of her body brushing against his warmth.

"What were you shopping for that is so important to the colonists?"

"We're a country, so that would be citizens," she corrected. "And carpets," she continued, answering his question.

"Did you steal them?"

"Of course not! I'm a merchant. I paid for them. And got a very good price, I might add."

"I believe you." He lifted a hand in surrender, while quickly scanning the streets for signs of danger.

"But . . ." she hesitated.

"Ah. The truth at last," he teased, pulling her along the edge of a narrow road.

"Well, there was this very, very old woman . . . and . . ."

"And?"

"And she kept insisting she knew me, but I know that's impossible."

There was a scuttle in the dark ahead of them. Alex was instantly pressed into a shallow doorway and obscured by the giant. She felt his sigh of relief before he freed her.

"Just a rat, scavenging for food," he informed.

"I've encountered a few of those this past day."

"Indeed," he said, studying her.

His hand came to her cheek in a caress before quickly falling away, leaving Alex wondering if he had meant to comfort her, or something else. He checked a street as they prepared to turn, and pulled her along. "Quick. This way."

After a moment he spoke again. "Was she welcoming or threatening?"

"The old lady?"

He nodded, and she continued, "Welcoming. Except for the part about the deadly prophecy, a monster rising from the sea, and the end of days . . ."

He laughed softly, "That doesn't sound entirely hospitable."

Alex sighed, convinced he would not believe the rest of it. She certainly didn't. "I must get back to my family and warn them about Paxton—that filthy bastard."

"Reginald Paxton?"

"You know him?" She froze in panic, wondering if she was in danger.

"Only by reputation. He is the most successful slave trader in South America—if ruthlessly trading in human flesh makes one successful."

"It doesn't. I must stop him."

"Of course. Where shall I escort my lady?"

Alex gave him the location.

Joshua recognized the name of Sir Thomas Morbay, and

his heart dropped a little. He was a friend of her family, she explained. A man of means, as he already knew. She had just stepped unequivocally out of his reach. Not that he could have any ambitions to know her. It would be useless. He focused back on the present. Now was all that mattered. Getting her to safety, then getting out of Morocco.

They were nearly at the end of the alley when an elegant, black carriage flashed by. It stopped. Joshua thrust her safely into the shadows. The horses pulled to a stop and the sound of a carriage door opening echoed in the darkness.

"Captain?"

Joshua exhaled with relief. "Raja. You truly are a prince, my friend."

A tall, dark native in robes beckoned. "Quickly. The streets are full of quiet hunters."

The two fugitives scrambled to the safety of the carriage.

The girl nearly tripped over a prone form on the floor of the carriage. She jumped backward onto Joshua's lap.

"I am sorry, miss," Raja said. "My cousin has overindulged and disgraced himself tonight. He is harmless."

There was a confirming groan from the carriage floor. The girl nodded but remained curled up in Joshua's arms, not protesting when he pulled her closer.

Joshua swallowed painfully as long, slender fingers moved up his chest, then crept slowly to the skin at his throat. She took a wobbly breath and he instinctively began to soothe her by caressing her silken layers of hair. He was rewarded when her body relaxed and she snuggled more comfortably against him, wrapping that same hand around the back of his neck.

She was his.

The drive to Sir Thomas's was over too soon for both of them.

The carriage pulled into a shadowed area not far from iron gates leading to a sprawling English-style mansion. No one spoke as her champion helped her to the ground. Alex stepped gingerly, her bare feet sore and miserable from their escape.

The Englishman started to accompany her, but Alex

stopped him. His presence might evolve into more scandal. The English, she knew, were big on scandal. It was unlikely anyone would believe her story as it was.

" 'Tis best I go alone," she said.

He gazed down into suspiciously sparkling eyes and studied her in the moonlight. Then he took off his coat and draped it around her. It went past her knees.

She shoved her arms into the sleeves appreciatively and stared up at him as if to imprint his image forever in her mind. "I have no words that can describe how truly grateful I am for all you have done. Both I and my family will be forever in your debt."

He bowed gallantly at her polite speech. "Ah, my lady, it was nothing." They both laughed. "Well," he amended, "it is rare to have the opportunity to save a truly beautiful damsel in distress. But in all fairness, I also owe you my own life in return."

That pleased her. "Then we are indebted to each other!"

"Nay. Let us say the debt is erased," he whispered, voice husky, "and we come to each other freely." With that he lifted her chin and caressed her full, soft lips with his.

Joshua meant it as a chaste farewell, but the longing that overcame him was a shock. She was young, brave, and beautiful, and he wanted to keep this girl for his own. When the fingers curling in the linen of his shirt crawled up to twine into his hair, he sighed, yearning for one last taste, and deepened the kiss. Just once he wanted something good, and pure. Knowing the impossibility, he finally pulled away.

Regret stabbed painfully. He had nothing to offer. Nor would he for some time. His life was at sea for now. Clearly she was from a good family and wealthy if she called Morbay a friend. Better to leave her with a happy memory than the truth.

The girl's eyes slowly fluttered open. She studied him with a fierceness that was nothing less than disconcerting. As if she could read his thoughts and was not happy with them.

"I'm not going to see you again, am I?"

"I am due to leave soon. After tonight, the sooner the better, I'd say."

"Come here. Tomorrow. My family will want to thank you." She reached down and pulled off a ring. "Return this for whatever favor you wish. I or my family will grant it." She gripped his vest with one hand, then pulled his head down with her other. "You must come. I have a fondness for this ring."

Taken aback by her forwardness, Joshua moved instinctively. His lips pressed down, hunger for her overcoming reason, and with a surprised gasp her mouth opened, taking in his warmth.

Joshua knew she had never been kissed before tonight, and he knew he would never again savor lips so sweet. His tongue slipped inside and tasted hers. He groaned, wanting more.

"I will come." He gave in, sighing against her cheek, his lips brushing against her skin in discovery. "We will be properly introduced. Have a bit of tea. And perhaps you will tell me more about this monster and the end of days."

"Perhaps," she teased. "What is your name? I shall let the butler know to expect you."

"Captain! Quickly," Raja called from the shadows. Her champion turned at the summons, distracted.

"I must go," he said. "Until tomorrow." He bent his head one last time and enveloped her in his arms, before lowering for a possessive kiss. When he came up for air she hugged him tightly. "Try to stay out of trouble for the rest of the night."

That won a smile. "I will."

Alex pushed away from him and spun off before she humiliated herself with tears. She walked quickly through the shadows ignoring the pain swelling in her feet, determined not to look back. Then she remembered. "Wait!"

"Leigh," he called back, knowing instinctively her desire.

Alex nodded and continued. Captain Leigh. Army or sea? The English needed ships in the Barbary Coast to protect vessels. It must be the sea, she decided. A very good sign.

Just then, the breeze picked up. Alex stopped and frowned,

her senses alert. She looked skyward, noting the stars had disappeared. A storm was coming. It was early in the season for a storm. A bad omen. She shook the thought away and continued carefully on her path. Luckily, she didn't believe in omens.

Another carriage pulled up just as she neared the entrance, and she ducked back into shadows. A large, fit man in his late forties stepped out. Alex gasped in shock. Her father's head was bent in utter dejection, and he pushed aside the comforting hand her brother Samuel offered. Samuel, too, appeared deeply distressed. Alex stepped out of the shadows.

"Papa?" she whispered, unable to move.

Robert Stafford froze as if hearing things. He turned, looking up now. Her brothers gasped in shock but didn't move either, as if afraid she was a ghost.

"Allie?"

"Papa!" She sobbed as she tried to run toward him, limping.

Robert Stafford straightened with new power and in quick strides held his daughter in a fierce hug. His body heaved as tears streamed down his rugged face.

Alex, too, was crying and laughing, and crying again as her brothers Samuel and Matthew spun her around, practically tossing her in the air, demanding to know what mischief she had gotten into and who was her new tailor.

Joshua watched the touching reunion from the shadows. She was truly loved. He envied them. She belonged with them, to them. Someday . . . no. That was foolishness. He would have tonight, and tomorrow. That would have to be enough. He was an outsider, and from the outside he watched the jubilant family start to go in. She stopped and looked back at him one last time. He knew she couldn't see him but he dared not move anyway. Her father caught the action immediately.

"What is it?"

"Nothing, Papa. A guardian angel perhaps."

When they were gone, Raja patted his shoulder from behind. "You have done well, my friend. Rest easy with the knowledge she is safe."

"She was shopping," he told Raja with a grin.

"Shopping?"

"Yes. And there was something about a prophecy with a terrible monster and the end of days." He laughed at it now. The danger of the evening over.

"How strange."

"Yes," Joshua agreed. "I shall find out more tomorrow. When I call on her."

Raja held the carriage door open for Joshua to climb in.

"Allie," Joshua whispered. Her name felt good on his lips.

She was his last thought before the butt of a gun to the back of his head sent him tumbling into the carriage.

"Ah, my friend." Raja sighed. "The prophecy brings only death and ruin to all who pursue it. I hope some day you will forgive me." Now he had two bodies to take care of tonight.

Then he needed to find out what that girl had to do with the ancient warning of the siren.

Reginald Paxton winced as the needle pierced skin near his eye.

"Hold still, cousin. It's the last one." Liz Beauveau tied a knot, and cut the thread.

Reginald turned to the mirror and observed the damage. There would be a scar. It was a blow to his vanity as well as his ego. He only hoped the girl was being beaten into submission right now by the sultan. The image was a comfort. He ran fingers through gold coins. Enough gold to build another ship. The Stafford chit had earned him as much as all the other women combined. His loins tightened at the memory. She had been tempting, but without the map, she was of no value to him.

There was a knock at the door. Falco. The man was stealthy on his feet and efficient with a knife. He could also organize raids at the drop of a hat.

Reginald bid him to enter. "Did you get it?"

Falco nodded. "We captured the entire shipment before it reached the wharf the Staffords guard. An old man got away, but the others were eliminated."

"And the map?" That's all he cared about. He didn't need crates of rugs.

Falco shoved his hands into the pockets of his loose pants. "Nothing. We went through everything carefully, and then a second time. Whatever the old lady gave her, it wasn't a map."

"Then it's a dead end. Literally," Liz said. "With the old lady dead and Stafford in the sultan's hands."

"Could it have been with the girl?" Falco asked.

"No," Reginald said. "I checked her myself. Twice." His lip curved up on the uninjured side, and Falco smirked back.

"What about the map, and the prophecy," his cousin asked. "Do we continue? What if the girl was the link?"

"She is no one," Falco answered. "Least of all 'one who commands the sea' if this legend is to be believed. And she is landlocked now. I don't see her rising up to bear destruction on all in her wake." He laughed derisively. "At the least, not soon, no?"

Liz shook her head with contempt. "She comes from a family of sea captains. She has some command over the oceans. At the very least, an understanding. And what of this?" She pulled the worn map from Reginald's desk where they had been studying it. "The one splash of color. Red. Her hair? Is that a coincidence?"

"All mermaids have red hair, cousin. It's maritime tradition. If she is connected to the prophecy she doesn't know it. And her ignorance is to our benefit. There will be fewer obstructions to our goal."

As he said the words, a heavy rumble vibrated the room.

A crewman pounded on the door before entering, in a panic. "Captain! The building's surrounded. By an army."

"What do you mean?" Reginald shot back, immediately reaching for arms.

"The Stafford woman escaped! Some giant monster that flies carried her away!"

"A flying monster?" Reginald disparaged. "Not bloody likely."

"Perhaps she commands power of which we were unaware,

cousin," Liz said, stepping back just as the sultan's guards burst in.

They demanded the girl. Reginald waved a hand for them to look around. Not finding her, they took the gold. When he resisted, their leader threatened, "Your life is spared. That is the sultan's mercy, after you sold him a witch." With that, they were gone.

Reginald cursed violently. The others waited for their leader's direction. It wasn't what they expected. "We leave tonight."

"But the weather, Captain!" His small crewman twitched, worried again. "There's said to be a storm coming through."

Reginald loaded a gun then reached for his knife. "Stafford has three ships in harbor, correct?"

"Yes," Falco confirmed. "But they are no doubt heavily guarded."

"Unless the doting father has every available man out looking for his daughter," he countered. "Prepare the crew. I'll get my new ship by one means or another."

"And the girl?" his cousin asked.

Reginald flipped the knife in his hand. "She's next."

Chapter Sour

Allie, think! What did Paxton want with this map?"

Alex had her feet in a bucket of water and a plate of food virtually untouched next to her. Now that her father's worst fears had been allayed, she was subjected to the full power of his inquisition and anger.

"He didn't say why he wanted it. The entire thing was so strange and absurd, Papa. Really."

Alex swallowed and reached for some ale that had been brought for her. Her brothers flanked the sides of the room. Samuel stood with his hands behind his back. Matthew methodically polished the array of knives encircling the hips of his personally designed knife belt. She knew they wanted to help, but were smart enough to wait for their father to finish.

"What else did this carpet seller say?" Her father paced the room not looking at her.

Alex hesitated, unsure how much to tell. "Just what I told you. That I had to protect the secret. Danger was near. If the prophecy came into being great things would occur. Among them . . . I think she said the end of days. I'm not sure. She was talking fast. And . . ."

Her father stopped pacing and turned at her pause. "And?"

"She kept calling me Kelile."

Her brothers' heads shot up. Kelile was her middle name.

"That's damned strange." Matthew looked to the others for an explanation.

"Father, you always told me I was named after a warrior prince. Do we have any other link to him? Did he ever mention a prophecy?"

"Enough!" Her father looked harried. "I don't want any of you to ever mention this prophecy. Or any other for that matter. It's all a legend. People are killing each other in the hopes of gaining some mythical power."

"And untold riches," Alex said.

"Alex," her father warned. "Your mother . . ." He choked on the memory. "Your mother died because of people who believed in this treasure. This prophecy holds only promises but can never deliver. Don't be duped. There will always be people looking for an easy way to riches. There isn't one. Only work. Don't forget it."

Her brothers nodded, but Alex thought there was more to be told. She also knew she wouldn't get it out of her father tonight.

"Birdie is okay?" she asked.

"Yes," her father responded. "I sent him to tell the crew you were safe and to prepare the ships for departure."

"We leave then?" Samuel asked.

"I'm leaving," their father corrected.

"What?" Samuel straightened to his full height. "I thought we stayed together. For safety."

"Head to Portsmouth. I'll meet you there."

Alex looked at her brother desperately, wanting him to intervene.

"Matthew will captain Alex's ship."

"What!" Alex stood, feet still in the bucket. "No offense, Matthew."

"None taken."

"Father, I'm perfectly able. I—"

"You were kidnapped and nearly raped and murdered. You are forbidden to return to Morocco with a Stafford ship. You are suspended from your captainship—for now."

Alex gasped, hurt. "But—"

Her father cut her off, relentlessly bearing down on her. He was tall. It was intimidating enough without the knowledge that she had disappointed him and he no longer trusted her. "Every man delivering that shipment from the market to the harbor is dead, Alex. They were your responsibility. Consider this lenient."

His words struck hard. "No . . ." she breathed, horrified at the loss.

Her father's tone softened, but only a little. "Skill is not good enough. You have to be smarter than every man out in the ocean, in the harbor, dealing with merchants, bankers . . ." He ran out of examples. "Everyone, everywhere, every moment. That is the choice you made. God knows I would rather you married off and having babies. But if you insist on captaining a ship, there are no excuses and no weaknesses. As a woman, you can't afford it. You are the first target for every ship out there, and don't think they won't find you."

Samuel stepped forward to her side and put a hand on her shoulder. "She's exhausted."

"I'd rather exhausted than dead." Robert Stafford spun away from his children and gathered himself. If Paxton believed in this prophecy and linked it to Alex or his family, they would never be safe. He had thought all the believers were dead. But always there seemed a carrier of the myth. Someone who spoke so beguiling of fortune and power that others listened and would do anything to gain part of it. His friend Kelile had died because of the legend. And Rebecca, his beloved wife, gone—murdered, saving their only daughter, a daughter who couldn't even remember that night.

Prophecy or not, Alex was a target, especially at sea. But the sea had been the only thing that made Alex happy after her mother was gone, and it had seemed wrong to keep her from it, especially since that's where her talents lay. Unfortunately, her uncanny knack for understanding the sea would only add to suspicions about the prophecy.

There was a knock at the door. "It's Birdie, sir."

"Come in," Robert said. "What's the news?"

"A lot of it and none good." Birdie shifted on his feet, gnarled fingers brushing back the remains of his hair. "Seems one of the ships is, uh . . . missing."

Four voices shouted at once with questions. "What? Whose ship? When?"

"Samuel's." Birdie looked at him. "Sorry, boy."

Alex breathed in relief while Samuel cursed. "Was it taken?" he asked.

"That's the word. A load full of pirates overwhelmed the crew."

"How long ago?"

"At least two hours. Some say they recognized the men. Part of Reginald Paxton's crew." Birdie spit in the fireplace when he said the name.

Samuel swore. "What does that bastard suddenly want with this family?"

"I'm going after him," Robert announced. "If it's a war he wants, it's a war he will get. Samuel, you're in charge. Keep everyone together until I return."

"I should go with you," Samuel insisted.

"I need you to lead, not fight." Robert laid a hand on his son's shoulder. "Do this for me."

Samuel reluctantly agreed.

"Birdie, you're with Alexandra. Stick to her like glue, would you?"

"Aye, Captain. A pleasure and a challenge," Birdie said.

Robert gave his sons a hug. His daughter stood defiant, feet still in the bucket.

"Papa, please. It doesn't feel right. There's a storm coming, I can smell it. *Feel* it. Wait one day to think it over."

"There's nothing to think over. When Samuel has a new ship, you can have yours back. That will give you time to think over what you really want."

"Yes, sir." She swallowed hard. "Please return safely and soon."

Robert nodded as his daughter's head drooped. She had her mother's green eyes. It was hard to deny her anything, but for her protection he would. This madness had to end. He couldn't risk his children.

There *was* a storm coming, and it had his name on it.

It was unnaturally quiet after her family left. Alex stepped gingerly on a towel to dry her feet, guilt eating at her. "Birdie.

I'm sorry. I should have never separated from you. I got distracted and put us both in danger."

"Now, don't you fret. It takes a lot more to kill me." Birdie patted her shoulder. "Fact is, we all know the dangers," he tried to comfort. She waved to the food and he helped himself to her unfinished meal. "It will work itself out."

"My father will capture Paxton. And when he does, it won't be a quick death." Despite her words, a sense of trepidation stayed with her. "Were you able to save it?"

"It's under your bed," Birdie said between bites.

Alex nearly tumbled to the floor in relief and unfurled the carpet. "Birdie, you are a prince."

Her hand brushed reverently over the stunning carpet that was more tapestry than rug. It wasn't the red-haired woman in the waves that intrigued her but something else, something behind her. The shape of a city or location.

Alex painfully returned to her feet and went to the small chest at her bedside. She pulled out the astrolabe. It was not complete, having only two pieces—the first disc and the decorative brass cover. Alex swore the maker had his or her maps completely wrong, but she loved it anyway for its beauty. It had been given to her at birth by a great warrior. Kelile. Her namesake. That only made it more special.

Only now, she was looking for something specific. At the top of the astrolabe, in the decorative area where the instrument connected to the chain, there was a distinct image etched into the brass. Alex laid it on the carpet next to the woman guarding the city. Well, she was either guarding it or destroying it. Regardless, the image was clear. Alex traced the lines. It matched the astrolabe. Perfectly.

"Did you tell my family about this, Birdie?"

Birdie shook his head. "I brought it straight here. Whatcha gonna do with it?"

Alex considered his question a long moment.

She lifted the astrolabe by its chain and slid it over her head. Then she rolled up the rug tightly. "I'm going to hide it," she said truthfully. "Somewhere no one can ever find it."

Chapter Five

England, three years later . . .

Would Paxton never give up?

"You'll never find it," Alex mumbled, not quite conscious, despite the unrelenting shake continuing to bear down on her shoulder. She smacked the annoyance away, eyes still closed.

"Alex! Wake up!"

Alex jumped. "What?"

Not yet awake, she reached out in confusion as her body fell unceremoniously sideways onto the cold, highly polished, and slippery wood floor. Realization flickered quickly. England. Stonewood Manor. Emma's party. She'd fallen asleep. Good lord! A social abomination if ever there was one.

"Damnation, Stephen! Must you yell?"

Her brother grinned down at her with distinct humor as she tried to right herself while wearing a dress that weighed more than she did.

"You wouldn't wake up," Stephen insisted.

She ignored him, trying to find her balance. "Damn, this dress has enough material to make an entire ship's sails."

"I thought you liked it."

"That was before I had to wear it for an entire evening. I'm ready to sink."

"You can't abandon ship yet. The party isn't half over."

"I never abandon ship. And I was up early! These damned affairs go on forever."

"Don't let Emma hear that," Stephen warned. "You'll hurt her feelings."

"Oh, I know." Alex fixed her dress, already feeling remorse. Emma was her one true friend. Actually, her first true friend, aside from family and her crew. But her family didn't have a choice and her crew was paid, so Emma's strange loyalty to her could only mean she liked her, right? God alone knew why. But Alex was learning friendship meant you did things for someone you wouldn't otherwise consider unless under the influence of a loaded barrel. Attending parties was one of them.

She sighed, exhausted. She was a shipping maven, not a social maven. Why wouldn't people accept that? The very question made her grumpy again.

If only she could get one night's sleep. It had been months since the last attack, and she was still rattled. That was not normal. Not for her. She'd dealt with worse. Perhaps it was the waiting and wondering for the next strike. Despite the reprieve, she had a sense of something closing in on her.

Stephen frowned, then immediately made work of circling his sister to make sure her skirts were in place. Not that he was an expert, but he didn't want Alex to see his worry. She was worried enough for them both these days, and it showed. He didn't know how to help, and likely if he did Alex wouldn't accept it anyway. She just wanted him to be happy. For now, he could only watch her back at social gatherings. Of course, that was no easy task.

He froze. There had been a glint of something suspicious at her wrist before she adjusted the sleeve. "Alex, you're not—"

"What are you two up to? Not hiding from my guests are you?"

Lady Emma Preston interrupted the siblings, gliding into their presence and completing the intimate circle of three they had become over the last months.

Alex welcomed her friend with a genuine smile and tried not to laugh at her brother's besotted adoration. His thoughts were easily distracted, much to her relief. She tapped her wrist to make sure everything was secure.

"I had to wake Stephen. He was dozing in the corner here. Very rude, I was saying. You must introduce him around some more. Perhaps the dance floor will keep him alert."

Stephen's mouth dropped in horror.

"Stephen," Emma cried, wounded, "you're not having fun?"

"Uh, I didn't say that. It was more like, umm . . . I was having so much fun, I needed a respite. Yes! And my dear, *dear* sister caught me unawares." Stephen locked eyes with Alex, promising revenge. Alex merely grinned broadly until her friend narrowed in on her.

"Alexandra, I haven't seen you dancing yet either."

"Ah. Yes, well. I am avoiding the dance floor for fear of embarrassing you, not to mention myself. I have a keen sense of survival if you haven't already discovered." Alex had mastered the complicated dance moves in the privacy of her sitting room, but had yet to put them to the test.

"Hummph." Emma seemed far from satisfied.

"I'm just going to have a quick breath of air, and then I will be back to converse intelligently with your many guests," Alex said. "I promise."

"All right, but don't be long. And stay within sight, please. I don't want a scandal at your first real ball." Emma knew she would be lucky if Alex listened, but she had to try. "And while you're out there, practice your gracious smile." Emma gestured in a mocking manner, her hand sweeping out to demonstrate how the smile should flow from within. "You looked quite pained earlier. *Gracious* smile," she added again, teasing.

Alex grimaced. The thought of practicing any more niceties was enough to make her run. Sighing helplessly, Emma gave one last warning, then draped her hand lightly over the arm Stephen offered.

Alex watched them go, giving a little wave when Emma peeked back over her shoulder as if to check on her. Then she slipped out onto the expansive terrace, grateful for the cool breeze on any part of her skin not covered in silk.

Once in the safety of shadows, she looked back at the people within. Some she quite liked, but most, she thought, were a bit odd. She grinned as Stephen was not so gently shoved off to the dance floor with a young girl suffering from nervous eye flutters.

Her heart swelled with pride as she watched him give 'the

gracious smile' to the girl. He had become such a gentleman. This part of their visit had been worth it. She wished her parents could see him now. It had been a priceless moment getting him to wear the proper attire, but it suited him surprisingly well. His shoulders were expanding into the shape of all the Stafford men and he was nearly as tall as the rest of her brothers now.

She leaned against a wall, thinking she actually missed her rude, pushy, domineering brothers. She wondered if being around women so much lately had made her unusually sentimental. She was never this way on the ship.

Alex scanned the crowd, smiling when she found her Aunt Maggie dancing with a handsome, older man. He looked somewhat besotted too. She nodded, thoughtful. Maggie deserved the attention. Her eyes continued to roam, stopped at the entrance of the grand room, then narrowed. With irritation. Lord Pillington. He wasn't on the guest list. She scowled more deeply, studying his companions and recognizing a prominent painter who had been to Aunt Maggie's when Alex first arrived in London. Her respect for the painter diminished immediately. Pillington must have persuaded him to gain an invitation. She watched the overbearing aristocrat with growing annoyance. Pillington searched the room, his smug look impossible to miss.

"Blast!" She watched as he was intercepted by Emma, who greeted him graciously while looking about quickly, no doubt to see if Alex was in sight. Alex stepped back from the window lest she be discovered by the potbellied, dandified lord. Emma was one of the few who knew of the nuisance Lord Pillington had become in his quest to wed Alex. Not that he cared for her at all. He simply needed to marry a rich heiress soon or be carted off to debtors' prison. It was apparently enough to make any Englishman desperate. She had advised him to seek employment.

A cool breeze ruffled the tendrils of hair at the back of her neck. She ventured to the remotest end of the veranda. She could probably hide here for sometime without being missed.

The idea held promise and gave her a moment to think back to the dream Stephen had so rudely interrupted.

Paxton had disappeared for awhile after her capture and subsequent escape in Morocco, but eventually he resurfaced. Unlike her father. She would never know if it was the storm or Paxton that became her father's ultimate doom. She tried not to think about either. Except when Paxton forced her to. Lately, that was a regular event. He was coming after her with renewed efforts and had gained a measure of wealth and power.

Pushing worry aside, Alex turned to enjoy the moon when something else caught her attention. A shadow moved along the back wall of Stonewood Manor. Her guard immediately up, she leaned her entire body over the side of the low marble wall to get a better look. The figure agilely scaled the manor and disappeared through a window. Who could it be? Had she been tracked to the countryside, or was this a random lothario escaping from an unwanted suitor . . . or husband? Alex flexed her wrist in preparation, grateful for the cold metal she always tucked away. If he was an intruder, he'd made a big mistake.

Joshua Leigh, Duke of Worthington and Marcus Hampton, Earl of Stonewood were grinning over the earl's twenty-year-old Scotch. Locked safely within the doors of the earl's library, they toasted their stealthy avoidance of the country ball going on outside.

"Damned good idea that was, Joshua. I couldn't face several hours of polite conversation after the ride from London."

"Nor I, though a hot bath would be pleasant enough." The duke had just lifted his friend, a good-sized man, through the library window and then climbed through himself. As a result he had mud on his hands and an inordinate amount of dust on his clothes. He tossed his riding coat on the floor before he got anything else dirty, and plopped comfortably in a large chair. The earl tossed him a small cloth next to the decanter to wipe his hands.

"I had forgotten all about this birthday celebration for Lady Margaret. She's been a helpful companion and kind neighbor to Emma since my mother died," Marcus explained. "I shall enjoy having her for a neighbor again."

The duke smiled, remembering Lady Margaret. She was a kind, down-to-earth woman who had been good to him and his mother when he was very young. Her husband passed away from a heart ailment shortly after he left for school, and she had gone abroad to visit with family. Joshua had left England as well, after the dean at Eton informed him his father was no longer paying for his education. After that, he had only stopped in London for business and to visit the few friends he had made in his youth. Marcus was one of those friends.

"Who else remains from the old set that I might remember?"

"Colin has yet to marry, but—" Marcus halted when the doorknob to the library rattled. They looked at each other, then in silence at the door, waiting for the person to move on. A scrape against metal and the sliding sound of the lock turning warned they were about to be found. Stealthily, Joshua reached for his jacket and Marcus made the signal to hide.

Alex heard the lock click and opened the door with extreme satisfaction. It had taken three hairpins. She bent them back into shape and slid them onto the cuff of her sleeve. Gently, she closed the door behind her and surveyed the room before venturing forward.

The window to her right was open, a breeze ruffling the curtains. This was definitely where the man had entered. There looked to be a bit of dirt near the carpet. She followed the path to the desk and spotted a crystal decanter. There were two clean glasses near it. On a small side table sat another glass. Even from the distance, she knew it had been recently used. Relief spread through her. Kidnappers and murderers didn't stop to have a drink. But where was the fourth glass? There were never just three. She laid her gloves and silk bag on the table near the door and quickly bent to the strap above her left ankle. If she was outnumbered, it paid to be prepared.

Alex had taken only a couple steps forward when the door swished behind her and the aristocrat she'd been avoiding entered. She covertly tucked her hands into the folds of her dress.

"Lord Pillington," she greeted disinterestedly, not bothering to mask her displeasure.

"Miss Stafford! What a charming coincidence. I've been looking for you. You left London without a word to anyone. Shame on you. Imagine how thrilled I was to hear you had turned up here. In Kent."

"I was just leaving." Her voice cool, she made for the door. "Enjoy your eve—" Alex stopped as Pillington blocked her exit, and the lock snapped loudly in place. With a silent curse on her lips, Alex retreated, unable to prevent a huff of exasperation.

Joshua tensed as the charming American accent cut off abruptly, followed by a husky sigh of irritation. He guessed the woman was too innocent to know the extent of her peril.

"I plan to enjoy my evening very much, Miss Stafford. Very much," Pillington repeated with a nefarious leer.

"Lord Pillington, if you will please step away from the door, I will leave you to relax alone. My brother will no doubt be wondering where I am."

"Not to bother, my dear. My companions are most accommodating. They will make sure no one finds you . . . quite yet," he threatened.

"Sir, I have no interest in parlor games, nor do I intend to marry you or anyone else in the near future. Please do not take it personally."

Joshua pressed flat against a wall, covered by thick drapes. He watched the figures in the room through the reflection of the window's glass on his left. Despite the confidence in her voice, the woman stepped backward slowly, circling a table defensively for distance. She was slim and gently curved. He calculated how long it would take him to reach the man's throat should it become necessary. He thought it would be a pleasure. At the same time, he was curious as to how and why this woman had come into the library in the first place. She was definitely not above suspicion. He listened further. The Pillington chap was confident of his success, and the girl, so far smart enough not to underestimate him.

"My lovely Miss Stafford. How foolish and naïve you are. You *will* marry me." He began as if patiently instructing a young child. "Let me set the scene for you. You are missing from the party, someone comments, 'Lo, how strange. Lord Pillington is missing as well!' A search party is formed and you are found alone, in a dimly lit room, with me, your lover, in a very compromising situation. The guests will pretend to be shocked, and some might be. Your aunt will be humiliated and scandalized. Your friends, what few you may have, will insist you do the right thing. I, of course, will save you—by announcing our engagement."

"Save me?" Her tone was derisive.

"Yes, my dear."

"Please, Lord Pillington. Do not force me to be unkind."

"It is done with now," he squeaked, oblivious to her growing impatience. "You must accept it. Come, Miss Stafford. Let us seal our future with a kiss."

"A kiss! Ha!" She laughed. "Pillington," she stated calmly, while mimicking his earlier condescending tone. "I would not kiss you if you were all that stood between life and a slow painful death. You are old enough to be my grandfather, fat enough to feed a family of four through a very *long* winter, and stupid enough to even think, for one moment, I would *ever*," she took a breath, "have anything to do with a cowardly, manipulative, shallow, money-grubbing, weak-chinned, foolishly attired, shadow of a man such as yourself."

Joshua listened to her assessment, rapt. He couldn't agree more. He thought he heard a grunt from Marcus as well. That about summed the man up, though in truth, he had no idea as to the cad's manner of dress and didn't think it particularly wise to provoke an overeager suitor.

Lord Pillington sputtered, furious and advancing. "You arrogant priss. You're nothing but American sea trash. You will marry me, Miss Stafford. You have no choice."

Joshua heard the click of a trigger and stepped from the curtain instantly, ready to defend. Instead, he froze, stunned at the scene. He stepped back and shook his head toward Marcus on the other side, also about to advance. This woman did not need their help. It was a pale Lord Pillington who was looking down the barrel of a gun. Her next words made Joshua shake his head in wonder.

"And herein, my lord," she said, "lies the difference between an Englishwoman and an American woman." Her voice was without humor. Her hand steady. Her face hard. She knew how to threaten and didn't waste the experience. God knows she tried to be polite about it.

Pillington turned ashen. Beaded sweat, once lingering in excitement, dripped from his brow and lip. "You wouldn't."

"My dear, Lord Pillington," Alex drawled, imitating him. "How foolish and naïve *you* are." Alex began to recount with cool logic a new scenario. "Let me set the scene for you. A shot is heard. Guests come rushing. I wasn't feeling well, you see, and came to the library to rest. Then you came." She mocked being frightened. "It was horrible. You tried to force yourself upon me. Lo, I only meant to scare you. But you wouldn't stop. The gun went off. It was a terrible accident. Such a waste." She pretended to weep. "But secretly everyone will think you deserved it. You were obsessed after all. And desperate, some will say. Your name will be ruined. You will be dead. But," Alex ended pleasantly, "at least you will not have to worry about your debts any longer." She advanced a step. "Do you wish to thank me before I pull the trigger?"

"Please—"

She cut him off impatiently. "Oh, don't beg. It's such a horrible waste of one's last words."

Pillington choked on a plea.

"Very well, since I consider myself both a generous and reasonable woman . . . tonight you will live."

Joshua wondered what kind of reasonable woman carried weapons to social events. Hell, carried weapons at all. He had no doubt Marcus was thinking the same thing.

Alex watched as Pillington slumped in relief. "Don't make me regret this," she said coldly.

Pillington swallowed fearfully. There was a long silence.

"I'm not going to regret this, am I?" she prompted harshly.

"No, no, of course not!" Pillington promised.

"Good." Alex motioned with the gun toward the open window.

Pillington looked confused.

"Well you can't leave by the door," she explained. "Someone might see you, and then I would have to kill you another way. Let's not make it messy. The window, please."

Pillington gazed out forlornly.

"Well?" Alex waited, wondering at the problem.

"My shoes. They are brand new."

Alex looked down at the shiny spectacle of footwear with continued dismay at the man's vanity. "So they are. And what snappy little buckles. Very well. Take them off."

"But—"

"Shoes. Now." Alex forced the humor from her voice, though her lips twitched from the effort. "I shall toss them down to you."

Pillington proceeded to take off his shoes. It took some wiggling. They were very tight. Then he sat on the sill, trying to get the courage to jump.

Eager to be done with the task, Alex lifted her foot and assisted him with a helpful shove. As promised, the shoes followed.

She leaned out the window. "Oh, dear. That wasn't your head, was it? So sorry. Well, do have a nice evening!"

Alex turned from the window with a satisfied huff and flounced over to a comfortable chair nearest the whisky decanter, carefully laying her gun on the table. "If that doesn't earn me a drink, I don't know what does." She poured a healthy splash of the amber liquid. Lifting her glass, she saluted the portrait of one of the earlier, stern-looking, dark-haired Stonewoods, and drank with pleasure. The amber liquid went down hot but smooth. The earl had excellent taste. "Nothing left to do now but go back and join the guests," she spoke out loud. Slowly she gathered her items together and made for the door.

The lock turned easily, and she peeked outside for witnesses before opening the door and closing it again.

There was a full minute of silence before he stepped out from behind the thick drapes with a sigh of relief and an empty glass still in hand.

As the immense shadow moved from behind the curtain, Alexandra Stafford thought she had just made the biggest mistake of her life. Danger set off the hairs on the back of her neck. The figure of the man came into view sparking a far-away memory at the back of her mind while self-preservation came to the front. The face she thought forgotten came into sharp focus then disappeared with the sheer impossibility. Alex forced unnecessary thoughts away. There was no time for reminiscing.

With her gun hand unwavering and her voice distinctly cool, she spoke. "And you are?"

His smile was disarming. His looks devastating. His size terrifying. This was not some pretty, English fop. This was a man.

He was well-dressed in traveling clothes that seemed to slide over muscles that rippled from hard work. Her mouth went dry taking in his white shirt, opened casually at the neck. A summer coat draped over one powerful arm. At the end of the arm was a large, tanned hand holding the missing glass. His free hand casually hooked the waist of his slim-fitted riding pants, drawing her attention to long legs and muscular thighs.

But it wasn't his looks that did her in. It was the sparkle of amusement and intelligence in his eyes—intense blue eyes reflecting an inner glow of vitality that so many pampered aristocrats lacked. She stiffened against the attraction.

Alex knew he was not a thief. He was a man of wealth. He was very comfortable in his surroundings and he smiled with much too much ease. To make matters worse, he was entirely too tall, too broad, too confident, and too attractive.

And too familiar.

"To answer your question, I am a friend of the Earl of Stonewood."

His voice was deep and rich and full of humor. It sent shivers down her spine. She ignored the sensation and debated the possibility with a frown. It could be the truth. If not, well, she doubted a small bullet would stop this man. Evidently he thought the same.

"You don't intend to shoot me with that?"

Alex slowly pulled out a knife from her sleeve and redirected the gun to the corner. "No. The knife is for your throat. The bullet for your friend in the corner."

If possible, his smile got bigger. "Ah, we have been found out."

There was a curse from the other side of the study as another man came out of hiding, a stubborn, lord-of-the-manner expression on his face.

When she turned to Marcus, Joshua took the opportunity to simply enjoy the woman before him. She appeared nearly five foot seven, lean but rounded with shapely hips and, he imagined, long legs. His gaze took in the golden skin at her swooping neckline then followed her features from stubborn chin to arched brow.

Each feature seemed a collection of sharp angles, but all fit together perfectly. Deep green eyes glittered at him from behind full, dark lashes. He liked the way her right brow arched provocatively when she had questioned him. He imagined the pink lips, when not pressed together with determination, were full and soft. Rich auburn hair was pulled back from her face and piled atop her head in an arrangement of shiny, stylish curls. Just one long strand fell over her cheek in a spiral, slightly obstructing her vision in a way that that made his loins tighten. She was exquisite.

He took one look at Marcus and realized his friend had not expected the unexpected. When he turned back to his angel, he realized she was experiencing the same thing. He watched with interest as her features turned to recognition, then dismay. She ventured a discreet peek at the large portrait of Marcus's father on the wall, and he held back a laugh as she visibly winced. The earl's high cheekbones, jet-black hair and dark eyes were hard to miss.

"Oh, dear." Alex shuddered in complete panic. Emma's dear Earl of Stonewood had returned! And quite unexpectedly. How damned rude! Alex wasn't sure it was at all possible to make a good impression at this point. Cringing at her predicament, she lowered her weapons. "One moment, please."

She hurriedly ducked behind the settee near the door, and sheathed her weapons. She straightened, catching them doing the same, eyeing her empty hands curiously. She ignored the earl's questioning look.

"So . . . you're friends of the earl? I've heard he is a nice man." Damn. Emma had really wanted her to make a good impression on the earl and he looked anything but pleased.

The blond giant laughed out loud. "Perhaps we should introduce ourselves."

"No!" Alex blurted out. "I mean it is obvious you are both well-mannered gentlemen, not thieves or anything equally notorious."

"Thieves?" The earl seemed affronted. *Great.*

"Yes, you know, the type to sneak in through windows and such. I thought I saw something earlier and only came in here to investigate. Otherwise, I would never presume to enter the earl's private domain," she explained as carefully as an innocent criminal before a judge.

"Investigate? By yourself?" The earl appeared astounded by the thought. The hole was getting deeper.

"Yes, well the earl is away right now, as you probably know, and so with no one to see to security, I thought, as a friend of Lady Emma, I should"—she swallowed—"make sure the wrong people weren't in the earl's private study."

"That's very noble of you," the blond man said. "But how did you get in?"

"How did I get in?" There was an awkward silence. She looked at him, annoyed. He wasn't being helpful. "Why, same as you." They looked surprised at that. "The door, of course."

She plucked a pin from her sleeve and lifted the wayward lock of hair back into place on top of her head. She followed up with the two additional pins, then reached for her gloves. Evidence gone, and properly attired, she smoothed her dress, took a deep breath and gave the gentlemen a *gracious* smile. It worked. They smiled back.

Joshua felt a catch in his gut. It was a feeling he hadn't experienced in years. She looked utterly sweet. He had to remind himself that minutes before she'd been ready and able to blow his head off. A dimple peeked out of her left cheek and her eyes lightened a bit, seeming unable to resist the humor of the situation.

She moved to the decanter and refilled both their glasses, acting the gracious hostess. "Please sit. I'm sorry I disturbed you. You look as though you had a long journey. You must be exhausted. I would like to hide with a drink . . . er, a refreshment as well after such a long journey. Have you come from London? Will the earl be joining you? I've heard he is a man of very good taste. And very forgiving. Is it true, he is forgiving?" she directed to the earl.

"I believe he's fair," Marcus answered with a winning smile. Joshua's friend was willing to be flattered by a beautiful and mysterious woman.

"Will you join us?" Joshua offered to pour some whisky for her. She nearly snapped at him when he reached for the glass she used earlier. He grinned with delight.

"A lady does not partake of such things," she recited dutifully.

Marcus looked at the used glass and his eyes filled with mirth.

She glanced at him sheepishly. "Well not in mixed company, and only when she has had a very trying evening."

"Yes," Marcus agreed. "I think the earl will definitely forgive you for requiring a drink. Would you have really injured him?"

"Of course not." She sat delicately on the edge of a chair that was offered and fixed the folds of her skirt in a way that all proper women did. "There were witnesses," she explained.

Joshua laughed. The earl choked.

"Oh, dear, are you okay?" Alex hurried to assist him with a whack on the back when they heard a commotion down the hall. "Oh, no!" she moved deftly and locked the door, then spoke with apology and panic. "Hurry! You must go."

Marcus shook his head in self-disgust, moving toward the curtains. "I'm taking my drink this time."

"It's Lord Pillington's friends. You cannot hide. They will be looking for him, and if they find you it's just as bad."

Marcus and Joshua both took offense at that.

"Well not nearly as bad," she amended. "It's just that I have no desire to be married, especially not to an Englishman!"

They feigned insult.

"Though I am sure you are the best of the lot," she reassured, politely. The study door jangled. Alex turned back to the window. "Would you like me to hand you your drinks?" She took their glasses, urging them, yet trying to be helpful.

The earl scowled. "I can't believe I'm doing this." He grabbed the whisky decanter.

"Jump or be fodder for husband-hunting mamas, my friend." Joshua winked knowingly at the red-haired beauty as his friend jumped out the window.

Alex leaned out. "I've heard the earl has a wonderful sense of humor. Is his humor unsurpassed?" An irritated grunt was her only answer. Alex hastened to the blond giant.

"Ah, alone at last," he teased. "Perhaps I should stay?"

Terror and consternation came at once. "No!"

"How rich are you?"

She gasped with disgust.

"Truly, no desire to be married to an Englishman?" he queried. She opened her mouth, ready with a tart response, but he stopped her. "No, don't say it. You'd sooner be shot.

And that wouldn't be well done of you. Being a lady," he mocked, before hopping easily to the ground.

Alex huffed at the impertinence of the man, decidedly relieved when he was gone. Then, just when she thought she was safe, he reached up and caught her wrists, sending heat up her arms. He held her still, and their eyes met with curious intensity as powerful hands slid deliberately over hers. The movement was both shockingly pleasant and achingly familiar.

He smiled knowingly. Then he relieved her of the two glasses.

Alex jolted back, annoyed at her unaccountable response.

"Careful, Miss Stafford, or I might change my mind about staying."

"You're too late." Alex said, feeling inexplicably hurt. For one moment there was a spark of question in his eyes. She slammed the window, but could not turn away. Not possible. Not at all. And yet . . . why did she feel so certain? Leigh, she recalled the name. Was it his given name or surname? It would be easy enough to find out. Determined, she pulled the thick curtains shut.

Outside, Joshua froze, staring at her. It was as if she could still see him. He couldn't make out her expression quite as well as he would've liked, but she shook her head. Was it in disbelief or dislike? What did she mean, he was too late? Surely he did not know her. And yet, there had been that spark of recognition. He shook it off. This woman was too elegant. Too high bred. Too competent? The image of her was right. He wondered, perhaps disheveled, with her hair down? Yes, then the gun in hand seemed to fit . . . but no, too incredible. The curtains closed and he dismissed further deliberation on the subject. He didn't really have time for a woman quite yet, still . . . when had that stopped him?

"I begin to wonder, Marcus, if that was not the most amazing woman I have ever met."

"She picked the lock of my study," Marcus pointed out.

"Resourceful," Joshua defended.

"More amazing than your long-lost slave girl?"

"Equally amazing," Joshua reflected. "Older, of course, and a bit pricklier. I'd have to hear her swear for a true comparison." This woman was much too well-spoken to swear like his star-crossed slave girl. But, if the possibility of finding that girl mere miles from his home wasn't so completely remote, he would question his own sanity. He was certain that girl had long ago married and no doubt had several children. Yes, that was the most likely circumstance.

"I hope you are up to the challenge, my friend. I don't think she liked you much."

"No?"

"No. She only scowled at you. She smiled at me. Obviously she thinks you lack charm."

"Impossible."

"But quite apparent. Whereas I am kind, forgiving, and full of humor," Marcus mocked. "You don't think I look too much like my father, do you?"

"Not at all," Joshua lied.

They laughed again, this time without holding back, and drank a toast to the strange woman they had just encountered, never once expecting their lives would soon be forever changed because of her.

Chapter Six

Emma laughed so hard she nearly fell from her mare.

Alex had just relayed her adventure from the night before, conveniently leaving out her awkward encounter with the earl and his companion.

"He actually went out the window?" Emma wiped the tears from her eyes.

"Well . . ." Alex hesitated, ". . . not without a little help."

"You pushed him?"

"He was forever dawdling," Alex defended. "And it wasn't that far down."

"At least that will be the last of him. I'm so sorry you had to deal with that." Emma sighed. "If I only had your troubles."

"You want to be married to some fat bore?"

"Not to some fat bore. I only wish Marcus would see me as a woman he could love."

"Ahhh. The earl again." Alex thought about the man with whom her friend believed herself in love. He was handsome. Nearly as tall as the blond giant and shoulders that seemed to appeal to women. She also guessed he possessed a bit of steel. Lean and fast. Dangerous if you got on his wrong side. Not as pampered as she had initially imagined. His hair had been ruffled and overlong for the current style, but not unattractive.

"He returned early this morning," Emma said. "Without even a warning. And drunk!"

"Drunk?"

"Well, I'm guessing quite intoxicated by the vague description, and disapproving expression on Langley's face. He said they entered singing."

"They?"

"Oh, yes," Emma gushed, clearly intending to play match-maker. "He and the duke."

"A duke!"

"Yes," Emma confirmed. "A tall, blond, broad, handsome, blue-eyed duke."

Alex thought of the impressive, albeit irritating giant and couldn't have been more annoyed.

"Also, your neighbor."

"Not Worthington?"

Her friend nodded.

Alex was wrong. She could be more annoyed. She loved the Worthington estate. She had even wanted to purchase it for herself only to be told it was subject to yet another foolish English law, entailment. Every time she visited she had explored and imagined the possibilities. Not that she would ever leave America, but she was in England enough to consider another home. She could share it with her brothers. Clearly the owners didn't care for the place as it had fallen into ruin. And Aunt Maggie hadn't had anything nice to say about the previous dukes, which didn't reflect well on the current one. She tried to picture the man she met last night as a duke. It was all wrong. His hands had been large and work worn. Not soft and pale like so many of the men she had met in the aristocracy. And his voice, the accent had been tempered by travel. The earthy timber, so deep, rich . . . and familiar. Goose bumps ran up her arms at the memory. She straightened, irked at herself. Silly to have thought they could be the same man.

"And does this duke have a name?" Alex managed. "A real name?"

"But of course. It's Joshua."

Alex nodded.

"Joshua Leigh," Emma finished.

Alex pulled the reins on Salem so hard he reared up.

"Alex!"

Emma reached over, and grabbed Salem's reins to prevent him from running. She needn't have worried. Alex quickly gained control of the horse. And herself.

"Well. That's a common enough name, I suppose."

"Not really," Emma answered.

"How long has he been a duke?"

"A year at least, but he didn't know it. He has spent most of his time in the West Indies," Emma explained. "But now he is home. Where he belongs. Are you sure you're okay?"

"Yes, yes. I'm fine." Alex breathed slowly, trying to calm the unusual pounding in her chest. "He will live here?"

"Well, I don't know exactly since I was asleep when they stumbled in, but I presume he wants to examine the estate and see what needs doing. You will like him. As much as you are able to like any Englishman," Emma offered. "And last time I saw him, he was very attractive."

"And what of the earl? Are you switching your affections?" Alex teased.

"No!" Emma blushed. "Marcus is the most handsome, wonderful man in the world. Just not the most intelligent," she clarified. "Otherwise he would realize I am perfect for him."

"Obviously," Alex drawled. She smiled and stroked Salem's mane thoughtfully, putting her own concerns aside. "You will have to make him jealous, you know. He must see you differently—as a woman, not a girl." She leaned down to whisper to her horse affectionately. "I may not know much about English society, but I do have three brothers. If you make him jealous, he will realize he has feelings for you. Then he will make a fool out of himself pursuing you. It's a tragedy to watch."

"So speaks the voice of wisdom." Emma mocked.

"Trust me, it's much easier to get men to obey you if they think it is their idea to begin with. However, I admit, I am not very good at it. Which is why I pay my crew to do as I say.

"Come to tea this afternoon," Alex continued. "Aunt Maggie wishes to thank you for the party. She will likely just be getting up by then. After, we will meet in the war room and plot your future romance. Come now. I'll race you back. I can't wait to hear how your earl is doing this morning."

"He's not my . . ." Emma stopped midsentence and urged her mare forward. Alex had to turn Salem around, and Emma took advantage to garner the lead.

Emma was a very accomplished rider, but so was Alex. The only edge Alex had was a fierce determination to win at all costs. She also had Salem. Salem was too arrogant to comprehend ever following another horse.

Alex saw Emma just ahead. The morning sunshine heated her skin as they raced. There was a border of shrubs too high for most horses to jump, and Emma made the turn to go around. Alex knew her only chance for winning was to make the jump. From there on it was open field to the stables. She pushed Salem on and felt his excitement at the obstacle ahead. Their timing had to be perfect.

Joshua Leigh, Duke of Worthington, had a hangover. He blamed the Earl of Stonewood entirely. After their intriguing encounter with the American woman, he had only wanted to plot how he would see her again. Marcus, on the other hand, was more concerned as to whether this new "friend" of Emma's would be a bad influence. The whole idea of having an arsenal under one's skirts did not sit well with him. Joshua smiled, wondering to himself what else she might have up her sleeves and skirts.

He went to the window, grateful for being in a room that didn't get morning sun blaring in too early. The weather in England had been unusually nice. He couldn't remember such a perfect spring, and summer was just around the corner. It made a pleasant change from the tropical humidity to which he had grown accustomed.

His eye caught a movement on the distant lawn. A rider came into view. A female rider he realized, recognizing the rush of Emma's blond hair flying onto the field. An instant later all he saw was black, as a huge stallion flew over a towering hedge. He gasped unconsciously, fearful for Emma, then fearful for how the other horse would land.

He needn't have worried. Horse and rider landed, completely as one. He also noted that the other rider was a woman. Her hat, like Emma's, had blown off and her long hair mixed with the horse's mane to create one magnificent, speeding blur as she gave the horse free rein across the long meadow.

Emma pushed her mare to keep up, and he laughed as he noted another thing for Marcus to worry about. Apparently Emma had grown comfortable riding astride.

Joshua admired the rider as she got closer. He knew instinctively that this was the same woman he met last night. Another accomplishment to add to Miss Stafford's list.

She glanced back at Emma, then pulled in the reins to stop, magnificent red hair swirling about in the sunlight. His heart jumped unexpectedly as he reached for a familiar chain lying on the table next to the bed. He slid the chain over his head and touched the ring at the end thoughtfully. He had given up on finding the owner, or so he had told Marcus. But he had still hoped that fate would one day smile on him. He had even tried to find Paxton once, when he learned the man was in the West Indies. But Paxton was gone before he arrived, as elusive as the woman who linked them.

He tucked the ring under his shirt as he dressed. Miss Stafford could not live far he estimated. With any luck, he could catch up with her on his morning ride. He smiled, his headache clearing. Perhaps this was his day.

A duke! That had to be practically the king of English pains in the arse. It took Alex's race on Salem and three long laps of swimming across the lake to be relieved of the tension she got when thinking of her aunt's new neighbor. Relaxed at last, she floated under a shady area, contemplating Emma and the earl. *There's a situation that will require a special strategy.*

It was a shame Emma wouldn't join her, but now that the earl was back it wouldn't do to show too much impropriety all at once. Emma was afraid he might think Alex was a bad influence. No one said this, but Alex knew.

Alex let her hair halo out around her as she paddled slowly on her back to a sunnier spot. The day was already warm, and the cool lake was her favorite place to visit after a morning ride. There was even a small, intimate waterfall at one end, hidden by rocks and overgrown trees. She thought the place had an element of magic to it. Apparently the first Duke of Worthington had good taste. He must have married badly she decided. Ruined all the offspring of future generations.

Alex dove underneath the water and swam several strokes before coming up for a deep breath of air. She lifted her head and stretched her arms to the sun in appreciation. It was rare that she could enjoy this kind of solitude.

A loud splash immediately disturbed her serenity. Her body froze in terror. To be discovered would be embarrassing to say the least, but she never thought bathing here would be dangerous. No one was ever at this end of the property. Which made it good for privacy, but dangerous if she needed assistance. No one would hear her if she cried for help, and her only weapons—a knife and long whip—were on shore with Salem and the rest of her clothes. She cursed her foolishness. Perhaps the intruder would not stay long.

A male body popped up less than a hundred yards away. Any hope that he would not see her disappeared when his head turned and he spotted her clothing. She heard Salem neigh at the intrusion. It was a warning too late. The man immediately began to turn to find the owner of the clothes. Alex got an impression of massive golden shoulders before she silently ducked underneath the water and swam as far as she could in the opposite direction. For good measure, she held her breath while making sure she was hidden behind the enclosure of rocks near the falls.

Joshua laughed to himself as he followed the gentle ripple in the water. He had caught up with Miss Stafford by pure luck and had been shocked to find his mysterious redhead swimming confidently across his very own lake. She had twisted gracefully on her back to float in the late morning sun and it was then that he thought a cooling swim was not a bad idea. This clearly was not Miss Stafford's first time in the lake, and apparently she did not believe in swimming costumes. He grinned rakishly at the boon and his decision to take her lead.

She was swimming toward the enclosed waterfall. He followed her and positioned himself on the other side of the rocks.

Alex carefully came up for air, causing only the slightest disturbance in the water. She listened desperately for sound. There was none. She forced her breathing to slow, resisting the temptation to gulp much-needed air. Perhaps he was a gentleman and after seeing her clothes quietly disappeared. Yes, that would be the gentlemanly thing. She hugged the rocks, waiting.

A whistle on the other side dashed her hopes. The hairs on her neck stood up straight. He was just feet away.

"Is someone there? Show yourself, friend." The male voice boomed with a tone of mild curiosity.

Alex panicked. Her long silence was interrupted by a deep sigh from the man, as if to indicate he had all the time in the world. She dare not speak and give away that she was female.

The silence continued until he spoke again. "Perhaps you need some assistance. Are you injured?"

She wanted to injure him. "Sir," she cried, alarmed. "You are trespassing on private property! I demand that you leave at once or I will be forced to call my groomsman. He is an excellent shot."

A splash of someone coming out of the water made her gasp. Rising on the other side of the rock was a giant figure of a man. He pulled himself up to his waist and leaned over the rock as if to observe her with the interest he would grant a small bug. His size blocked out the sun behind him, rendering his figure in silhouette.

Alex realized she had never genuinely screamed before. The shocked sound that came out of her throat was strangled in terror, indicating she needed practice at the activity.

He smiled with good humor, observing her panicked expression with obvious amusement. When his eyes lowered

and lingered she lifted a hand to cover her bare breasts underneath the water, and instinctively swam backward with the
other.

"Actually miss, you are the one who is trespassing, and if
you did have a groomsman, he definitely would have shot me
by now."

Alex recognized the duke's voice and was immediately infuriated. She quickly tried to swim away and heard a disturbing
splash behind her. Her heart quickened. When her ankle was
clasped in a big hand, she nearly blacked out from panic only to
be tugged underwater until she was completely submerged. In
other circumstances it might have been described as playful.

He released her ankle while pulling her thrashing body closer
to him. They surfaced together with only a foot between them.
He was blocking the way to the main portion of the lake where
her horse and clothing awaited. Her only choice was to fight in
the water or climb out and expose herself.

She chose the water. Her eyes focused on the giant in front
of her. He seemed even larger without clothes, a thought she
preferred not to dwell on. His blond-streaked hair was dark
and plastered to his head. Two hands came out of the water
to comb it back, exposing large, muscled arms that flexed
nearly as big as her thighs. She would be wise not to underestimate his strength. She did not know yet if he recognized
her from the night before, but likely her accent would give
her away if it hadn't already.

Joshua enjoyed looking at his water nymph. He had the
benefit of the sun behind him and didn't waste the advantage.
Long dark hair floated in a shield around Miss Stafford. Eyes
shimmered in the sunlight, willing daggers in his direction. Her
expression said she was prepared to kill him, and still she managed to look utterly enchanting.

"Hello." He smiled broadly. She did not respond. He could
tell by the direction of her gaze that she was assessing her
escape route options. "Hmmm." He made the sound seem
thoughtful. "Not the friendly type, I see."

Alex sputtered. "Sir, you did try to drown me just now."

"Oh, that." He shrugged, grinning mischievously. "I had to see if you were real or a mermaid."

"Mermaid?" His damn grin was beginning to annoy her immensely.

"Yes. Half maiden, half fish."

"I know what a mermaid is, sir."

"Then why did you ask?" He appeared genuinely perplexed. Alex thought him either a complete dolt or the most infuriating person she ever had the misfortune to meet.

"It was not a question regarding definitions. It was a question as to your answer. The truth of it to be more specific."

"Oh, I see. You don't even know me and yet you accuse me of being a liar? Well. I wonder what the duke would say to having guests of his insulted by trespassers?"

"You're a friend of the duke?" she asked, knowing full well exactly who he was.

"Yes, and you?"

Alex's eyes narrowed to slits. "I would never be friends with a prissy, pompous, ignorant blue blood who doesn't know his head from his arse."

"Oh, I see. You know him well then?"

Alex smiled at that. "Enough to last a lifetime."

"How pleasant for you."

"On the contrary."

"Truly? You didn't find him incredibly handsome?" The duke firmed his shoulders as if preening.

Alex wanted to laugh. "Handsome? Oh, no! Ghastly features at best, sir. Not the type any woman could gaze upon without becoming quite ill."

"Ghastly, you say?" Worthington looked disappointed. "But what of his fine and manly figure?" Alex tried to tread water around the wall of muscle in front of her.

"Lace and puffy clothes can hide a lot. I have no doubt his spindly legs can barely support him. And the protruding belly is uncommonly grotesque," she added for good measure.

He appeared deflated. "Spindly legs and a protruding belly? I can hardly believe we speak of the same man."

Alex pretended to soften up, while inching away. " 'Tis unfortunate, but men do tend to have a rather overinflated view of themselves."

"And what of his wit?" the duke persisted.

"Witless," Alex stated, as if a foregone fact.

"Is there not one good thing you can say about the poor man?"

"Aye. He's not here," she stated, daring him to deny the truth. With a smirk, Alex ducked underwater and made a desperate swim out into the center of the lake, away from the intimate confines of the rocks. He followed her, keeping pace easily. After a short swim he pulled at her ankle again, drawing her body even with his so that he could pass in front of her. Alex tried to control her fit of temper as she surfaced, but not before cupping her hand to send a splash of water in his face. She regretted the impulse immediately.

Worthington grabbed the offending hand with ease and returned the splash with his other. He laughed outright at her outrage.

"Let me go, you beast! Have you no common decency? You should have left when you saw my clothes instead of hunting me down to humiliate me. What kind of man are you?"

"An Englishman." The duke grinned, as if knowing to her that was the worst kind of curse.

"Damn bloody right!" Alex struggled to get away, but kicking in the water was futile. Her feet only came into contact with bare thighs that felt like granite beneath her toes. The more she struggled the closer they came together. She was acutely conscious that they were both bare skinned. Her entire body flushed with the thoughts that raced through her head and the speed at which her heart beat made it most difficult to breathe.

Worthington laced both his hands with hers, holding them firmly without causing pain. Slowly his hands pulled hers as he stretched them out sideways, thus pulling her body inexorably closer to him. His steely, blue gaze locked with hers. She dared not look away.

Alex recognized her anticipation and feared it. Her mouth went dry despite the moisture of the lake glistening on her lips. Her breasts were taut with unwanted desire, hovering just below the water's surface. One good pull would splay her body to his.

Stillness emanated all around. Alex vaguely recognized Salem neighing before her head was forcefully plunged in the water by his large hand. She immediately struggled against the duke's strong-arming until she heard him speaking. The words were difficult to understand as she froze underwater, but there was no mistaking one thing.

They were not alone.

Chapter Seven

Joshua's hand guided her around his back, where Miss Stafford was able to come up for air and still remain hidden. She pressed her face to the center of his back, arms holding his flanks in obvious fear of being caught. The sensation of her body against his back, legs tangling in the water with his, was almost more than he could bear. He swallowed painfully for control before addressing his friend.

"Marcus. Good morning."

"And to you, Joshua." Marcus moved closer to shore, still astride his stallion. "Are you alone? I thought I heard you talking."

Joshua grinned as warning fingers bit into his skin. He was relieved Miss Stafford's horse was blocked from his friend's view. "Just me and Cyclone. I was planning renovations and didn't realize I was talking aloud." He changed the subject. "Are you riding or would you like to join me?"

Nails dug into his ribs at the suggestion.

"Not today. I just came to find you. Langley said you came out this way," Marcus explained. "Your things from London have arrived along with Michaels and several servants. They are in need of direction."

"Ah, thank you. I'll be right there," Joshua said, but didn't move. Stonewood stayed on the shore, not inclined to leave either it seemed.

"Oh, and I found out a bit about that Stafford woman. None of it good, sorry to say."

"Well, no one's perfect." Joshua winced as the nails dug deeper. "I'm just going to do a couple more laps and I'll be right along. Let Michaels know, won't you?"

Marcus nodded with a grin. Joshua knew his friend suspected something, but he was not willing to give up protection of the delicious creature holding him so desperately at the moment. The nails were torturous, but everything had a price.

Stonewood reined his horse. "Very well. I'll tell Michaels you'll be there shortly." He saluted and disappeared down a path in the woods.

"Is he gone?" Alex whispered. The one man she needed to make a good impression with had nearly caught her naked in a lake with his friend. Could a woman be *more* compromised? She didn't know for sure, but this was definitely an indiscretion she *wouldn't* be inquiring about.

The duke turned in the water, and she immediately tried to get away. Having her body pressed against slick, hard muscles was surely more than any woman should have to endure.

"Yes, miss, you're safe." Worthington let her swim a few feet away. The water was cold now without his heat. He followed, keeping a little distance. "Not even a thank you?"

Alex registered the mock disappointment in his tone and turned fully in the water to face him, her exasperation clear. "No, Duke. I'll not be thanking you until the good Lord sees fit to take you. Then I'll count my blessings."

"My spindly legs and protruding belly save your reputation from harm and you wish me dead?" Alex fought the twitch at her lips, refusing to be humored. "That's not very neighborly, Miss Stafford. Not very neighborly at all."

The sound of her name whisked away all evidence of humor. So he knew who she was all along. Bastard. She wanted to take a swing at the arrogant, good-for-nothing English brute.

"Call me Joshua. It's easier than *Your Grace*," he said, emphasizing the proper title. "And perchance you would share your name?"

"Miss Stafford will do."

"Decidedly unfriendly. I thought Americans were known for their welcome."

She swam toward shore, ignoring him.

"Ah, silence. Refreshing in your company, no doubt."

"What? I beg your pardon—"

"Please do. I assume you mean for swimming in my lake, but being a gentleman and your neighbor, of course it's quite all right. I accept your apology."

Alex couldn't speak. The words she wanted to say would ban her from polite society for the rest of her less than sainted life.

"Back to silence then," he noted. "Well, if you don't mind, it's a bit cold here now." Worthington indicated the shore. "Unless you prefer to go first?"

"By all means." She motioned her hand, allowing him to make the first exit. He was waist deep when he turned to see her still watching. She grinned and turned around to give him privacy.

Alex dunked her hot cheeks underwater again to cool her burning skin and hide the shameless grin on her face. She had looked away, but only to turn her head again for a full view of his glorious backside. His shoulders were immense. His back tapered down to a firm waist. And the rest—she gulped her appreciation—the rest brought one word to mind: thoroughbred.

Wasting no time contemplating her easy fall from grace, Alex made her way down shore from the duke. She felt uncomfortable leaving the protection of water, but her skin was pruning up and there was no chance he could see her from this vantage point. She darted for her clothes and dressed in seconds flat.

Alex leapt on Salem as Worthington turned down the path, sitting regally on a nearly all white stallion. The two horses faced each other just as the two humans. Assessing. Scrutinizing. Wondering.

Alex propped her hat on her head and applied her most haughty air to the situation, nudging Salem forward. She reached up and grabbed the whip wrapped around a branch, and hooked it to her saddle before riding parallel to him.

"Perhaps I was wrong," she relented.

He was wary. "Yes?"

"About the spindly legs," she answered, her eyes dropping pointedly to his thighs.

Joshua was speechless. She was, without remorse, letting him know that she had looked at him while he was getting out of the water. A good look, judging by the sudden flush on her cheeks and her complete inability to suppress that wicked, lopsided grin.

"Good day, Duke." She left before he could return the farewell.

His chest began to shake with humor. A rascal of a woman. He would find out her name. But in his heart, he already knew.

Chapter Eight

Alexandra Stafford?" Joshua let the name linger on his lips. Allie? It must be. How many rich, red-haired, wild American women could there be? God help them if there were more than one.

"Yes, Alexandra Stafford," Marcus said, hands entwined behind his back, as he paced.

"Of Stafford Shipping?" Joshua inquired, connecting the clues. Some of their ships had come through the West Indies. He knew them by reputation, not acquaintance.

"So it seems. And a demon by all accounts!"

"Infamous, perhaps," Joshua suggested. "But a demon, no. I've heard of Captain Alex Stafford, but did not know he was a she." That was a bit mind twisting to be sure. Not what he expected. Not married. No children. He corrected, no known children. Just as quickly, he wiped that ill-suggested notion from his mind.

"She travels the seas without a chaperone. And carries weapons," Marcus pointed out. "We have seen that proof ourselves."

"Well, if she is traveling the seas alone, she would need the protection," Joshua offered logically, humoring his friend. Marcus was pacing. Not a good sign. He hoped Emma would show up soon.

"And Langley says she carries a whip. A long one. I cannot have Emma associating with her." He lifted the *London Daily* to emphasize. "Two young woman of society have already ruined themselves from bad judgment. Lady Millicent Fairbanks. We know her father. Harrington. She ran off with their groom." He tossed the paper back on the desk. "And just last week Cherise White disappeared. It's presumed she jumped in the river to get out of a marriage she did not want. Drastic measures indeed to not fulfill one's duty."

Joshua sprawled on a settee and crossed a leg. "Drastic indeed, when one's duty is so simple."

Marcus frowned at him. "I know Emma is lonely, but she will understand this is for her own good. Next she will be hanging around docks with this woman. I can't allow that."

"Really?" Joshua tilted whisky to his lips. "And you think Emma will go along with your plans?"

"I'll tell her at dinner."

"And ruin my meal? Perfect." Joshua finished his drink and set the glass down with a knowing shake of his head. "You deceive yourself, Marcus. Emma is loyal if nothing else."

Marcus ignored him, but poured an extra splash of courage. A sure sign he wasn't confident.

"I think this Miss Stafford is an interesting and resourceful woman. Let us not judge too quickly without further acquaintance. And certainly the Stafford company is known for reliability and talent at turning a profit. I should like to see what they know."

"The sooner I tell Emma, the better," Marcus insisted, planning his course of action.

"Tell me what?"

Emma had entered and stood in the doorway.

Joshua choked. A quick look to Marcus captured his friend's dropped jaw and frozen pose.

Good lord. Emma had grown up.

Lady Emma rushed to the earl's private library and paused to calm herself outside. The earl had left the manor to look around the estate before she had arrived for breakfast that morning. She thought to catch up with him, but pride prevented her from chasing him down. He had not waited to greet her, but had simply left word of his arrival and that he would see her at dinner.

Emma sighed over it for a moment then cleared her mind to deal with more important matters. She and Alex had had a very productive session in the "war room" over tea. Langley and Mary, both trusted servants and friends, had been subtly drawn into the plan. This first part was all up to her.

With a deep breath and a lift of her chin, Emma opened the doors and made her grand entrance. She was clothed in a silver-blue gown that shimmered when she walked and brought out the highlights in her curls. At least that's what Alex had told her. Curls that had been painstakingly piled atop her head—a look they both agreed was designed to show off as much skin and cleavage as possible.

The earl's glass froze midair when he turned to her.

She determined phase one to be a success.

Emma noted with pleasure the careful swallow of liquid that followed. The duke, after recovering from a slight cough, expressed pleasure to see her, causing Marcus's expression to become something between watchful and territorial. Either way, it gave her a wealth of confidence.

Marcus couldn't believe the woman before him. His ward, he quickly reminded himself, while getting his fill of the view. He resisted the urge to carry her up to her room and cover her from the eyes of his friend. A friend who was ogling as amateurishly as him, he noted with irritation. Then Joshua recovered and proceeded to bow over Emma's hand. His words of praise were playful but annoying. Marcus noted Emma's reaction. Yes, very annoying.

"Emma, your beauty is incomparable. You outshine the sun. The fair moon laments that you have stolen her glow. The—"

"Do stop with attempts at poetic flattery, Josh. I shall become sick and spoil the wonderful dinner Emma has so carefully arranged."

"Let me finish, Marcus." Worthington pulled her hand to his breast. "The flowers bloom in praise of your glory. The birds sing a new song this eve. The—"

Emma laughed, and Marcus pointedly took her hand from

Joshua's chest, then bent to kiss her on the cheek she lifted dutifully.

"Welcome home, Marcus. I'm sorry I was not here when you awoke. You had an adventurous evening, I gather?"

"It was rather." Marcus smiled. He tucked her hand on his arm and guided her effectively away from Joshua.

"You were going to tell me something?" she asked.

"Oh. Er . . . it can wait until dinner." Marcus cleared his throat. "Which, I believe is ready. Shall we?"

Emma nodded and politely turned for Joshua with her other hand. She glanced coyly back up at Marcus and tightened her hand on his arm to get his attention.

"This will be nice. I've missed you."

Marcus softened. "I've missed you, too, Emma. I'm sorry I stayed away so long."

She smiled. "You are here now."

Dinner was a complete success as far as Emma was concerned. She just followed Alex's advice. *Lull them into a false sense of security, then pounce.*

The earl was relaxed despite the occasional scowl at Joshua's blatantly flirtatious looks. Emma kept the conversation lively with stories of the village people, the trials of the orphanage, and some local politics. Any questions about Alex and their adventures she sidestepped lightly, knowing there were some things the earl would not approve. By the time the last course had ended she had given him a complete rundown of the estate. She ended with a casual mention of the next topic on her mind.

"But don't worry about remembering all this, my lord. I have made copious notes so that all will be in order and run smoothly when I am gone," Emma smiled. She had just begun phase two of the Alex Stafford Stratagem.

For the second time that evening, the earl's glass froze midair. Emma pretended not to notice. She turned to Joshua. "Did you enjoy the meal, Your Grace?"

"It was superb. But when did we become so formal?"

"Since you became a duke, of course."

"I hope I will always be Joshua to you, my love."

Marcus barely prevented his wine from spilling when his glass came down too hard on the table, making Emma jump in surprise.

"Where exactly do you plan on going, Emma?"

"Wherever my husband is of course, my lord. You would not have us stay here?"

"Husband?" Marcus looked at her as if she had lost her mind.

"Yes, Marcus. I must marry someday. I will be eighteen next month, and it is time to be done with the task."

"Task? I'm not sure your future husband will appreciate being referred to in that way," he said sarcastically.

Emma shrugged as if it was of no consequence. "I believe men think of it more as a business transaction. It is all the same." She directed the conversation away from the matter as if it were no consequence, but Marcus was not done. As hoped.

"And who is this husband you have picked out?"

Emma pulled out a piece of paper hidden in the folds of her dress. "I have made a list of nine, but I believe I have narrowed it down to three. Let us retire to the study and I shall brief you on the offerings."

"The offerings?" Marcus raised a brow, which Emma ignored.

Instead, she stood briskly, all business now, and strolled in the direction of the study after directing a servant to bring dessert and after-meal drinks.

Joshua recognized the set look of determination beneath Emma's calm demeanor and knew trouble was coming. He rose to his feet, waiting for Stonewood.

Mary, the housekeeper, cleared away the table with a deep sigh. "We shall miss her when she's gone. 'Tis sad."

Marcus scowled deeper as he got up. "She has a list of the 'offerings,'" he repeated.

"I heard," Joshua smiled calmly.

"This should prove very entertaining."

"This whole day has been entertaining," Joshua commented.

"Will Hilton!" Marcus roared with distaste. "He is a scrawny lad, and a half-wit to top!"

"William is twenty and a squire, and his family likes me."

"What's not to like?" Joshua asked.

"Lord Frederick is widowed and much too old," Marcus said, rejecting the second choice instantly.

"Is he not the same age as you, my lord?"

Marcus reeled.

Joshua resisted the temptation to laugh.

"He is a good eighteen years older than I!"

"Oh. I hadn't realized," Emma commented innocently. "He seems young compared to Lord Franklin, I guess."

"Lord Franklin is seventy-two. He is your third choice?" Marcus questioned. "What can you be thinking?"

"What all women think. That he will be dead soon," she responded bluntly.

Joshua coughed violently. Both pairs of eyes looked over. He held up a hand. "I'm okay."

Emma continued, "The others are of course possibilities, but these three are willing to take me as I am."

"Damn well, they should!" Marcus exclaimed, clearly outraged that anyone might insult her.

"Don't swear, Marcus. I only mean having no assets of my own. The others are all respectable, but they don't have much money, and I know how important that is to men like you. Since I have no dowry of my own I think it is very generous of these men to take me. They recognize my talents, feel I would make a useful wife, and barring any difficulty in child-bearing, a good mother."

Childbearing! The very thought of her with another man made Marcus's stomach twist with unaccountable violence.

"You are not without assets, Emma. I would provide you with a very generous dowry." He added meaningfully, "When the time comes."

"I will not take a penny from you, my lord. I came here with nothing, and I will leave with nothing, and if you dare insult me by selling me off with a 'generous dowry,' I will run away and never return."

Marcus panicked. Surely this was the behavior akin to what he had just read in the paper! "Where would you run to? What would you do? You are being ridiculous."

Emma swallowed slowly. "It is you who are being ridiculous, by stubbornly refusing to see what is right in front of you. Many girls are married or betrothed by now. I missed my season due to the mourning period. I am practically an old maid compared to others. Once my looks are gone, no one will have me. Humor, intelligence, and wit are not appreciated in wives."

"None of which you have any worry of showing at this moment," Marcus remarked sharply.

Emma gasped. His comment stung, but she recovered her composure, Alex's warning in her head. *Business is business, and when you're a woman, you can't let emotions be involved.* "If you refuse to do your duty I will be forced to leave and find work regardless."

"Why, pray tell, is that?"

"Marcus, why do you insist on being completely obtuse?"

"Why indeed?" Joshua chimed reproachfully.

Emma explained as if to a child. This was phase three. "Even though I think of you as a kind, old uncle, the truth is we are not even related. Some people will think it unseemly that we should be in the same house without a chaperone. Once I turn eighteen it shall not be tolerated too gently. I shall be compromised and rendered completely worthless. Even work in England will be difficult if that should happen. I could go to America. Miss Stafford, who is a dear friend— have I mentioned her?" It was a rhetorical question. She had avoided mention of Alex all evening. "Anyway, Miss Stafford said I could work for her in Boston. She also has two single older brothers, in addition to Stephen, who is currently visiting with her, and they are all very rich so I could marry any one of them and be well provided for."

"I won't have you marrying any American upstart," Marcus assured with a menacing edge. "And speaking of which, I'm not at all certain Miss Stafford is a suitable companion for you."

Emma continued, completely ignoring him. "Miss Stafford says Americans aren't as obsessed with money and titles like we are."

"I'm sure Miss Stafford knows very little about English society. Another reason why it is unwise to associate with her any further," Marcus stated.

Emma laughed. "Well if that's the criteria, then we can take you off the list as well, Marcus. But this is not about Miss Stafford. Or you. It's about my future. And it's difficult enough having to leave my home, but to leave my country on top of that. I would never see you again . . . which, despite your slightly elitist behavior, would make me very sad." She gazed at Marcus with a hurt expression. "Or maybe you have in mind suitors farther away. Then you wouldn't have to think about me at all and your duty will be complete."

"I do not consider you a duty."

"Yes, you do. You always say I am your duty as your ward, and it is your duty to watch out for my interests. Yet now I think you are behaving horribly selfish and unfair to me. You would have me humiliated in front of the entire household."

"I have never humiliated you."

"You will marry one day, and then what will become of me? I cannot remain the mistress here. I will be reduced to nothing. You would have me reduced to nothing?" Emma looked genuinely distressed.

"I am—" Marcus wasn't sure what he was. Baffled for one. Frustrated came to mind. Hell, he'd just returned home. Was it too much to ask for one day of peace?

"I see you have no plan currently in progress." Emma got up and proceeded regally to the door.

"Where are you going now?"

"To my room," Emma said. "I've suddenly acquired a tremendous headache."

"We will discuss this further at breakfast."

"Fine," Emma retorted, "assuming your advanced age permits you to rise that early." It was a deliberate dig, but Marcus was certain Emma didn't see the innuendo, so he refrained from responding. He also managed to ignore the irksome fact that Joshua was choking again.

Marcus surveyed the determined woman in front of him. Her cheeks were flushed with what he presumed to be temper. Her eyes flared to a dark blue that he found utterly fascinating. The result was a beauty. He would give her anything, he admitted. He just didn't want to give her away. Now it seemed she was determined to expand her horizons. Maybe he *was* getting old. He imagined that he used to be quite adroit at handling women.

"I will be awake," he answered.

"I will see you in the morning then. Good night, my lord. Your Grace." She made a polite, but stiff bow.

"Good night, Emma," the duke replied. The earl didn't respond but instead turned away with a deep sigh and poured a drink.

Emma stared a moment at his back, wanting to throw herself into his arms and tell him she would never leave, no matter what the circumstance. But Alex had gone over this relentlessly. She must not waver over phase three. *In any negotiation, you have to be able to walk away.* Only Alex hadn't told her how hard it would be.

"Oh. And welcome home, my lord."

Outside the doors Emma paused and took a deep breath. It was the performance of her life. She hoped her bluff would pay off.

Joshua filled their drinks, then sprawled in his usual manner in a comfortable chair near the window, while Marcus paced, hands folded in the low of his back. As if pacing would help him solve the problem.

"Welcome home? This is my welcome? Indeed." Marcus turned to pace the other way.

Joshua merely smiled. Stonewood didn't know how good

he had it. Based on the number of times his friend had brought up Emma, he knew she was more than a passing concern. By all accounts, Marcus had dismissed all mistresses well over eight months ago, and no one had caught his fancy since then. Still, he insisted on this self-imposed exile from everything and everyone he obviously cared about. Emma adored Marcus. That much could not have changed. He wasn't at all convinced it was brotherly hero worship either. Not with that last, well-choreographed episode under her belt. He hoped his friend would recognize his luck and grasp it while he was able.

"I can only guess boredom has put this notion of marriage in her head. It was not well done of me to leave her here without a chaperone. I shall send a letter to Aunt Matilda immediately."

"Lady Emma is both sensible and competent, my lord," Langley offered, entering the room with a new bottle of port. "And on the contrary, I don't believe boredom is an issue. She has been a model of industry."

"A model of industry?"

"Yes," Langley said. "I believe the influence of Miss Stafford has increased her ambitions and given her remarkable confidence."

"Miss Stafford." Marcus looked at Joshua significantly. "Again. Strange how Emma seemed willing enough to talk about everyone in Kent, yet little about Miss Stafford."

"Except for the fact that she has a number of wealthy, handsome brothers," he reminded pointedly.

"Are they handsome as well now?" Marcus's irritation increased.

"One can only assume."

"But we digress." Marcus returned to Langley. "You were speaking of Miss Stafford."

"Everyone knows Miss Stafford, my lord. Perhaps Lady Emma wanted to spare you the distress. It does take some time to get accustomed to her. She is Lady Margaret's niece from the colonies. Excuse me," Langley corrected, "America. She is quite particular about that colony reference," Langley informed, wickedly. "Her younger brother is with her. Stephen. A fine young man. Unfortunately, easily led by his elder sibling whom I blame personally for any bad behavior on his part, though he has always been studiously correct in my presence."

"That's something," Joshua noted encouragingly for Marcus.

"And I do believe Lady Emma has been a positive influence on Miss Stafford. Miss Stafford is much tamer than when she first arrived." Langley wiped a brow as if reliving the trauma, causing both the earl and the duke to wonder at what they'd missed.

"And what of this brother?" Marcus asked.

"Ah. Master Stephen. He is quite besotted with Lady Emma. Why I heard him propose again the other day."

"Propose!" Marcus cursed. They were back to that.

"Marriage, of course, my lord. His intentions are entirely honorable."

"I don't give a damn—" He turned to the window to gain his composure.

"We shall miss her when she's gone," Langley lamented.

"She is not getting married, Langley!"

"Of course, my lord." Langley agreed in a way that indicated the earl didn't know what he was talking about. He made to exit, then paused at the door remembering something else. "Oh, and, Your Grace, I have not had the opportunity to offer my sincere condolences on the death of your brother."

"Thank you, Langley. It is no secret I did not get on well with my family. I have more regret over the state of the lands than his passing."

Marcus stopped his pacing once the butler had left and stood in the center of the room.

"What do you make of it all, Josh? Perhaps it's the age. That's why fathers marry them off immediately." He thought that over. "But Emma was never difficult. Or hysterical. Or overly interested in social affairs. And now she is industrious! Isn't it enough that I *give* her everything she wants?"

"Some things cannot be given, Marcus. You know that."

"Yes." He sat down, temporarily defeated. "Then it must be this Miss Stafford who is making her want different things. That's the only factor that is new."

"Then," Joshua encouraged him, "let us learn more about this new factor. It's time we called on Lady Margaret and renewed our acquaintances."

He swiveled the amber liquor in his glass. Indeed, it was time to be formally introduced to the intriguing woman who tormented his thoughts.

Chapter Nine

Alex called out to her father, but he didn't turn. Soon it would be too late. She was disappearing into the darkness, pulled relentlessly under by the current. She strained for air, but choked instead. It was useless. The weight of an ocean pressed her down. Dark. Icy.

Just when she thought she would suffocate from lack of oxygen, it occurred to her that this wasn't right. She couldn't die this way. She reached out one last time, a final act of desperation, and released a pained gasp. Air.

Alex thrashed in the sheets, confused. It took only a moment for relief to sweep through her as she recognized her room in Aunt Maggie's home. Lilyfield. Thank God.

It was dawn. The rest, merely a nightmare.

Alex fell back on the pillows and swung a hand over her eyes. What did that one mean? Guilt? Yes, she had a lot of that. But drowning? Of course, if you spent most of your time at sea, it was a likely source of worry. Alex turned on her side and squeezed her eyes tightly to push away the thoughts.

She never told her brothers, but she still looked for her father. She guessed that they did too.

She should have hugged him that last day. Told him she loved him. Told him about the mysterious tapestry rug. But she didn't. She had kept it to herself. And now she was cursed. Cursed with an awful mixture of guilt and hope. Guilt, that it was her fault to begin with. Hope, that her father would one day return home.

It was a slow process, building her reputation with Stafford Shipping. Even her brothers had been nervous to let her out on her own. But they needn't have been. The sea was the one place where she understood what was going on. It was changeable, but it made sense. It wasn't about who had more money, or how to flutter your eyes, or saying the right things in the right order. The sea obeyed different rules, and only those who respected them survived.

She always had an instinct for the water. Being captain she finally felt that she had come into her own. She had navigated the roughest waters, remained steadfast in the toughest negotiations, and protected and fought with her crew against the French, and even some Corsairs looking to poach on American ships no longer protected by the great English navy. She had been injured but survived, and always the sea was on her side, aiding in her triumphs.

Alex stumbled out of bed and opened a heavy curtain to check for light. Dawn crept over the thick forest of trees that separated Lilyfield from Worthington Park. Time to start the day. It would not do to get accustomed to sleeping the hours of the privileged.

Alex went to a trunk she kept locked in the corner. It was filled with fabrics. Not particularly suspicious. She selected a yellow and green silk, pulled it free, and released the Berber carpet hidden in its folds. She unfurled it and laid it at the foot of the bed. Using another key, she opened her shoe trunk. It was mostly empty. She turned a circular lever, lifted a false bottom, and seized her journal.

She huddled back on the bed studying the carpet, the tips of her fingers running lightly over the short silky threads. This had not been made as other carpets. That's why it originally caught her attention. The threads were thin, painstakingly drawn through a tightly woven back allowing the artist to express more detail in the design. She traced the woman's hair in the figure. The waves surrounded her bottom half. One hand was over her womb. The other spread wide, more active. But protecting or wreaking destruction was the question. Alex hoped protecting.

She still recalled the words of the old woman in Salé three years ago. Despite everything that had happened afterward and since, the conversation was burned into her mind in a way that was unnatural. *You are the last kelile of the prophecy. On you rests the end of time. Keep the secrets safe, that we may pass the hour of destruction, or be the source of that destruction, turning the seas upon the land. The kelile must protect the treasure or join the monster of the sea.*

Kelile. It meant "my protector, my gate."

If Alex had understood the old woman right, she was the protector of the prophecy. But how, she didn't know. She just knew that Paxton had only evil purposes, and if she could thwart him, she'd done her job.

The silhouette of the city behind the woman she had yet to discover in her travels. Her best guess was it was an ancient city, either long destroyed, or irrevocably changed so as not to be recognizable.

Or it represented civilization—just another symbol. So much of the story in the richly colored threads was symbolic. Arabic star symbols framed the edges, divided by six Berber images in the corners and at the top and bottom center points. The next layer within that frame had symbols of animals. In the center there were images of the dolphinlike sea monsters on each side of the woman. While made by someone of Berber descent, this was not a Berber carpet. It was a story of some kind. The mysteries of which she might never unravel.

Impatient for the sanity of daylight, Alex dressed and grabbed her bag with a bundle of tools to practice with. Knives and her whip. Birdie had come in last night with news from London. He would be awake soon enough, and they could discuss next steps.

Her first mate found her an hour later in the farthest corner of the garden. Twelve knives lined up vertically in a tree. Not bad handiwork, if she said so herself.

"You're going to scar yourself permanently with that thing," Birdie reprimanded, a rare scowl on his face as he observed the whip in her hand.

"Stay back," Alex warned. "I'm going to master this weapon if it's the last thing I do." She had already failed near a hundred times to capture a knife with the tail, but that didn't mean it couldn't be done. "I'm getting closer," she told him. Catch and release. Catch and release.

With a quick flick, she unleashed twelve feet of leather and struck. The end wrapped thrice around a blade. "Catch!" Thrilled with her success, she tugged and flicked back. "And release."

It was a mistake.

Having not practiced this part, she didn't have any control of the knife. When it released, a streak of silver flew toward Birdie. As if she planned it. He froze. The knife landed with a firm thunk. On the ground. Between his legs.

"Holy, son of—" A long string of curses expelled from his mouth.

Alex rushed over to him. "Oh! Birdie, oh, I'm so sorry. I'm so sorry." Her oldest friend looked ashen.

"All I do fer ya! And this is the thanks!"

Alex stifled a laugh and helped him to sit. He wouldn't let her touch him. Especially now that he was okay, and her chest was shaking with relief and laughter.

"You tryin' ta' take off me privates?!"

Alex blushed. "I told you to stay back."

"Well, I didn't think you'd catch one, not to mention wield it on me innocent self!"

Alex took off the leather coat and leggings she wore over her garments for protection. Birdie was going to go on about this one for a while. She saw another figure coming to join them. Whitley, one of the youngest on her crew. He was seventeen and a friend of Stephen's. She had asked him to join Birdie as her friend was getting on in age and she didn't like him traveling back and forth from London alone.

Birdie immediately tried to pull the younger man into the hazing. "Did ya see that? The captain used me fer target practice."

"Yes, sir," Whitley agreed with him.

"Ach. No sympathy," Birdie grouched.

"Can I sharpen your knives, Captain?"

"Thanks, Whitley." She handed him the knife belt, along with wrist and ankle sheaths, and he went to the tree to collect the blades. Normally she would do it herself, but she had been teaching Whitley, and he had proven quick to learn what she liked. "I'll have my correspondence ready in a few hours. Before luncheon. Be sure to wake Stephen soon. He is getting fat and lazy." She gave the gentle, brown-haired boy a wink, and handed him the rolled whip. "Clean and oil that for me."

"Will do, Captain."

Alex tossed her protective leathers over one arm and locked her free elbow with one of Birdie's. "Now that's how crew are supposed to behave, Birdie."

She received a grunt in response. "He's too young ta know better."

"Yep. That's why I like him," she teased. "Let me change and I'll meet you in the study. What would you like? Scones, minipies, strawberries, and some fine whipped cream?"

"That'll be a start," Birdie relented a bit. "I've got some news."

Alex knew by his tone, it was serious. "Okay. Give me ten minutes."

They met in Maggie's study. It was unused by her aunt, and Alex had taken it over. The house was beginning to stir, and Stephen popped in to see if she wanted to go for a morning ride with him and Whitley. She shook her head, and got down to business with Birdie.

"So?"

Birdie laid the latest news periodicals on her desk. "A ship came in yesterday. Another American carrier, *The New Yorker*, with news from the continent. Yer not going to believe this."

"Tell me." Alex was both excited and worried.

"A house was broken into in Paris."

"That doesn't sound unusual."

"Hold on, no patience for a story, have you? Listen up. This marquis guy was a collector in books of astrology and prophecies."

"Was?" She straightened.

"Aye. They found him dead. Throat slit. Anyways, not much was taken. Whatever basics they could get quickly, and an old book and an ancient astrolabe. Rumor has it, they belonged to some astrologer, Nostrodamu or something," Birdie emphasized.

"Nostradamus?" Alex asked. She had heard of him, but only vaguely. He had been a French physician to the king. According to some reports, he often predicted the future.

"Yeah. That might be it. Anyways, astrology. Prophecy. Astrolabe. A connection mayhap?"

"It's unusual."

"Yer not appreciating it yet, I see." Birdie wiped a thick layer of jam over a scone. "But here's this. The feller from *The New Yorker*, he thought it was not so odd at first. Until he learned that an even older relic was stolen from Alhambra Palace. In Spain," Birdie emphasized.

"I know where Alhambra is, Birdie."

He bit into the scone and chewed. "Them's Moors," he went on, ignoring her. "As in your Morocco Moors." He waited for her reaction and nodded when none was forthcoming. "And I suppose you'll want to know what was taken?"

"I'm waiting patiently."

"A box."

"A box," she repeated.

"Yup." He swallowed the rest of the scone in his mouth before continuing.

"Anything in this box?"

"Sure there was. Sure there was," Birdie nodded his eyes widening. "An astrolabe. Supposedly over two thousand years old. That's pretty old. Maybe as old as your astrolabe," he noted. "But here's the clincher." He waited for a dramatic pause, then leaned forward to whisper. "It's supposedly the key to a great treasure, protected by a devilish siren. Only, none know the location."

"You're exaggerating."

"Only about the devilish part," Birdie admitted.

"So the astrolabe is a key of some kind?" she said.

"Could be." Birdie sat back and spread cream on a second scone.

"That's it?"

"That ain't enough?" He bit into his breakfast with pleasure. "Just thinkin', you got that appointment with the museum. Ya might wanta hurry."

"You think this is Paxton's work?"

"Word on the docks is that ol' Reggie is in port. We know he likes the nice girls," Birdie stated frankly. "The man has connections to sell the girls, so maybe that's him in town doing his shoppin', the bastard. The money he earns supports these other activities," he theorized. "Chasin' the siren. Maybe he's learned about the astrolabe. He learned about the siren's map right enough."

"Do you think it's a siren or a mermaid?" Alex wondered. "It might make a difference."

"Don't know. Don't care. They're both man-eaters. Ye oughta listen to yer pa's last request and stay clear."

"I can't if Paxton keeps pursuing us, Birdie."

Birdie swallowed the last of his second scone. "Aye. That's a problem, ain't it." He took some milk and sat back. "You gonna call in your brothers, or do I need to?"

"There's nothing to tell them yet."

Birdie pressed his lips together, nodding. "Right you are." He drank some milk before continuing. "Just some crazies looking for maps, and old astrolabes, and ancient prophecies. All o'which you coincidently got hoarded up there in your room. Safe and sound, I'm sure. Nothin' to worry 'bout here."

"You're a pain, Birdie."

"Yup," he agreed, finishing off his milk and dabbing daintily at his mouth with one of Aunt Maggie's elegant serviettes.

"I'll go to London tomorrow. Meet with the curator, then send word to Samuel." Birdie nodded again, as if that sounded like a wise plan. "I'll send Whitley ahead when he returns. We'll need to double the men on watch."

"Already done." Birdie grinned. "An' I told 'em all not to be yakking about company business to anyone or we'd dock their pay. It's a good deal they have with ya."

Alex nodded her thanks. It seemed Paxton was gathering information about the prophecy. The frightening thing was that information existed. And likely Paxton wasn't the only one searching for clues.

Alex wanted justice, but mostly she wanted to stop Paxton from hurting anyone else. That terrified her the most. She swallowed the emotion and straightened her back. Too many people relied on her for her to indulge in self-pity.

"It's all enough to make me crazy, Birdie."

Stephen burst through the door just then, causing Birdie and Alex to jump up nervously. Guiltily. "Did I hear you finally admit to being crazy?"

"You heard no such thing. And you shouldn't be eaves—" Alex stopped midsentence. Right behind Stephen was Emma, the Earl of Stonewood, Lady Margaret and the Duke of Worthington. Her attention was caught primarily by the latter. She stared at the blond giant, stunned. The last thing she expected was to see him escorting her blushing aunt into her workspace. Granted, the family inevitably ended up gathered in here since Alex was always here working, but entertaining strangers was another thing.

"Guess who we ran into?" Stephen said by way of introduction.

Margaret stepped in. "Such a pleasant surprise, my dear. I'm so glad Stephen was able to convince them to come by. I haven't seen these boys in years," Maggie explained. "This is such a treat."

"Boys?" Alex looked again at the massive duke and the sophisticated earl, wondering if she meant *those* boys. From their wry looks, she guessed it was true.

"Your Grace, may I present my niece, Miss Alexandra Stafford from Boston. And er . . . her associate, Mr. Birdie. My neighbors, Joshua Leigh, Duke of Worthington, and Marcus Hampton, Earl of Stonewood."

"Just Birdie, ma'am." The old man glinted with humor.

"My pleasure." Worthington bowed to them with an easy smile, but his eyes were fixed on Alex. She didn't need to look at him to know it.

Stonewood bowed as well. Emma stepped forward with less formality and took both of Birdie's hands in greeting.

"It's a rare joy seein' your purty face again, m'lady." Birdie smiled with genuine pleasure.

Joshua studied his prey while greetings were exchanged. She stood behind the ebony desk in a plain, green day dress. Not quite as tall as he remembered. Her hair was folded in a simple plait that fell over her left shoulder. The sunlight behind her caught the reddish gold highlights as she quickly but methodically folded some papers that were on her desk, then secreted them away in a drawer. Clearly they had come upon her during a serious discussion. He'd caught a look of concerned determination in her expression, and something else. Worry. He thought her brother had seen it as well.

"What were you saying about being crazy?" Stephen repeated, curious.

"Something about how your constant eavesdropping makes me crazy," Alex turned it back on him, managing a good-natured dig.

"Blame yourself. I learned all my spying techniques from you."

"Is that so?" Marcus asked.

Alex fought the blush creeping over her skin. Great, she thought, trying not to squirm. So much for convincing the earl her intrusion was an exception.

"You're even taller than I remember, Your Grace," Maggie intervened.

Alex watched as Worthington elegantly seated her aunt in a blue chair at the other end of the library. "You, my lady, have not changed a bit."

Alex smiled at that truth. Lady Margaret remained a petite figure with curly reddish-brown hair liberally mixed with gray. She wore her hair in the same style as when Alex first met her as a child . . . something akin to a disorganized mop of curls that always looked like she just came back from a tumble in the barn.

Kendall, the butler, and another servant entered with trays of tea and refreshments as the others took their seats. Alex sighed resentfully, realizing they were here for the duration. She would have to join them on the other side of the desk. The only open seat was next to Emma, across from the duke and earl.

She was halfway seated when Worthington's curious observance of the hem of her dress got her attention. She began to glare at him when she realized why he was staring. She was barefoot. The act of sitting down was about to expose her. Having no idea the extent of that social error, she jumped back up as if she had just sat on fire.

The action drew everyone's surprised attention.

"I've been sitting all day," she explained, glancing at the earl to see if he had caught her lack of footwear. He smiled pleasantly, appearing not to notice. She wondered if that was a skill all the blue bloods had, pretending they didn't see what was right in front of them. Birdie took the opportunity to excuse himself.

"Think I'll butter up that young pretty in the kitchen for a bit o' lunch. The cap'n here hardly ever feeds me."

Alex protested, "I just fed you!"

"Aye, but you're a taskmaster. Need me strength to keep up. Not a sympathetic bone in ya," he teased.

"And that 'young pretty' you speak of is at least fifty."

"That she is. A pretty baby, too. Thinkin' I'll be cradle snatchin, are ya?" Birdie gave the men a wicked grin.

Alex suppressed a laugh, shaking her head at him. "We'll see you at dinner then."

"Aye, lass, but if I ain't there," Birdie warned, "don't come knocking on m'door, eh?"

"Birdie!" She hoped the guests weren't overly shocked by the conversation. Maggie was blushing. Birdie just chuckled.

"Good luck, sir," the duke said, as he shook the old man's hand in farewell.

"Ack. You boys'll be needin' it more than me, lad." Birdie bowed to Emma and Lady Margaret on the way out. Alex used the distraction to collect her soft-soled shoes under the desk and slide them on.

"Your Grace, you must catch me up on all your adventures since we last met," Maggie insisted. "You were returning to Eton at the time. I gather you left England shortly after."

"I joined the employ of a Hungarian merchantman with shares in a number of ships. I worked on one of his ships until I earned captain, something that happened more through mishap than experience, I'm afraid. Our leader was killed in battle, which left me as next in line."

"In battle?" Margaret gasped, questioning.

"Off the Barbary Coast."

"A notorious area," Maggie commented, glancing toward Alex.

"Quite." Alex confirmed nonchalantly. "Few of our ships have traded in the Mediterranean or around Morocco in the last several years. The risks don't make it entirely worthwhile. I certainly don't have any desire to return."

"You've been there?" Stonewood inquired.

She hesitated. "With my father. It's several years ago now."

"Have you seen the area as well, Your Grace?" Stephen asked. "I'm told it's very exotic. And what of the pirates?"

"Did I say pirates?" Worthington teased.

"Even I know that," Maggie said.

"It was a fog-infested night when they caught up to us, but we were prepared. Our captain was the only loss. A gut wound slowly took his life. We buried him at sea. Then I was the captain."

"You pirated?" Alex asked.

Margaret gasped at her niece's rude suggestion.

Worthington grinned. "We prefer 'privateer,' Miss Stafford. And it's patriotic, which I'm sure you can appreciate. We defended what was ours. Our attackers happened to have a greedy streak. What they already had, we claimed. In that way, I was somewhat fortunate."

"Well," Emma said without thought of what to say next. She looked to the earl for help. He just smiled curiously, waiting for her to continue. "Well," she said again, a little desperate. "Alex, you and His Grace have so much in common. And now you will be renovating Worthington Park, are you not, Joshua? Alex is extremely fond of the place. You must consult her on your plans. She has remarkably thorough opinions on what needs to be done."

"She does?" the duke asked.

"Not really," Alex denied.

"I'll say," Stephen added. "She's been in there enough times drawing up notes."

Alex blushed guiltily. "I thought it abandoned, not entailed."

Marcus nodded. "One of those English things."

"Exactly."

"And how did you get in?" Stonewood inquired much too innocently.

She smiled back, equally innocent. "The cellar door leading to the kitchen is unlocked. I was concerned there could be squatters or wild animals burrowing away, else I would never presume to enter."

"Of course," the earl agreed.

"Last I had heard the duke was dead. No one thought to inform me there was another on the way." She added that last bit pointedly toward her aunt.

"But what a happy surprise for us all," Maggie remarked.

Worthington smiled. "I shall expect you to visit me regularly to consult, Miss Stafford. I am not nearly up to the task as you seem to be. May I take her away from you a bit, Lady Margaret?"

"Why of course, Your Grace. Alexandra would be delighted to help you. And she is most efficient, I can assure you."

Delighted? Alex raised a brow to her aunt, wondering if she had lost her mind. "I'm very busy . . ." Alex began her excuses, which Worthington ignored.

"And have you had the opportunity to survey the rest of the estate, Miss Stafford? You must have seen a bit on your rides over to visit Lady Emma. I have a wonderful lake. Quite magical actually." He grinned wickedly as her teacup began to rattle on its saucer. "Why just the other day, I thought I saw—"

"I have seen some of the estate," Alex jumped in. "The land is so lovely this time of year, isn't it?"

"And that's not the only thing. As I was saying, I could have sworn I saw—"

Dear lord, he was going to expose her. Certain ruin in Emma's eyes, not to mention the earl's.

Chapter Ten

Alex jumped up in panic and said the first word she could think of to distract Worthington from shredding her reputation. "Butterflies!"

"Butterflies?" the duke repeated.

Yes," she enthused. "Butterflies! I have seen some of the most amazing butterflies of late."

"What about mermaids?" Worthington asked, a wicked glint in his eyes.

"Have you seen one, Your Grace?" Maggie said.

"Once. I thought it was a mermaid, but she swam away before I could find out."

"Scared off by your homely face, no doubt," Marcus suggested.

"Or appalling manners," Alex grumbled quietly.

Maggie stepped in graciously. "We must ride some morning, Your Grace. My niece and I can show you the wonderful changes she has made to the estate. Alexandra has been a godsend to me. I don't know what I would have done without her regular visits this past year. I'm so glad Samuel assigned you the English route, dear." Maggie explained to them, "Samuel is the eldest."

"Yes. Well, it seemed the safest, and I didn't get much choice," Alex explained.

She looked up as Worthington cleared his throat meaningfully. "And of course you get the number one benefit of seeing your beloved aunt regularly."

Alex, horrified at her oversight, quickly jumped in. "Oh, yes. Seeing Aunt Maggie was why I suggested it would be good as well. She is like a mother to us. For many years now,"

Alex explained. "I'm sorry, Aunt. You are much more important than a shipping route."

"Absolutely," Stephen agreed before turning the conversation again. "My sister is actually very bossy, Your Grace. I would steer your horse clear of her."

"And Stephen is a continual delight," Maggie added, supportively.

"It comes naturally," Stephen quipped back, earning some grins.

Alex focused her attention back to Worthington. "So you were a sea captain? I met a British sea captain once."

"Is that so?" he said.

She nodded. "He was quite mad."

Stonewood laughed out loud. "We seem to have a long way toward proving ourselves, Joshua."

"Oh, not you, my lord," Alex insisted. "Emma has spoken most kindly of your character and integrity." The earl smiled at that. She turned to Emma deliberately. "Have you decided yet if you will marry locally, or come home with me?"

Stonewood nearly sputtered. Emma rejoined sweetly, "I am still undecided."

"America is very beautiful. I think you would love it." Alex thought Stonewood was about to have a fit. She smiled inwardly and moved on. "Perhaps we could take a turn outside. I have been in this room all day and a change of scenery would certainly improve my disposition."

"One can only hope, my dear," Maggie drawled wryly.

"Yes, Aunt Maggie. Isn't hope a powerful draw, though?" The others followed her lead outside, with Worthington offering his arm to her aunt. Alex was nearly out the door when she realized the earl and Stephen had not followed. She raced back into the study in time to catch her brother stating his case for Emma's hand in marriage.

"Sir, I beg you, with all sincerity, to allow me to take Emma as my wife."

Alex nearly burst out laughing. Instead she apologized for

her brother. "I'm sorry, my lord. My brother is . . . um, as you can see, besotted."

"Besotted?" Stonewood questioned.

"In love!" Stephen corrected passionately, looking highly offended.

"Besotted," Alex repeated as if his response confirmed it. "And you are too young."

"My lord, I will be eighteen soon—"

"That old?" Stonewood acted impressed.

"Yes, my lord, eighteen. And I will, at that time, come into my inheritance. I can give Emma anything she desires and would do so happily, with your permission that is."

"Hmmm."

Alex had to give the earl credit. He looked as if he seriously considered Stephen's offer before answering diplomatically. He was also much more likeable than she thought he would be.

"I'm afraid, Stephen, that I have recently learned Emma has plans of her own and I cannot commit to an engagement without consulting her first as to the nature of her feelings."

Stephen sighed deeply then flung himself dejectedly into a chair. "Rejection again."

Stonewood raised a brow to Alex, who just smiled at her lovelorn sibling, then mouthed the word, *besotted* back at him. The earl grinned.

"Alas, she has turned me down several times already," Stephen confessed with another heartfelt but exaggerated sigh. "To be loved as a brother. Was there ever a more woeful curse?"

Alex turned to leave. "Do join us, Stephen, once you have recovered."

"I shall, but though I smile, my heart will be breaking."

Stephen changed the subject and told of one of Alex's mishaps on the way to London their first day in England. By the time he finished telling his side of the story, Alex was laughing as well.

"Were you my sister, Miss Stafford, I would be constantly

filled with worry over your misadventures," Stonewood confessed.

"Don't worry too much, my lord. My family has the ability to turn a walk home into a story of legendary proportions. It is how we entertained ourselves growing up. I promise you, I am very careful." She added, "And I would never put Emma in any danger."

Marcus didn't think she would do it deliberately, but she was still young regardless of her experiences. He would keep that to himself. They followed the others at a short distance, strolling the gardens, and he brought up the subject of her aunt's estate. He was surprised at her thorough knowledge of agriculture, though she claimed it was new to her.

"I have a wonderful book that teaches the basics," Miss Stafford explained. "Emma was able to fill the rest of the gaps in my knowledge. She is very adept at running an estate, as I am sure you know already."

Marcus wasn't sure, but nodded politely. He couldn't deny that Emma had a talent for organization.

"And how is it you acquired such a talent with locks?"

"Locks?" Miss Stafford asked, feigning ignorance.

"Door locks, to be specific." Marcus smiled blandly.

"Oh, dear."

"Yes, I'd say so. It doesn't bode well for your character, Miss Stafford." He was teasing, but she looked painfully contrite. He thought any apology on her behalf would be torturous. She bent her head in humble submission. It was entirely at odds with the mischief she had in her eyes.

"I beg you to forgive me, my lord. It is the result of trying to live with two older, ugly, mean brothers. They continually locked me in my room as a child. I used to climb upon the tree branch near my window to escape, but then they cut down all the branches on that side of the tree. It was an odd sight I assure you."

"So you found another way out?"

"Yes. 'Twas the beginning of a whole new career. Samuel and Matthew found me most useful after that."

"The mean, older brothers?"

"Don't forget ugly."

"Of course not, it's their most endearing quality," Marcus said.

"I have passed my talent on to Stephen, but the others are undeserving."

"No doubt."

"I am very sorry about the, uh, disturbance, my lord. I truly thought someone might be up to mischief."

"Um-hmm." She looked sincere, but Marcus suspected she was the cause of more mischief they had yet to discover. The silence spilled over a bit.

"I can see this is very difficult for you, Miss Stafford."

"Yes, my lord, humility is always a painful pill for a Stafford, especially in front of an Englishman."

Marcus grinned. Langley was right. The girl was completely incorrigible.

"And then there is the fact that Emma was on your ship for a number of voyages."

"Oh, dear. Am I to get the full lecture then?"

Marcus balked in surprise. "Lecture?"

"Yes, on safety and women being unable to protect themselves, and that we have no idea about the unimaginable dangers that could befall us."

He was on the defense now. "You must understand that I worry about the very idea of Emma traveling so freely without protection. And," he added, "she is very different since I returned."

"She is a woman with ideas and desires and needs of her own, my lord. In some cultures that is valued."

Marcus lifted a questioning brow, waiting for her to name one.

"Trust me," she smiled. "There is at least one."

"Regardless, those things are not always practical."

"Not practical when found in a woman?" Why couldn't she keep her mouth shut when it had been going so well?

Marcus answered, "Less practical in a woman."

"Sometimes, all I see is that practical behavior prevents one from living properly. Our time may not be long on this earth. I surely do not want my epitaph to read, 'She led a practical life.' It is much too deserving of death."

"I see we could debate this for hours."

"Yes, I'm certain we could. I have enjoyed our visit, though, my lord. You are not nearly as stuffy as I thought you would be," she confessed.

"Who said I was stuffy?"

"Oh, just the way Langley described you, the proper English gentleman and all. It must get quite dull for you."

"I'm plagued by dullness, Miss Stafford," he said.

She laughed at that. "You make me miss my horrible brothers, my lord . . . though with you I needn't worry about getting strong-armed aside if I disagree. They are merciless, I assure you."

He studied her freely a moment, her attention caught by Lady Margaret, who was laughing at something Worthington was saying. She was beautiful, without doubt, and in a way that was entirely natural. For all the experience she had in business and sailing, there was something guileless about her. And when she watched her family, he saw a yearning to take part. As if she wasn't quite part of it. Which was strange.

"Your brothers?" Marcus said, wounded. "It has been a long time since I have been compared to such a lot. Ugly, mean, American ones at that. I thought I was well past Stephen's woes. Perhaps I am losing my touch."

He watched as the American blushed prettily at the unexpected flirtation, but covered it with bravado. "I assure, my lord, such is not the case. But in truth, I think you may have a penchant for blondes."

"Ummm." Marcus neither confirmed, nor denied. "And you, Miss Stafford? Do you favor blonds?"

"I have no interest in any man, my lord. Stafford Shipping promises to keep me very busy for the moment, and there are . . ." She shrugged delicately, fading off as she watched her brother. He had tricked Worthington into giving up his seat on a bench next to Emma, only to take it himself. She smiled at his antics, but worry unconsciously showed behind the polite reply she gave him. "I have enough to think about already."

Marcus rather thought she did. A shadow had crossed over her that was entirely not right. Whatever the problems, her brothers should be handling it. He thought she was taking too much on herself. She was the type to do that no doubt. Overprotective, he added to himself before realizing how similar they were. Unfortunately, all those things did not necessarily add up to a good companion for Emma. He guessed Miss Stafford's life had much too much drama.

Joshua watched them and had seen the change of expression as well. It was much like the one earlier when they first came upon Miss Stafford in the study. He walked over to his friend and disengaged Marcus's arm skillfully from Miss Stafford before she could resist.

"I've come to save you from boredom, Miss Stafford."

"Don't be ridiculous, Josh. Miss Stafford has already informed me I am not nearly as dull as she expected."

Joshua grinned delightedly at that. "Best to leave now then, friend, while you've still made a good impression." Joshua guided her away from the group to a nearby path through the roses. To her credit, she resisted as politely as possible the entire way until he had her out of earshot of the others. Then she scowled at him fiercely. He thought himself rather devilish for enjoying it so much.

"I have no desire to be alone with you."

"We are not alone, Miss Stafford. Even now your aunt is watching us. Do try to look pleasant. I don't want her to be distressed by your manners."

"I don't want her distressed either. By anything," Alex clarified. "And my manners are fine. Yours, sir, are appalling."

Joshua sighed. "I knew I should have kissed you at the lake. You are going to make it most difficult for me now, aren't you, my sweet mermaid?" He added that last bit just to bait her. It worked.

"Don't call me that! And do not speak of that day, ever," she whispered furiously. "If you promise that, I will be less difficult."

"You will kiss me?"

"No!"

"Then you are going to be difficult. You just said you would be less difficult. I begin to doubt your word, Miss Stafford."

"You are infuriating. You cannot kiss me."

"Don't you want to be kissed?"

"No!"

"Perhaps you prefer the earl . . ."

"No!" she said again. "Emma is . . ."

"Yes?"

She paused, gathering herself. "I imagine that someone like Emma would be much more suited for the earl. Don't you agree?"

"Yes. There. We have something in common it seems."

"Highly remarkable." Alex was sarcastic.

"And we both like to swim."

"I'm warning you . . ."

"And we are both sea captains, very unusual that one. Let's see, we are both well traveled." He paused thoughtfully. "Have you ever been to Morocco, Miss Stafford?"

That stopped her.

"Yes. I did not like it much. Why do you ask?"

"No reason. You remind me of someone. Though she had a way of cursing that was a spectacle to behold. Have you a sister, perchance?"

"No. And I never swear. It isn't ladylike."

"Of course not. You're nothing if not ladylike."

"Damned right." Did the man realize he had just insulted her? She caught herself. Did he realize it was her? Did she want him to? That man in Morocco had been gallant and brave and gentle and good-humored. She went over the list of virtues in her head. The duke was not her dream man. He was her nightmare. Best he not realize. Then Stonewood would learn, and any hope of her appearing respectable would vanish faster than an auctioneer could say "sold."

It was strange, though. Meeting him again through completely different connections did not seem possible. The world was too big for it. But there was no doubt in her mind it was him. She recognized the essence of him. The power he exuded yet held back. Dislike him she might, but why then did she feel strangely safe? She stared at him, angry, trying to work out the puzzle.

"Miss Stafford? Miss Stafford, are you okay?" He squeezed her hands, jolting her back to the world.

She cleared her head, and immediately reclaimed her limbs. "I don't think I like you much."

"I gathered that already."

"You are not upset?"

"What you think has little relevance in this case, Miss Stafford."

"I beg your pardon?" She halted again, outraged.

"You don't want to like me but you do, despite everything."

"Really?" she drawled.

"Yes," he responded easily. "What you really don't like is the fact that you do like me."

"I don't."

"You do, and you are simply getting the two confused, not wanting to adore me and adoring me."

"I'm adoring now? Surely that is stretching it."

He ignored her, and continued, "Because to love me . . ."

"Love!" She laughed outright at that, actually humored.

"Because to love me would mean you have to be nice to the man who owns the sprawling mansion you also love and the lake you love to swim in," he explained with patience, "and who is a bloody, British nobleman to boot."

Alex looked him square in the eye. "Yes, I definitely hate you."

"Progress already."

She walked toward the others, who had made a move to

depart. Smiling sweetly, she informed him privately, "You are conceited beyond belief." She tried to take away the hand he had tucked politely on his arm, but his other hand wrapped over hers firmly in an immovable grip. "And your arrogance is despicable, even in an Englishman," she spat, nearly pouting as he didn't adjust his long stride and she was nearly dragged along by him, forced to keep pace.

"I will see you at the Davenport ball," he told her.

"I'm not going. In fact, I leave for London tomorrow."

Alex's aunt overheard the comment and questioned her. "Tomorrow? I thought you weren't going to go until Monday?"

"Sorry, Aunt Maggie. Something came up. I will be back with all possible haste."

"I will escort you," Worthington stated.

"No, thank you," she replied.

"No thanks needed. The roads are not safe. And I need to order supplies and materials, now that I have had a chance to see the sad condition of the estate."

"Oh, thank you, Your Grace," Maggie said. "I so worry about them. And they are not nearly as familiar with the countryside as you."

"The duke has been away for a long time." Alex was going to add that there was no reason to think he knew the roads better than anyone else. She rephrased after catching her aunt's disapproving look. "I have Stephen and Birdie. I hate to put the duke to any trouble, especially with such new acquaintance. It's taking advantage," Alex finished lamely.

Worthington bent over her hand in farewell. "No trouble at all, Miss Stafford. It is the least one can do for a neighbor."

"How wonderful," she said, less than enthusiastic. She turned to the earl more easily and curtsied exactly as Emma had taught her. "My lord, it was a pleasure to make your acquaintance. I hope we will have the honor of your company again very soon."

Stonewood smiled readily, clearly humored by her good behavior toward him. It wasn't her fault the duke was difficult.

Damn if she was going to curtsey to someone who insisted on stepping in where he didn't belong. Which made it even stranger when she recognized an unusual twitch of jealousy while watching Worthington solicitously help Emma into the saddle.

"I will be here tomorrow morning at seven, Miss Stafford."

"Ugh!" Stephen complained. "Another early riser."

"Seven," Worthington confirmed, looking her in the eye and waiting for agreement.

"Umm." She gave a half nod, followed by a muffled, "Maybe."

He grinned and nodded, as if understanding what she said. It made her want to scowl even harder. Damned arrogance of the man.

Once the visitors had taken leave, Alex took her aunt's arm and walked with her indoors.

"I think that went well," Alex said to her aunt.

Maggie answered agreeably, "Yes, dear. You only insulted the duke seven times, and all things British, let me see . . ." She counted in her head. "Yes. Three times. Then of course there was the exposing of your ankles. But who could recall that accidental faux pas amidst so many other well-chosen ones. Of course, I'm not counting all the indiscretions you might have muttered while alone with the duke, but I trust you were all that is genteel and amiable. Yes, indeed. All in all, quite a morning's achievement. You must be starved for lunch."

"Thank you, Aunt. I find I am quite ravenous." Alex took the ribbing with good humor.

"Eat up. You shall need your strength to deal with Joshua Leigh, Duke of Worthington. On that I can be sure."

"Huh! We'll see." She planned to defy him if it was the last thing she did.

Unfortunately, she was now counting the hours to when she could do just that.

Chapter Eleven

Alex stamped another document with unusual force.

The day had not gone as planned.

Seated at her desk in the offices of Stafford Shipping, she was having more than a little trouble focusing on trade orders and tariffs. It wasn't that she minded the duke besting her. She was simply tired. She'd had another restless night. So what if the duke had been waiting for her at six thirty when she snuck out? And she certainly didn't mind that he only spoke to the men the entire ride. He was obviously trying to get at her.

It was working.

Stamp.

She tore the paper. Damn. That was a little too vicious.

It was just that his behavior made her dislike him even more, and she was trying to like him for the sake of her aunt. Yes, that was right. But he was so polite she wanted to scream. It had been a relief to come to the office while the men went off to the Crow's Nest for refreshment and ale. She had hoped they would continue to town without her, but Worthington was nothing if not dedicated to his duty—which apparently meant her protection. Irritating . . . and comforting.

She slammed another stamp on a transaction and smiled, this time reading the purchase. Ah. Now this was a good deal. Dynamite. They were going to sail early in the morn to Dover and make a handy profit reselling it. And she'd keep a little for herself. It was always nice to have at least one sparkly accessory that went with everything. Hadn't Aunt Maggie said that?

Birdie entered a moment later from the reception office, followed by two men. "Sorry to disturb you, Miss Stafford."

Alex went on instant alert, sliding a knife from her wrist sheath, her hands thankfully hidden by the large mahogany desk.

Birdie never called her Miss Stafford.

Unless there was trouble. It was one of their codes.

Knife in hand she reached for the gun holstered under the desk. They didn't keep much of value at the office on the wharf, but she had wages for her crew, and that was enough to tempt any thief. Today it seemed there was a party of two.

"We have company," Birdie explained. One man pushed a gun into Birdie's back, forcing him farther into the room. "Sorry, Captain. They got the jump on me." The second man closed the door behind them. Since the office was just big enough for a desk, some shelves and two large chairs, it instantly felt crowded. Alex stayed perfectly still, waiting for one of them to make a mistake. Or for Birdie to be safely away from the gun.

"Don't worry, Birdie. These things happen." She smiled at the men, her gracious smile. It took them off guard. "Can I help you gentlemen?"

"We'll kill him if you try anything sneaky, lady," the man with the gun said.

"I see that." Alex breathed slowly through her nose, trying to slow the anger and energy coursing through her. "What is it you want?"

"Whatever's in that safe behind you," the other said.

Alex leaned and turned her head to look at the early Gainsborough landscape behind her. Then she turned back, her face quizzical. "You mean behind the painting? I didn't put the safe there. It would have been too obvious."

The man with the gun gave a momentary glimmer of panic. Birdie snorted with disgust. "Aye, they must think we all be idiots."

"In any case, I already paid my crew for the week. We don't have anything here but documents and paperwork. Boring stuff really."

"We want the map," the nervous gunman said.

"Shut up, ya idiot," the other told him. He was clearly the leader. Much calmer.

"I have lots of maps," Alex offered. "Right there on the shelf. You can look for yourself. Charts to just about every known land."

"There's a specific map," the leader said.

"Ah. I see." Alex studied them quietly, wondering how Paxton had found her. She took a chance on fishing out the truth. "The mermaid map, perhaps?"

Slow satisfaction spread across their faces.

"Aye. That's the one. Hand it over, and I'll not kill ya. Least not today." He poked at Birdie with his gun. "Him, I'm not so sure about."

Alex made eye contact with Birdie and shrugged, her face dispassionate. "He's old."

Birdie's captor wheezed. "She's a cold one."

"Stop with your yappin'!" the leader shouted. "I see what you're trying to do."

"I'm just trying to be helpful, gentlemen, and get this cleared up with the least amount of tragedy. In fact, if you both leave right now, I promise not kill *you*," she smiled encouragingly. "Least not today."

They laughed. "Aye, you're a sassy one. But time to give in. We were told the safe is behind the painting."

"Oh," Alex said. "Well, that's true." They nodded, finally getting her concurrence. Then she explained further. "But not this painting." She nodded to a smaller one on the wall behind them. "That painting."

The two villains turned in sync, and Alex fired a shot at the gunman before he had a chance. She regretted that she had to kill him, but shooting his hand or somewhere else could make him accidentally trigger the gun, and it was too close to Birdie for her to take a risk.

The leader panicked and pulled his gun on her, destroying the leather of her chair by putting a bullet right where her heart had been. Alex hit the floor hard, sliding on her back, knife wielded.

"Birdie! Down!"

The old man didn't listen. He hurled himself at the second opponent with enough force to crash through the door to the outer office. Alex bent her knee, pulled a smaller pocket pistol from her ankle sheath, and scrambled to her feet in time to see Birdie flying in her direction. She stepped backward to let him go by, and he landed with a mouthful of curses on top of the dead man.

"Are you okay?"

"Bloody, damned, foul hell, yes!"

The second man was already escaping out the front. She jumped behind the desk, grabbed her knife belt and attached it.

"Take care of this." She indicated the man on the floor. Then she ran.

Her office was on the second story of a small building on the wharf, in a space shared by several other merchants. The villain was escaping out the front door. She leapt off the stairwell of the low second floor and landed in the center of the entrance, gaining precious time and surprising a bespectacled building mate coming in.

"Excuse me." She nodded past the man, dashed out, and jumped the entry steps at top speed, pistol in hand. With a rushed breath, she shouted for help. "Someone stop that man!"

No one did.

They never did.

Damned if she was going to let him go. She had questions she wanted answered. And she had an arsenal on hand. Decent odds all in all.

She turned and sprinted after him down a narrow alley.

Joshua had enjoyed the last couple hours with Stephen. A few pitchers of ale had softened the ride from Kent and relaxed the men into an easy comradeship. Stephen was entirely likeable—sharp-witted, loyal, curious about the world, humble about his knowledge, and completely dedicated to his sister. Joshua gathered it was mutual.

They weren't far from the Stafford office when Joshua

thought he heard a strange pop. In other circumstances, he would have guessed a pistol, but shook the thought off, thinking he was not completely in charge of his wits after a few glasses of ale. When a woman flew out the building in front of them like the devil was at her feet, he pulled the rein on his horse.

"Wasn't that your sister, Stephen?"

Alex was unaware of anyone other than the man she pursued. She threw her first knife and got lucky. It hit the man in the calf. He cursed and limped, and turned his gun on her. She was ready. She aimed, shot her pistol, and hit her target strong and clean. The gun flew from his hand, followed by a pained cry. She pulled another knife, preparing. He pulled the bloodied one from his calf, holding it up protectively, inching toward his fallen pistol.

"Take it easy," she said. "I just want to talk." Before she could say another word he hurled the knife. With surprising accuracy.

Alex dove to the ground sideways, and the blade caught the material of her left sleeve. Too close. *Don't underestimate him*, she thought. She looked up, and he had the gun in hand, aimed her way. Twenty feet. Damn. Definitely too close.

A shot went off as she rolled away, hoping it would miss. She finished the movement by rolling onto her feet, another knife ready. Her next image was of the man crumpling to his knees, gun arm wobbling until the weapon fell loose and hit the turf.

She rushed to him, upset, looking around to see what happened. That's when she saw *him*. High on his white horse, riding toward her. Bloody Brit. What the hell was he thinking?

In fury, she shouted. "You killed him!" Clearly not the thanks he was expecting, as he shouted back.

"He was going to kill you!"

"I had it under control! I wanted him alive. For information," she panted, a little breathless from the run, and the near injury.

Worthington examined the man's hand where she had hit

him moments before, then looked her in the eye, only inches away before stating quietly and searchingly, "It *is* you."

"Of course it's me," she responded. "Who else has my aim?"

He shook his head, seemingly in disbelief. Back in Morocco, she had thought him a different man. She had thought he *liked* her. They had *kissed*. She doubted he even remembered that part. She had been young and stupid. Now shoulder to shoulder with him over the dying man, his presence was still unnervingly attractive, particularly this close. Which, she decided, made her old and stupid.

Alex felt for a pulse at the fallen man's throat. Still there. She shook him by the collar and slapped his face. Not too hard of course. He was dying after all. God help her. She was probably going to hell after today.

Eyes fluttered open. "Too late." The man smiled up at her with yellowed, crooked teeth. It was not a smile of regret. It was a smile of success. It sent chills down her spine.

"Too late for what?" Alex asked. When he laughed, she shook him with increasing fear. "Answer me. Too late for what?"

"Boom. Boom." He said the words like an innocent child. Then closed his eyes again. Dead.

"That was odd," Joshua commented.

Boom, boom? Alex went cold. Her ship. Could they know about the load of dynamite?

She dropped the man's collar and his head hit the ground with a thud. Not bothering to explain, or even retrieve her weapons, she ran. Faster than she had ever run in her life.

Alex made for the water. It was less than two hundred yards. Her ship was in the Pool of London, a very congested area of the Thames. They had just loaded cargo today, so the ship was still close to port, only a hundred feet out. But how to get to it quickly? Smaller barges and launches carted people and small freight.

Alex squinted, trying to see who was on watch. She didn't see anyone. There should have been at least four crewmen. And one on land. Good God. She prayed they were okay.

Running parallel to her ship, she searched the nearby docks. She saw his feet first. He was resting against a wood pole, his hat pulled down over his eyes, head dipped over chest. One of hers. Alex called his name, already knowing. Not wanting to believe it. She forced herself to lift his hat. To look at skin no longer supple with warmth. To see his mouth no longer stretched in a smile, but sagging, eerily cool to the touch. Blood had dried at his throat, and the slit that caused his death was covered by a decorative scarf made, she knew, by his younger sister in Baltimore. Her throat tightened unbearably.

Whitley.

Alex bit back the cry of pain and the tears that threatened to burden her vision. Carefully, she covered his face again and looked out to her ship with determination.

In a red-hot flash, a path across the water manifested in her vision.

Alex ran to the farthest edge of the dock and boarded the nearest ship. Thankfully, it was American. She shouted out who she was and what she needed, giving them little time to affirm or deny. Fury overwhelmed sanity and burned with increasing ferocity as she saw a stranger running across the deck of her ship. Without thinking of the consequences, she found the fore topmast mainstay. It was one of the longest ropes. Ignoring the shouts of the crew, she climbed the square shrouds as high as she could, and did something she never would have done had she stopped to think about it.

She swung.

Somewhere, midair, she thought, *big mistake.*

Alex made it within reach of her ship. Unfortunately, her landing position required her to drop a good number of feet to the hardwood deck. Wood she had picked out herself because of its hardness. Wood that lived up to its reputation.

She dropped, rolled, and rolled some more until she hit the farthest rail. Her bones jarred, her body shook, and her legs were more than a little wobbly when she stood. Testing that her rope-burned hands worked and the knife belt that bruised her hips was still in place, she headed below deck.

There was no time to take satisfaction over her first ship-to-ship mainstay swing, as Alex quickly realized she was alone and she didn't know how many enemies still lay in wait.

Joshua had never met anyone who could move so fast. Even after calling Cyclone, she was steps ahead of him. As she dropped from one ship onto another he realized she was insane.

And God help him, he was going to save her, even if it was from herself.

Joshua spotted a flat barge, not far off the dock, slowly making its way out to midriver between the docked ships. Some of the men yelled when they saw Alex flying onto the ship. He hoped that meant they were friendly. He called out, getting their attention. Then he did something he never would have done had he stopped to think about it.

He spurred Cyclone to top speed toward the edge of the dock. Then jumped.

Somewhere, midair, he thought, *I'm a genius.*

Then he landed.

Fortunately, Cyclone had excellent courage, aim, and landing skills. Unfortunately, for Joshua, he didn't accurately calculate the force of landing and having his horse stop instantly on a moving seacraft holding five men. Cyclone stopped dead.

Joshua kept going. And going.

Into the inky, polluted depths of the Thames.

Chapter Twelve

Alone on the deck of her ship, it was unnaturally quiet, despite the crowd of other crafts jostling for position on the Thames. Guarded, Alex made her way slowly aft, listening for movement, praying she was mistaken, but knowing there was at least one enemy aboard. The sound of wood cracking caught her ear as she made way to her cabin. Someone was in there. And in a rush. She snuck into the chart room next door and secured a gun from her weapons cage.

Creeping back, she waited outside for some indication of where the occupant was and when he would come out. Sudden and continued crashing trumped her patience. She opened the door quietly and pushed with her foot.

The door swung open, and the man looked up from his destruction. Into the barrel of her gun. And smiled.

It was safe to say that was not the reaction she was expecting.

Alex stepped into the cabin. Her aim was secure, but her hand shook. Not because of his evil grin. Nor was it from fear. Okay, a little fear, she admitted to herself, straining for control. More than anything, it was surprise. And the recognition of the scar running down his cheek that she had left on him three years ago.

He stroked it, as if remembering that moment as well.

"Miss Stafford. This is an unexpected pleasure. You weren't due back for several days." He waved a hand inviting her in. "Not that I mind. My, you *have* grown up nicely."

Alex swallowed, her gun unwavering, even as he pulled out the chair by her small desk and took a seat like he didn't have a care in the world, adjusting the cross-hilt, short sword at his side.

"Mr. Paxton. This was an unwise move on your part." Just as she spoke the words, she noticed the cabin door moving toward her and caught the motion of a third person revealing himself. The click of a trigger seemed to echo unusually loud in the space.

Paxton stretched a leg to rest a foot on her desk. "Funny, my dear. I was just thinking that about you." He waved his fingers to the corner. "Meet my associate."

"Lower the weapon, miss," the man commanded.

"It's Captain," Alex corrected, keeping her pistol directed at Paxton. "And I'll take my chances."

Paxton said his next words simply. Without hesitation. "Kill her."

With swift reflexes, Alex dove at an angle toward the henchman and shot at Paxton in the same movement, certain she could get him. Unfortunately, Paxton seemed to have nine lives, and this one wasn't over.

She landed in a heap on the floor. Paxton's man stepped on her hand and pressed his weight down until she was forced to release the weapon. Then he yanked her up by her hair, twisting one arm behind her back.

With her chin thrust upward, her neck tilted back uncomfortably, her nearest weapon disarmed, and her archenemy still uninjured and advancing, Alex decided a little polite conversation might be helpful before she made her next move.

"What do you want, Paxton?"

He sauntered the three steps it took to reach her. "I want what you have, my dear." He ran a finger down her cheek—a caress and a threat. Alex instantly thought not of the map, but the necklace she was wearing under her shirt. Her astrolabe. Would he recognize the symbol if he saw it? She breathed slowly to hide her panic. She had kept the necklace on her body for safekeeping. Now that seemed a bad idea.

"I don't have anything."

Paxton grabbed her by the throat with one hand. He was taller than she was, but shorter than most of her brothers. Nearly six feet, she guessed. His chest was barrel thick with muscles. His arms flexed tightly under his light shirt. He was built tough. Standing on her toes to curb the power of his chokehold made her realize his strength and the ease with which he could toss her, should he so choose.

"You've made this much more difficult than it needs to be, Miss Stafford. Whether you like it or not, you and I are connected. Only I'm destined to win. And you? You don't even know the truth about your own mother. Or why she died."

Alex struggled for air, her eyes not leaving him, trying to discern if he really knew anything about her mother, or was bluffing. Her mother died ten years ago. What could he know about it?

"Ah! I see *now* you're interested?" He released his grip on her throat.

Her voice rasped. "I don't see why we can't share information. Assuming you really have something to share." Damn. He could be an expert now on all things prophecy related, and she still suffered from trying to be discreet, hiding what she knew, even from her family.

"I've been following the prophecy for eleven years, Miss Stafford. I know a fair lot more than you, I'm guessing. But then, all the protectors of the prophecy seem to have taken a code of silence."

Alex stiffened. Did he know she was one of the protectors? Or at least she thought she was one. There were others? Did they know about her?

"I'm not familiar with this prophecy. Can you please explain, Mr. Paxton?" It hurt, but she gave the gracious smile. She would put her newly acquired etiquette skills to good use even if it killed her—something that was looking to be a more likely scenario just now.

Paxton trailed a finger down her throat to the collar, where the top button was undone.

He looked up at her, as if tempted to be distracted, but instead trailed the finger over a breast to her waist. She hid her relief that he'd missed the necklace, but felt the release of her knife belt as he swung it loose in his hand and tossed it to the other side of the room.

"I first learned of the prophecy from a gambling man."

"Why does that not surprise me?"

"Everyone needs to make a living, Miss Stafford."

"I prefer Captain Stafford, if you will. This is my ship that you unlawfully boarded. But you were saying?"

Paxton sneered with pleasure. "So it is, Miss Stafford, so it is. Right. The gambling man. Yes, now . . . I ran into him in Barbados. He had just arrived from the diamond mines in Brazil, after stealing a map from his employer. Of course the map is a copy of the original."

"Or a copy of a copy of a copy of someone's fairy tale," Alex suggested.

"Possibly," Paxton nodded. "But if so, why so protected? I ask myself."

"What is the story of this map? What does it lead to?" Alex kept the questions going. She was certain Joshua and her men were not far behind her. Help was on the way. She would capture Paxton and put him away for a very long time.

"The legend, Miss Stafford, is that there was a queen who lived three thousand years ago, maybe more. She was very powerful and had a great kingdom, but it was not enough. She wished to conquer her enemies and obtain complete reign over an empire that some say stretched larger than Alexander the Great's."

"And? Did she conquer them?" Alex asked.

"Yes. So it seems," Paxton explained, enjoying his story. "There was a great battle, and it appeared as though she would lose, but suddenly the skies darkened, there was a great quake, and the sea rose up and devoured her enemy."

"Bad luck," Alex said. "But very timely for her."

"It's believed that upon sensing defeat the queen sold her soul—to whom, we can only guess—and gained the power to command the oceans. She then used that command over the seas to defeat her enemy."

"Uh-huh." Alex arched a brow to indicate she was not a believer, though in truth, she was fascinated. He told the story well, she had to give him that. "You've collected quite a tale, Paxton. I'm all admiration."

"Ah! But the price she had to pay. As there always is one."
His finger lingered on her blouse again and expertly popped
the second button. "Was to give her child back to the sea.
Only she did not want to comply. And perhaps she thought
she was strong enough to beat that which gave her the
power." He popped another button. "So she took the child
of one of her captive enemies, and offered it as a sacrifice,
thinking to outwit the gods." He slid a finger across her col-
larbone and fingered the chain under her shirt.

"Seems like a god would know," Alex said, trying to distract
him.

"But of course. The innocent child died. Three days later,
the oceans reared up and the kingdom disappeared. The
queen died with all her subjects. Those who survived left the
cursed place, but shared the story generation to generation, as
a warning to all."

Alex felt the ship rock. Not the gentle movement of the
river, but the subtle movement of weight. Her crew was boarding. She had only to keep Paxton a little longer. She tapped the
arm around her throat. "Getting a little uncomfortable there,
sir." The man loosened his hold. "Better. Thank you." Good
manners could win even the nastiest antagonist, according to
Aunt Maggie. She eyed Paxton again. Of course Maggie didn't
have Paxton in mind when she said that. "That's a wonderful
story, Paxton. But what does it have to do with you and me?"

"Ah," he caressed her cheek. She attempted to disguise her
revulsion at his continued touch. "That, Miss Stafford, will
have to wait for another day." He opened the door to exit.
"Assuming of course that you survive this one." He gave a
signal to the man behind her.

The man released her hair and instead locked his arm
around her neck. Alex's vision darkened. She pulled down on
his arm with her free one, turned her face, crushed his foot,
and squeezed out of his grip while striking backward several
times with an elbow, making contact before her legs gave out
from the blood loss to her brain.

Paxton wasted no time. "We need to go. Leave her."

She wobbled and fell to her knees as they escaped. Alex heard something slide across the deck on the outside. She tried the door. Damn! What was that? She was a prisoner in her own cabin. Scrambling, she hooked her knife belt, grabbed a short sword from her wardrobe, took the coiled whip on the wall and secured it over her shoulders, then pulled up the carpet by her bed and jumped down the secret trap door. She had customized her ship for all possible scenarios. A quick escape from her cabin was one of them.

Alex opened another secret door, one deck down, and ran up a ladder to the upper deck. She and Paxton were both surprised when they ran smack into each other. She swung instinctively and he countered, sword in hand. He was stronger, taller, and struck fiercely, the vibration of blade on blade jarring her muscles. But she was fast, agile, and determined. And he had underestimated her.

Alex vaguely recognized the sound of Joshua's voice not far off, but dared not turn. She tossed the whip to the deck for more freedom. Paxton was bearing down on her. Her shoulder burned from effort, and she sought to distract him. "You defend well for your age, Paxton."

"I'm not too old to teach you a few things."

"I'll pass," she retorted.

He grinned, but advanced like a predatory beast. He thought he had her. She stepped back and feigned fear, allowing him to move in. When he did, she stepped aside and arched her weapon, surprising him with a slash to his sleeve, drawing blood, and pushing him back.

"Sorry about the face, by they way," Alex taunted. She moved sideways to avoid the heat of his next fury-driven strike. "I didn't mean to injure you." Her sword clashed with his dangerously close to her heart and she used both arms to stop the blade, shoulders and back straining. "I meant to kill you." Quick feet aided her as she danced to the right before he parried sharply, his blade cutting the air with a swoosh, then colliding again with hers.

"No one's perfect, Miss Stafford, least of all you." He kicked out and sent her sprawling backward. She rolled to her feet and took cover behind some barrels on deck separating her and Paxton. They eyed each other, assessing. Just then there was a loud whistle, and another man came hurtling onto the deck.

"Go!" the man shouted.

Paxton nodded to her as if to politely say good-bye and ran after the man. Panic filled her. They must have learned about the dynamite. Oh, God. Two more men followed Paxton. Neither interested in her. She turned in time to see Joshua crush one of them with his fist. She hurled a knife to take down another. The first of her crew were climbing the Jacob's ladder aft.

Alex ran to the men, shouting. "Get off the ship! Get off the ship!" The sailors' faces looked confused until she screamed at the top of her lungs, seeing her brother and some others in a rowboat not far from them. "Get back! It's going to blow!" The sailor let go of the ladder, and she heard a splash. He knew about their cargo. They all did. They scrambled for distance. All except the duke.

"Get off the ship, Joshua! Please!" She ran past him, leaping down steps to the farthest cargo hold, worrying the entire way. She opened the door fully expecting an explosion in her face.

Instead, she found two bodies. And one of her three crates of dynamite was open. Panic and horror increased. She held her breath and listened. There. To her right. A sizzling sound. She searched, spotted the rapidly shortening fuse and leapt. With her bare hand she extinguished the light, heedless of the burning sensation. She looked up at the sound of thundering footfalls, and Joshua was there. From her prone position on the floor, all she could do was lift a finger to her lips, hoping he would be silent. She could hear another faint sizzle.

"Over there! Quick." She scrambled to her feet next to him. Paxton's men had set a long fuse to get off the ship in time. She could still hear it.

Joshua picked up the two bodies and tossed them. Without thought he squashed the fuse that had been underneath with his wet boot, pressing firmly and holding it an extra long time.

"Any more?" he whispered.

"Guess we'll find out in the next couple of seconds." She gave a wan smile, sorry that this might be their last moment together.

He reached out his hand, and she took it, grateful for the squeeze of comfort. Then he too stood silent, listening. For what seemed like a full minute.

Finally Alex pulled her hand away, and inspected around the crates.

"Shopping again?" he asked.

Amidst the recent danger and stress, he managed to make her laugh. A couple of tears edged out with it, the shock of seeing her men lifeless taking hold.

"I got a great deal," she answered. "And a buyer in Dover willing to pay double my cost and expenses."

"Perhaps you could start trading in safer commodities. Shoes, Miss Stafford. Have you considered shoes?"

"Dynamite is safe," she defended. "Except for when you cap it with a fuse and light it."

"Exactly."

She ignored him and continued to inspect. It appeared safe. She counted how many were missing in the opened box.

"How many?" he asked.

"Five," she said, worried. "They come in packs of five. We only got two."

"Hell."

Regretting that she couldn't stop for her two dead crewmen, she pushed past Joshua and raced up to the deck. It was empty. She ran forward and found Paxton being rowed away to the opposite shore. He stood up in his craft, aimed, and threw. The dynamite landed at her feet. Joshua instantly tossed it back and it exploded midair. A second one hit the rail, and exploded, sending wood shattering near them. Joshua grabbed her and turned away, shielding her with his back, while she fought to be free in order to detect a third stick.

It took a moment. Then it came.

She cursed loudly. It landed in the foresail and got stuck in the rolled-up material, the bottom end sticking out. She ran for it, swiping her whip from the deck on the way, thinking to stop the inevitable. Catch and release. No problem. She flicked her whip, aiming carefully. The next instant she was thrown forcefully to the ground.

"Have you lost your mind?" he shouted.

Alex wasn't sure what hurt most—knowing her ship would be damaged, the explosion assaulting her ears, or the crushing power of being thrown to the damned hard deck by two hundred pounds of wet male. She winced, pressing her head into Joshua's throat while debris shot up and landed around them, grateful that at least the big pieces would hit him first.

Finally, it was silent.

Joshua lifted his head, and moved an arm gingerly to the side, lifting up on an elbow. "Bloody hard decks."

She grunted agreement. "Southern live oak. Only the best for Stafford Shipping." Alex didn't move. She was certain several ribs had been cracked between him and the hardwood deck. And her clothes were becoming damp. "Did you swim all the way to my ship?"

"Not exactly," he answered, inexplicably.

"You stink of the Thames."

He rolled to his side. "I'll take that as a kindly, 'Thank you, Your Grace.' "

"I didn't ask for your help. You could have been killed," she added, furious at him for taking the risk of following her. "And you know what? Everyone would have blamed me."

He rolled back on top of her. His eyes blazed a hot blue, the intensity of them sharpening her awareness. They were both on fire with postbattle energy, so she wasn't surprised when he grabbed a fistful of her hair like he was going to shake the life out her, and spat his words with barely concealed passion. "You chased down a man. Alone. Down a dangerous alley in the docks of London. You were nearly shot, leapt from a ship—the fall of which should have knocked some sense into you. I'm not sure what happened before I arrived. Honestly, I'm too afraid to ask. Then you went down into a hold of live dynamite, knowing it was about to go off."

"And?" Alex couldn't help herself. She said it cavalierly, just to aggravate him.

"And I don't know *what* you were thinking just a moment ago!" He squeezed her hair more tightly, forcing her head off the deck. "You've been lucky before, Alex. You should be smarter now. You risked your life for a damn ship!"

If he did not have her arm trapped she would have slapped him. As it was she struggled uselessly under his weight. Giving up, she elucidated on what he did not know. "It's not just a ship," she choked. "It's all I have—my home, my family, my livelihood. Who I am. The only place I belong." Alex felt the emotional stranglehold around her throat from so many losses. "Today I lost three of my crew. Three men who entrusted their lives to me. Men who were like family. And one a dear friend of Stephen's." Her eyes burned. "He was only seventeen. And I have to tell Stephen. And Whitley's family. And when I do, I want to be able to tell them I did everything possible to capture the ones who did this." A single drop of moisture slid from her eye down her left temple. "If you can't understand that, *Your Grace,* then you have no hope of ever understanding me."

Their eyes locked. Each, she thought, trying to conquer the other. He shook his head. "Damn the Thames." And he crushed her lips with his, as if to punish. As if she had done something to hurt him and he wanted revenge. A thought skittered across her consciousness that this wasn't at all how she had long dreamed their reunion would be.

At first his lips tasted of salt, their movement harsh and cruel. He used his power to remind her that she was not as strong as she thought. At least that was how it felt. But then it changed. A different power took over. She recognized a pained curse from him. A regret. And just as suddenly, he softened his grip, his mouth explored, and he took possession, branding her with increasing heat. Her skin pulsed to life, responding to the coaxing movement of his lips on hers. Her mouth opened with a hungry gasp, and her body arched to be closer, all of her wanting all of him, reveling in his control, welcoming the unexpected freedom she felt in his arms.

When he lifted his face from hers, Alex opened her eyes, slightly bereft. Then on guard, as she saw a shutter come down over his. A hardening against her. It hurt.

"My apologies for not coming to you sooner. There were unexpected circumstances, but you seem to have fared well." He paused. "And clearly there is little room in your life for anything or anyone new."

He should have slapped her. It would have hurt less.

"But—" Alex stopped and started again, "Fire."

He nodded, mockingly, "Yes, we have that—"

"No," she corrected, looking past him. "Fire!"

Forgetting her aching muscles, jarred joints, and bruised flesh, she shoved the giant off her and ran for water.

Joshua stood up like he couldn't believe there was more. He took off his damp shirt, and walked to the smoke, ruined boots still squeaking annoyingly with each step. Wearily he put an arm out to have her step aside. "The Thames and I have this one, madam."

Alex watched as he climbed to the smoking sail, and used his shirt to put out the threat. Not a bad scene all in all. She should enjoy the moment while she could. The next week was going to be awful. She needed to meet with the crew, gather information on Paxton, bury her men, deliver the dynamite, repair the ship, and talk with the authorities. Explosions in the Pool of London would not go unnoticed, and if the authorities could track Paxton, she would accept their help.

Exhausted by the thought of it all, Alex went to the port-side rail to wave her crew aboard. For a long moment she stood staring in astonishment at the sight before her, barely registering the duke when he joined her side.

"Joshua?" she queried.

"Yes?" he replied with a bone-deep sigh.

She pointed to a beast swimming through the water. "Isn't that your horse?"

Chapter Thirteen

Alex met the crew of her second ship, *Sea Fire,* four days later in Portsmouth. Stephen and some of her other crew joined her to participate in the spreading of the ashes.

Alex liked Portsmouth. It was smaller and friendlier than London, and closer to the open sea. She felt contentment walking toward her ship in port, taking pride in the vessel she had designed almost wholly on her own. There was another sleek ship docked just ahead of hers, and she couldn't help admiring its elegant lines. She estimated it could capture some speed. Not as fast as hers, but worth the match.

She had sent a trusted Stafford mate to Dover with the damaged ship, to deliver the sealed dynamite, then continue to Portsmouth for repairs. At least most of the dynamite. She was keeping a little for herself. Port authorities had a warrant for Paxton, but she guessed him long gone. Either that, or he used another name, as he was nowhere to be found. Neither was Joshua. She assumed he was back in Kent, beginning repairs on Worthington. She tried not to think about him. It was too confusing. And she needed to be clearheaded.

The crew was ready. Stephen came toward her, ready to board. She reached for his hand and squeezed. He nodded. He hadn't spoken much since Whitley's death. She had little enough explanation for the reason behind it all. Stephen didn't know about the prophecy or the map. He thought her study of ancient sea lore merely a hobby. She would need to tell him something. Perhaps sooner than she wanted. Especially if danger still lay in wait.

Alex noticed Stephen's attention directed behind her, his mood appearing to lift.

"Joshua!" he announced, astonished but pleased.

She turned. The duke stood before her in all his ducal glory. Well, not that bad. Actually, quite good. Definitely distracting. He was garbed more casually than she had seen him of late. More like the first night she had met him in Morocco. His gaze wasn't hostile, but neither was it welcoming. He took Stephen's hand, then amazingly pulled her brother in tightly and slapped him twice on the back before releasing him. Alex was stunned at their man hug. It was unexpected. Her brother, after his initial surprise, welcomed it. Joshua had a way of comforting. It seemed her brother felt it too. She nodded to him, grateful for his compassion toward Stephen.

"It's good of you to see us off. We should be back in Kent by the end of the week. Perhaps we will meet again then." She put the offer forward. She would like to talk to him and get to know him when things were not quite so impossible, and she could have time to figure out if he was or wasn't quite so impossible.

His grin widened toward her. "Actually, I'm here to escort you, Miss Stafford."

"Captain," she corrected, automatically. "And just where do you plan to escort me?"

"Out to sea and back. With Paxton's whereabouts unknown, two ships are better than one."

"Two ships?" Then it clicked. He motioned to the sleek vessel she'd been admiring.

"She's a beauty," Stephen chimed.

"You're welcome to sail with us," Joshua offered.

Stephen laughed. "No thanks. I'll stick with the sure thing." He nodded to his sister.

"A challenge?" Joshua surveyed them.

"I doubt it would be much of one," Alex rejoined, grateful for her brother's improved humor along with his loyalty. "For us that is." She gave him the course plots followed by a breezy, "Try to keep up."

"We'll wait for you there," Joshua returned. "Don't feel bad. None have beaten her."

"Ha, there's a first time for everything, Duke. But we'll let you lead us out to sea before setting the record straight."

He smiled at her genuinely for the first time in a while. "I think the sea air is going to suit me, Captain Stafford."

"Aye, I think the same, Captain Leigh."

They shook hands and prepared to outwit each other.

"So that's her, eh?"

Joshua's first mate, Mick Leeds, stood at the rail and watched Alex inspect the deck. In fact, several of his crew watched her. Curiosity, envy, or desire, he wasn't sure. Her antics had already made it around London. It was scandalous to society, but on the wharves, and amongst men of the sea, she had gained notoriety—and respect. And with the new stories, old ones surfaced. Stories from crew who no longer sailed with her. Stories about how she could manipulate the sea to her whim and all the creatures in it. An exaggeration to be sure, but curious.

Joshua called his crew to hand. He gave his instruction, and they made the ship ready. "Mick, you're at the helm. I have only one order," he commanded. "Don't let them pass us."

Later that afternoon, Joshua lazily made his way back on deck, enjoying the full sail of *Sultan's Prize*. It had been pure ego, having her made for speed, but he liked to win. They would go two days out, spread the ashes of her men at sea, then two days back. Plenty of time to think about the beautiful captain.

Joining Mick at the helm, he looked back at Alex's ship. "How's she doing?" he asked.

"Keeping up," Mick grunted.

Joshua returned to him quizzically. "What's wrong?" Mick was near sixty, still lean and fit, but more important, experienced. Joshua caught some frustration.

"Nothing. Can't lose her. That's all. Been staying steady on our tail without worry or effort, it seems."

Joshua went farthest aft and gazed out. As if spotting him on deck the *Sea Fire* sped up on their leeward side, then mysteriously she pulled in some sails and made to turn.

"She's turning."

"I see that! But, she's going to lose the wind. It's lunacy." Mick shook his head. "Women."

Then they heard the sharp sound of a whistle. A warning from the *Sea Fire*.

Mick laughed. "She intends to overtake us?"

"And apparently is being very polite about it," Joshua noted, for the warning wasn't required, and none expected an American to show them courtesy at sea. Hell, anywhere, for that matter.

"Well, good luck to her. I guess we'll have the opportunity to teach the cocky young lass a thing or two about real sailors," he said, relishing the opportunity.

Joshua slapped the older man good-naturedly and turned his attention back to the American vessel, curious. Mick was right; they had a strong wind. No need to switch course midsail. What was Alex thinking? He watched as each of her sails unfurled. He could barely make out the sound of commands being shouted from across the water. And strangely, as each sail opened, wind seemed to fill it. He was so enamored by the scene, he didn't notice his own ship losing wind. Not until Mick shouted out to the crew, then to him.

"Blimey! The wind changed! Just like that. How did she know it?"

Joshua laughed. Mick had the crew scrambling, their pride about to take a hit, as the American ship gained on them. Joshua had underestimated the ship, thinking it merely designed to be a merchant vessel. Clearly the Staffords had earned their reputation for delivering on time. Alex's *Sea Fire* seemed to glide across the water like it had wings, tilting magnificently against the wind, and to his amazement, dolphins rode the crest ahead of the ship creating a magical vision.

He spotted Stephen at the helm, a cheeky grin splitting his face, and Alex behind him, a hand on his shoulder as she pointed something out in the sails, guiding him. Then she turned his way. He waved. He realized it was with a bit of awe, for she was truly as magnificent as her ship. She stood with pure confidence, her hair in a tie behind her, flapping wildly. Her blouse and skirtlike pants billowed to reveal the outline of her figure. And her smile, relaxed and carefree—something he hadn't seen before. A smile that said in that moment, she didn't have a care.

She seemed the picture of something joyous.

It struck him hard what a beautiful window into her being, into her life, he was being allowed to witness. And doubly hard when he realized how desperately he wanted to protect that woman. The woman she was at sea. The one who didn't have the cares of a business and social pressures, and threats on her life.

The *Sea Fire* was close enough now for him to hear her captain's orders. If he was not mistaken, the command was, "Crew, give a wave to our British mates!" A lineup of men came to the windward rail, and just as the two ships were parallel, the Americans quietly, uniformly, lifted their hands in a ceremonial wave. Wicked smiles on them all, Joshua noted.

Joshua checked on Mick, who still scrambled to catch up. He tapped the older man on the shoulder before he missed the sight of his life.

"Mick, wave to the lovely lady, my friend."

Mick pressed his lips, shook his head with defeat, then turned from the helm. At the sight before him, he did what any gracious seaman would do. He saluted. Looking somewhat surprised, Alex bowed humbly, accepting the honor.

"Good God, she's a beauty, Your Grace. The ship and her captain."

"Yes," Joshua thought, watching the sight of them pulling away for as long as he could.

Mick grinned, then turned to their crew. "Come on, ya rascals. Going to let some rebels get the lead on us?"

The morning of the second day, Alex was anchored and had lowered a longboat to the water so she could visit with the dolphins. Stephen and a few men joined her while others tossed bits of fish they had netted the night before over the side.

The dolphins clicked noisily and Alex clicked back playfully, having some fun before she had to address her more serious duties.

When it was time, later that morning, Joshua and his men joined them while the minister prayed some final rites over the remains of her men, doing his duty with the utmost sincerity. Only his words were so somber that Alex felt compelled to intervene before the ashes were released.

Each small urn was held by a friend of that seaman. She started with the lowest rank and as Stephen came forward to lead them, she added something that she hoped was kinder, more personal. She'd never had to do this before and faltered at first, the emotion of remembering Whitley painful. But she knew this was the time to comfort her crew, not think of herself.

The men released the ashes, more solemn than monks. Then they waited a moment in silence. It was quiet but for the sound of a very light wind and the gentle lapping of water on the ship. Then there was something else. A shiver crawled up her arms. She sensed something familiar, but even knowing it, doubted herself. A sound, but not a sound. A vibration. With a hand to her crew for silence, she climbed the shrouds to the foretop, standing on the platform and looking out. She saw a spout of water shoot up in the distance and smiled. Sure enough. Whales. A double pleasure to be had this day.

Joshua and the crews of each ship watched bemused as Alex climbed the mast, each jostling to get a view of what she apparently had spotted. Some of his crew, he could tell, became uneasy. The whales had been behind them. She could not have seen them, and she could not have heard them. But perhaps the sea had already shared some of its mysteries with her. He knew some sailors could sense certain animals, though how was unknown. It was usually something eerie and uncommon. But what unsettled the men the most was what she did after spotting them. She held to the mast and began a long, low tune that was picked up by the wind and carried out to sea.

Mick whispered by his side, "Is she singing to them?"

"I believe so," Joshua answered.

"Do you think they can hear it?" he asked.

"I don't know, but . . ." Joshua swallowed at the sight of several waterspouts shooting out of the sea. ". . . I believe they are coming to visit."

Mick released a curse of fearful amazement. "Who *is* she, Your Grace?"

Joshua gave him a questioning look.

"I've been around the sea a long time. I've witnessed glories untold. But this? Legends coming true? I did not think I would live to see it."

"What legend is that, Mick?"

"The sirens, Your Grace. The legend of the sirens."

"She sings to whales, not men. And there's no land near for us to be shipwrecked upon." He could see his assertion was useless. "It's not like you to be superstitious, Mick."

"I never was, before today."

Alex rejoined them at the rail for a view of the whales. She called out to his crew to assure them. "Gentlemen, be steady!"

It seemed to be a family of whales. Five in all. Joshua watched as Alex waved delightedly and called out to the mammoth creatures. The first surfaced miraculously between the two ships, causing waves to rock both vessels, revealing an immensely long, brownish grey form.

"Good lord, a leviathan!" Mick expressed, somewhere between awe and fear.

"No, sir," Alex corrected, "*balaenoptera physalus*."

"What gibberish is that, Captain Stafford?"

"Science. This is a fin whale. One of the biggest, I'm certain. I have seen them before. I have a book in my library if you would like to borrow it. I always get a funny feeling when they are around. Do you feel it?"

"Aye," Mick agreed. "Guess I do."

The crew was more relaxed now, enjoying the antics of some baby whales that circled around them. One practiced an acrobatic leap from the water, earning loud gasps of awe from both crews. Another lifted its tail and slapped it down so near his own ship that some of the men got wet. He heard their surprised laughter.

"Wait!" Alex cried out. "There's one more!"

It was the largest yet, following at the back. Joshua estimated nearly eighty feet. It, too, surfaced between their ships, but this one blew from the furrowed spout, causing a spectacular display. It was perhaps the most remarkable demonstration of sea life, nay, any animal life, that Joshua had ever observed. And it was over too quickly.

"Spectacular!" Mick stated it most succinctly. "Strange," he added, "but absolutely spectacular!"

When at last the whales dove into the depths, Alex gathered her men, and made a final declaration. "Though their death untimely, let it be known that it was their time. And this day, the sea has blessed their passing and welcomed our friends home to the place that they loved and that loved them back."

A cheer went up. When it settled down she continued.

"Birdie, each man who wants it, may have three cups of ale, one for each passing soul." Another cheer went up. "Three cups," she warned. "No more. We make sail at midday. For now, enjoy a meal and some remembrance."

Mick turned to him and made a request. "I should like my burial to be done like that, Your Grace. You'll make the arrangements, won't you?" Clearly the old sailor was more relaxed now that it was over and nothing sinister had happened. "She missed her calling, though. Should have been a whaler." Mick winked, before preparing to depart for their ship.

Joshua watched as Mick made his farewells to Alex, followed by the reverend, who said something that caused a shadow to fall across her face. Joshua was immediately at her side.

"Your Grace," Alex greeted him. "The reverend has asked that he might return on your ship. He believes your men would benefit from some ministering."

Joshua laughed. "My men?"

"Your service is complete, Reverend. If the duke," she corrected, "if His Grace, permits, you may collect your items and return with him. Come see me for payment before you leave." With that she was gone. Joshua watched her leave, stopping to say a few words to others before she disappeared.

"No offense to her, Your Grace, but there's something evil about," the reverend said.

Joshua scowled. "Evil?" He deliberately looked about. "Where?"

"It's not proper for a woman to be among men, alone. Not good for the men. And sure enough there's something not right with that woman. Only God can call to His creatures. God," he paused knowingly, "or the other."

Joshua gripped the man by the shirt, tasting bile at the suggestion Alex could in anyway be evil. Crazy, insane, brash, hotheaded, and a lot more. But never evil. He let the man go. It wasn't worth the effort. But it saddened him that a man of God could not appreciate the beauty of what they had just observed.

"Mick!" he shouted. "The reverend will sail back with us. Make the arrangements."

"Aye, Your Grace."

Joshua made one last scan for Alex. The world had encroached on her domain and she was in hiding. For the moment.

Chapter Sourteen

A short time later, Joshua knocked lightly on the door of Alex's cabin. There was a light step on the floor as if she had been lying down and just stood up. Then he heard her response.

"Come in."

When he entered, Alex was standing in the middle of the room. Her hair was free and tangled about her shoulders. Though she'd worn a hat most of the morning, it seemed as though the sun had kissed wayward strands with dashes of gold. He caught her brief look of surprise before she frowned and folded arms across her chest protectively, her stance widening. He smiled gently and ducked his head to enter, closing the door behind him. The action caused her brow to arch in a familiar way, but leaving a door open at sea would soon become annoying, as they both knew.

"I came to see how you were faring," Joshua offered.

She ignored his explanation, still on the defensive. "We pull anchor soon. You should get back to your ship."

"I've switched places with the reverend. There were no extra cabins on my ship so I gave him mine. Stephen offered the reverend's in exchange." It was a blatant lie. He had plenty of room on his ship. He just couldn't stand knowing that Alex had been hurt by the reverend's inability to accept her. Worse, that she knew the man thought there was something so wrong with her that he wanted to get off her ship as quickly as possible. Alex had been relaxed, uninhibited, different than when she was trying to fit in and follow the social rules. She had not expected to be emotionally slapped when she was unguarded and in the place she thought of as her home. And certainly not from an unexpected source.

Knowing he couldn't say any of that, he offered a different clarification. "And I wanted to sail with 'a sure thing.' Thought I might learn something."

Alex smiled, or tried to. Failing it, she turned her back on him. "Please . . ." She swallowed, her voice husky. "Please don't be nice to me. I'm too tired for it."

Joshua understood instantly. That's why he pressed forward and touched her shoulder. She stiffened and shrugged him off, moving away. He let her recover some composure, then persevered, turned her around, and enfolded her stiff body in his arms. Eventually, as if too tired to keep her head up by herself, she leaned in and rested her cheek on his chest. It was her undoing.

And his.

He felt her tremble, fighting the weakness of tears, and pulled her tighter. After a moment or so, she released a heavy sigh and accepted the embrace, wrapping her arms around his waist.

Alex took another slow breath, closing her eyes, grateful that she had at least been able to maintain control until she reached the privacy of her cabin. Though she blamed Joshua for making her weepy now, after all her efforts. This last week felt like a lifetime. Too much to do. Too little time to sleep. And when she did find time, her dreams left her restless.

Joshua stroked her back lightly with one hand, as if to communicate support. Or sympathy. Or simply that he was there. A gesture of friendship, she supposed. She didn't care. He was warm. And surprisingly comfortable despite the hard muscles underneath her cheek and hands. She relaxed heavily, finding it easy to shut off her mind and drift off under the addictive motion of his fingers stroking through her hair.

She woke up seconds later, still on her feet.

"Come here." Joshua led her to a chair and tugged her down on his lap.

Alex complied, curling up comfortably, forcing him to adjust to her position. She smiled happily when he did. Not because she had control, but because it was very nice of him.

More like the Joshua she remembered from Morocco. The one she liked.

Her muscles relaxed. He took one hand and threaded his fingers with hers. Despite herself, a lazy desire spread through her body, warming her several degrees. She ventured a look upward, wondering if he knew the effect he was having on her. What she saw was disquieting.

Serious eyes stared back. The blue darker than usual. More intense. Hotter. His focus and concern completely on her. Her mouth went dry.

He began to pull her hand toward his mouth. Stunned, she resisted, drawing his eyes back to her own. Her hands were more roughened than most women, calloused from working ropes throughout her teen years and tanned from being so much in the sun.

"My hands," she sought to explain.

"Are beautiful." His expression softened. He gave a gentle tug this time, as if asking consent. Curious, she relented and watched as he lifted her hand to his lips with an incredible patience that caused goose bumps to trail up her arm before he even made contact.

When his lips finally touched her knuckle, the softness of the contact was a surprise. The sensation of the small movement was a mere brush, yet the delicate pressure mixed with the heat of his breath, emotionally stirring.

The entire experience shocked her.

Wordless, their eyes met again and this time what stunned Alex the most was the remarkable tenderness in his gaze. A tenderness that made the dangerous possibility of hope grow in her heart. That she could be with him, safe and accepted at last. She smiled back at him tremulously as he caressed her hand against his whisker-roughened cheek.

Mesmerized by the care he took in holding her, she could only obey his unspoken command allowing him to turn her palm to his mouth. Her heart pounded as he leisurely kissed the inside of her wrist, lingering until the desire for his kiss made her squirm to be closer. Then he quickly dipped in again, pressing a second kiss to the same spot, nipping the skin, transforming her lethargy to excitement, and earning a surprised gasp of pleasure. Her eyes closed and her head tilted back over his arm. When his breath came closer, and his lips touched the pulse near her throat, she arched unconsciously, knowing only that she was lost.

It was several moments before she opened her eyes. She thought to gauge his intentions. If the desire in his eyes was any measure, his intentions were serious.

He pulled her hand over his heart and held it there. She was relieved to find his heart pounded as quickly as her own.

"We need to talk," he rasped.

"We do?" That usually meant she was in trouble.

"It would help," he explained.

Comprehending his need for distraction, Alex grinned with delight. He scowled. She knew it was false. Feeling very confident in her position she rested her head against his chest and asked what he would like to talk about. Her fingers slid inside his shirt to feel the heat of his skin, and he quickly captured the stray hand, holding it firmly.

"Why is Paxton still after you?"

She stiffened, pulling away, but he tightened his hold—as if to offer safety. Something that she knew would never be possible. Not until Paxton was dead.

"I told you."

"No, you didn't."

"Yes, I did."

"When?" he asked.

"The first time we met. But you don't seem to remember any of that." It came out a little more plaintive than she intended.

"I remember every moment of our first meeting."

"No, you don't. You didn't even recognize me."

"Because you cleaned up so nicely I was blinded by your beauty, and then I was paying more attention to your gun. I might also point out that you were very rude to me, not showing the least bit of gratitude of one who was previously rescued by my dashing courage."

"Madness, you mean."

"Not the least bit of gratitude," he repeated. "So. Paxton is still on about this prophecy and thinks you have a map to a secret treasure?"

"You do remember." Alex wondered what else he remembered. Their kiss. Her ring. Did he still have it? He hadn't brought it up. She didn't want to ask and be disappointed.

"Of course I remember. And it's not polite to doubt a duke. I realize you may not have had time to learn that yet."

"No, but there are so many useless rules, it's easy to forget."

"Sassy. Must be feeling better," he noted. "Do you have this map?"

Alex didn't answer. It was better if no one believed she had the map. Her brothers still didn't know. After her father died, she couldn't tell them. She felt too guilty. He had left to hunt Paxton without all the information. She still wondered if it would have made a difference. If maybe he would have stayed.

"I see," he said.

"What?"

"You do have the map."

"Sort of."

"Sort of?" he repeated.

"It's not really what Paxton thinks it is, and I'm hiding it. I don't have it with me."

"So, the answer is 'yes.'"

"No."

"No?"

"Yes," she agreed.

Joshua thought kissing the woman was enough to make his head spin. Talking to her was just a damn mistake.

"Joshua," she begged. "My family doesn't know about the map. At least not that I have it. Please. Promise me you won't ever tell them. If I have to someday, I will. I just can't bear . . . Please, this is really important."

"You need help, Alex. Your brothers would want to protect you, wouldn't they?"

"Yes, but they don't need to know about the map. And I'm supposed to protect it and its secrets. Trust me. The fewer people who know the better."

"I won't say anything for now. But you need to tell them."

"I'm telling you. They don't need to know," Alex insisted.

Joshua sighed. He would fight that battle when he got there. "What do you know about the map? Where does it lead to?"

"I don't know. It's more of a story. Or a riddle."

"And did you ever figure out why the old lady gave it to you?"

"You do remember!" she said, surprised.

"I thought we covered that already."

"She gave it to me because I'm the kelile," Alex explained, solemnly. "It means 'my protector' or 'my gate.'"

"And why did she think you were the kelile?"

"I don't know. I think she was a seer."

"And you believed her? Did you have a chance to go back and talk to her?"

"My father found her when he was looking for me. She was already dead."

"Oh. Highly unfortunate." Joshua thought it over. "Did Paxton kill her?"

"I don't know, but I believed her." She sat up more in his lap, as if she wanted to ascertain his reaction. "Because Kelile is my middle name. And no one but you and my family know that."

He said calmly, "That's a very odd coincidence." *That is bloody strange.*

"For once we agree."

"Did anyone know you were in Morocco? Did this woman perhaps know your family?"

"I don't know."

"Does Paxton believe you are the kelile?"

"I don't think he knows about it. But when he was on my ship, he told me about the prophecy."

"You had time to converse with a murderous bastard who

was trying to blow up your ship? Good God, Alex! He could have killed you right then. You should have waited for me before you went aboard."

"I knew you were coming and I just had to keep him talking. It's too late to lecture now. Besides, he told me things I didn't know."

"It could all be more trickery," Joshua countered.

"I think it might be true. Or at least he thinks it's true."

Joshua listened as Alex proceeded to tell him an ancient myth about a very ambitious queen, the child sacrifice, and the lost kingdom.

"Why did your parents name you Kelile?" he asked.

"My parents were in Morocco, or somewhere east of there, when I was born. They had an adventure, and were helped by an African warrior—Prince Kelile," she explained. "So they named me after him. My middle name, that is."

"So, it's possible the old woman could have known you. Or your mother. Do you look like your mother?"

"Yes, but she had dark hair. I have my father's coloring." She looked at him hesitantly as if to decide what else to tell him. "There's more," she offered.

He nodded to proceed.

"When I was born, Prince Kelile gave me a necklace." She pulled it from her shirt, where it hung on a long, sturdy chain.

"It's an astrolabe."

"Yes. Well, part of one. And it's very, very old."

"And?"

Alex didn't say anything. Joshua realized she was wary of trusting him. That realization was disturbing. Especially since he needed all the information in order to protect her.

"Nothing. It's just my talisman. My lucky charm. It doesn't actually work since the rest of the pieces are missing. There's usually five or six disks."

She didn't elaborate, and Joshua thought he would have to be satisfied for now. "Tell me more about the map. What does it look like?"

"Very pretty," she enthused, surprising him. "The one thing that worries me—"

"Only *one* thing worries you!"

She ignored him. "In the center of the map is a woman. With red hair." Alex paused, collecting her thoughts. "I keep wondering if it's a woman, or a mermaid, or a siren, and what if she is the one causing the destruction behind her? And what if that woman is me? What if I'm the one who brings the end of days?"

"Okay. Let's not get ahead of ourselves."

"I can't help it. Since I've had the map, people have been dying in my wake, Joshua! The men who were there when I first got it, my father, Whitley, my crew. Who else?" Alex started to panic just thinking about it.

"How can you tell she's causing destruction?"

"She is," Alex stated knowingly.

"Well, most likely, if any of this is true, the woman represents the first queen who was able to make the seas rise up against her enemy."

Alex thought it over. "Yes. That could be." She rested back against his chest, stifling another yawn. When his hand threaded through her hair to comfort, she closed her eyes and decided not to think about it for a while. This was much nicer. Until she remembered . . .

"Wait." She sat up again, vaguely registering a pained look on Joshua's face when she adjusted her bottom on his lap. "Sorry," she said, getting comfortable. "My mother too."

"What about her?"

"We can add her to my path of destruction. She died because of me. Paxton said I didn't even know why, and he's right. I don't remember what happened. I only found out because I did something stupid."

"You never do that."

"I know," she agreed, as if outraged at the unfair complaints. Then she calmed down and confessed, "But I did that time."

"Tell me."

"I got stabbed and caught an infection."

Joshua swallowed, afraid to ask. "And almost died?"

"I got very sick, and my brother was mad because, really, he was worried, and he said I should take better care. That our mother died for me, and I shouldn't . . ." Alex trailed off, her voice becoming harsh. "I shouldn't take that sacrifice so lightly."

"Can I kill him?"

"No."

Joshua looked down at her. She gave a slight shrug.

"He didn't mean to tell me. At least not like that. And I never told anyone else that he told me because everyone was trying to protect me and I didn't want them to feel bad. But . . ."

"But then you blamed yourself."

"Sort of."

Joshua pulled her head back down to his chest. "What happened?"

"There was an invasion of our home, and some servants were killed. My mother and I were out by the water . . ." Alex pressed closer, squeezing her eyes shut. "My mother protected me and even killed two men before they could get me. But the last man killed her. I learned all that later. She fought so I would have time to get away. They said I ran to the water and thought I had drowned. But then I showed up on a beach several miles away."

"You sound a lot like your mother."

"No," Alex said. "She was brave, and kind, and compassionate. And her first season out she was an incomparable. Everyone loved her." Alex sighed. "Even though she was English."

"Everyone loves you," Joshua insisted, sensing she felt lacking by comparison.

"No," Alex said. "Only my family. Because they have to. And if they knew everything, they might not." She was quiet a moment. "My last memory of my mother was looking at her through a mirror as she stood behind me, braiding my hair. I remember thinking she was so beautiful. And I asked her if I would ever be pretty, because I was so gangly and baby faced. It sounds so stupid now."

"It's not." Joshua bent to kiss the top of her head and rested his cheek against her hair.

"The next I remember it was the morning of her funeral. It's so strange. I hate that Paxton may know something. Maybe he could explain what happen. But why would he know?"

"I don't know. I'm hoping you won't be seeing him again. I didn't get a chance to tell you, but I spoke to a friend who works in the government. He made some inquiries." Joshua decided not to add that he had hired private help as well to see where Paxton might be hiding. So far no luck. "He must be sailing under a different name. There are no records of him in the logs—"

Joshua was about to continue when he noticed a steady breath against his chest. "Alex?" He tilted his head carefully to peek at her and laughed. He must be losing his touch. She was sound asleep.

Chapter Fifteen

Alex couldn't seem to get rid of the duke. They had been back in London two days, and every time she turned, he was there. He even offered to escort her to the British Museum, only Lord Heatherly, the museum's professor of ancient maritime history, sent her a note changing their plans. He was preparing for a trip, and it would be much easier for him to call on her.

"It's really not necessary for you to stay, Your Dukeness." She frowned when he smiled. Nothing she said could irritate him lately. "I'm sure I'm perfectly safe with Lord Heatherly."

"I shall see for myself. And it's my pleasure to spend time in your company."

The frown deepened. She didn't know if he was mocking or serious.

"Perhaps we can take a stroll in the park afterward."

Alex's pleasure at the offer was marred by her complete displeasure at not understanding why he wanted to stroll in the park with her. To protect her? Definitely not to be seen with her. She had recently been cut by a number of the ladies in the ruling class. It seemed the reverend had warned the good people of London about her. Of course, there were just as many invitations from those who were curiosity seekers.

"You must have other things to do, Your Grace."

"But none so enjoyable."

Entirely too accommodating. It wasn't right. Dissatisfied, she ignored him and proceeded to make a production of arranging her skirts on the small settee where she sat. She'd seen women who could arrange their dresses for fifteen minutes at a time. She thought she could manage one minute in order to gather her thoughts. She ventured a glance to the duke. He stood by the fireplace, seemingly relaxed and content just to watch her. He even smiled when she looked his way. Very strange. Perhaps she should lay the skirts another direction. Yes, that would give her another full minute to think some more.

Stephen ambled through the open doors of the drawing room to join them. He stopped short at the sight of his sister fussing with her dress and glanced from her to the duke to ascertain the situation.

"What are you doing?" he asked his sister.

Alex answered, distracted, "I'm fixing my skirt."

"No," Stephen repeated, implying she must be up to no good. "What are you *really* doing?"

She didn't spare him her look of annoyance. "Weren't you going riding?"

"Yes. Is that librarian still coming?"

"He should be here any minute." Alex hoped her brother would leave soon.

"Would you like to join me, Josh? Sounds like this is going to be a bore."

"Another time perhaps, my friend."

Stephen nodded, looking thoughtfully at both of them. "All right then. Everything is all right, isn't it? I can stay if you need me."

Alex stopped with her skirts and turned her attention to her younger brother, realizing he was becoming worried and perhaps feeling a little left out. She didn't want him to be hurt, but she didn't want him to stay either. "Please go. It's too beautiful to stay indoors. This will be short. Then we'll meet you in the park. His Grace wants to take a stroll."

"Excellent. Then I'll see you both in a bit."

She nodded agreement and Stephen left, just before their stocky Irish butler announced the arrival of Lord Heatherly and his assistant, Miss Rule.

Lord Heatherly was just as Alex thought he would be. Very serious in manner, not too tall, silver-haired, carrying spectacles, and walking with the help of a charming wood walking cane. His assistant was equally somber, much taller, and in all black. A widow, it seemed. She looked to be in her midforties, and bore her role very obsequiously.

Alex introduced the duke, and a servant brought some refreshments.

"Oh, thank you, my dear," Lord Heatherly said. "But we don't have much time. Let's just get straight to business, shall we?"

"Of course," Alex agreed. "Thank you so much for making the time. I truly appreciate it."

Heatherly nodded, waiting.

A little disconcerted by his directness, Alex guided them to the table nearest the window. "I wanted to get your opinion on a design I came across." Alex pulled the worn paper copy of her map from the desk and unfolded it for all to examine. She knew she'd get some answers when Miss Rule straightened up. It was almost imperceptible, but Alex caught the action and inquired curiously.

"You recognize this, Miss Rule?"

"No, ma'am," she answered. "Just the image of the mermaid seems very familiar. Does it not, Lord Heatherly?"

"It does indeed." He lifted his spectacles a moment, then put them down. "What do you make of these symbols around the edge?"

"They are Arabic," Alex said. Then she stopped. No need to share anything he didn't know. "What I was hoping to learn, Lord Heatherly, was if anything seemed familiar to you. See this behind the . . . the mermaid." Alex traced the line that matched her astrolabe, the silhouette she thought might be buildings or a palace. "I was wondering if it's a location that you would recognize, or that might have been documented elsewhere, perhaps on other maps at the museum."

"Well, I can't be sure, but I think it is similar to a very ancient, uh, text that I know." He lifted the map to examine it more closely, then nodded and rolled it up. "Yes, I believe it is. I will take this and compare the two for you."

"Oh!" Alex did not want to part with the map, but also did

not want to seem rude or ungrateful to so valuable a resource. "That's not necessary. I can wait and bring it myself." She reached for the paper.

Miss Rule took it from Heatherly. "He's right, Miss Stafford. If you wish an answer, the easiest way is for us to do the initial work and we must have the map available to do so. Fear not, it shall be in very good hands."

"Do you think it's a map?" Alex inquired. "If so, a strange one."

"Yes, well, clearly it is a location of something, Miss Stafford. I have learned that much from my work with Lord Heatherly. And that he is most responsible and dedicated."

"Of course, I did not mean to imply otherwise—" Alex felt trapped.

"Where are you going on your trip, Heatherly?" Worthington interjected.

Heatherly looked to Miss Rule, a moment of uncertainty glimmering in his eyes. Alex wondered if he didn't want people to know where he was going.

"To Egypt, Your Grace."

"Yes," Miss Rule agreed. "But we will have time to help you with this first."

"Nonsense." Joshua took the map from her hand, and folded his hands behind his back, blocking further dispute. "You are too kind, but I'm sure you have much to prepare before such a long journey. And you're leaving soon, are you not?"

"Uh, yes," Heatherly agreed.

"This is not so important. I'm sure Miss Stafford would be happy to wait until you return."

"Yes, yes," Alex concurred.

"I can help you," Heatherly insisted.

"No, no. This is merely a hobby. A curiosity. Please do not worry yourself," Alex said.

"Well then," Miss Rule spoke tightly. "We have made a needless trip it seems."

Alex was struck by the woman's remark. "My apologies. Please enjoy refreshment with us. I should love to hear more about your travels." She couldn't wait to get rid of the woman, but damned if she would let her know it.

"As His Grace said, our time is very valuable, Miss Stafford. We cannot all afford to chase our whims."

"I shall make sure the museum is compensated for your time." Alex stood, dismissing them, angered by the woman's outright rudeness and implication that Alex's days were so empty she spent them looking for ways to waste people's time.

Lord Heatherly tsk'd at the woman, and shook his head. "Don't be ridiculous. It was a pleasure to meet you, Miss Stafford."

"And you, Lord Heatherly," Alex offered warmly. "Miss Rule." She nodded farewell, less interested in the woman's feelings.

When they were gone, Joshua returned the map to her.

"It's just a copy," she explained. "A drawing to see if he recognized anything on it."

"I understand," he said.

"It just felt strange giving it to them. And I did not like Miss Rule. She was rude. I have never been that rude, have I, Joshua? I swear I haven't."

"Impossible, my dear." Joshua smiled at her.

Alex unrolled the map, and folded it back up to fit inside her journal. "I apologize if I have ever been that rude to you. Except for the times you deserved it, of course."

"Of course. And I certainly have earned your wrath, my love."

"Hmph."

He changed the subject. "But I agree that something was not altogether right about those two."

"Lord Heatherly seemed all right. I thought he would be more helpful. But that woman was very suspicious. You don't think she is up to something, do you?"

Joshua flexed his hand as if ready for a fight. "I think we don't have enough information, my sweet."

Alex lifted her journal to her chest, protectively. "You cannot keep saying things like that."

"That we don't have enough information?" He grinned.

"You know, Your Grace." She stood stiffly.

He laughed quietly, tilting her chin up to him, and brushing her lips lightly with his. "Regretfully, I cannot keep my promise of a stroll. Will you please make my regrets to Stephen?"

"Of course. You are English, after all."

She said it with bite, but Joshua caught the glimmer of disappointment before her face became a mask of aloofness. One step forward, two back. A shame he had to leave so abruptly.

"There is something I have recalled that I must do. You are heading back to Kent tomorrow?"

"Yes." Her body remained stiff and inflexible in his hold.

"I shall see you at Emma's ball in a few days. Promise me you will be safe until then?"

She shrugged.

"Promise me," he repeated.

She nodded reluctantly. He wanted to say more, to reassure her. He certainly did not want to leave her. But before he could enjoy her company, he needed to find out more about Lord Heatherly and his companion. Something was not right. And with Alex suspecting that Paxton was still at hand, he could not take any risks.

He pecked the top of her head with his lips, allowing himself nothing more. He was fully aware of her confusion over his behavior, but decided to let her think on it a bit longer.

Eventually she would figure out that he was courting her.

Chapter Sixteen

$\mathcal{A}$lex flicked her wrist impatiently, visualizing. "Catch and release. Catch—"

"Alex, hold still! You've lost weight in the last week," Maggie complained to her niece. "Your gown must be altered."

"Not that you don't look very nice, Alexandra," Emma hastened to add.

"She is sunburned and skinny. It's a wonder any man would be interested," Maggie said.

"I'm rich," Alex retorted. The comment earned her the poke of a needle. "Ouch! That was cruel."

"But fun." Maggie finished her stitches. "Now let's see."

Alex turned around to face Maggie, Emma, and one of Maggie's housemaids. There was a collective sigh. Then nods of approval.

"It's perfect," Emma exclaimed. "I'm a genius!"

Alex arched a brow at her friend. "It's just a dress."

"It's a miracle!" Maggie exclaimed. "Come see in the mirror."

Hesitant, Alex looked, then looked again. Yes, she definitely appeared different. Her hand touched her breasts where they heaved at the low neckline. The pale gold material did make her skin glow. And her hair—it stood out too much.

"It makes my hair look red."

"Your hair *is* red!" Maggie said, exasperated.

"Don't you like it?" Emma asked, worried. "Oh, Alex, I think you look beautiful. But if you don't like it . . ." Emma trailed off biting her lip anxiously, studying her friend in the mirror. She pulled some of Alex's hair forward. "Not red. Like rich rosewood."

"It's just that I don't look like me."

"That's the point!" The fact that Maggie and Emma said it in unison left little room to guess what they really thought about her regular mode of dress. It also sent the housemaid into a fit of indiscreet giggles. Alex glowered.

"I think I should wear the green. And it won't do to compete with the birthday girl."

"Oh, don't worry," Emma promised. "My gown is spectacular. And it's silver, so when we are next to each other we will complement!"

Alex shook her head with a light laugh, giving in. In this dress, it was in fact hard to do much more than give a light laugh. Regardless of her discomfort, it was difficult not to be swayed by Emma's enthusiasm.

"I'll help her undress, Lady Maggie," Emma offered, dismissing the maid as well.

"Thank you, Emma. And thank you for helping us find such a wonderful dress on short notice. Perhaps your genteel company will put Alexandra in a more grateful mood."

"My green dress was perfectly fine!" Alex caught her aunt's censure and added. "But truly, this is much more magnificent. Thank you, Emma."

"You're welcome. You shall be fighting off suitors."

"Ugh. Then I take my thanks back!"

Emma laughed and helped with the buttons once they were alone. Very carefully they laid the dress out and then sat by the window to catch up.

"I'm very excited about the ball tomorrow," Emma confessed.

"Well, of course. Eighteen is a milestone."

"What did you do for your eighteenth birthday?"

"I worked."

"You worked?" Emma was outraged.

"It was a Wednesday, after all. And everyone was out on their ships, making deliveries. My father was in Savannah purchasing wood for a new ship. Matthew got called away to help deliver a baby. Only Stephen was home. He had our housekeeper make a cake and a special dinner, and we celebrated."

"Oh." Emma sounded like she felt rather bad about that.

"But," Alex continued, "that Saturday, when my father returned home, he took me down to the harbor for a special lunch. Just me and him. It was very nice. We had fresh lobster cooked right there on the docks, and we talked about the business. I told him how I wanted to open an emporium and start selling products to regular people. You know, offer folks a little variety. Then we argued about how we should design the hull of the next ship. It was wonderful," Alex reflected. "With so many of us, and with the demands on my father, I wasn't alone with him often. Least not for a whole afternoon. He gave me some pointers on managing my brothers, told me about a couple tough negotiations. I had been working in the business my whole life, but that day, I felt like he really accepted me as part of it. And then the most amazing thing happened."

"What?"

"There was a small point with a lighthouse, and as we sat and talked this beautiful ship came into the harbor at full sail, slowly revealing itself. Eventually it got close enough for me to hear shouts and I recognized all my brothers were aboard and waving to us. I jumped up and exclaimed to my father that it was in fact them. He said, 'Of course it is. Someone had to deliver your gift.'"

Alex stopped and hugged her knees to her chest, remembering. "He put his arm around me, said happy birthday, and I couldn't believe it."

"He gave you a ship!"

"Yes." Alex grinned. "But it wasn't just that. I knew then, he really did believe in me. More than even I believed in myself." Alex sighed, closing her eyes. "It was the most perfect day of my life."

"Oh," Emma said again. This time her eyes were watery. "I don't remember my father really. But that sounds much better than a ball."

Alex reached out to her friend, "But you are getting more than a ball." She gave Emma a quick squeeze. "You're getting the chance to dance with the man of your dreams."

"Yes," Emma hesitated. "Alex, I'm sorry Marcus is so stuffy about some things. I'm hoping he will learn how wonderful you are in time. He does like you."

"He just doesn't want me becoming a bad influence."

"It's not that," Emma denied. Though both knew it was exactly that. It was silent a moment before Emma continued. "I just want everything to go well. You promise to behave? Just for one night. There are a lot of Marcus's friends coming in from London."

Emma had tried to make it sound teasing, but Alex knew her friend was anxious for Marcus to accept her and to make a good impression. Merchant class was merchant class, no matter how much money you had. Alex assured Emma all would be well.

"I promise I will be a model of decorum, and as boring as humanly possible."

"Thank you. I know I'm just fretting over nothing. I do want you to have fun. You will try to dance, won't you?"

"I'm wearing the dress and I'm promising to be genteel. Two out of three is very good, Lady Emma."

Laughing, her friend relented. "But Joshua will surely want to dance with you."

"Please. I cannot figure out that man. He has been acting very strange of late."

"Tell me," Emma insisted, curious.

Alex explained that he sailed back on her ship, and was very engaging company for the most part. Then in London, he kept showing up. "And he wanted to talk and spend time with me. He even suggested a stroll in the park." Alex shook her head bewildered. "Do you think he feels he must protect me or something?"

Emma burst out laughing.

"Emma! It's not funny. Surely he has more important things to do than take tea and escort me around town. For heaven's sake, his roof needs to be fixed."

"Yes. He most certainly does have other things to do," Emma agreed. "But his roof is almost done. He made arrangements."

"Then why are you laughing?"

"Alexandra." Emma looked undecided about revealing the answer to the puzzle. "Have you never been courted?"

Alex balked. Then she blinked. Then she sat in stunned silence.

"Oh, dear," Emma worried. "Do you not want him to court you? You seem like such a good match. Have you no affection for Joshua, Alex?"

"I don't know." Alex thought on it. "It's more that," she tried to explain, "I don't have room for affection quite yet."

"Well. There's no rush." Emma got up to go. "Think on it, Alex."

Think on it. Alex turned again. It was all she had been able to do for the last twenty-four hours. She needed to figure out how to stop Paxton, and now she was obsessed with a duke. She would be seeing him in a mere sixteen hours. She must decide quickly how she felt. She knew she wanted to get to know him more. They had yet to talk about the past. He seemed to avoid it. As did she. It felt too intimate to bring up.

Frustrated, she kicked off the bedsheets. Another sleepless night. She would be lectured in the morning for bags under her eyes.

There might be a growing affection between her and Joshua, but Alex knew she was not duchess material. And she couldn't stay in England. It was completely impractical. The Stafford Emporium was in Boston, and her business took her to various ports. Hell, she would be blind if she hadn't noticed that he could be kind. And his employees seemed to adore him. And he occasionally challenged her with his wit. What if he wasn't courting her? Her heart dropped. Not a good reaction.

It must be the weather.

Summer had definitely arrived. Uncomfortable from the heat, Alex got up to open the windows. Her mind worked too much for her to sleep. Frustrated, she donned some riding clothes and made her way down to the stables.

Salem was already aware of his mistress and whining impatiently from his stall. She slipped on his saddle and within minutes they were quietly making their way out toward the lake. It had been on Alex's mind to take a swim, and at this time of the morning it was safe to assume everyone at Worthington was asleep and in bed. Plus, the duke had not returned.

The moon guided their path and Alex enjoyed the refreshing water in no time. She knew better than to linger, and after just a couple laps dried off with a towel she brought, then dressed again before lying out on the grass to admire the sky. It was the most relaxed she felt in days. Within minutes of closing her eyes she was fast asleep.

She dreamed of him, as she was prone to do lately. Only instead of being on the run across the buildings of Morocco, they were dancing. As the dance ended he drew closer, tracing a long, tanned finger down her cheek. It feathered across her lips, easing a sigh of pleasure from her before gliding over her chin and throat to the open neckline of her shirt.

Alex turned on her side, shivering slightly. The dance ended, and he was running his fingers through her wet hair, fanning it out to dry. It was strange, she thought, that her hair had become wet while they were dancing. It must have rained, her dream consciousness decided. She leaned into him for warmth. He was solid and warm, and his arm made a nice pillow. She snuggled closer using her hands to pull at his shirt indicating she wanted more. He put his other arm around her, obeying, and she mumbled that this was "perfect" to nobody in general. She could have slept for days if it weren't for that wandering hand of his.

Alex grinned sleepily, enjoying the feel of that large hand gliding over her waist and thighs before feeling the curve of her buttocks. It massaged nicely too, she thought as a knot of desire grew. She stretched against him, arching with need. When that expert hand cupped her chin and cheek, and his body rolled her back on the grass, her lips were already parted for his kiss.

It was the gentlest of caresses, but every nerve ending in

her lips came alive. He brushed their lips together once more, barely touching. It was enough to make Alex fight through her confusing dream and open her eyes. She struggled to focus, still in the depths of sleep, her body aching for more of his touch. She couldn't reconcile that he was here with her. She saw his face close to her, the stars behind him, his body warm and protective against her, waiting.

"It is you," she whispered huskily, confused.

He only nodded silently while she struggled to wake up. Her eyes couldn't determine if he was an illusion or not. Her hands reached out to help and came into contact with a wall of muscle. Alertness shot through her. Panic as well.

"It's okay, Alex. It's me. Joshua." He caught her as she tried to break free.

His voice broke through the chaos of her mind and instantly calmed her. She thought it was strange that it would. She relaxed. Salem was by a tree near Cyclone, nibbling on grass. Joshua rolled away and seated himself beside her, not moving. She sat up as well, ducking her head between her legs to calm the pounding in her chest until she could speak.

"What were you doing?"

"Guarding you, of course." She saw his smile clearly. Dawn was about to break and the sky had begun to lighten in anticipation.

"You could have done it from over there." She pointed to the horses.

"You were cold."

She threw herself back on the grass and laid a forearm over her eyes. Embarrassment was starting to take over. Had she curled up to him and pressed against him, or was that her dream? Please, God, let that have been a dream.

"Are you okay?" He leaned closer.

"Are you still here?" she inquired, deliberately provoking. She peeked out and saw him smiling. She shivered, her attraction to him undeniable.

"Are you still cold?" He grinned, rolled a little closer and propped his head up on an elbow, inches from her face.

"No."

He touched her arm and felt the goose bumps. "Are you sure?"

"Yes." She pushed his hand away and sat up. He followed her movement and sat as well, still watching her. "Did you kiss me?"

He gave a roguish smile, confirming what she already knew. "It was hardly a kiss."

"Why?"

"Why was it hardly a kiss?"

She shook her head. "No. Why did you kiss me?"

"You wanted me to."

Alex laughed despite herself. "No, I didn't. I don't even like you."

"No?" he questioned. "Come, you must like me a little bit by now." He wrapped a strand of red hair around his finger and tugged her down to her elbows. "I have been a model neighbor."

"You just accosted me while I slept. Had I not awakened, who knows what vile activity you might have engaged in."

"It is my lake," he reminded her. "But being a good neighbor, I welcome you to use it anytime. Naturally, when I saw you on the ground earlier, I feared foul play."

"Foul play?"

"Yes, dear. Murder, mayhem, and such. It seems to follow you around."

"Um-hmm."

"You were so still, I had to be sure you were alive. Then you were cold and I had nothing other than myself to provide you with heat. And you were sleeping so peacefully and smiling so happily in your dreams . . . I just didn't have the heart to wake you."

"But you kissed me." She pointed out.

"Hardly a kiss," he reminded her. "Certainly not memorable." Long fingers tugged on her hair again, pulling her closer to him.

She pressed a hand against his chest, to keep some distance. "It's not very nice of you to insult my kissing like that."

"I'm sorry. I'm sure there are other things you are better at."

Alex slapped his chest, laughing. "That's cruel, Duke."

"Call me Joshua." He leaned over to kiss the tresses wrapped around his fingers, bringing his face inches from her own. "It sounds so pretty on your lips."

Her heart slammed in her chest. She attempted cool sophistication she did not feel.

"Are you flirting with me . . . Joshua?"

"Is it working?" he whispered back. His hopeful smile was the only clue that he teased.

It was working. "I refuse to answer that question."

He rolled on top of her triumphantly. "Ah! Success at last."

She struggled, laughter making her attempts ineffectual. "I didn't say you were succeeding! You oaf. Get off me."

To her dismay he bent his head and nuzzled her neck and ear, causing every nerve ending in her body to jolt to attention. "But you didn't say I wasn't succeeding."

"I was being polite."

"You're never polite!" He said it as proof of his victory, leaning up to stare into her face. She gasped at his insult, before laughing again. Her body shaking against his. A sensation he apparently did not like as he immediately rolled off her and took a deep breath.

Alex felt bereft the instant he moved away. He sat up with his arms draped casually across his knees. She did the same, watching the dawn barely touch the sky with a glimmer of pink. Then she looked at him. He still watched the sky, ignoring her.

Alex wanted to kiss him. In another minute it would be daylight. Servants would be up. Work would need tending to. And she would definitely lose her nerve.

"Have you kissed many women?"

"Of course."

"Oh."

"I'm irresistible, you know. Not jealous are you?"

"No," she denied, embarrassed. "Just curious in general." They were both silent. Alex sighed and drew up on her knees

to face him. Her chest touched his muscled arm, her right
hand rested on the shoulder nearest her. His hair was getting
long. A sun-streaked lock fell over his cheek and she brushed
it back, enjoying the soft texture under her fingertips in
contrast to the rough stubble along his jaw. She reached her
free hand around and turned his face toward her, holding his
cheek in her hand so that she could examine him.

His eyes reflected the golden glow of the sunrise slowly
spreading across the earth. He didn't move. He just watched
her, curious, waiting.

"Joshua."

"Yes?"

Joshua swallowed hard. His voice sounded harsh even to
his own ears. She was too innocent to know her closeness was
driving him crazy.

"I would like to kiss you."

They were the last words he expected to hear her say. His
mood lightened, his body warming with delight.

"You may," he said, causing her to blush hotly.

She moved closer. Joshua's stomach clenched. He wasn't
sure she was serious until she leaned in. Until she pressed lips
tentatively against his. He waited. She drew back dissatisfied,
then pressed closer to him again. This time taking his bottom
lip between her own and tasting. After that experiment, she
leaned back to assess his reaction, daring to look him in the
eyes. "I think you should help me."

It was all the invitation he needed. He smiled, relieved to
have the opportunity.

"With pleasure."

Joshua turned fully and wrapped both arms around her,
tilting her backward and off balance so that she instinctively
wrapped her arms around his neck to hang on. She gasped at
the quickness of the reversal, but never took her eyes from his,
the intensity of her gaze filled with both anxiety and excitement. Her sea green eyes seemed to darken mysteriously as he
studied her at his leisure, lying beneath him on the grass.

Joshua rubbed his thumb over the tender, innocent lips that

had just caressed him. He dipped his head forward and slowly kissed a feather light path from her brow to her ear, nibbling on the lobe gently. Her skin tasted fresh and cool against his lips. He released a breath into her ear, whispering, "Are you ready?"

Her answer was a satisfying and throaty, "Yes."

She was eager, but Joshua was patient, tutoring her in the movements of passion. His tongue slowly began an exploration, tasting her, caressing until her mouth opened on a sigh of pleasure. She was as sweet as he knew she would be. His thumb caressed the curve of her breast, firm and round under his touch. Slow circles eventually brought him in touch with a taut nipple that hardened in reaction. She emitted an aching groan and arched hungrily against him.

Alex didn't know when tenderness turned to passion. All she knew was she needed this man. His kiss and his touch burned her. She was panting when his head lifted to plunder her throat and scorch a path to where her shirt now lay open, golden skin exposed to his gaze.

He lifted his eyes to hers, his thumb stroking the delicate curve of her cheek. "You're so incredible. So beautiful," he confessed huskily. "It takes my breath away."

Her heart opened then, and she smiled shyly, wondrous.

With excruciating slowness, not breaking contact with her eyes, he lowered his lips to hers.

It was very nearly the last thing she remembered.

Demonstrating patience he didn't know he possessed, Joshua continued his assault until she was once again begging with need. He decided he loved the sound of her voice when she begged and was unable to prevent the arrogant smile curving his lips as he lifted his head and watched her squirm with passion.

It wasn't without a price. His own body was throbbing with agonizing need as well. He forced his desire away and focused on her.

She moaned. "Please." Her body pressed against his.

He sighed. Pained.

Knowing he must stop now, or not at all, Joshua pulled back and rolled on his side facing her, trying not to be so pleased by her expression of open contentment.

He took a slow breath, closing his eyes as he fought for control against the sharp desire. His forehead tilted until it touched the hot skin of a curved shoulder, and he breathed in the dizzying, fresh scent of her. Thinking better of the direction his mouth and mind were heading, he leaned back once more and carefully brushed his lips across hers, slowly bringing her back to her earthly senses.

Alex fought his withdrawal.

He soothed her with a quick, searing kiss that blinded her to all other thoughts.

"As much as I would love to take you right here and now"—he looked at her hungrily, as if still debating the possibility—"I can't."

Her body demanded him. "Why not?"

"Because." He buttoned up her blouse. "It would not be well done of me."

She flung herself backward on the grass, sulking. "Well, damnation." Confused, she turned away. His rejection hurt.

As if understanding, he pulled her back. "Alex." His eyes scorched her with a devastating power. "Don't think for a second that I don't want to divest you of all this unnecessary clothing and kiss every inch of your delectable body." His hand traced the outline of her figure to the soft curve of her backside, garnering an unconscious sigh of pleasure that fluttered across his chest. "In fact"—he tugged her hair back to look into glowing eyes, dark with a mixture of emotions—"you're still far from safe."

"I'm far from satisfied."

Joshua laughed. "So you like me a little bit now?"

"Hardly." Her body was throbbing with pleasure and she owed it to him whether she liked it or not. She decided she liked it. No need to share that quite yet.

"Ah, you're a tough woman. What happened to 'Joshua, please Joshua, I need you, Joshua'?"

If possible her entire body blushed now. She tried to hit him but he caught both her hands firmly, his body shaking with laughter. To prove his point, he spread her arms by her sides and assaulted her lips.

She pulled away with a breathless plea.

"Admit you like me a little?" he teased again.

"Yes," she agreed, gaining his attention. "Very, very little."

Satisfied, he resumed kissing her, this time on her neck and down to the pulse beating frantically at her throat. "And do you forgive me for almost having my way with you?"

"Yes, Joshua," she said, obediently before adding, "I did start it after all."

"True," he agreed.

"Though, I admit, I was quite hoping you'd finish it."

He groaned in agony.

Alex smiled in wonder at this unexpected control she had over him. And he over her. Her heart skipped several beats. She caught her breath. "You are a bit more expert in this area after all."

"Very true." He laughed at her blush, then sat up and pulled her onto his lap. "You are beautiful, Alex. Not just on the outside." He stroked her cheek, earning a brilliant smile from her. Then he pinched her bottom and set her on her feet before he lost complete command of his senses.

Alex yelped in response. For revenge she bent over to slide on her boots, deliberately giving him a view of her backside. His moan of distress was all the satisfaction she needed as she flipped her hair smartly and widened her eyes to inquire if he was okay.

He nodded, wincing.

"Are you coming?"

He shook his head negatively. "I'm going to take a long swim."

Alex nodded, reluctant to leave. She allowed Joshua to help her into the saddle, taking feminine pleasure in his solicitous care. A warm glow spread through her as he reached for her hand and laced her fingers with his. Turning her hand open to him, he held her gaze with his eyes while his lips brushed over her knuckles. "I will see you later," he promised.

"Yes," she confirmed, touching his cheek, memorizing his thoughtful features. She wanted him and from the look on his face he felt the same. He truly was the man she remembered. The rest would take care of itself. With a quiet farewell she guided Salem toward home, her face lifting to the morning sun with joy. She'd never felt so free.

Chapter Seventeen

Good God. She was trapped. Tied, knotted, buttoned, secured, and about to be announced. No turning back now. Good and trapped. The things one did for friends.

Alex let her aunt precede her into Stonewood Manor as she waited for Stephen. It seemed he had disappeared already. She found him back by the carriage, chatting up a groom, and pinched his arm. "There's no way I'm going in alone, dear brother. Besides, Emma would miss you."

He perked up. "Do you think? She's besotted with the earl you know. It's unbearable."

"I know, Stephen. I'm sorry."

"He's not entirely awful, which makes it more difficult. But Joshua is much more down to earth. Don't you think?"

Alex managed to avoid discussing the duke. Her lips still tingled when she thought about him. She hoped he would like this dress. *Something* good should come of wearing it.

Stephen hesitated again. She stopped. "What is it?"

"It's just . . . it seems strange to celebrate after burying three of our own."

"I know, Stephen. I know." Alex put a hand in his sympathetically. "If it weren't Emma's birthday, it would be different. But life is so much briefer than we ever know. Those we love are always with us. So put the pain away for a short time, and see what other diversions might await. Mayhap some true happiness will work its way in the mix." She pulled him along. "And if not, then the earl will no doubt have the finest refreshments on display for his guests and you can imbibe at will."

Stephen nodded. "Ah. Always looking on the bright side, sister. I do love that about you."

Marcus had planned every detail of the night with the help of Lady Maggie and his Aunt Matilda, who had arrived in time to play hostess and chaperone to Emma. What he had not planned was how his breath would escape him at the sight of Emma. She made her entrance to gasps of admiration, his own lost in the throng of admirers. He now regretted inviting so many of his friends and colleagues from London. Two had already inquired as to whether or not she was spoken for. It irritated him beyond measure. Still, he could not yet manage to be close to her. She was exuding a mysterious feminine power of late, and tonight it was in full bloom. Unfortunately, that didn't stop his feeling of consternation when he saw Emma smile beguilingly at Joshua on the dance floor while he watched from the side with their longtime friend Colin Weyford, now Lord Merriton.

"Emma has become quite stunning, Marcus." Colin added, "You should know I have half a mind to ask for her hand."

"What?"

"You heard me, old man," Colin said. "Just giving you fair warning. Unless you had Josh in mind? You have no intentions I understand?"

"I—" Marcus swallowed and was saved from answering when the subjects of their conversation joined them. He recovered somewhat when Emma moved to stand next to him and he felt her hand briefly squeeze his.

"Everything is wonderful. Thank you."

Marcus smiled down at her, lost for a moment absorbing her bright eyes and flushed cheeks. Her lips were just close enough to lean down and—

Emma's heart jumped in her throat at Marcus's intent gaze on her. On her lips! Did he intend to kiss her? The sound of Lord Merriton clearing his throat alerted her. She turned to Marcus's friend, promising a dance with him soon. They shared pleasantries, but Emma noted Joshua was markedly distracted, his eyes straying habitually to the entrance of the grand ballroom. When Lady Margaret and her family were announced, he perked up considerably.

Lord Merriton gaped. "That is the sea captain?"

Emma noted that Joshua didn't answer. All he could do was nod and swallow. It was no wonder. Alexandra looked . . . unrecognizable.

"She is magnificent," Lord Merriton said in awe.

"She's my sea captain." Joshua finally found his voice.

"She cleans up well," Stonewood said. "But," he lifted Emma's hand to his lips, "none can hold a light to my Emma."

Surprised and delighted, Emma smiled brilliantly at Marcus, forgiving his earlier indiscretions.

Joshua breathed in with pleasure, ignoring the sudden, possessive response to Alex's appearance. Her dress shimmered, her hair shined, and her eyes glittered with life. She had entered alone, but was immediately followed by Stephen, who hurried to catch up. Joshua's head buzzed with desire. Then his heart lightened with humor as he caught the off-guard moment when she placed a hand on her hip as if preparing for battle and reaching for a weapon. She looked nothing short of magnificent—but not at all certain about it. Her chin lifted a notch at the attention she had unknowingly roused. It reminded him of the first time he saw her, standing on an auction block, surveying the hungry wolves. Not so different from now, he realized. Only now, he knew her better. She was looking for a friend in the crowd.

He waited. He knew their gazes would meet in just another second. Her body stiffened. He smiled with a nod, and she looked away, but he noted that her lips curved with pleasure and she relaxed, ever so slightly, the change almost imperceptible. Yes. Progress. She made a comment to Stephen. Her brother, dressed in his finest, and looking only slightly less uncomfortable than his sister, nodded in agreement. Stephen offered his arm as if imitating a prince. They shared a look of resignation that seemed to say, "Here we go." Clearly, large gatherings were not their favorite.

Alex smiled graciously as her aunt led them through a series of introductions en route to Joshua. With every step, her anticipation increased, eager and excited. Her eyes locked with his a moment before she tore them away and smiled at Emma, reminding herself the main focus of tonight was to be a perfect guest, and impress Emma's earl—even if it meant she'd starve tonight from an inability to do anything but smile politely in this constrictive dress.

Stephen clicked his heels and bowed over Emma's hand, wishing her all the appropriate salutations, albeit with a slightly impish gleam.

"He's been practicing all day," Alex informed her dryly, before turning to Marcus. "My lord, your home looks resplendent tonight. Only Emma outshines it."

"Thank you, Miss Stafford. You look simply stunning." The earl bowed over her hand in a way she found both polite and charming. It put her more at ease. She shared a glance with Emma, and tilted her head to Marcus as if to indicate it was going well so far.

"She ought to look good. It took her long enough to get ready," Stephen complained. "I could have sailed to America and back—ouch!" Stephen winced as his sister neatly rapped his hand with a small fan.

Alex examined the fan as if inspecting for damage, "Hmmph. Now I understand why women carry these. Very handy."

The group laughed. Alex looked curiously at the man she did not know and gave him a friendly smile, forcing patience until someone made an introduction.

"You look magnificent, Miss Stafford." Joshua finally addressed her, his eyes speaking volumes more than the few words and causing her to suddenly fan herself in an effort to cool off.

Stephen's eyes narrowed and he stepped closer to his sister, recognizing the predatory looks. "Keep your distance, gentlemen. My brothers would have locked her up."

"I doubt that would help," Stonewood murmured, making

Alex aware that she had not fully won over him after stealing into his study. At the looks from the others he added, "I only mean to say that your sister is very resourceful."

Worried at the inappropriate attention, Alex changed the subject. "Your Grace, you completed your business in town? Successfully, I hope?"

"Indeed. In fact, there is someone I wish you to meet. Only he has not yet arrived."

"That's mysterious." She wanted to ask more, but he turned to the man she did not know and made the introductions. "May I introduce Colin Weyford, Earl of Merriton."

Lord Merriton was charming despite throwing her off balance a bit with his immediate request. "Miss Stafford. It's a pleasure. I hope I may call on you for a dance later."

"Oh. No!"

All eyes turned to Alex in surprise. Emma gave her an admonishing eye that she thought only Aunt Maggie had mastered. Alex scrambled to correct herself. "I mean, that is, yes. Later. Dancing is such a . . . healthy activity after all." She swallowed with horror. Not a great start, but she could recover. Preferably without having to dance later.

The conversation began to flow again, and Alex was able to relax a moment and simply look at Joshua. He'd cut his hair for the occasion. It made him appear more formidable, and his blue eyes were stark against his freshly shaven, gold skin. She realized too late that she had not been paying attention when he offered to lead her to the dance floor.

"Oh!" She swore mentally. "No, thank you. That is, we have not had time to greet anyone, and it would be rude to disappear so quickly to the dance floor." She was dissembling and not very well. She turned to Emma, praying panic was not written on her face. Her friend looked equally worried—whether at Alex's continued rudeness or fear she would fail her on the dance floor, Alex would never know. Her brother intervened.

"Certainly, she would love to dance. Alex loves nothing if not a turn around the old dance floor." Stephen pushed her forward helpfully, a wicked grin plastered on his face.

Alex thought she would learn what a swoon really was. "Emma," she entreated, praying for intervention, her voice breathy with alarm.

Misunderstanding Alex's concern, the earl invited Emma out to dance, leaving Alex with no recourse but to accept Joshua's arm. She gripped him, and went reluctantly, her eyes promising revenge on her brother.

Alex struggled at the edge of the dance floor, as close to panic as she had ever been in her life. Damn. What to do now? She glanced around desperately. Was it her imagination or was everyone staring at them? Not good. Definitely not good. Emma glanced back over her shoulder, and Alex tossed a little wave of the hand that all was well. Right. *Thanks for nothing, dear beloved friend.* She took a deep breath and squared her shoulders, daring to lift her head to the duke. Meeting his eyes was a mistake. They were the most beautiful color of indigo. She swallowed painfully, recalling how he had kissed her that very morning. Oh, God. The memory alone made her skin prickle with heat.

"Ah, your color is coming back. I thought perhaps you regretted being in my company?"

She could see her reflection in his eyes and his devilish wink did nothing to put her at ease. Discomfort turned to alarm. She decided honesty was her only option. "I don't really enjoy dancing, Duke."

"Truly? Or is it you just don't know how. That's fine, of course. Americans are certainly not known for their grace on the dance floor. I can understand you not wanting to embarrass your family name." He inclined his head to her brother, who had snatched a pretty maiden to join them on the floor. "Though Stephen seems to have a knack for it."

Alex sighed. "You are the most damned irritating man I have ever had the misfortune to meet. I know the moves. I just cannot—"

He pulled her forward. "So you do dance."

Alex swallowed painfully. She would disgrace her family for sure. It was one thing to know her failures, another to make them public. She stepped back unconsciously as couples swept by within bare inches of them. A hand went to her upset stomach.

"No!"

"It's not nearly so bad as you think." He held her hand tighter as she struggled to free it.

"I can't!"

"We have already been seen, we must go through with it. It would be scandalous otherwise."

Her dismay increased. Alex prayed he could not feel her tremble as he pulled her deftly into his embrace and into the first turn—into the middle of the floor! She instantly grabbed hold of him in fear, seeking protection from the confusing pattern of bodies twirling about.

"There you go, my sweet. Step, step, turn."

She followed quickly then faced him again. "Don't call me that."

"And one more time, my love," he instructed.

"Someone will hear—" Her words were cut off when Joshua expertly swirled her out to the music. She made a desperate attempt to keep her footing as he spun her back to face him.

"It is appropriate to keep your eyes on your partner . . . darling," he teased rakishly. "And now would be a good time to breathe."

Alex laughed. She had been holding her breath. She was dancing, she realized. In a real ballroom. She looked around. Astounded.

It was a mistake.

All she saw was chaos. She pulled away in panic and missed a step. He caught her more firmly, focusing her attention back on him. "Alex, my love, the guests would doubt your affection for me, should you abandon me on the dance floor with such passion. On the count of eight. And turn and bow." Joshua led her through the steps.

"We have no relationship for anyone to ponder, let alone doubt."

Joshua ignored her. "Why don't you give me a smile. Just to be polite."

Alex arched a brow.

"Yes, I know, you'd rather give me a kick."

She did smile then, despite herself. "I'm sorry, this dress has squeezed the humor out of me."

He glanced wickedly lower, down her dress, and leisurely back up. "Happily, the rest is still intact."

Her cheeks pinkened. "Careful, Your Grace. I'm armed."

"As I've just noted, Miss Stafford."

She gasped, her face getting hotter, while he laughed at her discomfit.

The dance ended and the music flowed into a slower, sweeping tune. Joshua pulled her closer before she could escape. It would improve her confidence. She didn't seem so fearful now, though he caught her trying to look beyond him several times, before quickly averting her eyes back to his. It amused him how she kept trying to overcome whatever fear gripped her.

He knew he should not have kept her for a second dance, but he also was letting everyone know he was staking claim. He gambled he could get away with it. For the moment, his American beauty did not seem to notice or think of it as an impropriety, so he decided not to mention it. He squeezed her hand gently, and it warmed him that he was granted a somewhat shy smile of pleasure from her as he guided her around the floor in a companionable truce.

Alex surprised herself. This dancing thing wasn't so bad after all. She moved with more ease around the floor.

"Alex," Joshua said softly.

She met his serious eyes in response.

"You do look spectacularly beautiful. An incomparable. Even in your mother's time."

Pleasure washed over her. Emma had indeed accomplished a miracle. "Thank you . . . Joshua."

"But, I still prefer my lakeside nymph. She is much more accommodating."

"Accommodation is easier without clothes."

He laughed out loud, and she hastened to add, "I mean, without these formal type clothes . . . oh, I give up. I'm just going to be silent for the rest of the evening before the earl thinks I'm a completely inappropriate companion."

"Ah. So that is what all this effort is for."

"Not all. Some is to entice you. Emma thinks you might be courting me."

"I see."

"Are you?" Alex asked. It seemed impossible, but maybe not.

"I thought you were going to be silent for the rest of the night," he answered.

She was disappointed. The idea that he might be courting her had become appealing. Not that she could love him. Oh, lord. Her steps faltered and Joshua steadied her instantly, inquiring with his eyes if she was okay. She stared in horror. She was not in love with him, was she?

"My sweet, that expression is not at all flattering. You're not going to be ill are you?"

She shook her head in denial. At him. At her stupidity.

"Hold on a bit longer. We're nearly done."

"I'm fine." She forced a smile at the man who continued to befuddle her. "Perfectly fine." She just needed to get as far away from him as possible, as soon as possible.

The evening progressed beautifully and was fast becoming the highlight of the summer. Alex wandered from the crowds to a second-floor balcony in order to view the event. Lady Matilda joined her, the two becoming fast friends when Alex freed the newly arrived chaperone after her dress became tangled in a planter on the veranda.

They watched as Emma was introduced to a young man at the far end of the ballroom. "Do you know that man?" Alex asked Lady Matilda.

"Yes, I met him earlier. Lord Heatherly. A nice young man. Clever as well. A professor with the British Museum."

"What!" Alex looked again. "That is not Lord Heatherly!"

She touched her wrist instinctively, wishing for knives. "Hurry. Find the Duke of Worthington. We must get Emma away from that man."

Lady Matilda turned with shock. "What do you mean?"

"I mean I have met Lord Heatherly. Just this week. And that," she pointed to the man, "is not Lord Heatherly."

"Impossible!" Lady Matilda was genuinely distressed.

"Please. Find Worthington or Stonewood," Alex implored, pushing the elder woman on her way. She reached for her ankle, then stopped, stuck in a half bend, her dress preventing further movement. "Wait!" she cried. Lady Matilda came back, her color unnaturally high. "I cannot reach my gun. Assist me." She lifted her right ankle while pulling up her skirt.

Lady Matilda lost all her color. "You have a gun under your skirts?"

"Believe me, there is room for plenty more, only . . ." She bent as far as she could to illustrate that she could not bend at all. ". . . impossible to reach!"

"Good lord. Marcus was right," Lady Matilda mumbled, handing her the gun between two fingers. "What will you do?"

Alex abandoned all hope of appearing genteel. "I'm going to stop him."

Hurrying away, Alex followed Emma's progress, strategizing. The imposter was leading Emma out onto the dark veranda. Alex would not make it in time. Looking across, the fastest route instantly appeared in her mind with a red-hot flash. Chandelier. Drapery rope. Floor. On another day, a distinct possibility. In this dress, a run for the stairs was the better option. She hurried, gun tucked in her skirts, and made her way back to the crowds. Unfortunately, in her rush, she did not account for the slide of polished floors, the edge of a carpet, and an old dowager fainting at the sight of Alex running full speed.

Lord Merriton sipped some champagne, enjoying conversation with Worthington as they caught up on news.

"Heatherly is coming, isn't he?" Joshua asked.

"Yes, yes. Don't worry. He probably got distracted reading or something," Colin promised.

"Excellent," Joshua forced himself to be patient. He had done some investigating and found that Heatherly and Miss Rule had been imposters. Unfortunately he had yet to track them. He did find the real Heatherly, and looked forward to introducing him to Alex, certain the man would have information that would be useful to her.

"I'm sure your sea captain will be very grateful for your help," Colin reassured. "By the way, she is not at all how you made her out. Why, I fully expected her to be swinging from the chandeliers, garnishing weapons, and causing—" Colin stopped, his attention caught by the vision in gold running across the second-floor viewing area and apparently unaware that when she turned the corner she would be faced with two elderly patronesses who had the power to cut her completely from London society with a mere word. "—general mayhem."

Joshua continued chatting, unaware of the scene behind him. "She's not a pirate, man. Just a very determined woman at times."

Colin nodded. The eldest dowager stumbled at the sight of Miss Stafford barreling toward her, a look of fear visible, even from the slight distance. The other woman fell over in an apparent faint, and Colin was certain all three women would tumble down the stairs an instant later. To his surprise, it didn't happen.

"I know Marcus has his doubts about her, but she is simply unaccustomed to our social habits. Her heart's in the right place."

"Uh-huh." Colin wanted to say something, but he didn't quite know how to tell his friend that Marcus might have reason for concern. Instead of colliding into the swooning dowager, Miss Stafford agilely leapt, albeit her upper body unnaturally stiff, slid on her bottom partially down the stair rail, and ultimately lost her balance, which he thought was no surprise in that delectable dress. She fell sideways to her certain death. But she didn't die. With one elegantly gloved hand she grabbed hold of the one of Stonewood's blue decorative banners, and caught herself midair, her dress ballooning out for what he might have otherwise appreciated to be a spectacular view. Until the banner ripped, with a distinctly loud tear, drawing a dangerous amount of attention. Miss Stafford fell the next ten feet with only her dress to slow her down.

Colin ventured a wary look to his doomed friend, who continued to plead her case. "In any event, she has been very anxious tonight to behave and I know it's an effort for her—though not as much as she would pretend—and meeting the real Heatherly would make her evening much more interesting. Then he can visit tomorrow to advise her, and—"

The duke stopped.

"Colin, what has you so *enraptured*?"

His friend turned around in time to see Miss Stafford straighten her legs and regain balance after a relatively successful landing. One hand, Colin noted, had a small pistol, which she shoved between the folds of her skirts, while the other hand attempted to discreetly pull up the top of her dress, which had temporarily exposed a delightful, but decidedly unacceptable amount of her breasts. A servant nearby nearly dropped a tray of champagne flutes at the shock of Miss Stafford landing in front of him. She steadied the tray with a helpful hand, only to turn around and have Langley drop his entire tray right next to her, causing an unholy clatter. Miss Stafford quickly sidestepped the disaster. Quite politely, to all appearances, and excused herself, moving to the veranda.

The next second, Lady Matilda came to an abrupt halt in front of them, flushed and worried.

"Gentlemen. We have a situation!" she whispered urgently.

"Miss Stafford," Colin guessed.

"Yes. There is a man here posing as another, and he has Emma, and Miss Stafford went to stop him, and she has a—"

"Pistol." Colin had noted that.

Chapter Eighteen

Alex found Emma and the imposter within seconds of going outside. Thankfully, he had not taken her far.

"Emma," Alex called sharply. "Come here." Emma, ever polite, invited Alex to come meet Lord Heatherly.

"Emma. Step away from the man."

"Alex, really—"

"Emma! Please. Step away from the man."

Emma stepped away, and Alex lifted her weapon. "I have met Lord Heatherly. He is a kindly old man in his sixties. *This* is not Lord Heatherly."

"Miss, truly I am. There has been a mistake."

Alex thought he was surprisingly calm, for one who had been caught in the act. "We will let the authorities sort that out, sir. Kindly do not move."

"Alex," Joshua called behind her. "Alex, put that away."

"Joshua, this man claims he is Lord Heatherly. Will you please dispose of him?" she requested, confident in his skills.

Joshua came behind her and slid the pistol from her trigger-ready grip. "Alex." He lowered the gun. "This is the man I wanted you to meet. *This* is Lord Heatherly."

Alex shook her head, but he confirmed.

"The other was the imposter. I stayed in London to check it out."

"Why did you not tell me?"

"I intended to."

"Why not this morning?"

"You had other things on your mind," he argued.

Alex turned around slowly, the full horror of the situation sinking in as she took in Emma's white face, along with the Earl of Stonewood's very stony face as he joined them. "Oh, no." Several other guests surrounded them, curious. "I thought Emma was in danger," she pleaded to the earl, knowing his was the only opinion that mattered in that moment.

"If I'm not mistaken, you nearly knocked Lady Wimbleton to her death, leapt ungainly from the staircase, exposed all my guests to your underskirts, and now threaten a peer of the realm."

Emma gasped in what Alex made out to be unspeakable shock at the quick summary of her recent antics. "Alex. No." She seemed to beg for a denial.

Alex winced sorrowfully and watched as the real Lord Heatherly helped her friend to sit.

"As for the underskirt," Colin offered, "it was by no means an entirely terrible vision."

Emma, Joshua, and Marcus turned to him appalled.

"Not helping, Colin." The earl's voice was tight with disapproval.

"I'm just pointing out that no real harm has been done. Lord Heatherly is aware that Miss Stafford was tricked by an imposter posing as him."

"And you all brought this into my home. Unthinking? On this occasion?"

Alex did not think the heat of her skin could get any hotter. "My lord, I am so sorry." She stepped toward her friend, who held a hand up for space. "Emma, I am so sorry."

"I know," Emma breathed out, soft and cheerless.

As if matters could not get worse, Aunt Maggie and Stephen joined them with more news. "Alex," Stephen spoke urgently. "We have to go."

Alex nodded. It seemed like the best idea.

He added, "There was a robbery at Aunt Maggie's. Some injuries."

Alex was torn, but Emma just said, "Go."

Alex looked to Lady Matilda for assistance. The elder woman nodded to confirm that she would stay with Emma—relieved no doubt to have Alex far away. Lord Merriton, Lord Heatherly, and Joshua would escort them to her aunt's home and investigate the situation. Rather than reenter the ballroom, the small party skirted Stonewood Manor and disappeared into the night.

Her aunt leaned toward her. "I hope you have a good explanation for tonight, Alex dear. And a tight dress preventing blood flow to your brain, thus hindering good judgment, is not going to be sufficient."

Disgraced, Alex thought. Completely and perfectly disgraced. And entirely her fault.

It was nearly dawn when the authorities left and the servants were put at ease. Maggie's butler, Kendall, had a lump on his head the size of a plum, but the doctor thought he would survive.

Alex's study area and the library had been torn apart, as had her bedroom. The intruders didn't find the map, though Alex guessed they had walked over it a dozen times in the study, never noticing. Even now, her friends did not think it amiss in the room. The astrolabe she had hidden in the secret bottom of a heavy statue. She secured it around her neck with relief.

The intruders had found her journal, though. It contained all the secrets her family had tried to protect regarding her connection to the prophecy. At least the ones she knew, including her connection to Prince Kelile and every symbol on the map that she had diligently researched. There had also been a number of private entries recalling dreams and some personal notes regarding the duke. The humiliation of having that read by strangers was nothing short of unbearable, though in truth the least of her worries.

Alex changed and joined Joshua, Lord Merriton, Lord Heatherly, and her brother. A servant brought breakfast, tea, and coffee for everyone. Joshua gave her an expectant look. If he thought she was going to share her losses and worries with him, he was mistaken. Tonight had shown her reality as it really was. She would never fit into this world. And certainly not into his life.

"Thank you, gentlemen, for your assistance with the magistrate. My aunt is in bed, but also sends her deepest thanks."

"You have your necklace?" Joshua asked.

"Yes." She gave no other response than to touch her medallion.

Lord Heatherly wandered the study where they gathered, collecting and stacking books left in disarray by the intruders. He was young, wiry framed, and not unattractive. She'd had no time to observe him earlier, when she'd been focused on blowing his head off. Not that she would have, but now that she had a moment to study him more clearly, she noted eyes that calculated and observed so as not to miss anything, matched with a manner that was meant to put one at ease, as if nothing were amiss. A dangerous combination.

He thumbed through a book. "Does your aunt have children?"

"No," Alex replied. "Why?"

"No reason." Heatherly answered in a way that told her there was definitely a reason. He handed her the thick volume. "This one. A rare piece. Your thieves were remiss in not taking it, if in fact they were searching for a bit of history."

"*Creation Myths*?"

He nodded. "Do you know the story of Lilith?"

"A little. I came across her in some reading." Alex didn't mention it was research on mermaids.

"Who is she?" Merriton asked.

"Some believe the first wife of Adam," Heatherly explained. "One of the oldest myths in civilization. She is often represented as a beautiful woman waist up, and a serpent waist down. A bit mermaidlike. Some call her the first siren. Enticing men to abandon themselves to become something new. To rebel against their spiritual nature, and embrace their physical nature. Some say she became the bride of Satan, abandoning Adam in favor of equality."

"Why are you sharing this, Lord Heatherly?"

"Sorry, Miss Stafford. I thought it obvious."

He had the attention of everyone in on the room. "That

necklace you wear. Not so old in comparison to the beginning of time, but an antique, 200 to 400 BC perhaps. The symbol on it, as you must have noticed, matches the symbol on your carpet, which I note is fairly new by comparison."

Everyone looked at the carpet. Everyone but Alex. She knew he didn't mean her aunt's carpet, but the smaller one by the desk, under her chair. She didn't say anything, uncertain as to the trustworthiness of the man. She covered her astrolabe with her hand, as if to protect it from him.

"That symbol on your astrolabe, Miss Stafford, is the ancient symbol for Lilith."

Alex went cold. "What does it mean?"

He shook his head. "I don't know. Nothing. Many people worship ancient gods. A follower of Lilith could have made that astrolabe, invoking her protection perhaps over their travels."

Stephen was confused, as Alex knew he had a right to be. "But Alex has had that necklace since birth." He turned to his sister. "What is this carpet?"

Alex went to the desk and brought out the carpet for them to view.

"Alex, you had it in plain site?" Joshua looked at her as though she was insane.

"And it has proven to be the safest place."

"When did you get this?" Stephen asked.

"A while ago," she temporized, unwilling to share the truth just yet, and risk her brother's trust and affection. "Lord Heatherly, would you know any more about Lilith, and could you tell me why anyone would be obsessed with collecting relics and information relating to her?"

Heatherly bent to the tapestry, examining. "This is an interpretation of the myth in some way. I'm not sure what all the symbols mean." He looked up. "At one point, Lilith came back to Adam and had an affair. She begot two daughters and shared her part of the earth equally between them."

"Only one sister was not satisfied," Alex said, recalling Paxton's tale.

"Yes. She waged war, conquering all in her path, collecting treasure and power until her realm was stronger than her sister's—but still her sister would not fall. Determined, the evil sister—if we can call her that—cried out to Lilith's husband during a great battle, and begged his assistance."

"She called upon Satan?" Alex asked.

"Well, if indeed, all that is true, Miss Stafford. It's really just a morality tale."

She nodded. "Please continue."

"The dark one aided her—in exchange for her first child. She agreed, conquered her sister, enjoyed a short reign of power, peace, and prosperity, then made the mistake of falling in love."

"Mistake?" Alex's stomach turned.

"She had a child, Miss Stafford. A beautiful child who was gifted in every way."

"But she had to give it back."

"Exactly," Heatherly continued. "The queen begged a reprieve, offering all the treasures she had attained, but it was not to be."

Alex added, "So she took another woman's child and sacrificed it instead."

"Not just any woman, Miss Stafford. Her sister's child."

"Her sister's? She destroyed her sister's realm *and* her child?"

He nodded. "When the child was sacrificed, its mother died of heartache, causing Lilith to return from her days of untamed promiscuity to see what had happened to the paradise that she left. Upon finding the truth, she sang a violent song so powerful that the earth and waves vibrated, rising up, and flooding the entire empire with everyone in it, spare a few to tell the tale.

"Some say the siren's song heard at sea is not meant to destroy unwary sailors. It is merely Lilith's lament over her lost daughters. Others say it is her revenge against Satan, calling him to engage in a final battle. A battle that all agree would be an apocalypse of sorts."

"The end of days?"

"As we know them," Heatherly said.

"I still don't understand," Stephen asked. "Why would anyone care about this? Is this why Paxton is still after us?"

Alex turned away, unable to face him, but answered best she could. "Treasure, Stephen. I think Paxton believes he can find this lost kingdom, and the wealth it contains."

"It's a myth. Surely no one would believe any of this?"

There was silence in the room.

"Alex? You don't believe this?"

She shrugged. "I don't know, Stephen. What matters is that Paxton believes it, and that makes him dangerous."

"Then give him what he wants. It's not worth it."

"I can't." Alex said it quietly, but with certainty.

Stephen turned to her.

"Whatever it is," she explained, "I am too connected to it. And so was our mother. I need to find out why this has all happened. To make sense of it somehow. If I can't do that, then at least I can stop the wrong people from getting their hands on anything until I am sure it's safe. I've failed at so many things . . . I need to do this. I'm sorry. But I will stop Paxton. I promise."

"That's madness," Joshua countered.

"I have to agree with Worthington, Miss Stafford," Lord Merriton said.

Alex turned to the men. "I think this has been enough for one night. Your Grace, if I may have a moment privately before you leave?"

Stephen scowled, his curiosity still not satisfied, but he nodded reluctantly when he realized she was not going to discuss this any further tonight and he left with everyone but Joshua.

Alex ran a hand over the carpet, pretending to study it, seeking a moment to gather herself.

Joshua came to her. Too close. She stepped to the other side of the desk. He frowned at that action, but she needed something between them before she could do what she needed to do.

"What is it?" he asked.

"I'm leaving England."

"That's ridiculous."

"As soon as arrangements can be made," she continued, ignoring him.

"Under what protection, I'd like to know?"

Alex swallowed. He inquired like he had a right to know. As if his protection was the only she was allowed. And as if she needed it.

"I can't remain here at Lilyfield and put my aunt or her people in any further danger."

"Agreed," he said, surprising her.

He took a pace closer, and Alex put up a hand to stop him. "Please! Please just let me finish. I understand what you are doing." He came around the desk, unrelenting, and a tingle of desire shot up her arms—a desire to lean in and trust him and let him take care of everything, a desire to simply be with him in every way possible. All of which was impossible. She circled the desk again to get away.

"What you think can never be," she explained.

"You're wrong."

"We are too different. *I'm* too different." She knew it, but it still hurt to say it to him. To make him see who she really was . . . and let her go. Because if he didn't, she didn't think that she could.

"Different is good."

She shook her head. "The Earl of Stonewood will hate me after tonight. And how long would it take before the rest of your friends turned against you because of me?"

"You're mistaken, Alex."

"I'm not! Joshua, I had only to get through one night. And I ruined it. For everyone."

"Because you took matters into your own hands instead of getting help first. But you'll learn."

She laughed, but it was with moisture burning her eyes. His words only proved that he did not know her yet. "I did send Lady Matilda to find you. But you would have had me wait?"

"Alex, I only ask that you not risk your life carelessly."

"I don't." She didn't. But everyone had risked their lives for her. She had so much to make up for. Her mother. Her father. They all had made sure she was protected. If the one thing she was meant to do was protect the map, then she would do it. And if part of that meant she had to stop Paxton, then that was best done alone—without risking the loss of anymore loved ones. Joshua would never understand that.

"Please understand. I can't be what you want. In the end, I would just disappoint you." She turned away from him. "And that would be more unbearable than this is now." She gathered her composure and turned back to him, offering a hand of farewell. "I only wanted to thank you for your friendship toward me and Stephen."

He didn't take the hand. In two strides he was in front of her, staring at the hand as if thunderstruck. She hadn't ever seen him truly angry before. It was upsetting. She had not meant to cause this. She didn't want their farewell to end in disagreement. After a moment she dropped her hand and folded both in front of her, unsure how to deal with him.

"And you know what I want?" he asked, his voice tight with control.

"Yes." Alex's temper flared. He didn't have to make this so difficult. "You want to marry a proper lady who will be your duchess, bear your many offspring, help you renovate Worthington Park to its former glory, and be the perfect companion to the perfect English lord."

"I'm flattered you think that I am so perfect."

"You're not," she said, sharp and instant. "But that doesn't mean you don't want perfection. I, on the other hand, have responsibilities to my family, and to Stafford Shipping. With Paxton in the mix, there is really no room for a frivolous affair with an English noble whose desires are at odds with my own. I am very flattered by your attention, but it could never work out."

He grabbed her by the shoulders and she held herself stiffly, turning her head away, knowing that to fight his superior strength would be a mistake.

"Look at me!"

When she didn't, he shook her and repeated the words.

"You don't know a damn thing about what I want," he hissed.

"Was I wrong?"

He hesitated, and in that hesitation, her heart dropped another inch, and she closed her eyes in defeat, all the while knowing she was doing the right thing.

His grip squeezed her arms a degree more, demanding her attention. She did not think her heart could take much more of doing the right thing. It hurt to look into those fierce blue eyes, but she made herself do it. There would be time for regrets later.

"You were not entirely wrong. I do want a duchess. And children. And to share a home with a woman who is my perfect mate. Not perfect, Alex. My perfect mate. There's a difference."

"I hope you find her," Alex parried, struggling to present a polite and uninterested demeanor. She must have succeeded. He shook his head with a bitter nod of acceptance, thrusting her away. She stumbled backward slightly, not fighting his wrath. She welcomed it. It was much easier to deal with. He moved away, toward the desk, as if needing to give himself distance in order to fight the temptation to strike her.

"We are not different, Alex. That's why I understand exactly what you're doing. And I admire you for it."

Alex looked at him, her first sense of uncertainty creeping in. Her stomach curled for one instant of hope.

"But," he paused, taking his time to study her. "It would be a mistake to care for someone who has so little sense of her own self-worth that she cannot accept help." He scrutinized the map on her desk and long fingers curled tightly around one corner of it, as if he would destroy it himself. She instinctively moved away from the violence etched on his face.

"You do leave a path of death and destruction, Alex." He pulled the carpet from the desk and threw it on the floor separating them. "Only you can change that."

Alex recoiled, her heart stopping at his words and her skin growing cold despite the summer temperature. He said nothing more, but turned and left. Not a farewell, or apology, or a bid of friendship. But in truth, she would have had trouble registering anything more.

She didn't move for a long time after. She couldn't. There was nothing left inside her. She was stunned by the shock of knowing she would not see him again. The shock of having him hate her so completely. And the shock of knowing that more and more she was becoming like the red-haired figure in the carpet. The one that stared up at her now while smiling mockingly with her arm directed toward devastation and ruin. The symbol of Lilith, Heatherly said. That was what she carried with her. The mark of evil, betrayal, and destruction. Every word Joshua had said was true, and she couldn't help wondering if she had not just destroyed something else.

Chapter Nineteen

"Precious." Reginal Paxton laughed in pure delight. "Absolutely precious!" He held up the journal to indicate his pleasure. "And the map, too!" He plopped into a chair of the luxurious apartment his cousin kept, appreciating the comforts of land. "Ah! Life is good."

His cousin, Lady Liz Beauveau, joined him. She looked a bit tired these days, her strong-boned face somewhat handsome, but deep lines of age were setting in despite a variety of treatments to fight the effects. Still, she was a shrewd partner in their high-end trading business.

"She is a kelile. Apparently the last," Reginald told his cousin. "She must be a descendant. But she doesn't seem to know it. We might have to kill her. Or . . ." His gaze turned thoughtful.

"What are you scheming?" Liz asked.

"I wonder what the sultan might pay to redeem his honor—and obtain the keeper of the prophecy. Damn. The chit is likely worth a lot more to us if she's alive."

"We have room to add more cargo, if that's what you are asking. But what of the rumors? Men are terrified to sail with her."

Reginald shrugged. "Stories get exaggerated." He turned the pages of the journal. "Whatever power she currently has is based on luck, experience, and money—three things that make anyone seem invincible to a commoner."

Liz poured herself some sherry and topped off his port. "And the astrolabe?"

"Yes. Odd, that bit." He pulled the chain from around his neck and fingered the disc at the end. "It seems her mother was not the only member of the family to have a portion of it.

It might be the final piece of the puzzle." He tucked the medallion away. "Or Miss Stafford might be. Only she doesn't know it."

Joshua left Lilyfield as if the hounds of hell were at his feet. He couldn't speak. A good thing, no doubt, after the damage he'd already inflicted. She'd flinched. From him. She'd tried to hide it, but he knew her too well not to see it. He had hurt her. Deliberately. Something he never wanted to do.

Damn, but she made him furious. And frustrated. She was being stubborn, pure and simple.

Colin returned to Stonewood Manor and Lord Heatherly to the Ashford Inn, both happy for well-deserved sleep, but Joshua spurred Cyclone on in the morning light until both horse and rider were exhausted. He could not stop thinking about her. He told his servants not to disturb him and for hours he paced his room, trying to figure out what went wrong, what went right, and all the reasons why he should just give up.

He could have mentioned Heatherly sooner. Or perhaps shared that he had asked Colin to use his government contacts to help search for Paxton. But until there were results, there was no point in getting her hopes up. Certainly, he had been wrong to say she left a path of death and destruction, but she needed to stop and think about her actions more. She constantly put herself in danger, as if she were invincible or— Joshua stopped in his tracks.

No. She couldn't really think that.

A chill went up his spine. She carried guilt for the death of both her parents. And how many more? Did she think she had to die to make it better? He paced more quickly, worried.

She didn't need to leave. They had only just found each other. He fingered the ring she had given him that first night they met. Her marker. He would use it if necessary.

"Marcus, honestly it was a wonderful evening. No harm was done in the end."

Marcus looked at Emma as if she'd lost her mind. The

guests had left, and the others were in bed, but she'd cornered him in his study where he waited for Lord Merriton's return.

"Quite frankly, you should be happy that I have friends who are so concerned about my well-being," she said.

"You will go with Aunt Matilda to London and she will introduce you to a number of appropriate companions."

"I don't want to go to London! My work is here. On the estate. Who will run it if I leave?"

This time Marcus looked incredulous. "A short visit to London will not bring ruin on the estate. Besides, I thought you wanted to marry. There will surely be better offerings in town."

Emma froze, then swallowed the bitter realization he had just inflicted on her. "Surely," she agreed.

She still had on her ball gown. For a short moment that night, she had thought he'd looked at her with more than just brotherly affection. She could not have been so mistaken. Could she? She walked over to him. Ha. That was the look. She smiled.

"Don't you wish to kiss me good night, Marcus?"

"It's morning."

"It's still my birthday." She stepped up to him and pressed her chest to his, pretending innocence as she lifted her cheek to the side for his lips. He gave her a quick peck and pressed her shoulders away, forcing her back. Interestingly, he did not let go.

"You do understand my position on Miss Stafford?"

"Completely."

He sighed with obvious relief. "Good." He released her and stepped back.

She laughed. "But I don't agree, and I have no intention of cutting my dearest friend because others are too shallow, pompous, and self-absorbed to recognize all the goodness inherent in everything she does for others."

"Killing people aside," Marcus mocked.

"And what would you have her do?" Emma shouted. "Would you have her leave me to potential villains because it would cause less scandal? Alex was protecting me. Would you not kill someone if they threatened me? Or perhaps you would be quite pleased to be done with this burden on your time!"

She had gone too far. She saw it instantly when he crossed the short distance between them and grabbed her firmly by the shoulders, his face inflexible.

"I would kill anyone who touched you. Make no mistake, Emma."

She breathed hard, his usual lordly mask stripped bare, something raw and violent in its place. Emotions he never let her see were now open to her. But she wondered sadly if it might be too late, for surely he was forcing her to make a choice that she could not.

"How can you doubt it? I want only to protect you."

She shook her head, a lone tear freeing itself from her lashes. "No, Marcus." She reached to him and touched one high-boned cheek. Then she did the one thing she wanted to do before it was too late. She kissed him.

It was only a brush of her lips. Enough to make them tingle. Enough for her to feel the sudden increased speed of his heartbeat under her fingertips. It wasn't nearly what she wanted, but it would have to be enough. She drew back.

"You don't want to protect me. You want to suffocate me." She wiped another offending tear from her cheek. "You want me to choose between you and Alex."

His stiff mask was back in place. "I ask only for a little common sense."

"Of course. So I should end my friendship with Alex, go to London, and find someone suitably boring to marry. I presume then that you would be free to do the same. And we would remain friends and our children would grow up to repeat our excessively boring and loveless lives, and all will be appropriate and quite common. Yes, I believe I am very clear, Marcus."

"You needn't be so dramatic." He smiled, as if relieved to have his way.

"Ah, but it is dramatic. Friends betrayed, love lost? All for the sake of leading a meaningless and dull life? That seems very dramatic."

Emma experienced a bitterness in her heart she hadn't previously known existed. She looked at the man she had loved so long and for so many reasons. This was a new side she had to accept. And it seemed he could not love her enough to trust her choice in friends. She was at the door when she turned to look at him one last time.

"Good-bye, Marcus."

"You mean, good night," he corrected.

She shrugged a shoulder to show she didn't care and it no longer mattered.

"Whatever you say."

Alex hadn't gone to bed yet. When Emma was brought to her room, she guessed her friend had not slept either. Upon seeing the disarray of open trunks, Emma was immediately on alert.

"What's going on?" Emma demanded.

Alex rushed to her, relieved to have the chance to apologize in person. "Oh, Emma! I am so, so sorry about last night." She reached for her friend's hands. "I never, never wanted it to turn out that way. It's all my fault. I ruined the most important occasion of your life because I am a complete idiot—"

Emma cut her off. "Nonsense. Joshua should have told you what was going on. I don't know why men think they need to keep all the information to themselves. I swear, they are hoarders. Is it too much to ask for a little communication?"

Emma turned from her, clearly frustrated. Alex chewed her lip, guessing it did not go well with the earl after she had left.

"But this . . ." Emma swung a hand around the room. "What is this?"

Alex spoke gently. "I'm going home."

Emma spun on her, voice sharp. "Because of last night?"

"Partially. Also because it's time. And I can't risk any further danger to Aunt Maggie," she explained. "I'll go to London today, and Stephen will follow in a couple days with the rest of our baggage."

Emma nodded. Surprisingly calm. "I'll come with you."

"I'll be in London for a little while. I would welcome your company if the earl doesn't mind. I could ask Aunt Maggie to join us as a proper chaperone. Or you have Lady Matilda as well. She is also welcome."

"To America," Emma elaborated.

"What?" Alex nearly dropped the blouse she was folding.

"There is nothing left for me here. Marcus will never love me. Not how I wish it. And on top of that, he is incredibly stupid." She paced to the bed and started to help fold Alex's clothing, albeit a little too enthusiastically. "Incredibly stupid!"

"I see." Alex waited a moment to see if she was done. "You are, of course, completely welcome to join me." She took the blouse Emma held before the material could accidentally get torn in her friend's passionate helpfulness. "What happened?"

"Nothing."

"You fought because of me."

"No!"

Alex looked at her friend in disbelief.

"Well, not exactly. It was more about him not trusting my judgment." Emma grabbed a skirt and began to roll and crush. "And being stupid!"

Alex winced at the tortured skirt. It was one of the few she actually liked.

"I can travel to London with Aunt Matilda. Marcus was sending me there anyway. To get away from you. Ha! He will have to be happy that I'm obedient about that at least!"

Emma reached for a green waist-cut jacket to fold and Alex snatched it before Emma did. Her friend stopped abruptly.

"You're leaving today?"

"Yes." Alex put the green jacket in a trunk to be brought to London later.

"Will you say good-bye to Joshua? Oh, I completely forgot! Is Kendall okay? No one else was hurt last night? The men were gone so long. What happened? You are going to say good-bye to Joshua, aren't you?" Emma repeated, confronting Alex.

"We said good-bye last night."

"And?"

Alex shrugged nonchalantly. "Nothing. We agreed we aren't right for each other."

"You were civilized?"

"Of course I was civilized!" Alex returned, defensive.

"No, I meant both of you. It was a civilized conversation?"

"Yes. Of course. We determined that I destroy everything I touch and leave a path of dead bodies behind me, which clearly is why Marcus does not want you within ten feet of me."

"Joshua said that?"

Alex shrugged to indicate it didn't matter. "It's true. And Marcus has good reason for his opinions. That's why I'm leaving. I can't bear to see anyone else I care about hurt by Paxton and his senseless ambitions for some legendary treasure." She fingered the astrolabe. As long as Paxton was alive, anyone near Alex could be a target.

"Joshua is not going to London with you?" Emma seemed confused about this still.

"Emma!" Alex breathed to calm herself. "I already told you, we said our good-byes."

"It's just . . ." Emma collapsed on the bed, dejected. "I don't want you to go."

Alex sat next to her and squeezed her friend's perfect, soft fingers in comfort. "I know."

Marcus woke up early in the afternoon, unable to sleep any longer. Something about what Emma said still bothered him. *Friends betrayed, love lost.* Whose love? he wondered. It was too much to think about. He was grateful when Langley announced the Duke of Worthington's appearance.

Joshua looked as tired as Marcus felt. "Did you sleep?"

"Not much. I came to apologize about the Heatherly incident. Entirely my fault."

"Really? I don't recall seeing you pull a gun on one of my guests."

"Don't be cruel to her. She was defending Emma. At least she thought so. Foolish though that impulse was. I don't understand what is wrong with women."

"We agree there." He waved to the refreshments. "Tea?"

"Something stronger if you've got it."

Joshua plopped in a chair. Marcus thought his friend looked worried. "What happened last night? At Lilyfield."

"A lot. Alex has been keeping some secrets for a long time." He accepted the glass of whisky Marcus handed over, and stared into it as if he had an unsolvable problem with no easy solution. "I can tell you some of the story. The rest is Alex's to keep. For now." He set the drink down untouched, and reached inside his shirt to pull out the small ring he kept on a thin, loose chain. He took it off, and swung it in front of Marcus.

"Remember this?"

"From your harem girl."

Joshua nodded. Then he surprised Marcus. "It's Alex's."

"What?" Marcus's teacup rattled when he put it down. "How?"

"How do you think?" Joshua laughed.

"Good God! She's the girl? Impossible!" Marcus grabbed at his hair making it stand on end, mystified by the revelation. "And yet," he looked at Joshua, working it out, "who else could it be? Her family's business, her penchant for mischief, her use of firearms. Indeed, she is very athletic and spirited." He shook his head with agreement. "I find this really should not astonish me so much. In fact, heaven help us if there had been more than one woman on earth who could cause this much trouble."

"Through no fault of her own, of course." Joshua smiled.

"Of course," Marcus said. "Tell me the rest."

Merriton entered at that moment. "Wait! Tell me as well. I could use a good tale. What did I miss? And does no one sleep in anymore?" He yawned, observing Joshua's drink. "Helluva night. I'll have what he's having."

Marcus poured another glass, and Joshua started over, getting their friend caught up. By the time he was done, they were all working on a second drink.

Colin leaned back from their huddle, finally able to put all the pieces together. "More intrigue than any assignment I have ever had. So . . ." Colin looked to Joshua to solve the most immediate problem. "If I am to understand correctly, you are concerned Miss Stafford won't speak to you after you told her she leaves a trail of destruction behind her."

"Actually," Joshua planted his forehead into his hand, "I said trail of *death* and destruction."

"You devil. That old English charm bedazzling the women again."

"It's the truth," Marcus defended. "But I'd never say it to her face. She might hurt me."

The three clinked glasses to that truth, then stood when the butler entered, announcing Stephen Stafford.

"Stephen," Colin greeted. "You are the only who looks to have slept."

Stephen nodded. "I cannot stay long, I only came to make my farewells and deliver these messages." He handed one to Colin and one to the Earl of Stonewood. "We are leaving for London tomorrow and will be heading back to America soon. Alex asked that I extend her apologies for being unable to say good-bye in person."

Joshua snapped straight. "What do you mean?" Stephen turned to him, more reserved than Joshua had seen before. Worry tingled the back of his neck.

"Alex left this morning. I will meet up with her tomorrow."

Joshua felt the gut punch. He knew she would leave, but he didn't think it would be so soon. He touched the ring through his shirt, catching Colin's eye on him.

Colin spoke for him, understanding. "Nothing for my friend, the duke?"

Stephen shook his head apologetically.

Colin opened his envelope and read parts aloud. "Alex extends her warmest regards and thanks for my assistance . . . I am 'most charming, kind, and helpful.' She would be honored to see me the next time she is in England or I am in Boston. Excellent! I've still got a fighting chance."

Joshua sighed.

Stephen tried to reassure. "She can't be leaving too soon. Emma is to join us for a stay. The marriage opportunities are thought to be much better in London, after all."

Marcus scowled.

Stephen flopped in a chair. "I'm only the messenger."

"Ah, I shall be surrounded by beauties," Colin crowed.

"The London house is not even prepared," Stonewood continued, frustrated.

"Oh, I don't think . . . that is . . ." Stephen winced. "I got the impression she would stay with us, then visit Boston if no husband could be found. But perhaps I misunderstood."

"Oh, I doubt it, dear boy." Colin patted his shoulder. "What of your note, Marcus? Any clues as to Miss Stafford's next move?"

The earl shook his head, but read with a sound of increasing guilt. "Only that I am everything Emma said I was. 'Funny, thoughtful, insightful, caring.'"

"That sounds more like me," Colin said.

Marcus scanned the rest of the letter before crumpling the paper in his hand. "I'm an idiot."

"Agreed," Colin offered placidly, pouring them all a drink. He looked at Stephen, then around the room. "So, I guess we are all off to London tomorrow?"

There were resigned nods.

Joshua thought the support of friends might be useful. Alex had left completely without protection. It made him uneasy. The sooner he reached her the better. And the sooner she admitted she needed him, the easier his life would be.

Chapter Twenty

Alex arrived at the Staffords' London house in near exhaustion. Usually she appreciated the elegant lines of their home near Hyde Park, but today she thought she would just make it up the steps. O'Neil, their man in charge, sent someone to attend to Salem. Wearily she peeled off her riding coat and let it fall to the tile floor where O'Neil caught it, tsking at her state of disarray and asking where her companions were. He hadn't had a chance to tell Alex the latest news when her brother Samuel walked into the foyer and revealed himself, having heard her voice.

"Samuel!" Alex was filled with new energy, more grateful than ever to see her eldest brother. He always made it seem like everything would be okay. She rushed to him with such exuberance she nearly knocked him over, which was saying something as he was equal in size to Joshua, whom she considered quite a giant. Samuel in turn spun her around until she was dizzy.

"Allie!" Samuel embraced her fiercely before putting her down and inspecting. "I thought Aunt Maggie would have had you in bows and curls by now, married of to some skinny, spineless twit."

"I'm not so easily married off." She brushed back some errant hair.

"Come along, I have a surprise that will perk you up." He pulled her into the study.

"You have not married and begot children, have you?" Alex inquired.

"No, you impertinent imp. Go see for yourself."

Alex walked into the study and saw nothing. She wondered what joke her brother was playing then noticed another glass of whisky had been poured. Just as she turned with suspicion, Matthew jumped out from behind the door and scared the life out of her.

Pleased with her surprised shriek, he proceeded to smother her with hugs. Samuel grinned, crossing his arms across his chest, satisfied at the reunion. There was some color on her cheeks now. Then he frowned, noticing something that looked suspiciously like moisture in her eyes. His gut tightened. When had she gotten so sentimental? What was wrong? She looked like she had not slept lately, but he knew she went through periods when sleep was difficult. He guessed her correspondence hadn't told nearly the full story. Yes, definitely moisture. Matthew stepped back to check what he had seen as well.

"Alex. I thought you'd be happy to see us," Matthew said.

"I am, you idiot." Alex wiped an eye before the tear could escape.

Samuel teased her hoping to lighten the mood. "We haven't ruined some secret rendezvous you were planning, have we?" The very thought made him laugh. It had the opposite effect on Alex.

She looked at him in shock.

Samuel reached for her apologetically, but she stepped away, the pain on her face acute.

"Alex?" Samuel said. "I didn't mean—"

He tried to explain, but fell silent when tears spilled over his sister's cheeks, seemingly unstoppable, and she ran from the room, her expression stark.

Matthew stalked quietly to his whisky tumbler. He was always the calm one. He swallowed the contents of his glass in one toss, then turned to his brother with murder in his eyes.

"I believe we arrived just in time."

Samuel agreed. Someone would pay for this. First they had to find out who.

She almost had them fooled into thinking she was just exhausted from so many parties. When Alex joined them again for dinner, she wore an emerald green dress and had her hair gleaming and displayed regally on top of her head. Matthew even gawked as he asked what she'd done with their sister. She laughed, appearing calm, and politely apologized for her earlier hysterics. They wanted to strangle her. She had definitely been in England too long.

Patiently, at least patiently for them, the brothers caught Alex up on all their news while plying her with alcohol. She shared tales of their aunt, Lady Emma, and all her new friends in Kent.

"So are all the men in England blind, Alex?" Matthew smiled charmingly. "I cannot believe they haven't been throwing themselves at you."

"Oh, they find my money attractive enough," Alex said, explaining how Pillington had plotted to compromise her and force her into marriage. "As if I would care about being compromised by an Englishman," she stated.

Samuel grunted. "We'd just kill him and be done with it."

"That's what I told him. He was quite surprised to be looking down the barrel of my flintlock."

"Well, I'm glad you haven't fallen for any snotty, simpering, silly-tongued dandies, Alex," Matthew commented casually. He wasn't easily diverted.

"Of course not," Alex assured.

"I pity this country, though," he continued, "that they have not one decent man worthy of your approval."

Alex opened her mouth to defend the Brits, then stopped and looked down to hide the truth. "Well," she said with honey in her voice, "certainly none who could hold a candle to any of my brothers. I guess I've just been spoiled."

Samuel barked out a laugh, shaking his head. "Allie, I believe you have become a liar!"

"But when they are sweet lies, it's permissible," Matthew said in her defense.

"Aye. Another round then." Samuel poured the drinks and, knowing they would get nothing else on the subject of men, turned the conversation to the recent attack on her ship. The tale left him cold, though he kept his expression calm. Matthew gripped and fiddled with silverware, ready to wield his fork like a weapon. By the time Alex told them of the robbery at Lilyfield, Matthew's fork was embedded in the table.

Samuel shared a look with his brother. Both knew Alex had her secrets and she guarded them well. But if Alex really did have the map Paxton sought, it was one secret that could get her killed.

Alex spent the next day on her ship. She watched the crew from the top deck and breathed in the warm air. Granted there was an unpleasant stench emanating from the water around the wharf, but just being there felt like being home. The smell was the same in nearly every harbor.

Her ship was anchored, its gangplank lowered to the dock while her crew prepped and loaded supplies. Alex spent the day working in the tactical area and meeting room. She kept most of the charts here and the table doubled for a dining space. She had another desk at the farthest end where she kept her ledgers and inventory notes. The door opposite led to her personal cabin.

A familiar, rhythmic knock interrupted. "Come in, Birdie."

He entered and bobbed his head while swiping his cap to show his shiny bald scalp. "Decks are sparkling like new. The fellows 'bout to take a break. Thought I'd see how ya are."

Alex smiled effusively, not wanting Birdie to fuss. "I'm fine, Birdie. Looking forward to the sail home."

"Lookin' forward to boredom, are ya?"

"Peace and quiet."

"Uh-huh." He didn't buy it. "Nothin' to do with that big, blond blue blood, is it? I seen how ya looked at him." Birdie unhooked a stool from the wall and sat down next to her at the chart table.

"With annoyance, you mean?" Alex deliberately misunderstood.

"You know what I mean, missy. Fixin' your hair an' all."

Alex laughed as Birdie stroked his imaginary long hair, mimicking a feminine mating ritual.

"Mind you, nothin' wrong with hankerin' for a Brit, other than their obvious flaws. Yer mom was one after all, so there gotta be somethin' good about them. 'Course, she married out of the country as soon as she was able and cain't says I blame her, but we're talkin' about you now." Birdie thought he should give some approval over her choice. "The duke seems an honest sort. I chatted up his crew."

"Birdie!"

"Now, don't go on, thankin' me." He winked at her irritation. "His crew spoke highly of him. He's feared and respected, and they say none fairer than he. High praise for a Brit, but then he's one of their own, and a smart man don't bite the hand that feeds it, eh?" Birdie huffed from the effort of saying something nice about a Brit. "Even so, I reckon he's all right, iffin' you like him."

Alex was certain it was the longest speech Birdie ever gave her. She was touched by his concern, but this was one situation that there was no solution for, only survival.

"So, what be the situation? Ya ain't runnin' off with your tail between yer feet, are ya? 'Cause ya know that ain't no way to find yer happiness."

Alex scowled, offended at the suggestion. "No. I'm not runnin' off, old man." With a resigned sigh, Alex confessed. "I'm not the kind of woman he really wants."

"What?" Birdie looked like the concept was impossible.

"It's true. He wants a peaceful, dutiful duchess to grace his home. Not . . . not me."

"You could be a duchess. Not peaceful and dutiful, but still good."

"We agreed it was impossible."

"Shortsighted bastard. Never liked him. Cold fish. All them Brits. Cold fish."

Alex laughed, then leaned over and kissed his cheek. "You're the only man I need, Birdie."

"Och." Birdie whacked her on the shoulder with his cap. "That's your mother's charm in ya."

"Thanks for making me feel better." She forced a grin she didn't feel, while helping reattach the stool to the hooks on the wall.

When he was gone Alex sat down, rubbed her eyes and wondered when she *would* ever be able to stop running.

By late that afternoon, Matthew was vexed. He joined Samuel in the study and pulled out the single malt. "She wants to stay on her ship tonight. A sure sign of something pitiful. I can see it plain as day but she won't tell me a thing. It's a man, though. I'm sure of it. Perhaps he's married?" He poured two glasses and handed one to his brother.

"He's not." Samuel took his drink and sipped, an intense satisfied expression on his face as he explained. "But he's a duke. Seventh Duke of Worthington. His home is between Aunt Maggie's and Lady Emma's. He's that Marcus fellow's best friend." He paused to let that sink in. "Funny she never mentioned him."

Matthew raised a quizzical brow.

"Ah, hell . . . I pumped the servants who arrived with her things." He relaxed in a chair and held out his glass for Matthew to top it.

"What sort of man is he?" Matthew asked.

"Does it matter? He'll be dead soon enough," Samuel said. Noise in the foyer got his attention. "Stephen." Matthew put down his drink, recognizing the voice. "Maybe now, some answers."

"From the sound if it, he's brought the entire countryside with him," Samuel noted.

Lady Emma entered the Stafford home with Stephen, and after one look at the two angry giants approaching them, knew she would remember this day for a long time to come.

They made an impressive sight, these Staffords. The largest, she knew to be Samuel. He strode into the foyer imperiously, his brother at his side, the two standing like warriors ready to kill, faces harsh and unyielding. Samuel had a barbaric look about him, and his lips were firmed, indicating he would be relentless when he went after something. The only thing that softened her to him was his obvious affection for young Stephen. And then the warmth was gone, and he folded his hulking arms across his extraordinarily large chest and waited. His younger brother did the same. When Emma looked back at her fellow travelers, she realized that Marcus and Colin had assumed a similar pose behind Joshua. She sighed loudly. Men! This would surely be entertaining, she thought, her brow arching with humor. A shame Alex was missing it.

"Friends, Stephen?" Samuel asked.

"Where's Alex?" Joshua didn't have time for this.

The second brother stepped forward, assessing whether the Englishman would put up much of a fight.

The elder held up a hand. Tension mounted. "And you are?"

"Joshua Leigh."

The duke didn't dress it up for them. A wise move, Emma thought. They seemed to appreciate that. Nor did he offer a hand, clearly realizing that none would be forthcoming.

"Worthington," Samuel said in recognition. It was a statement of disgust. Emma swallowed, waiting to see how that would be received.

"The same." Joshua took another step forward, facing the American. They matched inch for inch in height, and likely shoulders as well. "I need to see Alex."

"That so? I don't recall her mentioning anyone by your name," Samuel commented, looking ready to inflict pain. Good lord. They were about to come to blows. Emma squeezed between the hulking bodies and hastened to introduce herself and the rest of the party, hoping good manners and salutations would encourage friendliness. It didn't work.

"Afraid we can't help you, old man. She's gone," the second brother said.

Samuel felt a tinge of sympathy when a pained look clouded Worthington's eyes. The man didn't look particularly well-rested either. That brought him a small degree of satisfaction.

"Tell me she has not left London?"

"Is she down at the ship?" Stephen asked.

"What business is it of his?" Samuel parried.

Stephen looked at Joshua. "He has feelings for Alex."

Emma nodded. "He's besotted. He can't think straight."

"Besotted," Samuel repeated, thinking it absurd. Though, Worthington did look a bit crazed. "What do you want with her, Worthington?"

"I would talk with her first."

Samuel shrugged. "Then what proof have we that your intentions are sincere?"

"You have my word."

"The word of a Brit," Matthew scoffed.

"Let's just say you owe me, Stafford." The duke's arrogant statement had everyone's attention now. Samuel's eyes narrowed, waiting.

Worthington continued, his gaze piercing Samuel in its intensity. "You were there, Stafford, three years ago, with your father and another. That night in Morocco." He pulled out the ring on the chain he kept next to his heart. The entire room was on edge, waiting to see what he held. "The night Alex gave me this." He opened his palm for Samuel to see the small signet ring displayed in his palm. Samuel was speechless.

Matthew grabbed the ring. "How did you get this?"

"She gave it to me."

"I was there," Matthew said, his expression still icy as he handed Samuel the ring. "She looked back. She said a crazy man helped her. She didn't say he was English." Matthew couldn't conceive it. "It was you?"

"Yes. We met again only by chance. I had hoped to call on her the next day, but circumstances prevented me. Will you take me to her? I at least deserve the chance to tell her how I feel. Then if she wants to leave—" Well, if that happened he would kidnap her and deal with it then, but he kept that part to himself.

Samuel held the ring. His mother's. Alex would not have given it lightly. Worthington had saved her that night. Reluctantly, he gave it back to the duke. "This needs to be worked out. For good or ill." Acquiescing, he nodded to the group. "Let's go."

Chapter Twenty-one

Alex lay on her bunk barefoot and dressed in only loose breeches and a linen shirt, unbuttoned a little for comfort. She stared dry-eyed into the oil lamp, trying to think of what else she could do to take her mind off Joshua. She thought about starting a new journal but decided it was best if everything just stayed in her head.

There was movement on the ship that disrupted the steady rhythm. She felt it before she heard the commotion. Out of habit and experience she slid a knife into her belt and went to make sure her pistol was loaded. She finished loading the second weapon when her cabin door burst open, and the visitor faced down her double-fisted attack.

"Joshua?" She gasped, stunned to find him in London, not to mention on her ship. Samuel and Stephen were in the doorway behind him, and by the sound of it, several others not far behind.

"Don't." He took one gun and put it on the desk, followed by the second. Spotting the knife, he took that, too. "Don't say a word," he commanded, turning on her and gripping her arms powerfully, nearly lifting her off the floor. "Don't speak. Don't ask. Don't talk."

Joshua closed the distance between them and took her mouth possessively. His hands raked through her hair until it fell wildly about, and he bent her into his body until she was forced to hold him or lose all balance. He kissed her with a need she didn't know existed in him, and she responded instinctively in kind.

A feminine gasp from behind caught their attention. Joshua lifted his head for air, taking a moment to gaze into her eyes and stroke a finger down her cheek.

"Just a minute."

He grinned. Turned. Then slammed the door on several astonished faces. There was a heavy latch that locked the door and he dropped it into place.

"Joshua?" Alex whispered, shocked. He had just slammed the door on Emma, Samuel, Stephen, and goodness knew whom else.

"No, Alex. Not a word. Not a sound," he threatened, stalking her. "Not until I am done."

She gasped when he took her in his arms again, scooping her close, this time with searching tenderness. "God, Alex, how could you leave me?"

She thought that a stupid question but kept her mouth shut. He was teasing her forehead, nose, and cheeks with gentle kisses.

"Stupid question. I was an idiot. I didn't mean the things I said."

"Yes." She sighed, melting into him, unable to resist his heat, touching his chest with eager hands while he pushed aside her linen shirt and tasted the soft exposed flesh at the base of her throat. A shiver of delight coursed through her.

She took his face in her palms and brought his lips back to hers, demanding. Alex tasted him as he had her, possessing his lips, then testing her skill with a lick of her tongue on the inside of his mouth. She completely forgot anyone else existed. Joshua was all there was, and her need for him was consuming. After wanting him so intensely, having him here was a miracle. His legs were hard as steel, the muscles flexed and firmed against her own as she pressed mindlessly closer, needing him with a desperation she didn't know how to satiate.

Their friends outside waited quietly. Emma blushed when the silence indicated Joshua's hunger showed no signs of abating.

Stephen's protective instincts surfaced. "He's supposed to be talking to her, not taking advantage."

"Give them a moment," Marcus insisted, thinking his friend owed him for holding off three hulking brothers right now. "It's only been a minute. What can happen with all of us standing nearby?"

Samuel nodded. It seemed reasonable. However, the next instant a distinctly feminine groan of desire changed his mind.

"That's enough!" Samuel raged, and with one strong kick, burst through the cabin door with four more men at his feet.

Worthington was sitting on the edge of the bed, cradling Alex on his lap. Her shirt was no longer tucked in her pants and was unbuttoned enough to show the man didn't have gentle thoughts on his mind. His sister's rosy, swollen lips and desire-filled eyes did nothing to ease Samuel's temper.

Alex caught only a flash of danger in her brother's eyes as he tackled Joshua, driving him across the bed and into the wall of the cabin behind them with enough force to rock the ship. Joshua, seeing the attack, tossed her aside just before he went flying backward. She screamed for them to stop, then watched helplessly as Matthew, Marcus, and Colin pounced. Alex didn't know if the other men intended to pull them apart or jump into the fray. There wasn't enough room to do either. She pressed against the wall near the head of the bed as two bodies fell in front of her, then were pulled off by Colin and Matthew. Joshua finally got a punch in that cleared him enough room to reach Alex.

A gun exploded, someone screamed, Emma nearly fainted, and everyone froze. Stephen shook his head in disgust.

Joshua grinned as the collective shock gave him an opportunity to pull Alex against him for a quick kiss. He stopped when Stephen pointed the smoking gun at him.

The men disentangled themselves, and Samuel stood over the bed that Joshua and Alex were now sprawled on.

"Well?" Samuel was the first to break the silence. "What's going on here?"

Alex was stunned. "I thought you knew."

"He said he wanted to *talk* to you," Samuel spit out, ready to pounce again.

"That was my way of saying hello." Joshua grinned.

Marcus sighed. "He's got a death wish."

"My love, you've been compromised," Joshua said.

She shrugged. "Oh, well."

The Stafford brothers looked at each other and nodded in agreement. There was only one thing to be done.

"Well, you've done it now, Worthington," Samuel threatened.

"Don't worry, gentlemen," Joshua responded. "I'm willing to marry her. Don't worry darling, your virtue is still safe—" He sucked for air as her fist hit him up under the ribs without warning.

Alex was outraged. "I'm not going to marry you, you bastard. Hell, I'm not going to marry anyone!"

"Yes, you are!" There was determination in his eyes, as he caught her hands.

"The hell I am!" Alex fought to get her wrist free so she could land another punch.

Matthew decided to intervene before determining whether or not to the kill the Englishman. "Alex, you do not want to marry this man, even though he has tried to seduce and compromise you?"

"Correct, dear brother," Alex spat, as if they were all idiots.

"Very well." Matthew nodded to Samuel. "We'll kill him instead." Matthew grabbed her second pistol and was checking it for ammunition.

"No!" Alex threw herself in front of Joshua.

"There you go." Joshua relaxed and grinned knowingly at her brothers. "She loves me."

Alex snorted in disgust, trying to remove the muscled arm that snaked possessively around her waist. "There are witnesses and nowhere to dump the body. It would ruin Christmas if you were all in jail."

Emma gasped. Marcus laughed. It was Stephen who got to the heart of the matter. "Alex, tell us this: Do you love him?"

The room was silent awaiting her answer. "I don't see why that matters since I'm not going to marry him," she announced, stubbornly.

"Of course it does," Matthew insisted. "If you love him, we won't kill him. We'll just torture him until he wishes he were dead."

Marcus shook his head in disbelief. "I love the way you Americans think."

Samuel shook his head gently at his sister. He recognized the unrelenting set of her jaw. "Allie, we only want you to be happy. Tell the truth. Do you love the man or not?"

They were backing her into a corner. She didn't like corners. "I think Joshua and I need to talk." She waited. *"Alone."* Her brothers grumbled, but got the hint. Samuel picked up the door and fit it back on the hinges on the way out.

When they were all gone, she turned on the source of her current trouble. His intense blue eyes were on her—angry, expectant. As if *she* owed *him* an explanation.

Weariness overcame anger. "Joshua, why are you doing this?"

He softened and shook his head at her. "Why do you think, you fool?" He touched her cheek gently with the back of his fingers. "I love you."

Alex's heart pounded and her eyes burned, disbelieving. He reached for her, and she stepped from his grasp. She wouldn't be fooled again. "I thought you wanted to marry some fellow blue blood with a fancy title and decent reputation."

"I never said that."

"What happens when you get to know me better? I can't change. I tried already. I'll just disappoint you like I have everyone else. Please," she waved to the door, weakening. "Leave, Joshua." She choked on the truth. "I don't want you to hate me."

He stalked her to the corner and lifted her chin. "Look at me, Alex." His hands curved up her shoulders and threaded through the hair at the base of her neck, tingling every nerve on their path and effectively holding her still.

"Alex, you might make me insane, furious, crazy, you name it. I still could not hate you." He searched her eyes, willing her to believe it.

"What if I'm cursed?" Alex leaned against him finally, exhausted.

"You're not cursed."

"I'm going to stop Paxton. What about that?"

Joshua sighed and pulled her against him, enfolding her protectively. "Let me help."

"Do you think there's a treasure?"

"No. If any of it were true and there was a treasure, someone has already found it." Joshua looked down at her. "You're the only treasure I care about." He kissed the top of her head, relieved to have earned a hint of her dimpled smile. "Do you know how terrified I was thinking you had slipped from my grasp again?"

She looked at him, questioning.

He pulled the ring off the chain around his neck and put it in her hands.

Alex closed her hand around the ring, tears in her eyes. "You had it." The next question was out before she could stop it. "Why didn't you come back the next day, after you saved me?"

"Prince Raja was the sultan's nephew. He knew both of us would be in danger if he didn't get me out of the country fast. He knocked me out from behind and brought me to my ship. When I woke up we were already out to sea, and I didn't have any way of finding out about you. I couldn't exactly return to Morocco anytime soon and, in truth, I had nothing to offer you. I was the second son of an impoverished line and had only just set out on my own. Hardly suitable material for some wealthy man's daughter." He bent and brushed his lips over hers, his voice husky. "I carried this with me always, Alex. Near my heart."

Joshua put the ring back on Alex's finger. "I loved you the minute I saw you fighting to survive three years ago, Alex, and I fell in love the instant I found you again. You have always been in my heart, not because of your beauty, or humor, or charm, all of which I adore, my sweet. But because of your spirit," he kissed her gently on the lips, "which has touched mine so deeply that I cannot bear the thought of living my life without you."

He cupped her face in his hands and tilted her chin until their eyes met. "Alexandra Stafford, you told me once I could return this ring for whatever I wanted." He brushed her hair away from her face tenderly. "I want you. Will you forgive me for not finding you sooner, and please marry me?"

"Oh, Joshua." Alex shook her head, tortured and uncertain. Maybe it would be okay. She only had to change a little. And once Paxton was stopped things would settle down. She desperately wanted to believe it was possible. Maybe he could accept her as she was. Maybe this was possible.

He wrapped her hand in his larger one. It felt safe and comforting.

"I do love you, Alex. I know it's soon. But I don't want to lose you."

"I don't want to lose you either. You promise not to get killed?"

"I promise. I'm going to live a long, healthy life and drive you crazy."

"Well then, I love you, too. I will marry you, Joshua."

Everyone eavesdropping outside the door breathed a collective sigh of relief. Emma sobbed and threw herself into Marcus's surprised arms. The older Stafford brothers slapped each other on the back, acting arrogantly responsible for bringing the couple together. Stephen grinned, satisfied at the scene and said the words no one ever thought they would hear. "Alex is getting married."

Chapter Twenty-two

Samuel was entertaining his future brother-in-law with the rest of the Stafford men when Alex and Aunt Maggie returned from shopping. Alex was so excited to see Worthington she dropped all her new purchases and ran into his arms.

"Joshua!"

Worthington greeted Lady Margaret, who excused herself to freshen up, then smiled tenderly at his fiancée, catching her in his arms with a half spin before planting a possessive kiss on her lips. Samuel waited. Then cleared his throat . . . patiently. By the third time he was tapping his foot.

"I think you'd better say hello to your brother before his throat dries up," Joshua said.

Alex launched herself with equal abandon on her brother. Samuel hugged her, overwhelmed by the happiness beaming out of her eyes.

When he let her go, Alex dropped her small hand purse on a side table and greeted the brothers with such energy he didn't recognize her at moments. Her face was transformed with joy, and she chattered about her day with such delight it made him think he didn't know who this woman was. He had seen her at her fiercest, he had seen her in battle, he knew her determination, her stubbornness, her loyalty, her compassion. He was proud of her and admired her abilities. So many things he knew, but he had missed this. They had never given her a chance to be a woman.

She was so open and full of love it was a powerful thing to witness. It also made him very protective of anything that might injure this newfound happiness.

"Your shopping went well, I take it?" Worthington inquired.

"Indeed," she said, excited. "I made several purchases. All good deals. And I have taken your advice and invested in shoes. A charming little store."

"I didn't—" The duke stopped when all eyes turned on him. Samuel waited to see if the man would pass this test.

"It's important to expand my business interests, as I will be spending more time in England now. Don't you agree, Joshua?"

"Of course."

"You do?"

"I just said so, love."

Worthington smiled, and Alex relaxed again. "Okay. I'm going to change then. I'll be back soon."

"Don't hurry," Samuel offered. "I have a feeling the duke will still be here."

"Of course he will," Alex agreed. She made her way up the staircase smiling. Slowly she was gaining confidence in the future and in Joshua. It was hard, though. She had brought up the map a couple times, only to have him tell her not to worry about it. And she had yet to tell her brothers about the map. She kept meaning to bring it up. They needed to know. But everything was so perfect at the moment. One more day of perfection wouldn't hurt anyone. She was halfway up the stairs when she remembered her purse and hurried back down. At the silence in the study, Alex slowed down, curious and on alert until she heard the voices of her brothers. Then she heard her own name mentioned. By Joshua.

"I can keep Alex up north for at least four weeks."

"Four weeks off the water?" Samuel asked. "Good luck."

Matthew grunted in agreement.

"Then we can go to the continent. There will be plenty to keep her busy," Joshua promised.

"We won't be able to get the astrolabe from Alex easily," Samuel said. "We might need to stage a theft."

"I can do that." The voice was whispered, but Alex recognized clearly that it was Joshua. More grunts of agreements. She put a hand protectively to her necklace, fear tingling up her arms that suddenly she was in enemy territory, her own family conspiring against her. She stood frozen, until Joshua continued, stunning not just her, but the rest of her family. "What of the map? That should be destroyed as well."

"The map?"

Even without seeing, Alex could sense Samuel stiffening. Heard it in his voice. In all their conversations she had never said anything about having the map. Only that Paxton still sought it. Samuel had a theory that the astrolabe might be the map. But now, he was about to know different. And this was not how she wanted him to learn of it.

"You know, the carpet," Joshua said. "Not exactly a map."

"A carpet?" That was Matthew. His voice cold, sharp. There would be no avoiding it now. "Explain please."

Alex pushed the door open. They all jumped at the same time. Guilty.

"Alex," Samuel spoke first. "You've had the map all this time?"

She looked at his disappointed face. Hurt and anger were masked, but not completely. Matthew didn't bother to mask his. Stephen was no longer there. They must have sent him away. Joshua had a moment to see the expressions of her family and remember her request not to tell them about the map—too late.

"Yes. I have it. I didn't know at first it was a map."

"You knew it was what Paxton was after, though," Samuel clarified.

She looked down guiltily and nodded. "Yes. I figured it out."

"Why didn't you tell Father? Before he left?" Matthew's voice was icy. "He might have reconsidered. He might have let Paxton go instead of chasing after him."

"I don't know," she said to her brothers. "I'm sorry. I thought I would have time when he returned. Everything happened so fast. And I just had a feeling the less people who knew about it, the better."

"We're your family," Matthew said quietly.

"Yes." She swallowed painfully, still holding her astrolabe.

"A family that was about to betray me. Utterly and without regard."

Joshua knew he was in trouble. Worse, Alex was in trouble. Because of him. Her face was white. Her expression when she finally turned on him—shattered. The fragile trust and love that had grown only recently was about to be tested. Severely.

At the questioning looks from Samuel and Matthew, she explained. "I was afraid. Of this."

"So you lied." The words from Matthew seemed to devastate Alex. She recoiled. Joshua stepped forward. She didn't look at him, but stepped away, causing him to pause.

Samuel spoke up, having gathered his composure and calm. "Father was determined to stop Paxton, Matthew. I doubt knowing about the map would have made a difference. There was something else driving him that night. Something about mother's death. You'll know it too if you recall. He didn't want anything to happen to Alex or us."

"It might have made a difference. Matthew is right," Alex said.

Joshua swallowed, pained to understand too late why she blamed herself for her father's death.

"We don't know. There is no sense in anyone looking back." Samuel made the statement final among the siblings.

"I have told you everything else," she promised. Then she turned to him. "Why would you go behind my back?" Alex directed her attention on Joshua.

"We're only trying to ease your burden," Joshua explained.

"By stealing my astrolabe?" she shouted.

Joshua took a step forward. She took two back.

"It's my birthright. Mama and Papa didn't deny me it," she told her brothers. "Even though they must have known the danger, they didn't hide from it. Or expect me to. This prophecy, that none of you want to believe, is real. Well, at least, the *people* who believe it are real. It's why mother died," Alex said. "And I had to hear about *that* from Paxton."

She shook her head, as if still unable to believe their plan.

"Alex, we want you to be happy," Samuel said. "Let us take care of Paxton."

Joshua reached to take her hand. She let him hold it, but it was lifeless. She stared at their connection, then slowly pulled away.

"I can't marry you. This was a mistake. I'm sorry."

"Dammit, Alex. This is a mess at the moment. I admit it. But we love each other."

Joshua needed to convince her and quick. She shook her head and shrugged helplessly, numb to the entire conversation. "It doesn't matter. Some things can't be changed. I was foolish to think otherwise. There is something I have to do, and you will only try to stop me."

"I'm trying to protect you!"

"No, Joshua." Her calm acceptance and understanding scared him more than anger and shouting. "You want to save me. And you can't."

She went to the table and retrieved a small beaded bag. "I forgot my handbag," she explained, before making for the door. Then she paused before leaving, deciding to share one more thing with her brothers and him.

"When the old lady gave me the carpet, she said I was the *last* kelile." Her brothers sharpened at that information. "I don't know if any of the prophecy is true. If there is an end of days. If there is some treasure or source of power that the map leads to. But I will protect the map and the astrolabe. Even from my family. Though I hope that is no longer necessary. If I am the last of some strange legacy, then I will do whatever necessary to make sure what needs to end, ends with me."

With that she turned, nearly bumping into her aunt on the way out, and leaving the three of them, Joshua thought, to feel like complete bastards despite their good intentions.

Maggie surveyed them all, and shook her head with a frown, clearly having heard the entire conversation. "I'll go talk to her."

Just then Stephen walked in and saluted Alex and his aunt as they left. He had an unopened bottle of port in hand, his face full of concern. "What did you do to Alex?"

Silence.

"That bad?" he asked.

The men let out a collective breath of frustration.

"She had the map all along," Matthew said.

"She heard us conspiring against her," Joshua admitted.

"She called off the wedding," Samuel added.

Stephen looked around the room, amazed. "I wasn't gone but five minutes."

Maggie joined her niece by the window seat in her room. The girl was pensive, confused, and definitely upset. She sighed, wondering if all her family would be cursed by the prophecy.

"Do you want to talk about it?"

"Oh, Aunt Maggie." Alex shook her head. "No. It's all so complicated."

"Hmm," Maggie nodded. "Let me talk instead, then, okay?"

Her niece nodded, and Maggie began. "I understand Lord Heatherly told you about Lilith?"

Alex looked at her in surprise. "I thought you were asleep?"

"Really, my dear. Nothing goes on in my home that I don't know about." She smiled. "Being eccentric is just my masquerade." That earned a smile from her niece. "So then, you know the myth of the two sisters—one destroys the other, then refuses to give her own child as payment for her success. Mother returns, destroys them all. Very dramatic." Maggie waved a hand, personally quite sick of the story. "As Lord Heatherly said, supposedly there were survivors of both women who left the cursed place with all its knowledge and beauty sealed, they hoped, until the curse could be broken, or balance restored."

"How is the balance to be restored?"

"Traditionally by a pure sacrifice of some kind."

"I hate that answer," Alex confessed.

"I know. Me too, dear." She continued. "Now you know the myth. Let me tell you the prophecy, at least as I understand it."

"You've known about this all along, Aunt Maggie?"

"Sadly, yes, though I've tried to put it behind me. But let me finish, as I really don't enjoy this part very much."

"Sorry. Please tell me."

"The prophecy, whether true or not, has been spread by various so-called seers throughout the ages. Essentially it is said that the lines of the two sisters would mix again, creating one, and from that line two new sisters would be born, creating the opportunity again for a sacrifice that could restore the balance. Sort of pay the original debt and win back the riches and power of a new realm. It's quite the fantasy, I always thought. A nice little bedtime story your mother and I were told as children."

"Only not a bedtime story?"

"Not to some people," Maggie agreed. "Because of my father's pride in our genealogy, many who followed the prophecy knew, or at least believed, he came from one of the lines." She paused. "And our mother from the other."

"Thus creating the new line?" Alex said the words with awe, concern on her face.

"It gets a bit stranger I'm afraid."

"That would be impossible, Aunt, but please feel free to try."

"Very well. Both of my parents, your grandparents, had a portion of a key. When your mother and I were born, we each received one of the keys—mine from your grandfather, your mother's from your grandmother. We never thought they meant anything, not really. Until you were born."

"I didn't have much say in that, Aunt Maggie."

"Of course not." Maggie patted Alex's hand. "But upon your birth, you were given a portion of the same key . . . by a stranger."

Alex reached for her necklace.

"Yes. Prince Kelile had another part of it and gave it to you just before he died. Mine was stolen eventually, and your mother's as well. Perhaps for the best. And quite frankly, if any of it is true, no doubt it's best that all the pieces of the puzzle are kept apart."

Alex still held her necklace, looking as anxious to learn more as she was not to. "There have been two astrolabes stolen recently. What are they the key to?"

Maggie shrugged. "No one knows. No one has all the parts of the puzzle." She touched Alex's necklace. "But someone or some group went to a lot of trouble to make sure this one was separated and sent to the ends of the earth."

"Are the others decoys?"

Maggie shook her head again. "I don't know. This one could be as well."

"What did you mean when you said, 'Until you were born.' "

Maggie hesitated. "Alex, when you were born, it was obvious even at an early age, you had an affinity for the sea . . . in a way, my dear, that was perhaps, shall we say, eerie to those who did not understand. It seems that there are some out there, followers of the prophecy, that believe you are the one to be sacrificed—that you have the gifts granted only to the last queen and her survivors."

Alex gasped, then paled. "I have an understanding of the sea. I don't have any magic!"

Maggie reached her hands out to Alex and held them. "Things not understood are magic to others, my dear."

Alex was beginning to understand the past. "My mother." Alex choked on the memories of her beautiful mother. "They wanted my mother to sacrifice me?"

Maggie nodded. "A group of fanatics. Yes. Naturally, your mother had no intention of following along. Nor would I. It's not even a question."

"So they killed her instead?"

"The true reason for her death, we may never know. Alex, I only want you to know this so you will not be foolish with your life. The prophecy requires the right sacrifice, at the right time, in the right place. My father believed that 'the place' is the altar where the first queen made the false sacrifice. So far as we know, that location is unknown. As for the time, I don't know that either."

"But you think I might be the target, and my map might have a clue as to the location."

Maggie nodded. "Trust me, Alex. Paxton is the least of your worries. He seeks only treasure and wealth. The real followers of the prophecy are out there. And they are watching."

"How do you know?" Alex asked, uneasy.

"A lifetime of living it, my dear," Maggie gave a wry smile of acceptance. "I take it the real map is safe somewhere?"

Alex looked at her aunt in surprise.

"It wouldn't have been entrusted to a fool, my dear. Don't tell me where it is. Don't tell anyone. While it is safe, you are safe. Though no doubt there are duplicates and copies out there." Maggie gave her parting advice. "I have had my losses in this life, as you have. I only want to enjoy the family I have and the friends that are dear. All else is foolishness. I want no part in the thing that has killed my parents, my sister, my husband, and everyone else in my life that I have loved, Alex. If you decide to chase after this legend, it will be without my help. I hope you will realize what you have and let it go."

"I don't believe in it, Aunt Maggie. And I don't want any part of it."

She sighed. "Your mother and I said the same things, and as we learned, sometimes there is no choice. Time will tell."

"Why did you wait until now to tell me all this?"

"I hoped you'd escaped this curse. It seemed happiness was very close at hand. It still can be, Alex. The duke is strong—in both character and health. If your future holds any kind of difficulty, he is a man who can survive it. Don't turn him away now because of something, that in the end, might be quite foolish."

"Marcus!" Alex sailed into the forward sitting room of the earl's London town house with Stephen at her feet. She stopped short, causing Stephen to bump into her. Joshua was there. He stood instantly.

"Alex."

She hadn't spoken to him yet, but he kept showing up anyway. She gave a cursory nod, then greeted the earl with an overly friendly smile. Unfortunately, ignoring Joshua did not stop the hairs on her arms from standing up in awareness, or stop the tingle at the back of her neck where his thumb had made a habit of brushing when they stood near each other. They had had a perfect week before she discovered his betrayal. She was still coming to terms with it and all that her aunt had told her. All she could think about was that if she had died, instead of her mother, none of this would be happening. The prophecy would be over. The curse ended.

"Where is Emma? Recovering from our endless shopping?" Alex struggled with small talk, eager to take her leave of the men.

"Reading in the garden right now. She is expecting you," Marcus said. "Any word on when you will forgive my dastardly friend?"

"Why, yes. Never, I believe was the answer." She smiled.

"That's progress," Stephen encouraged the duke.

"Your brothers forgave you for not mentioning the map. Don't you think you can forgive me for loving you so much I want to keep you alive?"

Alex spun, angry. "Don't use love on me! You were going to destroy the map, steal my astrolabe, and kidnap me so I wouldn't be able to go after Paxton. My brothers told me it was all your idea!"

"Joshua!" Marcus straightened in surprise. "Brilliant plan."

"Thank you."

Alex could feel the tension rising in her chest. "I did consider forgiving you this morning, but I've changed my mind. Excuse me, while I join Emma so you men can smoke and gossip."

"Men do not gossip, Alex," her brother informed her with a haughty look. "They discuss the quality and character of contemporary society."

"Well said, Stephen." Marcus grinned.

Alex gave her brother a level look. "My, Stephen, you sounded English just then." It worked. She said to Marcus: "I'm glad you decided to accompany Emma to London. You are showing her the sights?"

"I'm trying. We are going to the opera tonight. I think she is very pleased about that."

"Excellent," Alex pronounced. "I want to keep her safe, and sadly that's not with me for now, but I know she enjoys your company."

"Wait," Joshua interrupted. "You are allowed to protect Emma from you, but I'm not allowed to protect you from you?"

"Kidnapping is not protecting. Destroying my birthright is not protecting. Not trusting me enough to share your stratagems is *not* protecting."

Joshua grunted, clearly intending to provoke her. "Obviously you do not take your duty as seriously as I do."

"Joshua has always taken his duties very, very seriously," Marcus assured.

Alex huffed. They evidently thought they were in the right. It boggled the mind. "Stephen, you explain. Excuse me, gentlemen, while I join Emma to discuss the quality and character of contemporary society and how it has dimmed the wits of modern man." She stalked to the door mumbling in disgust. She ran into a servant halfway out and swiped his tray of tea to bring to the garden.

"She'll come around once we are married," Joshua teased.

"I heard that!" Alex's voice yelled from down the hall. "And I won't!" They laughed in response, and she accepted she would not get the last word when it was three against one.

She followed the hallway out to a small garden patio. It was quiet. Unnaturally quiet.

Alex put the tray down on the marble table and picked up a book that looked to have fallen open on the ground. She closed it and put it back on the table, enjoying the shade and privacy created by several trees and a large, enclosed wall.

Emma must have gone in. Odd, she left her book. Likely she planned on coming back.

Alex stood still a moment longer, trying to figure out what did not seem right. The garden gate was swinging slightly, the sound of it turning her attention. An instant later, a shiver of warning went up her spine as the movement of a figure flickered in the silver teapot.

Trusting instinct, Alex reached for the teapot and spun sharply. Hot tea flew into the face of a masked attacker. It burned the material covering his face, distracting him long enough for Alex to see Emma's feet on the ground near the farthest edge of the patio. In a second she had reached the knife in her boot and launched it at the man as he was pulling off his burning mask. It landed in his throat. A wet spray of blood hit her face.

A warning cry broke from her lungs and was quickly muffled as another attacker grabbed her from behind pressing a wet cloth over her mouth and nose. She recognized the ether and held her breath, slamming her elbow several times into the man holding her, and stomping his foot to get free. It worked. She gasped for a breath of air just as something hammered her head. She thought she heard a woman's voice before blackness drowned all thought.

"At least she didn't deny you would be married, Joshua," Marcus noted.

Stephen agreed. It had been three days since Alex called off the wedding. "She was much calmer today," Stephen confided to Joshua and Marcus. "Maggie says she will come around, that Alex just wants you to suffer a little. And Matthew was very complimentary today."

"About what? My horseflesh?"

Stephen laughed. "Uh, actually, it was along those lines. But that speaks of good taste. Um, and it was after he had to do his full day of escorting her around London shopping. I believe he would have pawned her off on even the enemy at that point."

Marcus couldn't stop his laugh.

Joshua cut his cigar and said dryly, "As always, refreshingly honest, Stephen."

"Then this morning she nearly killed all the house staff practicing in the yard." Stephen flicked his arm imitating, " 'Catch and release.' She wants to master the whip. So far it's catch, and . . ." Stephen cupped his hands around his mouth, pretending to yell. "Take coverrrr!" He took a weary breath. "We finally got her to practice with spoons."

Joshua rubbed his jaw, as Marcus shook his head.

"Samuel had the best duty so far," Stephen said. "She spent the day on her ship arranging dynamite in strategic locations."

"I thought she sold it all."

"Nope. Something about the importance of sparkly accessories. You'll need to come up with something soon, Josh," Stephen warned. "Her ship in London is ready, and repairs are complete in Portsmouth. She could set sail any day."

"One can only hope," Marcus teased lightly. "Dynamite, indeed." He was about to light a cigar when his butler burst into the room, pale as a ghost and a fearful look in his eyes.

It took Joshua less than a second to register his ultimate fear. Alex.

He was on his feet and running for her before he even heard the man speak. Marcus and Stephen were at his back.

Dread chilled his skin when he stepped out onto the patio. A silver teapot lay on the ground and blood covered the white marble table. He fought back the nausea that burst from fear in his gut. There was a trail of blood going around the corner of the marble deck. Stephen and he reached the victim at the same time. He was so relieved it wasn't Alex or Emma, he couldn't speak for a full minute.

"He's dead." Stephen pulled out the knife. "This is Alex's. She didn't go without a fight."

"They're both gone," Marcus said, his voice cold. "Morton, the gardener, is dead as well."

Joshua jumped over the deck wall and ran to the garden gate. He looked out into the alley. It was empty. He ran up to the main street. The world around him seemed to proceed as normal. Carriages went by. People chatted in the park. Only nothing was normal. Terror like he had never experienced gripped him. He reached for the ring that had always given him comfort and wanted to weep realizing it was no longer there. He took a calming breath and cleared his head. She was still alive. No one would go to this much trouble just to kill her or Emma right away. He would find her. But, there was no time to lose. Every minute counted.

Chapter Twenty-three

Liz Beauveau had taken a risk, but it paid off. The Stafford home had been guarded like a fortress, and there had been very little opportunity to intercept the girl. She had waited patiently at Lady Emma's, knowing it was only a matter of time before the two women would have a visit.

Two crates were brought into the warehouse, and her mouth widened in malicious satisfaction. She brushed the dirt from her gloves. Too bad about the Crowley fellow, but the Stafford girl had proven quick with the knife. At least dead men didn't talk.

"Get them up to the room," Liz instructed.

Emma was conscious and listening to every sound. She tried desperately not to panic while inside a crate that made her feel like she was about to be buried alive. A latch opened and cold, damp air greeted her. She was pulled roughly to her feet in what appeared to be a dark warehouse, and by the sound of it, near the water. Carefully finding her balance, she watched as another crate was opened and gasped at the sight of Alex. Her friend was unconscious and, by the look of things, injured. Emma ran to Alexandra, fear knotting her stomach as she reached to examine the blood on her friend's pale face.

A rough arm yanked her back, and she stumbled to cold earth. She shook her attacker away with outrage and got to her feet, intending to reach Alex again. There was a woman present who seemed to be in charge. She was richly dressed, but what struck Emma most was the icy hardness on her face. She apparently didn't like to get her hands dirty either. There were seven henchmen surrounding them, willing to do it for her.

"Who are you?" Emma asked with open disgust.

"A friend of the family," the woman answered, indicating Alex. "Now take off your shoes."

"No."

"Yes," she demanded, slapping Emma hard to emphasize.

Emma jumped for her, surprising the woman, but not the men. One of them grabbed her. Another had taken Alex, now barefoot, and swung her over his shoulder. He was carrying her up some stairs.

The woman came closer to where Emma was held back and slapped her again, causing blood to spurt from her lip. "So feisty. I hear Arab men like that in their slaves." She smiled with satisfaction at the glimmer of fear in the girl's eyes.

"Let us go now . . . while you can still live," Emma warned, fighting back fear.

"I'm going to make a small fortune on you." She turned to one of the men. "Get her shoes and tie her up with the others."

Emma fought as they dragged her up the stairs. She was thrown into a room and was shocked to see several other bedraggled and weary girls, eyes dark with fear, some only half conscious. Her immediate thoughts were for Alex, who lay curled on her side in the center of the room. The door was locked behind her as Emma hurried to Alex and knelt in front of her.

"Alex? Alex?" Emma listened for a heartbeat. There were no apparent wounds. The blood must not be hers. Alex's eyes fluttered.

"My head," she mumbled. Emma felt around her friend's scalp and found a knot the size of an egg.

"Dear God," Emma worried. She looked around at the other girls. One slowly came over beside her and Alex.

"My name is Cherise White. Can I help you?"

Emma gasped at the name. This was the girl everyone believed had killed herself by drowning in the river. Emma told Cherise the story.

"So no one has been looking for me," Cherise said. "Will anyone be looking for you?"

"Yes," Emma said. "Don't worry. The Earl of Stonewood

is my guardian, and the Duke of Worthington is my friend's fiancé, sort of. . . . Anyway, they will tear the city apart until we are found. I promise."

A tear slipped down the girl's face. "There isn't much time. They are going to move us before sunrise. To a ship." Worry and hope mixed on her face.

"We will get out of here somehow. I promise you. Be strong." Emma held a sleeve to her mouth and wiped the blood. It wasn't too bad. She focused on Alex, giving her a couple light slaps on the cheek. "Please Alex, wake up," Emma begged, fighting back her own tears. She swallowed another lump of fear and slapped Alex's cheek more urgently.

"How can I sleep with you hitting me," Alex mumbled, wishing Emma away. Thoughts started to jumble through her head as she tried to make sense of what was going on. "What happened?"

"We've been kidnapped."

Something registered, and Alex's eyes opened, as if struggling to comprehend.

"I'm so sorry Alex. I'm afraid I've gotten us in an awful mess. I should have never told the gardener to open the gate and give the man directions."

"Well," Alex whispered, trying to focus on her friend through confused and blurry vision, "I'm glad it's your fault for a change."

Her pained smile turned to a grimace as she tried to sit up. They were losing daylight.

"You have blood on you." A new voice whispered to her. Alex turned to the girl.

"I killed a man. But then another one got me from behind and hit me." Alex slowly remembered. "I saw you unconscious." She looked at Emma. "The ether?"

Emma nodded.

"Joshua and Stephen were there. As soon as they see the mess on the patio they will hunt down our kidnappers."

"Who are they? Why would they want us?" Emma queried.

"She goes by the name Lady Beauveau," Cherise said.

"She called herself a friend of the family, Alex," Emma said. "I think she meant your family. And she's not very friendly either."

"That must be the understatement of the year." This time the jest worked. Emma smiled. Cherise looked awed that they could make light at a time like this.

"This is Cherise White."

"Oh, no." Alex saw the fear and understanding on Emma's face when she made the introduction.

"Yes," Emma agreed. "There are others."

Alex struggled to pull herself together. A headache and stomachache made her want to curl back up, but she knew time was all they had, and there was not much of it.

"According to Cherise, there's a ship due in, and all of us are going to be transported before dawn."

Damn, even less time than she hoped. Alex's gaze pierced Emma, knowing what their fate would be. She couldn't let it get that far. They may not be found by morning. Daylight was nearly gone. She looked around. There were no windows. How did she know that? She tilted her head and saw the vent in the ceiling. A small skylight. Ugh. Looking up made her dizzy. She tucked her head between her knees and breathed carefully while she thought.

"One of us has to get out," she stated. "Cherise, will they be checking on us regularly?"

Cherise shook her head. "I think there is one guard, but sometimes he doesn't come in here. Tonight may be different though, since they want to move us."

"Emma, can you help me stand?" Emma and Cherise both helped Alex as she fought the nausea that swept her when she moved. Slowly she tilted her head again to assess the height from a standing position. The vent was not taller than nine feet above the floor. A slow smile cracked her cheeks. Definitely in reach.

It was ten P.M. Six hours since the women had disappeared.

The Stafford brothers were murderous. They nearly killed the constable while in the Earl of Stonewood's parlor. They had already tried to strangle Joshua and Marcus. The women were kidnapped from under their noses! Samuel knew that Joshua loved Alex as much as they did. It was all that prevented his death. The man looked like he had already died several times that evening, but he'd stayed deadly calm and focused.

"Clearly they were after Lady Preston." Constable Pierce tried to put some order in the room. "Miss Stafford must have interrupted." He handled the knife as if wondering what kind of woman knew how to use one as effectively as she had.

"Self-defense." The Duke of Worthington interrupted his thoughts, daring the man to hint otherwise.

Frustrated, Matthew hissed at Pierce. "We questioned the neighborhood. All anyone saw were crates being loaded into a carriage. They must have been in them. The dead man, what's the line on him? This can't be his first trouble with the law."

"His name was Crowley. He is known to do odd jobs, lawful and unlawful. He is also known to frequent the harbor district."

"We have all of our crews working the waterfront," Samuel informed the inspector. "They will check in again at midnight and every two hours after."

Pierce lifted a suspicious brow to the duke. "According to one of the servants, Miss Stafford was not so keen on getting married."

Joshua grabbed the man ready to throw him against the wall. Joshua thought of Alex. Before his blunder she had been ecstatic. They both were. Samuel pulled him off just as there was a commotion at the door. Birdie was trying to get past and about to clock the butler a good one when Marcus intervened.

"Quick, lads! Lady Emma. She's at the ship and says ya must hurry. Ain't much time." Birdie was out of breath.

Joshua pushed the others away and grabbed the man by the

shoulders. "Alex? Where is she? Is she okay? Is she with Emma?"

"Nay. Injured, but okay, accordin' to m'lady. There be several women from what I reckon. All held captive by some filthy, scum-sucking, lowlife, dirt-crawling bastards." Birdie relished each slur. "Thay's going to transport the girlies a'for morning."

Joshua shot out the door, a black look on his face that would have frightened the devil himself.

"By God!" The inspector gasped, sickened at the thought, and excited to make the capture. "White slavery."

"I think, maybe." Birdie wiped one of his few hairs across his head. He didn't want to alarm the Staffords. "Emma feared she wouldn't be able to find her way back to the warehouse. She awaits us on the *Sea Fire*."

"Is she okay?" Marcus was asking. There were a hundred questions being asked by all the men. "Aye, sir. Roughed up and scratched something awful, but okay."

Joshua was already on his horse with the Staffords and a grateful Marcus at his heels. The inspector and his crew jumped in their carriages not far behind.

"Bloody country," Samuel swore. "Damn, bloody country." For once, all the Staffords were in agreement.

Alex would have been climbing out the roof herself if she didn't feel so ill. The plan had gone well. Now it was up to Emma. She hoped her friend had found a way off the two-story building and wasn't lying in a heap somewhere.

Half an hour after Emma's escape, a man walked into the room, followed by several others. He lifted a lantern, illuminating his face. Coldness gripped her soul and foreboding chills ran down her spine. Paxton. Time had just run out.

He walked over to where the women crowded behind Alex.

His eyes stayed on her and he laughed with supreme delight. "Well, well. Liz was indeed successful. We meet again Miss Stafford." He smirked with delight. "Or should I say, Kelile?"

Alex didn't speak, but her jaw tightened. She wished she had a knife and that she wasn't so weak from the miserable bump on the head.

"Where is your duke now, I wonder. He didn't tire of you already?"

Alex swallowed, the dig hitting its mark.

"Perhaps he prefers a more delicate sort. A woman without calloused hands and sunburned skin, who is not quite so socially inept?"

She hissed in fury, fighting to keep her face neutral. He had read her journal. Of course. Alex had known he would. She visualized murdering him slowly to keep from attempting it now. They were vastly overpowered.

Paxton handed his lamp to one of his men. He reached down and pulled Alex up by the hair. She struggled when he grabbed the collar of her blouse, knowing what he was after. Her struggles were futile. He tore the shirt from her throat with one easy tug, revealing the necklace. Her astrolabe. Now the journal, a copy of the map, and the astrolabe were his.

He managed to get the chain from around her head, while one of the men held her. Alex watched as he pulled his own necklace from under his shirt, revealing a disk. A disk that was suspiciously similar in size and style.

Alex gasped in wonder.

"Yes, my dear. I told you we were connected."

Alex watched in astonishment as he turned the center screw that held her disk in place below the ornamental design with the mark of Lilith etched at the top. His disk fit behind hers perfectly, and a slow one-sided smile curled his cheek into a twisted look of satisfaction. He began to laugh low and deep, his chest shaking with triumph, hungry ambition seeming to grow stronger in front of her very eyes.

"I suppose you are wondering where I got this?" he said to Alex.

She didn't respond.

"I told you, you didn't know why your mother died. You

still don't, do you?" He held up his disk for her inspection, now attached to her disk. "She died protecting this."

Alex's blood burned hot, clearing any befuddlement that remained from her injury. "You killed her?"

"No." Paxton shook his head at her sympathetically putting the chain with the astrolabe around his neck. "No, no, my dear. She was much too beautiful to kill." He walked over to her and caressed her cheek as if to comfort. His false gentleness turned cruel a second later when he scraped a sharp fingernail down her cheek. It wasn't enough to leave a mark, but enough to warn her he wanted to do harm. "I took this from the man who killed your mother. Right before I killed him." He taunted her further, "So it seems, Miss Stafford, that you owe me.

"Of course, had either of us known the little whelp running into the water had another piece . . ." He looked at her, letting her know he had been there when her mother died. "Then we would have made more of an effort to fish you out. As it was, having you drown seemed best. No witnesses. Strange that you didn't drown though."

"Yes," Alex agreed, outwardly calm. "Strange." Inside she struggled with this information, her head pounding to remember something from the past, something to tell her whether or not what he said was true, but nothing came. Only images of her mother braiding her hair. Then water.

Paxton turned to the guards. "Tell Liz I'll take this one now as the advance on my payment. I'll pick up the rest at the meeting place in a few hours."

Alex wasn't going anywhere. She gripped her hands together and swung upward at his chin with all the strength she had in her. It wasn't nearly strong enough, and not a wise thing to do. He blocked her strike and made one of his own, the back of his hand hitting the side of her head, knocking her off her feet. She rolled to her knees and defended herself against the next kick in the ribs. She vaguely heard the whimpers and tears of the girls behind her.

Chapter Twenty-four

Emma thought she had lost the way. All the warehouses looked the same. She had wedged a piece of her skirt in the side of a building when she turned the first corner. She should be able to see it now. Worried tears brimmed in her eyes.

"Don't panic, Emma." Marcus held her comfortingly, and encouraged, "You've gotten us this far."

Marcus slipped from his horse to see if there was a piece of cloth visible from a different view. He helped her down as she started off the horse. Between the Staffords, the constable's men, and the Stafford crew they had picked up on the way, easily fifteen men waited on her in silence. She prayed she wasn't lost.

Emma looked. There was no cloth where she left it. She stepped toward the shadow of the building. "Here!" She gasped with relief and triumph. The strip had fallen on the ground. She picked it up. "The warehouse is the fourth one down on the left."

Marcus hugged her and planted a kiss on her forehead. "Good work, my love."

The men dismounted and drew their weapons. Joshua led the way. "Stephen, take Emma, and stay here with some men."

Samuel assessed the constable. "Pierce, unless you're prepared to accept the bloodshed, stay here with your men."

Pierce looked into the elder Stafford's face. He had no doubt that these Americans were ready to kill the kidnappers with their bare hands and enjoy it. They were also bigger than any of his men, who truth be known, did not look easy about being around the waterfront this time of night. "I'll be going in. No need to risk my other men." Pierce had his men follow but keep a distance.

Joshua held up a hand. Two men had just entered the building. Two others guarded a carriage loaded with three large crates. The driver got down for a smoke and it was the last thing he ever did. Matthew reclaimed his knife. Samuel spared a second man by only choking him until he passed out. Pierce took the surviving man away for questioning.

Matthew and Marcus were across the doorway from Joshua. They could hear hammering going on inside, and cries that were definitely feminine. Joshua counted the men. Four hammering crates closed and two trying to get a girl into one. She was kicking and screaming all the way. Her screams became louder the closer to the crate she got. Though she struggled, she was clearly no more than an irritation to the men who ruthlessly dragged her toward the wooden box.

Matthew swallowed his fury and calmly began to slide knives from his belt into his hand. When he saw the bastard strike the small girl trying so valiantly to fight, he decided that man would be the first. He followed Joshua silently, deeper into the warehouse.

The duke noted the knives in the American's hand. The nearest assailant was about thirty feet away. "Are you as good as Alex?"

"I taught her," Matthew said coldly.

Joshua nodded. "Help the girl. I'm going right. Give me ten seconds."

Marcus followed Joshua. Matthew started to count. The girl kicked to free herself and the man slapped her hard enough to send her several feet. Matthew checked his emotion.

"Ay, can someone help me with this bloody bitch?"

Matthew couldn't have been happier. He stood up and a knife sliced through the man's heart with deadly accuracy. "Happy to oblige," Matthew voiced calmly, directing all their attention his way. Another knife landed in the back of the neck of one man who turned to run. Samuel blackened a man with a bullet as the villain raised a gun toward Matthew, then shot another with a second gun, sending him down the stairs.

Joshua broke the neck of one man and knocked another out with a single punch.

Marcus saw the man reach for a knife in his waist and stepped on his throat, warning, "It makes no difference to me if you die tonight."

It was over in seconds, and triumphant, they searched for Alex.

Joshua called Alex's name repeatedly as he intently ripped apart crates with his bare hands. Alex didn't answer. With every crate cover he tore open, dread ripped his heart. He shredded the last cover to reveal a strange girl bound and gagged. His roar thundered through the warehouse as he threw the remains of the crate into a wall.

The girl who had been fighting earlier jumped backward, getting Joshua's attention. She seemed to be the only coherent woman here. Joshua pounced on her. "Alex. Alex Stafford. Where is she?"

Matthew moved in front of the girl, his medical instincts coming out. "The girl's in shock. Frightening her isn't going to help."

"It's okay." She peeked out from Matthew's side, slowly getting the courage to stand next to the man who just tried to protect her. "Did Emma find you?" They nodded. "After Emma escaped, a man came for us. He knew Alex." She started trembling violently now and tears filled her eyes. "You have to help her!"

Matthew checked her pulse. "What's your name?"

"Cherise White. We've been held for two weeks now. Please help the others. I'm okay."

Matthew doubted that very much. He put his jacket around her to stop the shivering then flipped over a crate so she could sit.

Samuel joined them. "Alex Stafford is my sister. Please. Tell us everything you can."

Cherise began her tale and Pierce took notes as fast as he could. She recounted the night, her voice dropping to a husky whisper as she finished revealing to the brothers, "He said he didn't kill her mother, but he was there. And then he took her necklace."

"The astrolabe?" Joshua asked.

"I think. Like a medallion?"

Joshua nodded.

"This mystery grows stranger by the minute," Pierce proclaimed. The rest ignored him, no longer able to be surprised by strangeness.

Samuel spoke softly, his voice harsh with worry. "Did he give a name?"

Cherise White nodded, confirming the fear that all had quietly hoped against. "He said his name was Paxton, Reginald Paxton."

Samuel hissed, falling to a knee as if his entire life force had been drawn out. Matthew spun in fury. He needed action, so he recovered the knives from his victims, before instructing the officials on how to care for the girls. He focused on what he could do for them, since at the moment there was nothing he could do for Alex. His hands were unsteady when he put his things back in his medical bag. All he could see was the image of his sister last week. So close to finding happiness. Floating into the parlor full of life and love. Laughing, innocent, hopeful. He felt fear for what was left of her innocence, and prayed that she would be spared the worst of Paxton's torture. He didn't need to look long at Joshua's face to see the man was equally tormented.

Joshua sought out their live captive and grabbed him by the throat, tempted to squeeze. "His ship is down at the dock," the man whispered hoarsely. "He's supposed to pay for the cargo—" Joshua lifted the man off his feet at that description, nearly stopping the flow of blood to the man's brain. Samuel stood by and nodded approvingly at Joshua's work. "The women—" the man corrected. His feet touched the floor again. "He's supposed to meet the contact for the final payment"—there was a warning squeeze—"before they board."

"Where?"

"I can take you," the man whispered.

Stephen ushered Emma to the warehouse when women started to come out. Emma ran to Cherise and hugged her. Both were teary. He looked around for Alex. Joshua stalked out alone, wordless, and jumped on his horse. Stephen didn't miss anything. He expected jubilation. If nothing else, a look of satisfaction. His brothers had the look of death. Cold fear ripped his stomach.

Emma saw it too. She rushed to Marcus for an explanation, still looking for Alex as if there were some mistake. They expected Alex to saunter out, laughing cockily at their success, asking what took so long. Stephen's throat tightened as he saw Marcus hold Emma back while Samuel approached him. He didn't miss the sympathetic look Marcus sent him and his hands clenched preparing himself, every muscle in his body tense.

"Where's Alex?" It was a command. It came out with anger. Matthew clutched his shoulder as if wanting to comfort him. Stephen shrugged him off, dismissing any coddling from his family.

Samuel didn't waste any time. "She's not here. Paxton has her."

Stephen froze. Then shook his head, unwilling to accept it.

Matthew nodded grim faced, confirming it, all the while wishing he could protect his young brother.

If possible, his muscles became even more rigid in his struggle for control. Alex at Paxton's mercy. It was unbearable. He pushed it away, a wall cutting his mind off from the pain. Finally, he nodded acceptance to his brothers. "I'm going to kill him."

It was a calm statement of the inevitable. Emotion in check. As if nothing would deter him from his goal. Samuel saw this, and regret filled his soul. In that instant he saw the man his brother would become and the boy he would never be again. Samuel nodded to his family and they joined the others.

"Let's go then."

The women were being ushered out when Samuel spotted the one who had helped them hurry over.

"Thank you," she whispered. "I hope you find your sister soon. I will pray for you all."

The brothers nodded acceptance.

She looked at the duke, as if just figuring out who he was. "Your Grace?"

Joshua turned to the girl. She looked too frightened to even speak to him.

"Miss Stafford," she gulped. "Before they took her. She turned to me and said, 'Tell Joshua, here's his chance. I'll be waiting.'" She added, "I'm not sure what she meant, but she smiled when she said it."

Joshua swallowed hard. Alex's words echoed in his mind. *You want to save me. And you can't.* He pulled the reins on Cyclone. He would prove Alex wrong if it was the last thing he did.

Their prisoner took them to the meeting place, but Paxton never showed. He must have been warned. But they did catch his partner.

"The Stafford girl was my target all along. The blonde was merely a bonus." Liz Beauveau, also known as Miss Rule, cackled at them.

Samuel pulled out his knife and began to polish it nonchalantly. He only kept one knife, but knew how to use it effectively. He was going to kill the woman.

"I might be able to help you," she said, "in exchange for my freedom and travel expenses."

"Madame." Pierce was amazed by her nerve. "Contrary to what you may think, you are not in a position to negotiate. Witnesses have named you as the head of a white slavery ring that spans the shores of England, France, and Spain. The punishment for your crimes will be nothing less than severe, I assure you."

He was awed when the woman shrugged.

"I think your friends here might think my information has value." She smiled maliciously at the Duke of Worthington and Samuel Stafford. "And every minute that you keep me here is another minute Reginald gets farther away." Her next words were saccharine. "He always had a thing for redheads."

Joshua leapt at the bitch the same time Samuel did. Joshua beat him to her throat, grabbing her by the neck and slamming her into a wall hard enough to stun her. She laughed wildly like a madwoman.

"Pierce, take your men and leave." Samuel bit out the words. "Stephen, please exit as well. Take the duke. No need for good British citizens to get their hands bloodied."

To the woman's surprise, the constable nodded mildly. Panic showed on her face for the first time. Seeing it, Joshua consented to leave. He would listen from outside. If Samuel killed her he would have to make do with the information they already had from the other two captives.

Samuel informed her harshly, "I don't give a damn about the laws of this country, woman, so don't think I will hesitate before killing you. You are either going to commit suicide in the next minute without the opportunity to atone for your life of sin, and thus spend eternity in hell, or you will live and I will hand you over to Pierce. There are no choices, exchanges, or escape plans. If you do not tell me everything you know, and every place that Paxton might conceivably take my sister, you will die. And," he added, "it will not be without a good amount of pain involved."

"I don't—" she protested.

"Wrong." He pressed his elbow against her throat, forcing her chin up, and brandished the knife in front of her. "Are you a vain woman, I wonder?" He let the blade slice slowly under her eye and waited for the blood to drip.

Liz Beauveau hissed, furious, "You bastard."

Samuel's knife tip touched the white of her left eye—and pressed.

"He's taking her to Al-Aziz. He follows the prophecy."

Samuel went cold and pulled back incrementally. "What do you mean?"

Her mouth twisted scornfully. "The prophecy? Your sister? If Reginald can prove the link, he thinks Al-Aziz will pay a fortune to have her in his control. The followers of the prophecy have gained power over the years in Morocco. He can use her to squash their hopes of regaining the realm. You know? Maybe hack her to pieces in the town square, or something equally civilized," she taunted.

"Are you sure?" Samuel pressed her neck to the wall.

She glared back. "I'm sure Reggie will find the highest bidder. He's good like that."

Samuel put the knife back to her throat and drew a shallow trail of blood. "You better be right. Or I'll be back for you."

Joshua listened quietly as Samuel conveyed the information they received from Liz Beauveau—every word of it, despite the increasing horror on the faces around him. Samuel finished by assuring Emma that the evil woman would never see the outside of prison again.

The sun rose outside, while Joshua stared thoughtfully. "Abda Al-Aziz."

"What, Josh?" Stephen said.

"Sultan Abda Al-Aziz." He repeated Liz Beauveau's words back to Samuel. "When Alex was auctioned, that was the sultan who bought her."

Emma gasped. Joshua realized she didn't know all the details. Perhaps her brothers didn't either. "I bid on her, hoping to save her the easy way. The Sultan Abda Al-Aziz won. He paid the equivalent of one thousand pounds for one night. Pocket change for him. He virtually rules Morocco."

"Dear God!" Emma leaned into Marcus, feeling ill.

"If it's true, and he believes in this prophecy, he'll pay even more to get his hands on her," Joshua said. "I have an old friend in Salé who might be of help. The sultan's nephew."

There was a long silence. Joshua looked around to see who was in. One by one they nodded. Samuel was the last. Joshua waited. He would leave with or without the Staffords, but their resources would help. What he needed most was their trust. Samuel looked at him hard, a leader clearly unwilling to leave a decision regarding his sister's life in the hands of someone who was still a stranger.

Joshua could offer no other argument as to why they should trust him—except, "I love her."

Samuel nodded. The decision was made. "To Salé."

Chapter Twenty-five

Alex struggled to be free of her guard's lusty grip, as he dragged her on deck. The sunlight on the ocean was blinding after three days of being caged and shackled in the prisoner's hold, but the fresh sea air was like food, filling her body with life again. There'd been hours where she thought they had forgotten her—something that was both welcoming and frightening.

Three days fighting hunger, nightmares, and fear. During the day she indulged herself with plotting her revenge, but at night, her dreams were a constant torment. Again and again, she was engulfed in darkness, a cold, oppressive weight suffocating her, her cries gone unheard as the dark ocean sucked her ever downward.

Today Paxton had decided to summon her on deck. She gathered he was bored.

Her eyes slowly adjusted while observing there was no sign of land. Her heart beat quicker when she spotted a ship on the horizon.

"Sorry, my dear." Paxton lifted his head from a book he was reading. "Not one of yours."

Alex ignored him and assumed a blank expression. Paxton was eating on deck, clearly entertained by the book on his lap. She forced herself to look straight ahead and not eye the crispy apples sitting in a bowl.

Paxton smiled pleasantly at the Stafford woman, while the rest of his men leered. Her bare feet peeked from her tattered skirt, and enough skin showed to make a man want to see more. "I'm torn, Miss Stafford, between keeping you for myself and satisfying the needs of my fine crew." The crew cheered at the suggestion. If he was hoping for a reaction of fear he was disappointed. Instead she looked up as if mildly surprised.

"You know as well as I, Captain, that I have little value if that happens. The price for a white virgin in Morocco is worth a small fortune."

Paxton sighed, waving to the disappointed faces. "You do know how to steal the fun, Miss Stafford. But . . . you know what is even better than a virgin?"

She lifted a brow as if waiting to be amused.

"One of Lilith's guardians."

Alex didn't move. She wasn't sure exactly what that meant, or what he knew—until he lifted the book on his lap and revealed her journal.

"I love this book. Entertaining, informative, full of insightful little bits of commentary on everything from sea life to seamen. Charming, my dear. Simply charming."

"Thank you," she returned.

"I couldn't help but wonder as I read, Miss Stafford, if the old woman in Morocco was right all those years ago." He read dramatically from her notes. " 'You are the last kelile of the prophecy. On you rests the end of times. Keep the treasure safe, that we may pass the hour of destruction, or be the source of that destruction, turning the monster of the sea upon the land.' " He snapped the journal shut. "Very strange. Very strange, indeed. Do you know where this treasure is, Miss Stafford?"

"If I did, I would have taken it by now. The story is a myth, Paxton, only real in the minds of those who make it real."

"Really?" Paxton thought on that. "Stranger things have been known to happen, my dear. Stranger things indeed."

"Indeed," she mocked. "The fact of your existence, for instance."

He laughed. "I see a few days in the cage have not trounced your spirit overmuch. But, as I was saying, the price for one of Lilith's guardian's is quite high."

"I'm not a guardian of some evil serpent lady."

He nodded. "Of course not, dear. But as you were saying,

some things are real in the minds of those who make them real. And I am here to help that matter along just a bit." He nodded to his men, who took hold of her again.

Alex panicked. Then she struggled, not knowing what they intended—murder, rape, torture? It took four men to drag her to a barrel and bend her over it, arms twisted back and almost broken in the effort to tame her.

"Calm down, Miss Stafford." Paxton strolled over, bending into her ear while crunching on an apple. "This will hurt much less, if you don't move."

"What are you going to do?" The terror of not knowing and being completely helpless brought furious tears to the surface. She couldn't fight. Her hair was pulled over her head and her blouse pulled down. A finger brushed across the back of her neck, a slow, threatening caress.

"Right here, I think," Paxton said.

"Aye, Captain."

Alex heard the voice of a new person, but saw only his feet as his legs pressed against her head until her chin was crushed in place between him and the hard, wooden barrel. "Don't move, miss, or this might kill you."

At the first sensation of sharp heat piercing the skin on her neck, Alex's body jolted. She twisted her head against the pain.

"Now, now." Paxton sat back on his haunches by her face and stroked her hair away from her cheek, sweat beading at her temples. "It's not so bad, Miss Stafford. Don't fight it. I'm giving you a tattoo. If you stay perfectly still it will come out quite beautiful, I promise."

"I don't want a bloody tattoo, you sick, filthy, bottom-feeding bastard from hell."

He continued to stroke. "I know dear. You don't always get what you want, do you?"

He stood back up, and the men continued, several more holding her down, forcing her skull into a painful position squeezed motionless by a man with a viselike grip.

"It will go faster if you don't move, miss."

Her body shook under their combined hold, despite all

their efforts. She could not control the natural flinching every time the sharp tool pricked and dug into her skin, a destiny being forced on her, not of her own choosing. The minutes stretched to what seemed like hours, and her quiet tears did not abate as she suffered the tattoo being embedded on her. It was not the physical pain that ultimately tortured her. It was the symbol they were leaving. A mark she already knew. A mark that would be a permanent statement for the rest of her days. A mark of evil.

The mark of Lilith.

Emma had packed a trunk of clothing for Alex. It had been easier than expected to escort the trunk and supplies to the ship. Sailors were small, and with the help of Alex's gear, including a wool cap, she had walked aboard the *Sea Fire* in the bustle of loading activities, and straight to Alex's cabin without anyone stopping her. She found the hidden compartment that Alex had told her about. The place where her friend kept a few emergency supplies that could only be accessed from the captain's quarters and two other cabins. The rooms connected to one another and the lower deck via a slender false wall at the stern of the ship. It was smaller than she imagined. She climbed in anyway with supplies for a couple days. What she hadn't counted on was the ongoing nausea once they set sail.

Stephen discovered her after the first night at sea. Despite her protests, he handed her over to Marcus on the *Sultan's Prize*.

Marcus took one look at her wool cap and cabin boy attire, and noted that Alex had indeed become a bad influence on his ward.

He didn't speak to Emma the first few days after she was discovered stowing away. It was worse than a deafening yell. Deafening silence. She ate in a cabin by herself, quarantined from the men. Eventually she was summoned on deck of *Sultan's Prize* and given lessons in loading, cleaning, and shooting a gun. Marcus issued the orders crisply until he was satisfied with her progress. They repeated this lesson every day until

Emma finally burst, spitting fire at his coldness with a fury that set off sparks. Marcus dragged her back to her cabin and locked her in.

Joshua had kept silent regarding the entire affair, until now. "You can take the ship back to England. I'll join Samuel."

"Forget it."

"Emma feels the same way as you do, Marcus. You would not abandon me when I need you. She is the same with Alex. The two of them are unreasonably loyal." Joshua smiled a little. "It's what I love most in them."

Joshua gazed out to sea, reflective. "I don't want Emma here, but I understand it. You do too. Punishing her is not going to help either of you. Don't waste the time you have together. I made a mistake with Alex. She was right. I wasn't trying to help her. I was trying to stop her. I only cared about us. Her need to guard this map is, I think, her desire to protect something much bigger than herself. Things might have been different if we had worked together from the beginning." He worried that now she might have to pay the price with her life. "Don't make the same mistake. Don't lose the very thing you hold most dear," Joshua finished quietly.

Marcus looked at his friend. Joshua had lost weight, and anxiety had wrought lines where laughter had once been. "Joshua, we are going to get her back. I swear it. Alex is one of the strongest women I've ever met. She will survive this." In his heart, Marcus had doubts, but he hoped against hope his words were true. His friend merely nodded.

Marcus decided it was time he talked to Emma.

Chapter Twenty-six

Prince Raja had his men looking for them. He was a minister in the sultan's inner circle and news traveled fast. If rumors about the red-haired woman were true, he needed to make sure he was not implicated in her original escape. Too much was at risk for a mistake to be made now.

He knew to look for the Stafford Shipping Line. He did not know his old friend Captain Leigh had finally caught up with them. The Englishman entered Prince Raja's home, accompanied by another man, Samuel Stafford. Raja assessed the men, then offered liquor rather than tea.

"So, my friend, you found your maiden, and now you have lost her again. What brings you here?"

"I have reason to believe Paxton will bring her to Al-Aziz."

Raja nodded. "There is a murmur around the palace that there is a sign—a woman."

Joshua's stomach filled with relief and dread. "That does not sound good."

"Please, sit." He encouraged the men, who reluctantly obeyed. Then he began to explain. "Years ago, there was a cult of believers who lived on the coast, south of Tangiers. Worshippers of a Berber sea goddess we call Tinjis. They were fishermen by trade. The fishing was very good, and because of their growing wealth, they were eventually attacked and driven into the desert by others who wished to take advantage of the riches of sea life. Only, shortly after the tribe was driven out, a terrible storm took over, and ever since that area has been unprofitable."

Samuel worried that superstition was about to get them mixed up in something very dangerous again. "What might this have to do with my sister?"

"I'll get to that, Mr. Stafford." Raja took a breath and explained further. "There is much discontent with my uncle's reign. One of the biggest dissenters is these followers of the sea goddess. They have joined with other groups, and are a constant source of rebellion. This man, Paxton, claims he has captured one of the sea goddess's guardians. You call her by a different name, but the story is the same. It is the ancient legend of creation, and the source of a prophecy that promises both triumph and destruction. Thus far, I have only seen it bring destruction. It is said your sister is one of the guardians who protects the mysteries of the goddess. The man, Paxton, has given proof of it. Proof that was very convincing."

"What do you mean?" Joshua asked.

"She bore the mark."

When the men balked, Raja questioned. "You did not know?" They had looks of both dismay and increasing trepidation.

"Paxton has already sold her to my uncle, who is making plans for a public execution the day after tomorrow. That is, she will be the finale to the other executions in a celebration of his twentieth anniversary in power."

He stopped. The men stared at him in horror, his old friend turning gray.

Samuel Stafford spoke. "Tell us. Please. Is she okay? How can we reach her?"

Raja sat back thoughtfully. "She is at the palace, not the prison. The sultan wishes to enjoy her. Perhaps he will like her enough not to destroy her right away," he said to offer hope.

"How well guarded is the palace?" Samuel asked.

"Any attempt to enter would be your death." Raja stated it calmly. "The sultan has little trust for anyone right now and has many enemies."

"Raja," Joshua pleaded. "You have no cause to help me and every reason to send us away. I would not think ill of you if you did. But, I have only just found Alex after three years. We are to be married. She is all to me. For whatever reason, Allah has put us both back in your hands." He paused. "Whatever it takes I am willing to risk it. Whatever you need, I am willing to give." Joshua held his palms out in humble supplication, his words a powerful plea. The other man backed his vow.

Allah must have some hand in this, Raja thought. The circumstances were too unusual, and very timely. This could possibly work to his advantage. His older brother had waited years to claim power, waiting patiently while their uncle's corruption slowly destroyed their people. This was perhaps a sign. He mulled it over in his head, knowing he would feel compelled to help these men regardless. Only, he couldn't let his sympathies get the better of him. They needed to make this work.

He stood up finally and nodded, causing the two men to breathe sighs of relief. "I heard the sultan paid a treasure for this girl. She must be very special."

"She is very special, Raja," Joshua said. "I wish you had time to get to know her."

"One of these days, perhaps. I will visit you in England. Now that you are a rich duke, eh?"

"I'm counting on that," Joshua promised.

Joshua conveyed the news to the others. It seemed a miracle. Though none understood the "mark" that Raja implied she bore. Joshua worried over what Paxton could have done to her, but forced the imaginings from his mind, only caring to get her back alive.

"The captain's a fighter, sure enough," Birdie promised. "I told you, Stephen. She's the most resourceful of the bunch of you."

Samuel grinned at Birdie's loyalty. He looked at his family, hopeful they would see another Christmas together. Matthew was missing. It was always a compulsion to know where they all were in times like this. And someone should bring Emma news on *Sultan's Prize.* He would send Birdie. He didn't want the older man getting caught in gunfire.

"Do all the ships have their instructions? If we miss the rendezvous point, get the hell out of the harbor," Joshua instructed. "According to Raja, this place is going to be bedlam tonight."

"What about Paxton?" Stephen asked. "We can't let him get away."

Joshua nodded agreement. "My first priority is getting Alex to safety."

Samuel concurred, though he had men making inquiries. "Has anyone heard from Matthew?" His brother chose that moment to walk in, holding a book. "Matthew, where in the hell—"

Matthew interrupted, tossing him the book. "Alex's journal."

Samuel frowned. "Where did you get it?"

"From Paxton's ship, of course." He grinned at his brother's surprised expression. "Which has recently joined the ranks of the Stafford Shipping Line. Nearly sufficient payback for Paxton stealing yours three years ago. However, if you wish me to return it . . ."

Samuel shook his head with a laugh. "I accept the gift. And the journal. Now we just need Alex."

Matthew nodded. "So what's the plan? We break into the palace, steal her away from an army, and make a run for it?"

"Good God," Marcus scowled. "That's not the plan." Everyone looked at him. "Please. Tell me that's not the plan . . ."

Joshua and Prince Raja laughed loudly at the sultan's joke made in broken English. They had been drinking and eating for the last six hours, and it was only right that they should be quite loud at this point. Joshua lifted his chalice again in salute.

"This time, Your Highness, we drink to your legacy! To your sons and your sons' sons, and their sons, and Allah help you, even to your daughters if you ever have any. May your royal line be long, healthy, wealthy, and blessed by Allah who is so great," he grinned drunkenly, looking highly self-satisfied. "I become more prolific as the night goes on!"

The sultan laughed. "And smarter too!"

"A long drink for a long toast." Joshua tipped his goblet dramatically then slammed it down in satisfaction and challenge to the sultan. Al-Aziz repeated the gesture that the duke insisted was English custom.

They had just negotiated a large trade of arms that promised the sultan would have the most technologically advanced army on the continent. None would challenge him now. They had shown a worthy sample today, and in two weeks Al-Aziz would get his first shipment—or so they promised. Joshua nodded heartily at the sultan. The man was feeling invincible.

"I would much like to stay, my friend, but I have another celebration I must attend tonight."

"Another?" Joshua asked, offended.

"Uncle has a woman who awaits him," Raja said.

Joshua laughed, and gave the sultan a manly slap on the back as he stood with him. "Just one? She must be some woman." The men laughed again.

"She is a flower," the sultan couldn't help bragging. "And tonight she will learn what it is to be loved, eh?" He puffed out, "By the sultan of love." They all laughed again and the sultan continued, "If she pleases me, I will not kill her. Not soon." The sultan burst out laughing again. After a stunned second Joshua joined in loudly, the effort painful.

"To my uncle, the sultan of love!" Another toast, then goblets hit the table.

Joshua thought he would strangle the sultan then and there, but there was a time for everything. He stood up swaying, reaching for the balance. "We retire then."

The sultan laughed at him. "I think you retire very quickly, English."

Raja agreed, giving him some male nudging.

"My thanks, sultan of love." Joshua lifted his goblet one last time. "To your fine home, good food, good wine, and that your 'flower' pleases you."

The sultan laughed and drank heartily, nearly falling over when he slammed the goblet down. Raja caught his uncle.

"Did you order the girl to my chambers, Raja?"

"Yes, Uncle. Not ten minutes ago. She will be on her way."

"Very good. I go await my pleasure."

"I will assist you, Uncle."

"We both will." Joshua jumped in swaying again, before letting out a loud belch that caused the sultan to chuckle. "And rejoice your good fortune as we go."

"To my good fortune."

The three left for the sultan's chambers, staggering and howling as they went. Raja's servant, a young Moroccan covered in a black robe, followed his master obediently. As they continued to the sultan's chambers two additional guards escorted discreetly behind. When Joshua and Raja reached the sultan's guarded doors they gave a drunken salute, and bade him good luck and farewell.

Alex walked as slow as humanly possible. The tile felt cool beneath her slipper-encased feet but she perspired with fear beneath the heavy caftan and veils covering her. Her new tattoo seemed to burn at her nape in response to her fear, reminding her that she was forever cursed. She itched to rub it and stop the power it had on her.

Her armed escorts marched in unison, leading her the short distance from the harem to the sultan's private quarters. She would have enjoyed the echo of their unified steps had they not been leading her to an untimely death, for she was determined that she would die before the sultan touched her.

Alex breathed slowly to prepare herself. She studied the swords in the guards' uniforms in front of her and knew the placement would be the same with those behind her. There was little time left for action. Purposely tripping on her long robe, she reached out to the guard behind her on the left, who reached to catch her instinctively. She smiled gratefully as she regained both her balance and his sword, slicing his wrist with one agile movement. She turned so quickly his partner didn't have time to respond before his leg spurted blood. The two front guards turned, only to panic as the woman whisked through their grasp and ran.

Alex sprinted to the end of the hall and not sure which way to turn, went left. At the end she had to turn again. This time she went right. It was a mistake.

Two giant men in traditional robes turned the corner at the end and there were two more guards behind them. She skidded on the tile, reaching back to the floor for balance as she slid to the ground, her sword clattering loudly. In her urgency to stop, Alex barely registered the dark faces before scrambling backward to regain her flight. She grabbed the sword, but when she turned around it was too late. The four guards were bearing down on her and the injured ones looked murderous. She swung defensively to keep them at a distance, knowing they could not kill her without incurring the sultan's wrath. With no time left, she turned the sword on herself, hoping the threat would make them pause.

"No!"

The command froze her. The deep baritone was harsh. It was followed by a drunken laugh. She dared not take her eyes off the guards to look back at the owner of the voice. It was achingly familiar. She shook her head. Best not to dream now. Two more guards had joined her escort and she was surrounded.

A man pushed his way through. Stumbled more like, she noticed.

"I say, what's going on here?" He showed no awareness of danger despite the weapon in her hand, and continued with his pompous line of questioning. "Shouldn't you be in bed with the other girls, young lady?"

Alex stared. Then she stared some more. Then she reversed the direction of the sword at him. She wouldn't have recognized him if not for his height, his eyes, and his voice. He was covered in a *jellaba* and what was visible of his face was darkened by several days' growth of moustache and beard. It was the eyes that caught her, an overbright blue. Eyes that seemed not to recognize her. He blinked hard—as if to focus. He was drunk. The scent of it was wafting to her. Dear God. She sucked in air for control. She was about to be served up to her enemy and he was drunk! Fury overcame fear.

The guards explained to Raja the girl was meant to go to the sultan. Raja hiccuped, appearing somewhat inebriated, and interpreted for the duke.

"What? This is his flower, eh?" He looked at the guards and gave what she supposed was the nudge for "guess he'll be having a good time tonight." Then he lifted his hands up to ward off the guards saying he had this under control. They looked doubtful, but after checking with Prince Raja, backed up a little.

Alex poked the sword at him threateningly.

"Now then, my lady, why don't you put that little knife away. Why your arms are surely getting tired by now, and I promise you the sultan is not nearly as bad as you think. Why he is a fine man. And his wine . . . well." He laughed, swaying. "I don't think I need to go on about that."

She glared at him.

"Come now, he is a sultan of love, nothing to fear."

Raja interpreted the joke for the nervous guards. They laughed discreetly.

Joshua nodded slowly to them. "Why he is. Self-proclaimed, but lotta love tha' man has." His words were definitely slurring now. "Thas' why he needs lotsa women. 'Cause he's lotsa man."

Alex knew she couldn't die. It was damn well up to her to save them both.

"You don't talk much, do you? Did they cut out your tongue? I heard they do that here. Not that I object. Many a woman's talked and nagged my ears near off." He swung an arm wildly, knocking a surprised guard in the face. "Oh wait! We haven't been introduced properly, have we?" He pulled himself up respectfully and again waved to his friend, this time causing the guard to duck for cover. "Thiz iz my fr-friend. Prince Raja."

Raja bowed . . . very carefully.

"And I am His Gracefulness, the Duke of Worthington."
He thumped his chest. "That's the seventh . . ." He counted
slowly on his fingers and held up eight in all. He stared blearily
at his thumb and pushed it down to make seven. It popped up
and he pushed it down again. When this happened a third
time, he gave up and just reiterated, "Seventh duke of . . .
of . . ." He forgot what he was saying. "Of, well . . . whatever." He waved a hand to the other side and whacked an
unsuspecting guard. "Oh, sorry, chap. Now that the introductions are made, I think you should lay down your weapon before these fine gentlemen get into trouble."

Alex seriously debated his request. She thought about
driving the sword through him. Did they bathe in alcohol?
Here she had been terrified for her life and virtue, and he had
been spending the evening getting thoroughly smashed with
the sultan. She desperately tried to figure out how getting
drunk could be part of any great rescue plan. You couldn't
leave anything to men!

"There you go, sweetlings. Jus' right here on the floor.
Nice an' safe. With the handle toward me if you don't mind.
Jus' in case you get an itch to change yer mind."

Alex finally did as she was told. Joshua bent to pick up the
sword. "Now then, who does this belong to?"

With lightning speed, he spun and dispatched the two
guards on his right and plunged through a third while Raja
silenced the fourth with a knife in the throat. Raja's two
guards helped them dump the four bodies into the darkness
of an adjoining garden.

Alex sucked in air, barely absorbing the quick action.

"Quickly!" Raja led them to a nearby room. Joshua had
Alex firmly by the wrist, and the second they were safe inside
the chamber, began pulling her clothes off. It was extremely
disconcerting. Then she noticed Raja's servant already had
his outer robe removed, and he wore an identical one underneath. Joshua threw her caftan at the boy and started on her
veils.

"I've got it. I've got it." Alex didn't like people pulling at her hair, and Joshua's lack of appreciation for the fine art of hair attire was noticeably missing. She smiled, loving him as she was stripped down to the filmy costume underneath meant to entice the sultan. A hand touched her waist and caressed lightly against her rib cage. She tilted her head upward, catching Joshua's admiration, his eyes intense and hot as he shook his head at her regretfully. As if wanting to admire some more.

His expression became a glare as he turned it on the other two standing by. Embarrassed, the boy looked away. Raja merely bit back a smile as he helped them get her into the folds of the black robe.

Alex followed the Arab man's directions and wrapped her hair while Raja aided with a black clothlike turban. She sensed his sudden stillness when she scooped it above her neck. Her hand instantly went to cover the tattoo and she turned around, defensive.

"What is it?" Joshua asked.

"Nothing," she said, pulling the hood of the robe over her head. She caught Raja's strange look, but he only nodded respectfully. Before she knew it, the boy was dressed to resemble her and ushered out by the two guards and led away. She heard Raja whisper a warning and worried for the child facing the sultan alone.

Raja recognized her expression.

"Fear not, my lady. He is small but fierce." To Joshua, "I will return in a moment."

The door closed and when Alex would have jumped into Joshua's arms, he held her still, quickly running his hands over her, checking for injuries.

"You are okay?" It was more command than question.

She nodded.

Joshua couldn't see any surface marks but that didn't mean anything. She was thinner. "Paxton and his men? They didn't hurt you?"

"No. I was worth more untouched. And he's greedy, but . . ."

"What?"

She turned and lowered the hood to reveal the tattoo. "This." Alex heard his intake of breath. She didn't move, waiting silently. Joshua slowly turned her back around.

He smiled gently. "So. A souvenir of your adventure?"

She breathed easily for the first time since the beginning of the ordeal and he pulled her against his chest in gratitude and relief—until she pulled away, desperate for something else.

His lips crushed hers, claiming. Desperation and urgency fought for control. She closed her eyes and allowed him his need, still trying to comprehend that he was here while her hips and body curved into him. He had come after her. He had found her. He really did love her. Then she tore her lips free, realizing something else.

"What were you thinking?" she demanded.

His desire must have befuddled his brain. "That I'm grateful you're alive."

"No, I mean coming into the palace. The sultan might have recognized you. You could have been killed."

He grinned, "Darling, *you* barely recognized me."

"And how much have you really had to drink?"

"Not enough to make me numb to your beauty."

"Hmmph. What's the plan?"

"The plan is we get out of here before a revolution breaks out."

"That's the plan?" her voice raised. "Who organized this rescue?"

"The man who's rescuing you." He pulled her to him again and ravished her mouth. "Just follow me. That is, two steps behind and your head bent humbly, as befits your station." He pulled her hood back up and bit back a grin. Humility really was a tough one for her.

Alex grunted, but smiled. She had complete confidence now that he was here. It didn't matter that they were still trapped in a heavily guarded palace in a foreign city about to be besieged by war. They were together, and the rest didn't matter for the moment. Just like old times.

Raja signaled to them, and they entered the hallway again.

The men resumed their drunken behavior so quickly that Alex rushed to catch Joshua before he fell over. He hung a heavy arm around her shoulders with a grateful hiccup, and the three staggered unsteadily through the palace. Alex observed her surroundings carefully, noting they were getting close to an exit. The guards in turn were increasing in numbers.

"I'm not feeling so well, Prince." Joshua grabbed his stomach, making some palace soldiers step back in alarm.

"Just another moment. Some fresh air will help. We are nearly there." The prince grinned to the guards. They needed no explanation for what was going on. The prince led them deep into the gardens before anyone else disturbed them.

There was shouting inside the castle, and Raja quickly pulled them aside onto another path of the mazelike gardens. He reached into his robe and pulled out two guns.

"I can shoot," Alex volunteered.

Raja handed her the guns and pulled two more. Alex thought he must have an arsenal underneath the folds of the dark material. She suspected Joshua had the same. She thought she saw the glint of silver beneath his robe.

"I'm good with knives, too, and they are much quieter."

Raja looked down at the small woman in surprise. Joshua nodded. Raja grinned in approval. She traded him the second gun for two knives, approving their weight and balance.

There was a shout for guards, followed by a rush of footsteps nearby. The three companions stepped silently into the bushes. Alex was about to move out again when Joshua pulled her back and slid a hand over her mouth. A single guard came by, casually swinging his finely sharpened cutlass back and forth into the plants on either side of the path.

When he passed, Raja stepped quickly from the hiding place, sliced the guard's throat from behind, and dragged him into the bushes. Then he hurried them into a small pavilion. They crouched below the ledge and pressed against the wall. Alex peeked out and saw lanterns lighting throughout the palace. Soon the gardens would be crawling with guards.

"You must try to get out." Raja pointed to two guards

standing by the wall farthest north from the pavilion. "Those men work for me. There is a hidden door in the wall below them. When you exit, turn right and keep walking. Do not run or do anything suspicious."

"What about you?" Alex asked, feeling guilty for the trouble she put him in.

"By now Sirac has killed the sultan, and left evidence that it was the red-haired slave."

Alex gulped.

"They will search the palace and the other side of the palace gardens near his chamber. If they catch you they will kill you instantly. Please go." He motioned to the short wall behind her. They needed only to hop over.

Alex looked at Joshua and shook her head negatively. "There are guards coming," she whispered. "We will help you first."

"You cannot help." Footsteps walked up the path. Alex leapt into the center of the pavilion and grabbed their attention. There were two men.

"Hello," she said, surprising them with her feminine voice.

Joshua killed one guard before his eyes could adjust. A knife from Alex found its mark in the heart of the other. She looked at Raja, very tempted to instruct him on women.

"Let's go," Raja said. They followed him, slowly making their way toward the outer wall. Freedom was a mere hundred yards away.

"You have less than a minute to reach the wall. I must return to the palace and conduct a search for the killer."

Joshua gripped Raja's hand in both of his, expressing without words his gratitude. "Until next time."

The prince nodded agreement, then turned to Alex. He bent to kiss her hand. Instead, Alex grabbed both of his hands and kissed each one gratefully. "Thank you. You always have a home with us. Good luck, and Godspeed." Then she turned to dash off before he could respond. Joshua was a breath behind her.

"Allah be with you too, Kelile. May you one day fulfill your destiny." He blessed them with a lifted hand until they were safely outside the wall. He hoped they would meet again. A noise nearby distracted him. He turned quickly and smiled at Sirac. The two returned to the palace. They still had a long battle ahead.

Alex kept her head down and tried to breathe calmly; the drunken routine seemed to be working for them. They walked outside, the palace wall on Alex's right, a small settlement on her left. There were evening fires and some tents set up for trading. A few buildings scattered the street up ahead. She was afraid to look up yet.

Joshua spotted the carriage not far away. "Almost there."

Alex looked, her steps quickening. A guard called out to them from the wall above. "He wants us to stop," Alex translated.

"Keep walking."

Alex didn't think it would be that easy. She felt for the gun with her free hand. The guard was determined and called to another on the ground.

"That was Arabic for 'stop them,'" Alex informed.

"Keep walking."

"Halt, or be killed," a man behind her said in Arabic.

They halted. Joshua bent over, grabbing his stomach as if ill. "I say, what's the—" And then he swung. The man fell instantly.

Joshua swore, recognizing the pattern—chaos was at hand, yet again. Shaking his head, he grabbed Alex and ran.

They had barely taken a few strides when a different guard on the wall fell in front of Alex, a knife in his chest.

Matthew was steps away. "Run, Alex! Run!"

She needed no urging. She leapt over the fallen guard and dashed forward while Joshua dragged her even faster. She had an instant of terror when the quiet fireside campers drew weapons and began to attack. Then she realized they were heading for the palace, running through the door from which she and Joshua had just exited, and throwing ladders up against the walls.

Alex saw her brother Samuel on top of the carriage aiming a long shotgun. Matthew caught up to her, grabbed her other arm and pulled her even faster to the carriage. She caught Samuel's eyes and smiled before Joshua tossed her onto the floor of the carriage and jumped in behind her. Marcus had the horses ready and they took off as Matthew leapt onto the back.

Alex didn't care what was going on around them as joy and relief poured out. She dropped the gun and knife and reached for Joshua.

"Oh, Joshua!" she nearly sobbed. "I was so afraid I would never see you again." She pressed kisses into his neck unable to hold him close enough. "I love you so much. I'm so sorry. I didn't mean for this to happen. I'm so sorry." Tears temporarily won out. "I can't believe you found me. I prayed you would, but . . ."

Joshua held her gratefully until her weeping subsided. "I know, I know, my love. I'm sorry I didn't reach you sooner." He stroked her hair gently down her back to calm both of them and relieve some of the shock. "I was wrong too. I should have been helping you."

"I know," she said against his chest.

He shook with humor.

"But you're helping me now." She looked up at him with a watery smile.

Joshua stroked her cheek. "You know you're all I want, right? The thought of losing you made me half mad." Joshua pulled her to him and pressed a savage kiss to her lips, letting her feel the hunger and fear he had suffered. She responded uninhibitedly, pressing into him and wrapping her arms around his neck, loving him as best she could while twined in robes, and bouncing uncomfortably on the floor of a moving carriage.

Outside, Matthew stood on the back and waved to the crewmen following behind on horses. His rare cheek-splitting grin spoke volumes. Samuel was also grinning as he slid into the driving seat next to Marcus.

Marcus knew they weren't exactly home free yet, but they had Alex, and now that they were away from the fighting he

Chapter Twenty-seven

Do you mind?" Paxton drawled with mild irritation. He was lounging unclothed on a large bed with two dark, accommodating women when Falco burst in.

"Captain! We've got to get out of here!"

"Now?" Paxton couldn't possibly imagine what could be so important that he needed to get out of bed at this moment. He eyed the women as if to make the point.

"The city is being attacked. The sultan's nephew has garnered an entire army. Word is every palace in the country is being besieged."

"So?" Paxton didn't care who killed whom, or who was in power. He was pleasantly numb from women and alcohol.

"I heard a rumor the sultan is dead." Paxton's eyes narrowed. "They are saying the new slave killed him and it's a sign of the prophecy coming true. She is taking revenge. Death and destruction will follow. She's started a religious war! And you brought her here!"

Paxton was awake now, scrambling and cursing.

"They are killing all foreigners on sight." Falco threw clothes at him. "And I have no doubt they are looking for us."

"Get the men up." Paxton checked his gold treasure then locked it. "Bloody . . ." A stream of curses spewed out his mouth. Not even a day to enjoy himself. He cursed again, and hoped the Stafford woman was dead and in hell.

She was in hell. Smoke and cannon fire permeated the air. The rancid smell of burning flesh reached her nostrils. It was still dark and no one knew who was friend or foe. Their only focus was reaching their remaining ships alive. Alex's hand tightened on one of Samuel's muskets she had grabbed from the carriage. Joshua motioned for her to come to him. She shook her head negatively. She almost had a shot.

Alex's elbows scraped bare along the gravelly road as she painfully repositioned herself, aimed the long American rifle and waited. If you were good, the gun was accurate up to a hundred yards. She calculated her target to be about half that. The man was hiding on top of a low building. She saw him peek twice. He too was patient, and he had a direct shot at Samuel. The smoke wafting toward her was oppressive, and she swallowed back the temptation to choke. She prayed the clouds would uncover the moon and give her some light.

Her patience was rewarded. As soon as she saw the shoulder lean over the side, she took the shot. At fifty yards, Alex was deadly. The enemy's gun fell at Samuel's feet.

Samuel jumped, his heart pounding unnaturally as he looked at the man hanging over the edge. He looked around and saw Alex roll into the safety of Joshua's arms. He thanked his sister silently, then cursed her, remembering she was why they were in this damned mess. The eldest Stafford motioned to some crew behind him and cursed again. In all fairness, and he did count himself a fair man, this mess was due to the lecher, Paxton. He hoped he'd get a shot at that bastard someday.

Joshua's arm snaked out for Alex as she rolled into him. "I'm glad you're on my side," he whispered against her lips, squeezing her closely to him between the stacked barrels that served as protection.

Raja's brother, Prince Khalid, had timed his troops well. They were all galvanized and enthusiastically killing everyone in sight. Mostly their targets were armed soldiers, as civilians remained hidden in their homes or running for the countryside in a panic. The armies of Sultan Al-Aziz appeared to be shooting all foreigners on sight. It was heavy on her spirit to think she was the cause of this, though according to Joshua, Raja had claimed the timing was very serendipitous. The confusion caused by the sultan's death would give Prince Khalid an upper hand in usurping the current powers that be.

Alex breathed in Joshua's breath, fought back a shiver, and

gave him a cocky smile to let him know he shouldn't worry about her.

Joshua brushed some hair off her face. "There's no one else I would rather have with me right now."

"Thanks, old man." Marcus popped up on an elbow behind Joshua, and cocked his weapon. "I'm going to make a run for the ship. Send Alex, then we'll cover you."

Joshua nodded and released Alex, rolling to Marcus's former position. He took a knee. Alex had already reloaded a musket ball and was looking around. There were enemy gunshots coming from three directions south on the road. Matthew had gone forward to the ship, while Samuel stayed back. Her oldest brother still needed to catch up. She knew three crewmen were waiting directly across from him. Two others were already dead, and one had made it to Joshua's ship. Her own ship was in view, sitting in the harbor waiting. She saw Marcus give the signal and prepared to cover him.

Stonewood darted stealthily toward some crates and jumped for cover. Matthew and another man moved to give him room. Marcus motioned north. There was new gunfire coming from the other direction. Joshua held Alex back. She wanted to go immediately, but wondered who else was shooting at them.

They both saw a little flicker in the harbor. Alex was the first to realize what it was. The *Sea Fire* had moved and was positioned to attack. She swore and prayed at the same time before jumping on Joshua to cover him. The cannonball hit about a hundred feet north. There were shouts of panic. Alex took the opportunity to make a dash. She was halfway across the wide road when she tripped on a body and fell, landing near yet another body. She scrambled only to stumble again in her black robe, trying blindly to reach Matthew and Marcus through thick smoke.

"Get down!" Alex heard Joshua holler.

Alex covered her head and flattened herself between the two fallen bodies. She waited. Another cannon hit and debris flew. A little too close for comfort, she thought, peeking up to see where she was. She couldn't quite make out which direction to go, so she dashed to an overturned carriage near the water and looked around. The men were only fifteen feet away. She estimated it was another fifty feet to the gangplank of Joshua's sleekly fitted schooner. She looked again and gasped. Marcus had fallen from a shot. She couldn't tell how badly he was hurt, except that Matthew had him around his shoulder. Alex motioned to the sailor to help them to the ship. He nodded and slid an extra gun to her before taking Marcus's other arm over his shoulders.

Emma peeked over the edge of the ship's deck and saw Alex. She guessed she was reloading. Her eyes hunted to find Matthew and the others. When Emma saw them coming up the narrow plank her stomach twisted in terror. As soon as they were on the ship, they lowered Marcus to the deck. He had a blackened mark in his chest under his right shoulder. Matthew ripped the shirt open to reveal the bloody wound.

"Is it bad?" Emma worried.

"Not deadly," Matthew stated grimly. "But not pretty." Emma nodded. Marcus's eyes fluttered opened. "He fell and hit his head. That may be a blessing."

She saw Matthew make a quick survey to see who could help. A sailor had already run to get medical supplies the duke had on board. Marcus's eyes closed again.

Emma slapped Marcus's face. "Marcus! Marcus! Wake up!" She was rewarded by fluttering eyelids and a pained grimace. She smiled, relieved. "Matthew says it's not bad. He is going to help you." Marcus nodded grimly in response. "I love you, Marcus. I wouldn't tell you before because you were so cold to me. I know you were just worried, but I have my pride too. You think only men have pride." Emma had to shout the last bit over the blast of another cannon.

"You're going to yell at me while I lay dying?" the earl bit out, gasping from the effort.

"You are not dying. You are too stubborn to die. You are going to get better just so you can yell at me for what I'm about to do." Emma worried she wouldn't see him again, but had already made up her mind. Alex needed help.

"What's that?"

"Never mind. Just get better and remember I love you, Marcus Nathanial Hampton. I love you with all my heart, do you hear me?" Emma didn't want him to pass out just yet. "And when we return home I expect you to marry me!"

"With a proposal like that, any man would come back from the dead." Matthew grinned while cleaning the wound expertly. Matthew looked up surprised when Emma took his gun and slipped it into her belt. "Emma?" It was a question and a reproach.

Marcus gasped at the pressure on his chest. He managed to smile at the woman glaring down at him with a remarkable amount of love in her eyes. "I already knew you loved me," he said. Emma huffed, very dissatisfied with that.

She packed small bullets into a pouch, which she attached to her belt. She could see he was losing consciousness and dreaded leaving him. She leaned down and pressed a simple kiss on his lips, whispering, "I know you love me too, Marcus. Someday you'll be able to tell me."

Emma got up and nodded to Matthew. Two sailors were already lifting Marcus on a board to take him below deck. "Emma?" Marcus called, searching for her through pain-fogged eyes. He was conscious enough to panic. She was headed for the gangplank. "Emma! Where are you going?"

"To be useful, Marcus," Emma shouted without apology, and ran to help her friend.

Marcus never heard four words strike more fear in his heart.

Matthew had to fight him down for several minutes before unconsciousness took over. The doctor shook his head. He was torn between going after Emma and helping Marcus. He knew Emma shouldn't have done it, but he also worried that his little sister would be out of ammunition soon and become a target. He was a selfish man, he decided. As soon as they moved Marcus he sent the two sailors out to help, and said a quick prayer for their safety.

Paxton saw a cabin boy run down the ship's plank and dive behind a barricade built around a fallen carriage. They shot toward the lad, inciting the other person to stand and shoot his way. It was dark, and dust had yet to clear from the last cannon, but Paxton could have sworn the figure was a woman. He ducked down and swore, hoping she didn't see him. There was a small American frigate in cannon's reach of the docks. He was surprised they hadn't left yet. Obviously waiting for the rest of the crew. Some were on the other side of the road. They would never make it, he thought. The schooner on the wharf was English. There was another large frigate behind it, sails unfurling. He looked around the dock. His ship was nowhere in sight. His crew would need to paddle toward the ship shooting the cannons and hope for the best. Had the Staffords followed him here and found his ship? What were the odds? The bastards must have been right on his tail.

Paxton crept around to get closer. He waved for his men to follow.

Alex was motioning for Joshua and Samuel to run while they were urging her to go. Joshua's face begged her. She stubbornly refused to budge. She pulled the trigger and swore. Another empty. She leaned against the cart and prayed. When she opened her eyes, Emma was shoving a loaded gun in her hand and starting to reload the others.

"Emma? What? How? You should be on the ship," Alex chastised with a grateful grin on her face. "You could be killed!"

"We are not going to die. Now shoot."

"Okay, m'lady." Alex leaned around the cart and caught a figure sneaking toward two sailors thirty feet away from her. She aimed and missed. The calibration was off. She would need to adjust for that next time. She took her newly loaded musket and tried again, this time catching the figure before he could fell any of the smaller Stafford sailors.

Alex took the moment to turn north. She didn't see anyone. It made her uneasy. Then there was a rumble in the ground. It was in the distance but surprisingly strong. She grabbed Emma's hand and pressed it down on the ground as well, to indicate something was up. Emma's eyes widened at the increasing vibration. Then she heard them. It sounded like an army of horses rampaging down on them. Alex crawled out on her belly to spy. Up the road, in the darkness, giant shadows were pulsing down on them.

She heard Emma make a muffled cry. Alex turned to warn her, only to face the wrong end of a gun—held in the hand of her archenemy.

Alex stepped back into the street, hands up, making herself a target, and making sure her brother knew she was in trouble. Paxton pulled her back, but not before Samuel had seen her.

"Hell! Someone's got Alex!"

They had to get to the ship before the horses bore down or they would have no chance of saving her.

Joshua only had thoughts of Alex. He ran across the road like a demon possessed.

Samuel followed, too stunned by the duke's courage and stupidity to do otherwise. The two were immediately besieged by deafening gunpowder and the pounding thunder of horses. Samuel guarded the rear and was closest to the impending danger. He could feel the heat of heavily breathing stallions. They neared the water. He could smell it as clearly as he could smell the horses.

"Jump!" Samuel bellowed. No one needed a second warning. They were midair when Prince Khalid's cavalry trampled the remaining forces of the late Sultan Al-Aziz.

Alex couldn't tell if Joshua had made it to the ship. She was thrown over the side of the wharf and landed in a rowboat with a painful thump next to Emma, who was smacking off prying hands. Alex realized Paxton hoped to board her ship.

She didn't know who remained of her crew. She wondered if they were ready for hand-to-hand combat. She debated the safety of all involved. The dark cavalry that had nearly trampled them didn't seem intent on pursuing. Part of the rebellion, she thought, wondering briefly how Prince Raja had succeeded after she left. She rubbed her bloodshot eyes, itchy from smoke and dust, and breathed in the first breath of fresh air in hours. As fresh as anything could be with Reginald Paxton in close proximity.

There were two rowing boats of men with twenty-four sailors in all if her count was correct. Her men were easily outnumbered and there was no doubt her ship was about to be boarded, with or without her consent. Alex swallowed angrily. She knew there wasn't one of her crew she wanted to risk, or another life she wanted to see claimed by the prophecy.

"Leave us here, Paxton. Take the ship and make a clean getaway," Alex offered coldly.

"Then who would I have to entertain me, Miss Stafford?" He smirked lewdly at Emma. "I do relish the idea of your friend here helping me to pass the long hours at sea."

Alex raised a brow in disgust. "She's a fool, not a friend. But suit yourself." Alex stretched her neck as if she didn't care either way. "If you take us, you will merely be hunted down until you and all your crew are shark bait."

Paxton laughed.

Alex caught Birdie's relieved look from the deck of the *Sea Fire* and shouted at him before he could open his mouth or throw the Jacob's ladder over the side. "Mr. Byrd!" His eyes squinted as if he didn't hear her correctly. She never called him "Mr." anything, and his surname was Carlisle. She shouted again, the code to escape, her voice filled with impatience and irritation. "Mr. Byrd!"

The old man looked down toward the boat floating alongside the ship. No doubt assessing the odds of disobeying her. She waited. Then she heard him shout to the crew. "Abandon ship or salute a new captain."

Paxton gave her a raised brow.

"Bloodshed is not always necessary, Paxton."

He pulled his gun. "But so much more fun." He shot at one of her men lowering a boat for escape and she threw an elbow to knock his aim off. Alex saw that Birdie stayed on deck. She prayed Paxton wouldn't hurt anyone who remained.

"Prepare the *Sea Fire* to be boarded by its new captain!" she commanded loudly with a nod toward Paxton. Paxton looked up at Birdie with an arrogant, self-satisfied smile and Birdie lifted a hand in salute to the man, keeping his gaze away from Alex.

The next two minutes were the longest of Alex's life. She saw some of the men leave their sails. The cannons ceased their fire. There was chaos on the shore but she could make the shape of Samuel's ship, *Avenger,* unfurling sails not far away. A light on the horizon hinted that sunrise was coming fast. Alex quickly covered different strategies in her head. She had to make sure Paxton didn't have any negotiating power. She saw Emma in the corner of her eye, and wondered what kind of chance she would have at throwing her friend overboard before they left the harbor.

Paxton yelled toward the deck, impatiently demanding a rope. His men in the second boat nestled against the ship and hooked a rope over the side. A sailor climbed aboard and threw down two more ropes and a ladder. Paxton scrambled up the side of the·ship in seconds, followed by his hostages. When he leapt onto the deck of the *Sea Fire* he appeared surprised that few remained. They'd rather take their chances with a war. He raced to the opposite side of the deck and in fury took aim at the longboats paddling off while several other sailors swam free in the water. Then he caught himself. This was easier after all. His first priority was to get the hell out of here and as far from Morocco and the Stafford men as possible.

Emma and Alex were tied together to a pole in the cargo hold. Alex was ill at the thought of another journey below deck, but knew it was ten times worse for Emma. Her friend was still trembling from nerves and Alex feared speaking to her at all while their guard could hear. She was thankful that Emma followed her lead, though her sharp comment earlier about being a fool may have been taken to heart. Alex only meant to keep up the charade that they were not particularly close to each other. She couldn't bear it if Paxton used Emma to hurt her. It was the type of torment he would most enjoy.

Alex waited until the guard left them to get a late breakfast. "Emma, listen to me." Alex turned her head over her shoulder and saw Emma nod silently. "No matter what happens, you must not indicate in anyway that you have sympathy or affection, or even natural human compassion for me or anyone else. Do you understand?" Emma was still and silent. "Emma, Paxton will use your emotions against us. Do you understand? If he thought that I cared for you, he might hurt you in order to hurt me. It's a game to him. He enjoys mental torture as much as physical torture. Perhaps more. Please. Promise me you will not let him or his crew see how you truly feel."

"I understand," Emma whispered. "Alex, I'm so scared. Wh-what will they do with us?"

"I don't know. But we are not going to wait to find out," Alex reassured her. "Even now Joshua and Marcus and my brothers are tracking us, waiting for the right opportunity to blow Paxton and his crew to smithereens."

"Smithereens?"

"Yes," Alex answered. "Millions of pieces."

"That's quite gruesome."

"Thank you. I was rather pleased with the . . ." Alex stopped, then added slowly, "Description." A thought formed in her head. She twisted around and surveyed the limited contents of her cargo hold. She didn't have much on the ship of value. She ticked through her list of supplies for the journey home: dresses, souvenirs, food, several caged chickens, water, ale, weapons, gunpowder, and of course—her bits of dynamite.

"Alex?"

"Yes?"

"Marcus was shot."

"I saw. Was it bad?"

"In the chest, somewhere below his shoulder. Matthew said it wasn't fatal."

"Then I'm sure he is fine. Matthew is the finest doctor in Boston, Emma. And he has treated several hundred gunshot wounds in worse circumstances and with no supplies or instruments."

"During the rebellion?" Emma asked, curious.

"Yes, the revolution," Alex corrected with a smile. She closed her eyes with a sigh. "I suppose Marcus will be very mad at me for getting you into this mess. Do you think he will forbid you from ever seeing me again?"

"I hope so."

"Thanks," Alex laughed.

Emma added, "I only meant I hope to see him soon so he can yell at me."

"All will be well. I promise. There are men on our side who stayed. Birdie for one. And, this is my ship." Alex twisted her wrists in the knots. "I assure you, I always have more than one escape plan."

"We were a good team on the docks," Emma recalled.

"We still are."

"I am feeling better," Emma said, sounding calmer.

"Me too." Though in truth, the details of her various escape plans made her stomach churn with tension. She would only get one chance to stop Paxton and it had to be tonight, before anything could happen to Emma. She knew it was already too late for her. Destiny had finally caught up. She must destroy Paxton and any copies of the map still existing. She inhaled the scent of wood and livestock, absorbing this part of the ship that she had not before spent much time in. It was just a ship, she reminded herself. The value of it was inconsequential when she looked at the bigger picture. And if she could destroy Paxton and all who followed him, it would be worth the ultimate price.

Alex took a calming breath, then started to tell Emma everything she needed to know about the *Sea Fire* and how they would escape.

Chapter Twenty-eight

ost of Paxton's crew had been indulging the previous night and were cranky that they had to work while the captain napped in a comfortable bed with the gold at his side. It was late afternoon by the time they were rewarded for their endeavors. The women were led onto the deck. Catcalls started from all around the ship.

Alex straightened her shoulders and strolled as if she were still in command. It was just the sort of thing to irritate Paxton, and the thought cheered her immensely. She observed where Birdie and Ilu were, then took bearings on the ship's location. A clear silhouette of a ship on the distant horizon encouraged her, though in truth she had hoped Joshua and her family would be closer.

Cheers from the crew greeted Paxton as he made a grand entrance on the deck, freshly dressed, giving a mocking bow to his men, and leisurely coiling her long whip in his hands. It looked like they would be getting a bit of entertainment. She made no acknowledgment of him, but rather, yawned delicately, aspiring for pleasantly bored. Paxton made a motion and they were hustled in front of him. A snap, and a man behind Paxton appeared with a rolled-up carpet, opening it for everyone to see.

Alex scowled, knowing it was expected. "So, Paxton, you finally found what has been at your feet all along."

"Yes, my dear. And it seems I no longer have any use for you."

"Perfect. Then set us off in a boat, and be on your way. You certainly don't want three Stafford ships catching up with you."

"Correction, Miss Stafford. I may not have any use for you, but my crew certainly does."

The cheers were deafening.

To Emma, he said, "The men have never sampled a true English blue blood. Don't see how I can deny them." He looked out to the eager faces and shouted, "Who wants to be first?"

The crew went wild and Emma shrank from the sound, paling visibly.

"Tie her to the mast, Monty. Time for a little sport."

Pale and terrified, Emma stumbled as she was forcibly dragged to the mast. Paxton smirked, and Alex smiled back, adding a wink. It seemed to thoroughly ruin his fun.

Paxton pretended to contemplate the whip, giving it a test strike in Emma's direction. Her friend flinched. Alex's knees went weak at the thought that he might consider using it on another human. She turned to the waves forcing her expression not to betray her fear.

Birdie's eyes shifted nervously to Alex, but she looked away.

"Captain Paxton," Alex said calmly. "If I may remind you, the prophecy calls for a pure sacrifice." She looked at the men. "I could be completely wrong, but it sounds like you'll need at least one of us intact. So, if I'm to be the prize, might I go to a cabin and clean up while you get on with this?" She checked the skies, like the professional navigator that she was. "You don't have much time to get where you're going if you intend to succeed." She paused and added carefully, "And your men seem to have us heading in the wrong direction. The treasure is south, not west."

He looked at her suspiciously, doubtful that she would help him. Pretending to misunderstand his expression, she acted as though she had stepped over a line, bowing her head. "My apologies." She lifted her bound hands in supplication and waved to Emma. "Please. Proceed."

Paxton wrapped the whip, stepped forward. He caressed her cheek. "What's your game, Alexandra dear?"

She shook her head. "No game. I just want to be done with it. The prophecy, the map, the astrolabe. It's all yours. Take it before the eclipse, and the secret's lost forever."

Paxton's face was expressionless. But she had succeeded. She'd piqued his interest, and he forgot Emma. Now she just had to find a way to get Emma to a cabin.

"Unfortunately, there is this other issue."

He stepped closer, trying to intimidate her, she guessed, but also not wanting the others to hear any of the secrets she had.

"And that would be?"

Reeling him in, she licked her lips and leaned forward, tilting her head to whisper in his ear. "You're not going to live long enough to succeed."

He thrust her from him, furiously. "The devil! You *are* a dangerous siren, Miss Stafford. Keep your mouth shut, and you might live another day."

"I don't need another day, Paxton." She smiled slyly. "Today will be quite enough."

He slapped her hard. She caught her head from snapping and tasted blood, but sensed uncertainty in his eyes. He stroked the curled whip in his hands, thoughtful.

"Careful. Don't want to hurt yourself with that, Paxton." She taunted him loud enough for the crew to hear, demanding that he recover his respect. She was ready for the next strike, but it rattled her brain nonetheless and sent a lightning jolt of pain down her neck.

Paxton walked away from her. "You show her who's boss, Cap'n!"

Alex let out a peel of laughter at that suggestion, inciting him further.

Paxton turned abruptly, and a wild strike with the whip in her direction let Alex know she had succeeded in goading him. Her hands moved instinctively to protect her face and deflect the whiptails that immediately lashed her wrists and arms. A sharp pull cinched her hands, and she was vaguely aware that the rope binding her actually saved a large portion of skin from this new assault. What wasn't saved burned like hell. A second yank and Paxton pulled Alex painfully to her knees. She gasped from the sting of the hard deck on her kneecaps. Yep. Nothing like solid American hardwood.

"I believe I shall want your friend alive and on her back for me." He motioned to Emma. "Take her to my cabin."

"No!" Emma screamed, struggling. Her eyes locked with Alex in terror. Hot tears spilled down her cheeks, and though her words sounded like they were for the evildoers, Alex knew they were for her. "Don't do this! Don't!"

"Now then, Miss Stafford. Tell me what I want to know and this will all go much easier for you."

"That's Captain Stafford to you." She looked him in the eye before adding, "Bastard."

He shook his head, chuckling indulgently. Then he gripped her hair and whipped her head backward, forcing her to her knees.

"When is the eclipse?"

"Tomorrow."

"You lie."

"When shadow crosses light. And light triumphs." She released a harsh breath. "Tomorrow, Paxton." She told him like it was already over. "Tomorrow is the eclipse."

"You speak in riddles. You're bluffing."

Alex smiled, knowing he hated it.

He tossed her away from him. "Tie her to the mast."

The sailors obeyed and cleared the area. Paxton slowly took off his shirt. He gave the whip a swirl to test and the crew gave shouts of encouragement.

"Wait!" Falco leapt to the deck. Alex thought for one instant the murderous first mate would save her. Then Falco took a knife, and before he could be stopped, sliced the back of her black robe and spread it to make a clean target for her nemesis.

A cheer went up.

The first crack of the whip was lost among cheers, but the dramatic flinching of the victim's body was not. Paxton looked at his crew and smiled with devilish pleasure. He enjoyed watching his victim arch painfully. A hot red mark opened on her back, revealing how easily her skin had broken.

Paxton stepped up and whispered in his victim's ear. "Did

you like that, my sweet? I can be nice, you know. If only you would give me a chance. If you beg me now, I might see my way to being merciful. The bed is very comfortable. But then you know that already since it used to be yours, isn't that right?"

She didn't say a word. She gasped for air painfully, trying to ignore the blazing sensation spreading from her back through her ribs, intensified by the simple act of breathing.

"Nothing to say?" He brushed her hair back to look in her eyes. "We could have been partners, you know."

Alex struggled to speak. "The siren and the snake?"

He sighed. "You do amuse me so."

Paxton walked back to his place and Alex braced herself for the next lash. A loud hiss squeezed from her clenched teeth as the whip seared flesh and muscle. She breathed in slowly trying to prepare herself for another, praying her whimper of pain was not discernible. Instead, her head was yanked back violently. Paxton was becoming incensed by her silence.

"Will you not beg, sweetling?"

Alex rasped, sweat burning her eyes. "Go to hell."

He slammed her head forward then stood behind her and kissed the back of her neck, on the tattoo where he had permanently claimed her. The more she denied him, the more it incited him. "Why do you make me punish you?"

The next lash struck her back across the middle, followed quickly by a second and third before she could even prepare. Her exhale of agonized breath seemed to garner sympathy from a few crewman, but none dared to challenge Paxton. Another long succession of strikes silenced the entire ship.

Alex crumbled against the wood, sucking in air during the pause. Her mouth was dry, her lips torn from biting back cries. Perspiration dripped at her temples as she fought to maintain consciousness against the blackness crowding the edge of her vision. That's when she decided swooning might work in her favor.

Paxton observed her limp body and lifted her tied hands

from the hook holding them in place. When he let go, she fell to the ground. He put his hands on his hips and gave her a push with his foot.

"She ain't dead already, is she?" someone yelled out, sounding disappointed.

"No," Paxton smiled. "But this sure as hell takes the fun out of it." He tossed the whip to the ground amid the laughter of the crew. An enterprising sailor grabbed a pail of salt water.

Seawater washed over the fresh wounds on her back. A wail erupted through her clenched teeth at the unexpected assault burning nearly as hot as her wrath toward Paxton and his men. She forced her eyelids downward to hide the murderous vengeance she felt. Adjusting her robe, she crawled a foot or two, struggling to see through wet, tangled hair and eyes rimmed with dirt, soot, and sweat. Reaching for the post that had moments earlier held her, she pulled herself up, straightening as much as she was able, every muscle protesting her proud stance. The raw skin remaining on her back resisted every movement, but determination to fight filled every part of her. At her feet she noted blood mixed with water dripping on the deck. She straightened herself further, shoulders back, head slowly lifting to Paxton. Her eyes glared, but her lips smiled. He needed to know there were some things you couldn't beat out of person.

Paxton knocked her sideways to her knees with a quick hook.

There were gasps of surprise.

Stubborn, Alex reached the deck with a hand for balance and stood again. This time she laughed. "Do I scare you, Paxton?" She took an unstable step closer to him. He didn't move.

"I'm very disappointed, Alexandra. Your father sustained at least thirty-five lashes before he fainted."

His taunt had caught her unaware. Paxton was pleased by the reaction.

"Of course he was crying like a baby until then." There

was doubt on her face. He finally found a crack in that steely armor. "He begged for mercy just before he died. It was very undignified."

"You're a bad liar, Paxton. My father was lost at sea."

Paxton laughed loudly at that. "Oh yes, my dear. He was certainly lost at sea." He winked to Falco, including him in the joke. "Piece by piece."

This time it was Paxton who smiled when Alex turned deadly white.

"You liar!" she screamed. "How dare you even speak my father's name on your foul lips, you pig!"

Falco chimed in, adding to the confusion. "Aye, Cap'n. Speaking of pigs, didn't her papa squeal like a pig when we did 'im in."

"Yep," Paxton embellished extravagantly. "I remember like it was yesterday. *Boston's Honor* was easily won that day. All her crew cowards. Ship went down in a blaze with your papa watching. Then we cut off his arm and fed it to the sharks."

Alex stared in disbelieving horror. She could not imagine her father's death like this. Never could she imagine anyone's death like this. Falco seemed to enjoy her sickened expression. A crewman asked another if it was true.

"Aye. That's when he started the squealing," Falco told her.

"But after his other arm went, it wasn't much fun. Not with all that blood getting on the deck," Paxton reminisced. "Fortunately the sharks were good and hungry when we finally tossed him over."

Alex stepped away from them, and spun with fury at the crew, then back at Paxton. She spoke loud, her voice scornful, her eyes burning with vengeance. "You, Paxton, who have followed the prophecy for so long. You who should have known better . . . have made an error in the extreme." She snarled her next words. "You don't control the seas, Paxton. I do!"

Alex took a deep, focused breath of ocean air, pulling in the power of the sea she had always known she was born with, and released a high, keening sound—a sound so cold it sent a chill down every sailor's spine.

At that moment, it seemed the wind ceased and the sails fell limp against the rigging. Sailors looked around them, eerie silence spreading to panic. The *Sea Fire* was in irons, and the strangeness of it was not lost on the crew.

Several looked at each other in terror, then all stared at the white, taut body of the woman who stood proudly before them in the tattered black robe, her red hair tangled and sticking to blood dripping down her back like an evil sorceress seeking revenge.

Birdie shivered at what he saw. He wasn't the only one. Her once warm green eyes appeared blacker than the depths of the darkest oceans, and ten times colder. They were the eyes of death. There was no life, no glitter, no reflection.

Paxton stepped back unconsciously.

Her lips curved slowly, but this time it was the smile of an animal that had turned feral.

Her voice came out calm and deliberate. "Thank you, Paxton."

He couldn't resist. "What for?"

She was unnervingly confident. "Now I know how you will die."

The crew gasped at her words, and Paxton struck her hard, as if chilled by her being. But this time she didn't fall.

Unaffected, she lifted her head and laughed in his face with the kind of cold delight one would imagine from a devil. He hit her again, this time in real fear, but nothing could wipe away the cold smirk or mocking eyes. He yelled for the crew to trim the damn sails and get her out of his sight. "Lock her up in the darkest corner of the ship. Where there is no scent or sight of the ocean."

A sailor whispered that they ought to toss her over now. Bad luck she was.

Her guards were afraid to get near her. She managed a cold nod to Paxton before falling into a sailor who jumped in terror, rattled by her clinging to him for balance. Recovering, she followed two guards below.

Falco issued orders to the men and all scurried to adjust

the sails, eager to move from this haunting spot in the sea. Despite their efforts, chaos reigned, and there was no wind to be found.

Alex was the only one who rested calmly. She relished the pain coursing through her body. It fueled her determination. She had used her knowledge of the sea and the prophecy to incite fear and uneasiness in the crew. It had been easier than she expected, even if the price was high. In the darkness of the cargo hold, her mind clicked coldly through the details of her plan, her fingers still clutching within the folds of her black robe the knife of the sailor she had fallen into. She touched her jaw to assess the damage. Not broken. She felt the tender skin near her eye. She could see. It would be several hours before any major swelling. That was fine. She probably wouldn't be alive that long.

Across the miles of open sea, another sailor stood alert, the tortured sound calling to him. The wind shifted and sails ruffled in urgent warning before being quickly trimmed by alert crewmen eager to please. He pressed a hand over his heart, as if half expecting to see a vision. A shiver of awareness washed over everyone on the schooner. A cry, like the echo of a whale, whispered on the water.

"Captain? What is it?"

He looked at the worried eyes turned to him, seeking answers, and more—reassurance. He didn't have it to give. Something had changed. A soul from the sea whispered urgently. He signaled to the helm. They were changing course.

Chapter Twenty-nine

Birdie unwrapped the dried herb celandine, which he used to help the pain in his side that Matthew referred to as his gallbladder. The doctor had given him a new supply of the medicine recently. Birdie made it into a tea once a day when the affliction came upon him. One time, when he was in a particular amount of pain he had thought to use more than the usual amount of celandine, which to Birdie's logic would match the more than usual amount of pain. It was a mistake he never made again. The herb had kept him in the ship's head, relieving himself, for a good twenty-four hours.

This time he tested his new potion on the appointed galley cook. The man had been in and out of the little kitchen ever since. Birdie stirred the entire contents of his celandine supply into the pot. It was the basis for the sauce the cook had directed him to fix just before he gripped his guts and made the now familiar dash.

The *Sea Fire* was still mysteriously becalmed, and the atmosphere was stifling. The crew grew more uneasy by the hour, but Birdie's cheerful encouragement to "eat up and all would be well in no time," echoed motherly advice some had once known. A gale picked up as bowels weakened. It was only then that Paxton went below deck to discover Lady Preston missing.

He looked under the bed, in the wardrobe. He banged around the cabin. The porthole of the cabin was open. She could have squeezed through, he knew. He just couldn't fathom that someone would throw themselves to their death. He looked out and reached, pulling a piece of material that had torn.

It was dusk and all of the crew went on deck searching

overboard for the body of Emma Preston. There were murmurs of fear and relief. Women were definitely bad luck on a ship any way you looked at it. Paxton ordered a second guard on the Stafford woman. He looked around. The two Stafford crewmen were accounted for, the old man was bent over with cramps cursing Africa for his pain. He went to the wheel and watched, alert for anything out of the ordinary.

Later, when all had given up hope of finding her, Emma lifted the trap door of the secret escape hatch, and reentered the captain's cabin. The treasure from the sultan was in plain sight next to the bed. The chest unlocked. Quickly scooping the gold into sacks, she passed them into the hidden passage below. She opened a drawer under the bed and reached for the belt Alex requested. It was heavy. Carefully she handed it to Birdie. Then something else got her attention. Coiled like a snake near the chest. The ends of leather were a damp reddish brown. She reached, trembling. She had heard every strike. She would not give Paxton another chance to do that again. Handing Birdie the whip, they shimmied along the wall of the ship awaiting nightfall, and freedom.

The threat of the lash was all that kept the night crew on their feet. The rest laid with eyes closed, in fetal positions, praying for oblivion. Paxton stayed on deck until the moon was high, though it was through pure determination. There was a ship within his sights, and he wouldn't risk battle in this state.

Birdie used the opportunity to gather supplies.

Alex sat in her cargo hold, focusing her mind and biding her time. Memories of her father were strong tonight. He had smuggled guns and ammunition during the Revolution. It was profitable as well as patriotic. One night he returned to town with news that he had set fire to the warehouse. Samuel had grinned when describing the looks of the British and how the building had blown to smithereens. She had loved that word as a little girl. It sounded funny. When her brother had

used it that night, it wasn't funny. She didn't understand why
they had done it. Her father's reminder stuck in her head for
years to come. *Better to cut off your hand, than to let it serve evil.*

Her brothers would reach them soon. Perhaps by morning.
If she didn't get Emma away now, they would be caught in
the crossfire, and she wasn't sure how long Emma could survive in the cramped wall of the ship before suffocating or being discovered. Alex let go of fear. She had to follow through
with her plan.

Paxton's voice echoed not far away. He was checking on
her. A sign he was wary. That was bad. He would be extra
careful. Fortunately, the sailors guarding her thought three
men were more than enough. Two would sleep and the other
would watch the girl. Alex pretended to sleep, but she was
waiting. And smiling. She had no doubt Paxton was the type
to count his gold before going to sleep. A shadow signaled
her. She pulled off ropes she had cut earlier, then got up and
walked over to the sailors on guard.

The man turned, "What the—!"

He was dead instantly. She ripped the knife out of his
throat as Birdie made sure the other two never awoke. A cold
chill went through her, but she proceeded, arming herself
with the weapons Birdie had gathered, then getting down to
work. She was nearly done rigging the dynamite next to the
gunpowder when she heard a shout of outrage on deck. Paxton reacted according to plan.

"Birdie, help me with the cannon." They had released one
cannon from its mount and repositioned it.

Footsteps alerted them to danger. "Captain wants everyone on—hey!"

Alex turned and released the knife. The man fell and Birdie
dragged him to the side. She reclaimed the knife, blocking the
image of death from her mind. They could hear the men
scrambling on deck above them, Paxton in a fury. It was time.
Alex stretched her back, ignoring the tearing of fragile skin
that had already tried to heal. She needed to be loose.

"Hurry and help Ilu with the boats. We only have two left

after Salé. Release them both. So there's no escape." With a premonition, she grabbed his arm. He looked back in the shadows. "Birdie," she ordered, "as soon as you hear the first blast, help Emma to the boat. If she doesn't jump, throw her. If something happens, you're the only one who can navigate the others to Las Palmas. Promise you'll do that."

"I'll see you on the boat, Captain."

"Promise you'll do it."

"I promise," Birdie murmured, his voice thick with worry. She told him one more thing, for Joshua. Just in case. That was when Birdie got scared.

She winked to reassure him. Then she gave her last vital instruction in a tone Birdie would someday describe as the typically cocky Stafford voice.

"Start counting."

Paxton was yelling madly when Birdie reached the deck. He wanted them all accounted for. The crew gathered, some stumbling onto the deck. Ilu slid from his nest and silently moved toward the bow, killing one nosey sailor on his way. While Paxton had the crew near the bow, Ilu, Birdie, and Emma were aft, pushing a boat over the side. Someone caught the movement and shouted a warning. A gunshot sliced the air, and Birdie threw Lady Emma over the side before she had a chance to think. Birdie turned at the sound of danger. Falco lifted a sword above his head just as Birdie finished counting in his head. Birdie waved at him, surprising Falco.

A cannon blasted through the frame of the ship, tossing Falco off balance. There was a cry from the crew. When Falco regained his footing, Birdie was gone. He turned back to see a fire crawling up the deck. Falco watched in dismay as a trail snaked to the surface, then split into two directions, one parting up to the sails. The crew panicked. The wind, which had been nonexistent earlier in the day, seemed to softly blow the flames, billowing fire into sails. An acrid mixture of ether and kerosene wafted through the air.

On the deck below, Alex finished her trail of kerosene up the opposite ladder. They would be here any second to see the damage. The ship was going down. They just didn't know it yet.

Ilu was already in the boat and reached with a paddle toward Emma. He pulled her out of the water and over the side of the boat, followed by Birdie, who was right behind. The fire on ship preoccupied the crew more than their escape did, but a few gunshots seemed too close for comfort. Birdie grabbed Ilu when he started to rapidly paddle away from the ship, but Ilu had his orders too.

"Wait!" Emma panicked. "Where's Alex?"

An explosion cut short the question, throwing her backward in the boat. Shouts grew aboard the ship but faded against the increasing roar of fire.

"My girl! Go back! I ain't leaving her, you bastard!" Birdie cried at Ilu. He knew Alex better than anyone. He bent over, holding his stomach, his heart aching, his eyes straining in the night for some sign of her.

"Dear God," Emma prayed, looking toward the fiery ship for some sign of her friend escaping. "Dear God."

The light alerted Joshua. They'd had the ship in sight most of the evening, slowly catching up with it. Then he saw the first blast light the darkness. Heard the explosion.

"Damn!" Samuel was out on the deck. He snapped orders to Joshua's crew that brooked no argument. Samuel's urgency only increased Joshua's worry. He had his scope out when Samuel reached him, yelling. "She's blowing up the damn ship!"

Samuel couldn't watch. He buried his head in his hands, waiting for what was to come.

The second and final blast went off, starting a series of explosions in succession, creating a fiery display that shot up into the sky like a fireball.

Joshua clutched the rail to remain standing.

Mick joined him and gripped his shoulder. "They must be on a boat already."

Joshua swallowed painfully, knowingly, and slowly shook

his head. "Someone had to be the trigger." Alex would never let anyone else do it. He knew her too well.

She was at the wrong end of the ship for her original escape plan to work. The first fuse didn't take, and she had to run back down to light the path of destruction. Now Alex was counting the seconds before barrels of gunpowder exploded, completely obliterating her beloved ship. This ship had been her sanctuary. Today it became her hell. She intended to re-claim it her own way.

She climbed out of the hold to see Paxton and several oth-ers blocking her path. She released four knives in succession, and all hit their mark except the one meant for Paxton. He deflected it with a sweep of the rolled up carpet. She ran to the side to get around him, aiming to get the farthest from the explosion before she jumped.

Bedlam surrounded her. Sails burned and men fell. Those who could swim leapt into the water. Midship, she was blocked by a crazed sailor, and a quick look revealed Paxton gaining on her. She swung aggressively with her knife and sliced through the man, blood spraying her face as she pushed him between herself and Paxton. One sailor left between her and freedom. She threw her last blade, cleared the path, and ran.

Something sharp hit her shoulder, knocking her from be-hind. She cried in pain, then stumbled to her knees, uncoiling her last weapon. A smaller explosion from below rocked the deck and caused Paxton to lose his balance. Desperate, she looked for an advantage. On her right, a possibility. With instinct born of practice, she flicked the whip hard. The end curled around the knife in a dead man's chest. "Catch," she breathed. Paxton stood, and grabbing the carpet and his sword he continued forward, hunting her, silhouetted by flames. She yanked hard, crossing the whip over her chest, hoping for di-rectional control. "And release."

The knife flew back to her and landed with a powerful thump in the wood of the mast. She turned her head a frac-tion to see her face reflected in the blade, and swallowed hard.

"That'll do."

She stumbled to her feet, struggling to stand upright, wrenched the knife free and gripped it to fight. Shadow crossed light, alerting her. She spun with force as his sword came down. He was going to finish her.

She struck first, ramming her blade into his heart.

Their eyes met in the light of incinerating wood and sail. The wind caught at her hair, whipping it wildly around, like the flames about to devour them. He dropped the carpet.

"On me, Paxton," she said bitterly, "rests the end of days. The end of your days."

Paxton's free arm went around her body, ripping further the sliced and raw skin on her back. His sword arm wobbled and finally his weapon dropped. Still, he could not let go. He could only stare.

"You *are* the kelile," he wheezed, his eyes shocked at the realization.

"No." Alex twisted the knife in his heart. "I'm not the kelile, Paxton." She reached out and tore the chain from his neck, reclaiming the ancient brass astrolabe.

"I'm the prophecy."

Emma screamed at the force of the last detonation. The ship's destruction was a passionate display of fury and finality.

Ilu jumped to cover them all. Wood and debris flew high, then slowly floated in the air as if suspended, before landing with a fiery splash. The cries of men stopped. Eventually there was only the silent burning of the *Sea Fire*, as she sank to her final resting place.

Emma called Alex's name for hours afterward. At first she was hopeful, then desperate, then angry, then begging. She kept up her ritual until her voice was hoarse and her eyes blind from smoke and tears, but nothing she did made a difference. Her friend was gone.

A cheer went up when they spotted the boat the following morning. As they got closer a quiet overtook again. Birdie was exhausted. His look of regret toward Joshua was enough for all of them to guess what had happened.

Someone had helped Marcus on deck, and when Emma spotted him she stumbled gratefully into his arms, her blonde hair nearly black with soot, her eyes red, her spirit destroyed. He held her tightly, tucked under his chin while her body shook wretchedly with a mixture of relief and heart-wrenching sorrow. He watched the others come aboard, knowing already that Alexandra wasn't among them.

They searched the wreckage for hours, finding few remains save bodies, debris, the occasional barrel, and the whip. Emma asked them to retrieve it. She would keep it she told them, promising Marcus that some day she would explain why. They decided any survivors would head toward nearest land, several days away. That's where Alex had directed Birdie. But no one expected survivors. " 'If anything happens, I'll meet you there,' " Birdie repeated. She had said it with a confident grin, knowing all the time, that she wouldn't be meeting him anywhere.

Still, Birdie thought, as he recounted the details to her loved ones, if anyone could survive, she would find a way. He wanted more than anything to give hope to the men sitting across from him. It was not easy, but he gave them every detail, including how she had been whipped, and each word Paxton taunted her with regarding their father's death.

"I heard her," Stephen said. He looked at the others. He would bet they had too. It had been a call for help, or justice. He had thought he was hearing things, but the time that Birdie described and the time he thought he heard the cry matched. Samuel merely looked at him as if to say "be quiet." Even Joshua looked away. No one wanted to admit to that strange moment on the water. Stephen closed his mouth. It was the stuff of legends and superstition.

"It was like she died in that moment." Birdie put a hand back up to his eyes. "It broke my own heart. Paxton was ruthless. 'Twas nothing a child should ever hear. She made a choice then. I saw it. She was going to kill them all, even if she died doing it."

Stephen refused to believe any of it. "She's a good swimmer. She could have found some debris. And what about the other boats aboard?"

"We released them, so's the crew would have no escape," Birdie confided, dabbing at his eyes. "And the others we dropped in Salé."

"Is there anything else?" Joshua hadn't spoken much. His voice seemed controlled, but had a taut edge. "Did she have no message for me?"

Birdie looked down, guiltily. He debated repeating her parting words, for they had been telling the moment she'd said them.

"Yes?" Joshua waited, eyes sharp.

"Her last words to me . . . they were for you." Birdie clasped his hands and took a breath. The man deserved the truth. It may be the only peace he would get.

"She said," he swallowed painfully, " 'Tell the duke I'm sorry.' "

Joshua drew in a sharp breath.

Birdie wept. "Aye, she knew it. She knew what she was going to do."

Matthew stared out the portal to the sea unwilling to believe it had taken another loved one.

Stephen leaned his forehead against the cool cedar wall of the cabin. "She must have had an escape plan. She wouldn't leave us. She wouldn't do this. It's too . . ." He closed his eyes, whispering, "It's too unbearable."

Samuel knew that any of them would have done the same thing their sister had done. It was in their blood. They wouldn't risk the life of a friend or crew, especially not if it was their responsibility as captain to protect them. His sister had been a Stafford through and through. Just like their father. If only she had known it.

Joshua shook his head. They all thought she was dead. He refused to believe it. He hated them all at this moment. He even hated Alex. He wanted to get drunk and find oblivion. Every logical thought said she was dead. She couldn't have survived. Even she knew she wouldn't survive, else why give him that message? But until he saw her body for himself, he would not give up. Not if it took his last breath.

"She's not dead." He spoke quietly, then with more certainty. "She wanted to kill that bastard, Paxton, but she's too damn stubborn to die in the ocean she's so fond of." He grabbed his scope. "I intend to find her." It was uncomfortably silent. "With or without your help."

He went back on deck to continue the search. One by one, the others followed.

Alex remembered her last moments on the *Sea Fire* vividly. She had become something she never thought she would be. Ruthless.

Her eyes had locked with Paxton's. His wide. With shock. A knife in his heart. Understanding too late what she was capable of. What she was willing to risk.

She watched, as he dropped to his knees, and crumpled over the carpet where it had unrolled at his feet. The woman's hand reached out across the waves.

His destiny. Not hers. She turned away. Done.

And then she ran.

Alex ran like her life depended on it because she knew it did. She was surrounded by flames, but she ran anyway. Through them when necessary. She kept moving, knowing water was on the other side. It hadn't taken more than eight steps to leap onto the edge. Her legs pushed off the deck with all her might. They were still spinning midair when she stretched toward freedom, her clothes partially on fire, making a path to the water. An explosive roar sounded off behind her and she saw the reflection of her body above the water before slamming into the cold depths of the ocean.

She struggled in desperation against the weight pressing down on her. Dark. Cold. No matter how hard she breathed, she couldn't seem to get any air. She panicked at the familiar dream, only to realize it wasn't a dream. Her arms stretched out, reaching blindly in the darkness uncertain as to which way was up. What had she done? Dear God, what had she done? She had destroyed it all. Everything she lived for. All for revenge.

She should have done it all for love.

Alex relaxed her body in the water, her struggles only impeding her. She unbuckled the leather knife belt weighing her down. Icy water washed around her, the burning of salt on the wounds of her back eventually numbing it into only a tight awareness. She floated in the water, listening. She had never been afraid of the water before. All her friends were here. A familiar sound encouraged her. Whales singing. Miles and miles away. Or maybe it was just her imagination. The whales were searching for land as well, but to avoid it. Slowly her body floated. She found her direction.

A vague light in the darkness glimmered through the deep Atlantic water. She kicked her legs forcefully, one arm stretching upward, reaching for air.

She cut the surface sucking in hard, gasping with desperate, life-giving breath.

The force of the explosion had tossed Alex farther away from the ship than she realized, but also safely away from the debris that continued to fly in all directions. Her head hurt, her skin burned everywhere, and her fingers cramped with cold, still clutching the astrolabe, its chain wrapped thrice around her good hand. For some reason she was alive. She wondered for how long.

Undulating waves brought her up and down in the ocean as she floated, looking for signs of life. On the upside of one wave she spotted something, a shadow afloat, barely lit by the flame of her beloved ship. Its shape was familiar. She looked back once more, nothing visible past the flames. There was an eerie crack of wood that echoed loudly, then new flames shot to the sky. That life was past. She turned again to the shadow floating away. It had drifted far from the ship. She swam with the current to catch it, her body protesting every movement, but her will forcing her to not give up.

It seemed an eternity before she succeeded. Alex laughed with delirium as she touched the wood. With no one to hear, she released a pained cry as she attempted to hoist her body over the side of the empty boat. It was almost too much. Finally, she lay unmoving and exhausted, adrift in the ocean. Slowly she regained her focus, strengthened her resolve.

She would not die out here.

She pulled herself up. She had to feel for the side of the boat, unable to see much in her current state. There was one oar. She propped it up. Then, unwrapping the astrolabe, she rewrapped it to hang from the oar, turning it so the shiny side faced out, a reflective beacon should anyone be looking.

With the very last bit of energy that she had left, she pulled in her breath and sang a song out to the whales. Then she collapsed, grateful that they still sang back.

The crew of the newly christened *Freedom* listened in the night to the strange sounds, and noted their captain was pensive, his brows furrowing with concern.

Koto, a dark, African man was their representative. He approached the captain and questioned humbly, "Captain, do we continue to the lights?"

The man shook his head, listening again, closing his eyes as if to concentrate on the sound coming across the sea. Finally he redirected.

"Southeast. Toward the song."

Koto swallowed nervously. He didn't think any good could come from following strange sounds in the night, and it didn't sound like any song he knew. Still, their new captain had saved them in Brazil. Freed them from bondage. And now he paid them like they were free men. They would follow him anywhere.

The captain seemed to recognize Koto's hesitation. He turned clear blue-green eyes on him that reflected the moonlight and spoke encouragingly.

"It's okay, Koto. It's not a ghost. It's a woman."

Koto nodded, still not understanding, for that explanation was even stranger.

Had he not been up with the sun, he might have missed it. The rising light catching something on the water and reflecting out. Bursting with hope, Joshua shouted to alert the crew and call to the men.

They all looked and saw nothing. Only the reflection of sun on water. A pretty illusion for the hopeful. Joshua knew what they thought. That he was tired, stubborn, afflicted with grief. Hell, he was. But this was something else. Stronger than just light on water. Every instinct told him so. The others on their accompanying ships looked out. They were sailing in a formation to stay together, but also cover as much water as possible in their search. Joshua continued to look out in the direction he had seen the light. Samuel joined him. Standing quietly, not judging. Perhaps as hopeful as he.

Minutes passed and none dared speak, though whispers had begun that it was nothing. Joshua wouldn't look away. He wouldn't risk that one instant. An hour later, Joshua was the only one remaining.

He might have missed it again, his eye aching so much from the glare. But this time they were closer. He was certain. A light shot out on the water.

There were gasps. "There!"

Joshua's chest filled with air. "There! Did you see?"

Suddenly it came again. Methodically.

Mick joined them. "It's a distress signal."

"Wait." Samuel had rushed to join him and was watching it clearly now. "She's using the astrolabe." His eyes filled with hope.

"It could be Paxton." Joshua voiced the other possibility, but Samuel grinned and shook his head.

"No. No, it's my sister. That's a uniquely Stafford pattern. Only our captains use it. Same with bells and whistles. It's Alex." He slapped Joshua's shoulder. "I'm sure of it."

It wasn't long before they also began to hear a ship's bell in the distance. A steady ring commonly used to indicate a need for help, but for Stafford's every fourth issued a double ring. Samuel was certain Alex had reached friendly help and had told them to do this.

The bell continued all day until they reached the ship. The Staffords surrounded a vessel called *Freedom*, its crew and passengers looking out at them from dark faces with worry and distrust. That's when Joshua discovered that Samuel had been entirely wrong.

Chapter Thirty

She was drifting. At some point Alex knew the wounds on her back were festering. She slept on and off, waking sometimes during the night to complete blackness except for the stars. That's when she felt most lucid. She would call out to the ocean or sing loudly to break the monotony, until her parched mouth begged for moisture. Then she would collapse again into a tortured sleep. She called to Joshua but he never answered. She could see him looking right at her but he never seemed to see her no matter how much she waved her hands with frustration.

What had she done? The image of the *Sea Fire* aflame taunted her. The sound of flames consuming wood and sail thundered in her ear along with imagined cries of innocent men. She was going to suffer slowly, then go to hell. She knew she didn't deserve a miracle, but she prayed for one anyway.

The crew of *Freedom* stood alert at the side of their ship. They had spotted what their captain seemed to be searching for, but he looked none too happy about it.

"It be a woman, Cap'n!"

"Aye," their captain nodded, seeing the long hair strewn about, covering the face and parts of the body. Some of the men jumped in the water and swam to the longboat, tying ropes to pull it alongside the ship. The captain released his tight grip on the rail, and lowered himself over the side, slowly boarding the smaller one as if afraid of what he might find.

Koto joined him to help in case the woman was alive.

The captain moved carefully, his first touch tentative at the throat, and then he breathed deeply.

"She's alive," he said, only loud enough for Koto to hear. Koto shouted the news back to the ship and told them to get a shroud they could use to bring her aboard.

The captain pulled her hair carefully aside, touching the black material that stuck to her back with tender care to inspect. They both recognized the fierce wounds on her back, blood dried in spots, other spots cracked and oozing infection. Koto gasped. If she lived, she would be scarred something awful. His captain pressed knuckles to his mouth, as if fighting for control.

The woman was in bad shape all around. Her legs were scraped and burned from exposure to the sun. The little bit of her face not covered by hair showed dry, cracked lips. She was skinny, young, and no doubt suffering from lack of water. Koto did not think she would live.

Gently, the captain turned her over, careful not to put pressure on her back injuries, while cursing inwardly that it was impossible to avoid it. He swallowed painfully as the delicate face was revealed. Still so young. Her hair more red than brown. The delicately arched brows were the same despite the sunburned face.

"My child," he choked, his heart shattered by this sight. "What have they done to you?"

He pushed away the heat in his eyes and focused on one thing. She was alive. That was all that mattered at the moment. She groaned, and he comforted her that she was safe. That she would be well. Her lids fluttered open, as if she struggled to wake up, and he saw the expressive deep green eyes fill with pain as she tried to focus, followed by a gasp when she tried to move.

"It's okay, Allie. I've got you."

His harsh voice got her attention, and she seemed to try even harder to force her eyes open. Her focus cleared and slowly recognition lit her face. A small, slender hand came up to touch his cheek and he covered it with his own, his heart skipping a beat when she spoke with both clarity and a hint of surprise.

"I'm dead then."

Then she fell into unconsciousness.

"You know her, Cap'n?" Koto asked him, the man's face mirroring astonishment.

"Yes, Koto." He wiped the moisture that spilled from his eyes, and explained. "She's my daughter."

From across the rails, the crews eyed each other.

"Careful, Joshua. They don't look overly friendly," Samuel warned. Mick grunted agreement.

"I'm going over." Joshua left the two men staring as he climbed the rigging to midlength on the mast.

"What are you doing?" Samuel shouted.

Joshua grabbed the line and freed it. "What Alex would do!" He gave a pull to test the strength, then jumped, swinging out and over the water, just high enough to cross the side of the other ship. Men scattered to give him room to land, and stared with undisguised shock.

"Hey! Send that rope back!" Samuel didn't want to be left behind.

Joshua was quickly surrounded, as much with curiosity as threat. He identified their leader, a tall, well-developed African with skin as black as night, holding in his hand a familiar medallion reflecting the sun. He eyed it, then the man, and held up his hands to show he meant no ill will.

"I'm looking for the owner of that. A woman with long, red hair. Her ship went down two nights ago." He was about to explain more, when all eyes turned to something behind him.

"I'm the captain here." The voice was low but full of deadly anger.

Joshua turned to a man his height. He frowned at the familiar face and brownish-red hair, then gasped.

"You're a Stafford."

The man nodded, not showing surprise at the acknowledgment.

"I'm looking for Alexandra Stafford." It was all he could manage, a terrible premonition beginning to settle in around his chest.

"I'm Robert Stafford." The man turned and walked to the captain's quarters, thrusting the door open before adding furiously, "You're too late."

A white sheet was pulled over the body, up to the edge of tangled, red hair, strewn off to the side. Joshua's very being felt ripped from him with one sharp strike.

"No." He rushed to the bedside. "No!" he shouted, pulling the sheet away.

What he saw stopped his heart.

He inhaled, falling to his knees. "Alex." Trembling, he reached out toward her neck, afraid to touch her skin. Terrified of the cold he might discover. The cold, hard skin of death.

He touched. Oh God. Cool. Slowly he stroked down toward her throat and pressed at her pulse point. Hope and surprise made him look up at the other man. Into dark, glittering strangely familiar eyes filled with fury—and pain.

"She's alive," Joshua said.

"Barely. Something's infected. I can't find it."

"We have a doctor," Joshua rasped. He couldn't halt the emotion as he looked at the woman he loved. Her back was raw, skin ripped away in spots, deep gashes dug lines to the bone, and swelling appeared in areas that could be healing or infection. One hand was set from palm to elbow with a length of stick and wrapped carefully to avoid what was left of her wrist and hand, the skin badly shredded.

"Are there any other injuries?"

"No major breaks. I cleaned splinters from her right arm and parts of her back. We salted the wounds best we could. She was conscious only a moment when we found her." He finished and gave Joshua an intense, penetrating look of pure hostility, before continuing. "What I'd like to know is who the son of a bitch is who did this, and why you weren't there to save her?"

Before Joshua could defend himself, there was a shout for the captain on deck.

"You better go before one of the Staffords get into a fight."

Enough time with the family had made him cynical. "Not much time left, by my account."

The man's expression was wry. Some of his anger faded, leaving only sadness. "Not the reunion I hoped for."

Robert Stafford returned to the deck. Weary. Afraid for his daughter and certain nothing could touch his heart. The expressions of his crew when he arrived told him otherwise. Their mouths dropped as they looked from him to the giant in their midst, then back to him. He knew his eldest in a way every parent knows their first born.

"Samuel."

Samuel froze. Then slowly turned—and swallowed. Samuel was the one who never needed an explanation. In three long strides, his son reached and embraced him. Robert held.

"Father."

There was a shout from below. Matthew was sending over supplies. More calls from the other ships indicated that people wanted to know what was going on. He instantly recognized the man swinging onto deck as Stephen.

Matthew was the last aboard, preferring to climb the traditional way, not willing to risk his physician's hands on foolishness. For that Robert was relieved. Matthew's greeting was cooler, wanting answers, but knowing this wasn't the time.

"Are you injured?" Matthew kept to basics.

Robert shook his head. "But—" He looked at his boys assembled around him. "I found your sister." His eyes filled. "You must prepare yourself." He looked to Matthew for help and his son nodded, a mask of cold control easing itself into place.

Joshua wouldn't leave Alex. She remained unconscious, but he continued to hold her good hand while Matthew worked methodically on her injuries. Joshua only started to worry when Matthew started swearing. And kept swearing.

Now covered in a good amount of blood, Matthew pushed between muscle around Alex's shoulder and demanded light. He swore some more and made a dozen more orders.

"She was shot. No surprise missing it in this mess," he choked. He pressed down and discolored infection oozed out. He started swearing more, panic evident on his face. "It's to the bone."

"Clean it," Joshua said.

"It's not that easy. The bone—"

"Take the bone too. I don't care. Save her." Joshua would not let him give up.

Samuel put a hand on Matthew's shoulder and gave a squeeze. Matthew nodded, his face assuming control again. It was hours of work. Removing the remains of the shot, absorbing the toxins already manifesting, scraping at the bone in hopes of preventing a fatal infection. Then, trying to find fresh skin to sew her back together. Through it all Alex remained abnormally still, causing Matthew to voice worries about possible injuries they could not see. The room became hot with all their combined worry. Joshua also noted that Alex's temperature had risen. They were keeping her cool with a constant change of dampened cloths.

Nothing made a difference. Alex was fading away. It was palpable.

Joshua read the fear on all their faces. He knew the same fear was likely expressed on his, as he desperately willed her to live. "Fight, Alex. You've fought for everyone else. Fight for yourself." He stroked limp hair from her check. "Fight for us."

The night came and went, then came again. Emma, Marcus, and the Staffords took turns keeping watch with Joshua, Matthew, and Alex's father.

In the early hours of the morning she shuddered.

"Matthew!" Joshua called in panic, but Matthew had already jumped. Alex struggled again. "She's having trouble breathing."

Matthew lifted his sister's hand and pressed it to his forehead. Finally, to his father, he said, "Get the others."

Joshua looked at him. "Don't say it. Don't say it, Matthew."

"I'm sorry."

"No." Joshua lifted her from her side to prop her up.

"She's having trouble breathing. Help her." He propped pillows up behind her as he lifted her limp body. She wasn't warm anymore. That should be good. "Matthew!"

Matthew shook his head once, helpless. Grief stricken.

The brothers entered and he panicked. Stephen's face was tortured, full of tears. He believed it as well. Emma stood in the doorway, pale, clutching the wall, struggling for composure. He recognized the expressions on everyone. They were letting her go.

Joshua wouldn't let them.

He pulled Alex into arms, onto his lap, to protect her. "She is not going to die. I won't allow it!" His hand captured her head as it fell backward, and he shuddered at the sudden decline in her temperature. "Fight, Alex. You deserve to live. You *deserve* to live!"

He held her close, willing her to take another breath.

"I know you blame yourself for your mother's death. But it wasn't your fault. None of it was your fault." His voice cracked, his forehead touching hers lightly. "I love you, Alex. Don't give up. I love you."

"Josh," Stephen, reached out to him.

Joshua knocked his arm away. "Get away!" He glared at the others and Robert Stafford held his hand up to halt the others, as if understanding. It was his right to fight for her. And he would not give up. He put a hand over her heart, certain there was still life. "Please, Alex. Fight. You are stronger than this. Fight."

He lost track of time in his pleading, rocking Alex gently until her body suddenly rattled and she expelled a gasped breath. Then she was still.

He heard Emma's gasp of pain from somewhere in his consciousness, the cursed lamentations from the others. Still he would not believe it. He pressed his lips to hers forcefully, his hands tightening in her hair.

"Dammit, Alex. Dammit." He touched his cheek to hers, then frustrated, shouted in her ear, "Wake up!"

No one was more startled than he, when she did.

With the weeping in the room, no one heard the weak cough but him. He pulled back, holding her gently, and she coughed again. More of a soft choke for air, but movement.

Matthew shouted, leaping at him. "Get back. Prop her up." He touched her throat and looked at him in awe. "She's back."

Everyone clustered forward, as if wanting to hear her breathe for themselves.

Joshua waited as Matthew examined Alex, before offering him a bemused smile. "It seems she's out of danger."

Joshua blinked at the man. "She listened to me?"

Stephen laughed hard, wiping at his tears of shock and relief. "You were a bit of nag."

Joshua nodded. "I told you she wasn't going to die."

The doctor contemplated him for a long moment, the intensity of his gaze disconcerting. "Who are you, Joshua Leigh, Duke of Worthington?"

"Just a man."

"No," Matthew considered. "You are definitely our sister's match."

Samuel grasped Joshua's shoulder from behind, deadpan. "But you still have our sympathy."

Marcus caught Emma as she stumbled. She wasn't going to make it, but she wouldn't ask for help. She fell into the door of the cabin next to Alex's, and he pushed it open with one hand, catching her with the other. It had been agonizing for Marcus to see Alex suffer, to watch her life ebb away and be helpless. It had been worse so, he knew, for Emma.

She grabbed toward a chair for balance, but he pulled her to him instead. Still she resisted, insisting she was okay, despite being blinded from the outpouring of emotion that she continued to rub away. He touched her cheek, desperate to ease her pain, and she smiled tremulously before giving up altogether and simply covering her face with her hands, her body shaking with quiet sobs, as she finally absorbed all that had happened. He pulled her to him and held tight, knowing he was unpracticed at comforting, useless at alleviating sorrow, and helpless to change anything in the past. He only knew he loved her. And in that moment he knew how Joshua had felt—that he would give his own life for one last smile from the woman he loved.

Joshua's grip on the rail was steadying, his breathing measured. The sun was rising again. Another day to hope.

There was a splash in the water near the ships. Surprised, he spotted whales nearby—a familiar sort if he was not mistaken.

"*Balaenoptera physalus,*" Robert said, joining him.

"Fin whale," Joshua said. Then added at the same time as Robert, "Alex has a book on it."

"Koto tells me they've been watching after us most of the night."

Joshua slowly turned to the man. "Is that unusual?"

Robert shrugged, facing him with a half grin. "Not in this family."

Joshua nodded, accepting the answer, wondering how this man had dealt with his wife's death. How he would deal with his daughter's future. "This prophecy. Do you think it's her destiny?"

Robert turned back to the sea. "Alex will have to decide that. I can tell you one thing. She'll always be the one stepping out in front to save others, fighting for what she deems the good fight." He sighed, as if pained by it, before warning him. "So, if it's the destiny *you* choose, enjoy the days you have."

Alex, didn't see anything for a long time. She knew there was pain, but she expected that. There was pain in hell. When she saw the light, it was a surprise. It was beautiful. That's when the dreams came, vivid and sure. Visions of things she was yet to do. The faces of women she was yet to meet. The voices around her spoke of love. It was comforting. And a little confusing. Then she was struggling. Against an impossible weight. Her body was stiff and immobile. Her eyes heavy. It hurt to breathe. But she did. And it felt like her greatest triumph.

Eyes opened. She stared unblinking. "You're still here." Her voice worked. It sounded raspy but it was hers.

"Yes."

He answered back. Maybe this was not a dream. "I'm not dead?"

"No."

She hesitated before the next question. "You're not dead either?"

He shook his head to emphasize. "No. I'm not dead either."

Her eyes filled with tears. "I'm glad."

"I'm relieved to hear it."

She smiled. Or thought she did. Every muscle hurt. She was laying on her side, a sheet covering her loosely. "Papa." She tried to reach out. Instead he came to her, listening to her struggled speech. "I had the map. In Morocco. Birdie saved it. It was woven into a tapestry."

"So, you've been chasing the prophecy, then?"

She shook head. "It's been chasing me." She touched the back of her neck, surprised the arm actually worked. "It caught up."

"Guess we should have armed you a bit more."

"I should have told you everything."

"I would have gone after Paxton anyway, Allie. It wouldn't have mattered."

She still had doubts. "What happened?"

"We both got caught in the storm, and I lost him for awhile. My ship had some damage, but we were seaworthy, and I managed to track him to Brazil. Unfortunately, that's an area friendlier to slave traders than abolitionists. He framed me for helping some slaves. I've been in prison until a few months ago. Tried to get home as quick as I could, only to find everyone gone. No surprise there, I guess."

She vaguely remembered being found. "The ship you have now . . . the crew—"

He gave her a half grin. "I served the time. Figured I ought to do the crime. We intercepted one of the Stafford Line out of Portsmouth and learned of your kidnapping. I followed to

Morocco and chased *Sea Fire* when I realized something wasn't right."

"I blew it to smithereens."

"That, you did. Very effectively, daughter."

"I couldn't let Paxton and his crew hurt Emma. I knew—" She shook her head not wanting to remember the past, then remembered her lost friends. "Emma! Birdie!"

"They're okay," he reassured. "Ilu too. You had to make that decision. Don't look back."

"But, Papa?" She put her hand out to him, and he held it companionably, comforting.

"Yes?"

"How did you find me?"

"Ah." He slanted his head, curiously. "Did you think you got all your seafaring powers from your mother then?"

She smiled. "Only the strange ones."

"I see." His chest rumbled with humor. "You were easy to track, daughter. Same as when you were a child," he enlightened. "I followed your song." Then he looked over her shoulder. "But I think the duke might have a different story." Her father pecked her forehead and excused himself with a faint smile. "I'll get Matthew and tell him you're awake."

Her father left, and Alex struggled to sit up. Joshua told her to stay and gave her some water before easing down next to her to make talking less difficult. Every move he made was careful so as not to disturb her. Though talking was not what he started with.

He kissed her forehead, his lips brushing tantalizingly over one brow. She lifted her good hand to cup his jaw, stroking several days of growth covering his face. He bent lower so his cheek could slide against hers, the soft whiskers tickling her skin, prickling her senses back to life.

"I missed you," she said, releasing a sigh.

"You haven't been acting like it."

She moved to kiss his lips and he permitted only the lightest of touches, his thumb following after, to explore with painstaking gentleness, as if she might break.

"I was sleeping," she chastised, softly. "I can hardly be enticing you every minute of the day."

His chest rumbled and his hard jaw transformed into a rueful smile before he lightly tapped his forehead to hers. "I'm sorry."

"It's okay," she promised. "As long as you still love me." His fingers teased the hairs at the back of her neck, making her want things she knew her body wasn't capable of doing . . . yet. He didn't reply so she added, "I understand if you're a little mad about the ship . . ."

He raised a brow.

"But you said you would love me even if you were mad at me."

"I'm not mad about the ship." He pecked her forehead. "Trust me. There are so many other things to be mad about."

"I still love you," she shared. Still, no response. "Joshua—"

"Alex," he cut her off. "I love you." He kissed her brow, her cheek, her lips. "I love you, I love you, I love you."

"I know."

He laughed. Finally. It was the one thing that reassured her. She held his sparkling blue eyes with her own. They were bloodshot and weary. Her hand went to his cheek again to comfort. He covered it gratefully with his own then turned his face to press a kiss to her palm, before lowering it between their hearts.

"There's just one more thing . . . my love. My darling." She tried out the endearments he seemed fond of, hoping he knew he could tell her anything. That whatever had happened to him, he would know she was there to comfort him. And no matter what he had done, she would still love him.

Having softened him with words and kisses, she finally said what was on her mind. "You look terrible. What happened?"

The weeks that followed were idyllic and would be looked back on by all as a perfect time in their lives. The ships and all their crews settled in at Las Palmas for the duration of Alex's recovery. Days were spent watching the men compete in games on the beach—Koto's team regularly trouncing Mick's smaller sailors in all games requiring strength. Her father would be returning all of Koto's people to Africa who wanted to go. The rest would continue on the ship, or take jobs back at the shipyard in Boston. Stephen would join their father on that trip. He looked forward to it before starting Harvard and continuing his studies as all the Stafford men had.

Meals were long and full of laughter, the evenings balmy with golden sunsets. There were late hours in the night when they caught up on all the Stafford family business with their father—the people and the ports they visited, favorite stories they all recalled, ideas and dreams they had, but had never shared.

Alex was still limited in sharing in much of the fun, but Joshua was always with her, engaging her in their plans for the future, teasing her about children, debating the location of their nursery; often when in the middle of one of these discussions, Alex would look up from their notes and get lost in his eyes. On such occasions, she had only to lift her face a fraction for him to know she needed his kiss.

As her health improved, Birdie and her father spent more time with her designing a new ship. Alex worried over Birdie constantly, the recent adventures having taken their toll on him. Emma proceeded with wedding plans—for Alex. She and Marcus would not announce anything until they were back in London, but it was agreed Alex and Joshua would marry on Las Palmas.

The day before their wedding, Joshua came upon her drawing in the journal Matthew had recovered. She was sketching the woman rising from the ocean, one hand over her womb, the other stretched out over the ocean. Alex looked up, not hiding the image.

"I've decided she is protecting the future, not destroying it."

"I'm glad to hear that, since I have something for you." Joshua pulled her astrolabe out from behind his back, hanging it from his fingers to show off the shiny new chain.

"Whatever this is, whatever this means"—Joshua widened the chain and slipped it over her head—"it's part of you." He took her scarred wrist and bent his lips reverently over it. "And there's no part of you that I don't want." He walked behind her and carefully lifted her hair away from the chain before kissing the mark at the back of her neck. "No part of you that isn't beautiful to me." He turned her. "And there's nothing," his voice got husky, "nothing, Alex, that could ever make me stop loving you."

Alex, smiled, fighting the glistening of emotion blinding her vision. She didn't move for a long moment, the astrolabe cutting into the skin of her palm from the force of her grip. She looked down at it briefly then released it to settle over her heart.

"It is part of me." She took his hands in hers. "But it doesn't rule me, or my destiny. I won't let it." She looked out over her family and friends, then back to him, wrapping her arms around his neck and pulling him down with force. He slanted his lips over hers possessively, and she gave back in equal measure, pressing passionately into him, loving every stroke of his tongue, caress of his lips, and groan of anticipation. Pulling back, she made a promise. "I choose life, Joshua. With you, and my family, and my friends. I'm not going to be the 'end of days.' I'm going to be the beginning of them."

He nodded, accepting. "Excellent. Because we are not going to be having anymore of this trouble." It sounded like a command.

"Hmmm."

"I'll take that as agreement." He kissed her affectionately on the top of her head. "We're going to lead a nice, peaceful, normal life."

Her body started to shake with laughter. He lifted his head to frown at her in warning. "You are not always going to get your way, you know."

They were surrounded by the love of family and friends, and Alex smiled with the knowledge that she could change, but some things need never change. It gave her immense confidence. She grinned mischievously, and teased him. "Oh, yes, Joshua. I am."

He sighed dramatically, giving in. "Are you upset about your carpet?"

She shook her head with certainty. "No. That's behind us."

He bent his head, laying kisses against her temple, her brow, and at her moan of frustration, down to her lips. Then he lifted her and spun her off her feet. She laughed with pure joy, holding on with everything she had. Her life perfect.

Some day, she promised herself, when it was time, she would tell him the truth about where the real map was.

After all, every legend has her secrets.

✂

☐ **YES!**

Sign me up for the Historical Romance Book Club and send my FREE BOOKS! If I choose to stay in the club, I will pay only $8.50* each month, a savings of $6.48!

NAME: _____

ADDRESS: _____

TELEPHONE: _____

EMAIL: _____

☐ I want to pay by credit card.

☐ **VISA**   ☐ **MasterCard.**   ☐ **DISCOVER**

ACCOUNT #: _____

EXPIRATION DATE: _____

SIGNATURE: _____

Mail this page along with $2.00 shipping and handling to:

Historical Romance Book Club
PO Box 6640
Wayne, PA 19087

Or fax (must include credit card information) to:

610-995-9274

You can also sign up online at **www.dorchesterpub.com**.

*Plus $2.00 for shipping. Offer open to residents of the U.S. and Canada only. Canadian residents please call 1-800-481-9191 for pricing information.

If under 18, a parent or guardian must sign. Terms, prices and conditions subject to change. Subscription subject to acceptance. Dorchester Publishing reserves the right to reject any order or cancel any subscription.